TRIPPER

When Ron Crusher is forced at gunpoint onto the parapet of a twelve-storey office block he suspects that he's being used to distract the police while a criminal gang escapes, and that his life will be spared. Minutes later he is sent plunging to his death, without ever knowing why. Meanwhile Sam Carew, ex-cop turned builder and private detective is hired to discover whether cruise ship crooner Joey Gladstone is cheating on his wife. Departing for Barbados where the *Caribbean Rose* is docked, little does Sam know that he will soon be drawn into the investigation of Ron Crusher's apparently motiveless murder.

TRIPPER

TRIPPER

by

Ken McCoy

Magna Large Print Books
Long Preston, North Yorkshire,
BD23 4ND, England.

British Library Cataloguing in Publication Data.

McCoy, Ken
    Tripper.

A catalogue record of this book is
available from the British Library

ISBN   978-0-7505-2687-6

First published in Great Britain in 2005 by Allison & Busby Ltd.

Copyright © 2005 by Ken Myers

Cover illustration © The Old Tin Dog by arrangement with
Allison & Busby Ltd.

The moral right of the author has been asserted

Published in Large Print 2007 by arrangement with
Allison & Busby Limited

Magna Large Print is an imprint of Library Magna Books Ltd.

Printed and bound in Great Britain by
T.J. (International) Ltd., Cornwall, PL28 8RW

Dedication

To my son Matthew

Acknowledgments

In 1977 Billy Byrne was locked up for murder. For a young man, barely out of his teens, freedom is such a precious thing that I can understand why such a man, even when guilty of murder, would deny this guilt until every avenue of appeal has been exhausted. At which point, if he had any grain of common sense he would stop lying, especially when faced with the prospect of indefinite imprisonment – people in denial of murder are considered unsafe to be let out on life licence.

Like most writers I have an abnormal imagination but, try as I might, I cannot understand why a guilty man would continue his claim of innocence when such a lie denies him his eventual parole. Once convicted of murder, admitting guilt is the quickest and most sensible road to freedom. However, many people find it simply impossible to admit to a murder they did not commit, and for these people the road to freedom is long and hard.

Although Billy Byrne was an undeniable scallywag and a pain in the arse of authority, I am convinced, for many reasons, that he is not a murderer. Such is his bloody-mindedness that he remained in jail, in denial of murder, for twenty-five years – thirteen years beyond his tariff – and would still be there had it not been for a ruling by the European Court of Human Rights. His story is horrific, fascinating, disturbing and in parts amusing. It's a story I will turn into a book in the near future. In the meantime I thank him for helping me with a few facts about life inside for a man on remand for a capital crime.

Thanks to my golfing pal Ian Harrison, ex-cop and ex-squaddie. Mind you, considering he was once one of the top five marksmen in the British Army, you'd think he'd be able to putt a bit straighter. If I've got anything wrong with my present day police procedure it's all his fault. Likewise to my good friend, Stephen Oldroyd of Zermansky's solicitors in Leeds, for his advice on legal matters.

He was known as 'Mad Carew' by the subs at
  Kathmandu.
He was hotter than they felt inclined to tell,
But, for all his foolish pranks, he was worshipped by
  the ranks,
And the Colonel's daughter smiled on him as well.

J MILTON HAYES
The Green Eye of the Little Yellow God

Chapter One

Unsworth, West Yorkshire: June 2004

Ron Crusher was dead and he never really knew why. A few minutes earlier what was undoubtedly a gun barrel had been pressed across his cheek from behind, then prodded into his back as he waited for the lift to take him down from the top floor of Ridings House. It was the voice that got to him, even more than the gun. 'Eyes front and walk up the fuckin' stairs.'

It was a voice of evil and the accompanying pungent halitosis suggested to him, just for a moment, that it might not be of this world. The hairs on the back of his neck stood on end and he had too much on his mind to notice the thieving hand that darted in and out of his coat pocket.

He had often wondered how he'd react if faced with a situation like this – a gun in his back. And he'd reacted in the way that most people would – he'd done as he was told. There was a depraved sincerity in this voice that persuaded him not to call any bluffs. Okay, so it might not be a real gun, but if it was a real gun he might end up dead. In fact by the sound of this thing behind him, he'd definitely end up dead. He had walked up that last flight of stairs and out on to the flat roof with a pounding heart, shaking knees and clenched buttocks. They were still clenched as he stepped up on the parapet. It wasn't so much the fear of a possible gun – he'd had a gun pointed at him before – it was the fear of heights and of the unknown nutter behind him.

'On the parapet.'

'What?'

'I said, stand on the parapet!'

'Look, I'm no good with heights, pal. Can't I just stand here?'

'Just do as yer fuckin' told!'

He put one foot on the parapet and drew it away. It was wet and windy and very dangerous out there.

'Do as yer told, yer bag o' shit. Stand on that parapet or I'll pull this trigger.'

Ron could swear he felt the bile that accompanied the rasping words, although the voice sounded some distance away.

'Okay, okay.'

Ridings House was a twelve storey office block and the tallest building in Unsworth. It was built of dull, grey concrete, and had the architectural lines and grace of an old filing cabinet. Ron stepped, gingerly, on to the concrete parapet, which was slightly convex and slippery with rain. As he really wasn't very good with heights, he faced forward but couldn't stop his eyes swivelling down. Some people were already looking up at him and pointing.

'What do you want me to do? I can't stay like this for long.'

'Yer won't have to.'

He was so tempted to look round. For all he knew this nutter didn't have a real gun. Half the scallies in Unsworth had replica guns stuck in their belts. The others had real ones. Status symbols. If this wasn't a real gun he had a chance. Ron Crusher was big and hard and had a decent chance against any unarmed man – even some malevolent ghoul with a voice like a farting camel.

It was a busy street below and it took no time at all for a crowd to gather. They had cleared the area below him – his dropping zone. How bloody thoughtful of them. No fear any of them breaking his fall then. He felt like shouting down that he wasn't going to jump; he was there because some nutcase bastard was pointing a gun at him, but he suspected that might not be a good idea.

'Look, my legs are going. I'm going to fall if I have to stand here much longer.'

'If yer want ter live, just do as yer told.'

He'd never heard so much hostility in a voice. 'But how long for? Why are you doing this to me? Look, mate, you're gonna have to let me down, I can't do with this much longer.'

Ron was pleading now, and pleading was something he didn't do much of. The last time he'd pleaded with anyone was to stop his dad leathering him with his belt. All that stopped the day he took the belt from his dad and gave him a leathering of his own. But that was then. He couldn't remember ever being this scared and he'd been through some scary times in the army in Northern Ireland back in the Seventies. Why would anyone want to do this to him? He supposed there were people around whom he might have upset, but he couldn't put his finger on anyone who had this much of a grudge against him. Well, maybe there were one or two, he wasn't exactly whiter than white, but then again, who was? Surely Milo wasn't behind this. No, he couldn't be. Milo didn't work like that. Then again he *was* standing immediately above Milo Morrell's office – the man to whom Ron had just given £150,000 for twenty kilos of cocaine. Ron had never dealt in drugs before, nor would he again. This was a definite one-off. It was surplus stock Milo was off-loading in preparation for going fully legit. Ron had laughed at the time. Fully legit, Milo Morrell? – that'll be the day. The cockney bastard wouldn't know fully legit if it bit him on the arse. But Milo had offered him a good deal and, when Milo makes an offer, refusal isn't an option. Ron had had to re-mortgage his house, but he wasn't unduly worried, he already had dealers lined up who would treble his investment within a few days. Jesus! What the hell was all this about? The nutter with the gun hadn't mentioned drugs or money, and Ron sure as hell wasn't going to broach the subject.

From his vantage point he could see the whole of the town centre. It was a typical June day in Unsworth and a light wind blew warm drizzle in to his face, mixing with the sweat that dampened his whole body. The clock on the Town Hall said five past two and the one on St Silas's church said quarter to five. The position of the sun, showing itself, fleetingly, behind grey clouds, indicated that the Town Hall clock was probably nearer the mark.

'Are there many people down there?'
'What?'

16

'I asked if there were many people down there! Don't make me ask questions twice. You only get one fuckin' chance in future.'

Ron took a deep breath to try and slow his hammering heart, then he allowed his eyes to swivel down again. 'Yeah, quite a few.'

'Any coppers?'

Ron answered quickly. 'Not that I can see.'

A police car arrived, with a flashing light but no siren, presumably so as not to disturb this potential suicide.

'One's just arrived.'

'Good. Hold your hands up in the air. Let them think you're gonna jump.' Then some of the malevolence went from the voice – not much, but some. 'Don't worry, it's all part of a plan we've got going.'

'A plan? Oh, I see. It's a plan is it?'

Ron raised his hands and released a slow sigh of relief. It was all clear now. There was a gang of them, not just a single nutter. He'd been brought here to distract the police from whatever villainy the rest of the gang was up to. If he was going to be killed this feller would have told him why by now. No one goes to all this trouble to kill someone without telling them why. Yes, it made perfect sense. In fact he'd no doubt be asked to stay like this long after the nutter had left. That's what they did, left people with a dire threat hanging over them to allow more time for the getaway. Ron was wondering if he should go along with this or should he immediately shout a warning down to the police below, in case they thought he was mixed up in the villainy? He

17

could well do without the cops sniffing round with the business he'd got lined up over the next couple of days.

First things first, he thought. *Just do as you're told. Be as helpful as possible. The main thing is to come out of this in one piece. Let the police do whatever they have to do. If you have to put business on hold then so be it.*

The people below could only see Ron. No one saw the hand that came from low behind him and pulled at his ankle, sending him off balance. The crowd shouted 'Oh no,' as he toppled forward, sending out a scream that didn't befit a man who, to the watchers below, was intent on suicide. His scream, which lasted maybe four seconds, was accompanied by loud gasps of horror from the crowd. During his one hundred and twenty foot descent he didn't quite reach the maximum velocity of a free-falling body but he was travelling at well over a hundred miles an hour when he hit the concrete. Most people had already turned their heads away as Ron splattered all over the pavement like a raw egg. His skin wasn't designed to contain such a violent redistribution of his innards, some of which splashed on to the watchers – blood, bone, brain, intestine. A man threw up over a weeping woman standing next to him, she followed suit and it caught on quickly, as vomiting does. People were now running around, vomiting and weeping; many of them splashed with important bits of Ron. The police were shouting for everyone to calm down and move away. In the midst of it all was Ron Crusher, who was dead and he never really knew why.

Chapter Two

The only thing worse than a miserable December day in the West Yorkshire town of Unsworth is a miserable December night. You just had to make the best of it. Sam Carew was in the bar of the Clog and Shovel, making the best of it with Alec Brownlow – his partner in Carew and Son (Builders) Ltd, and Detective Constable Owen Price, who, at the age of forty two, had recently got a much awaited transfer from uniform to CID. He and Owen had been pals since Sam's detective sergeant days; sadly Sam had been kicked out of the force because of a practical joke that had electrocuted Detective Inspector Brownlow, with whom he had never got on.

Dark, spiky rain spat at the windows in flurries, blown in on a gusting wind. Sam and Owen had just arrived. Alec, who was looking out of the window, had been in for quite some time. He wasn't normally a big drinker but the site had been rained-off since half past three and he had drunk more than his fair share. He gave them an accurate weather report.

'Spissin' down.'

Owen took off his saturated coat. 'Thank you, Michael Fish.'

'I've seen the forecast.' Alec jabbed a thumb towards the television. 'Sinfer the week.'

'I don't mind the rain, look you.' Owen was from

Merthyr Tydfil and made no pretence to come from anywhere else. 'Give me a cleansing shower to a cancerous heatwave any day of the week.'

'We'll have to find some under-cover work,' decided Alec, before returning his attention to his dwindling pint. 'Mus' keep the job moving.'

'That lets me out,' said Sam. 'There's no inside work for me. How sad, never mind.' He enjoyed laying bricks during the summer but hated winters. Dave, the landlord, responded to his signal to pull three more pints of Bootham's.

'I've got a bit of under-cover work on myself,' mentioned Owen. 'There's been some unseemly activity going on in the Unsworth public lavatories, look you. I'm going round them, posing as a member of the public.'

Sam lit a cigarette. 'We used to call it bog patrol,' he remembered. 'They had me doing that once. Very hard on the nose, bog patrol.'

'Hell of a responsibility that,' said Alec. 'Guardian of the public pisspots. All your police training didn't go to waste then.'

Owen bristled. 'It's not as easy as it sounds. Pretending to evacuate your bladder when there's nothing to evacuate takes a certain expertise.'

'Who is it you're looking for?' Sam asked. 'It was a phantom wanker in my day. Left his mark, like the Scarlet Pimpernel, only it wasn't scarlet. Never caught him.'

'This man's more of your exhibitionist, see,' said Owen. 'The great mystery is that he doesn't appear to have much to exhibit. What there is of it he's apparently painted red – either that or he's got some strange tropical disease of the willy.

20

Most peculiar, isn't it?'

'You could call him the Scarlet Pimple,' suggested Alec. 'We could make up a poem about him to arouse the public's interest.'

The three of them were composing the poem when a middle-aged man came into the pub and had a word with Dave before coming over to Sam's table.

'Which one of you is Sam Carew?'

'Who's asking?' enquired Sam. His lifestyle led him to mistrust such people. His was a name that could get him into trouble if he wasn't careful.

'Come on, I know it's one of you.'

Alec stood up, unsteadily, and declared, with his hand on his heart, *'I'm* Spartacus,' before sitting down, heavily.

With a few more pints inside them Owen and Sam might have followed suit. The Welshman just sat there and grinned, Sam was mildly embarrassed. The man seemed to pose no threat. 'That'd be me,' he said, 'and you are?'

'Philip Sims. I rang your office earlier and the young lady said I'd find you in here this evening. I might have a job for you. Could we talk somewhere more private?' He glanced, apologetically, at Owen and Alec. 'Sorry to spoil the party gents, it's a bit personal.'

Sam got up and led the man to an empty table in the corner of the room. Fifteen minutes later he and Philip Sims shook hands. Sims left. Sam rejoined Alec and Owen. He was examining a card Sims had given him.

'That was Philip Sims BCHD – what's a BCHD?'

'Bachelor of Dental Surgery,' said Owen. 'Do you know nothing about higher education?'

'Hey, I got two A Levels – and that's when they were worth having. They give them away with cornflakes nowadays.'

'A bricklayer with A Levels,' commented Owen. 'You'd have been better off with a spirit level.'

'The old man had great ambitions for me,' Sam said. 'I thought learning a trade would come in handy – if all else failed.'

'They'd be more useful nowadays if they printed A Levels on something a bit more absorbent,' said Alec. 'Maybe in a nice pastel colour. I'm a pale blue man myself. What about you, Owen? I see you as a daffodil yellow type.'

'I got A Levels in Welsh Language and Biology,'

'What's Welsh Biology?'

'It's–' Owen stared at Alec, wondering if he was kidding. He could never tell.

'He thinks his son-in-law's playing away,' Sam said, examining the card once again.

'Who does?' Alec enquired.

'Philip Simms BCHD. He wants me to catch him at it. He's offering good money – and a success bonus.'

'That'll be when you told him you don't do that sort of thing any more,' said Owen. 'As you once told me, catching adulterers isn't real detective work.'

Sam's eyes dropped in mild embarrassment. Owen persisted. 'You *don't* do that sort of thing any more, do you, boyo?'

'I do if it's in Barbados and it's pissing down in Unsworth.'

Chapter Three

In the basement of The Queen of Clubs in Unsworth was a furnace which heated a boiler that ran the central heating. It had been there since the place was built as a toffee factory just before the First World War and it still heated part of the building with rumbling inefficiency. Milo Morrell, the club owner, kept the furnace because it had a far more useful function than just heating radiators.

He knew the two black men standing in front of him only by their street names: Teargas and Zoo Blue. Where they'd got their names from was of no interest to him, other than they sounded as stupid as their owners looked. Milo smiled at them to put them at their ease. A few minutes ago Tony Ferris had asked them to stand with their backs to the wall, which had unnerved them somewhat, but Milo's smile told them everything was okay. It had not occurred to either of the men to ask why they were standing on a polythene sheet.

'We've done some good business over the years,' Milo said it with his smile intact, 'which is why I've asked you here.'

'You always been fair with us, Mr Morrell,' said Zoo Blue.

'An' we always pay you up front,' Teargas reminded him.

'You're a credit to your profession,' agreed Milo. He turned to Ferris. 'Wouldn't you say they're a credit to their profession, Tony?'

'If you say so.' Tony didn't smile as much as his boss. He looked impatient and slightly irritated.

Milo held out his hands, expansively. 'But all good things must come to an end.'

'To an end, Mr Morrell – what's that mean?'

'It means, Teargas, that we've done well out of each other. You both drive brand new Beamers and look at you – there's more bling on you than in H Samuel's window.'

Teargas gave a wide grin that showed off two rows of perfect teeth that he hadn't had when Milo began to do business him.

'And look at those teeth. You must give Tony the name of your dentist, Teargas. Those teeth must have cost you a nice few quid.'

Tony scowled and kept his mouth shut. His teeth weren't his best feature.

'They goes with the territory, Mr Morrell,' said Teargas. 'No one trusts a man with bad teeth.'

'Trust is good,' said Milo, 'but in this business respect is the thing.'

'We's the mos' respected faces in the business,' said Zoo Blue. 'Our dealers know they can't take liberties with us, but they also know we only supply high quality merchandise. What you supply we sell. We don' cut it, we don' fake it, we don' burn it, man.'

'Scag, blow, rocks, brown stuff, speedballs, Dr White, black hash, acid, ecky or jus' good ole Mary Warner,' added Teargas, 'we're the men. We got more varieties than Mr Heinz an' yer don'

24

need no tin opener.'

'Sounds like a good spiel,' said Milo with a grin neither as wide nor as genuine as that of Teargas. 'What do you think, Tony? Do you think it sounds a good spiel?'

'I'm totally fuckin' impressed, boss.' Ferris stifled a yawn and looked at his watch.

'You're the only connections between me and the street dealers,' Morrell told them. 'Well, there were three of you, as we all know, but Frankie's employment had to be terminated. And you're right about trust. We do need trust in business and I've been able to trust you to keep your mouths shut about who your main man is. You see I have people out there who tell me things and I know you're trustworthy people.'

'Well, you did mention how you'd blow us fuckin' heads off if we shot our mouths off like Frankie did,' said Zoo Blue, who remembered finding Frankie with a bullet hole in his head where his left eye should have been, and an even bigger hole at the back where the bullet had exited.

'And you've kept my identity a secret from all your dealers on the streets. So the only people who can connect me with the drugs business are you two and Tony here. I know this to be a fact and it is admirable.' Milo looked at Tony for his confirmation.

'Absolutely fuckin' admirable, boss. I'd like 'em facin' the wall.'

'What?' There was fear in Teargas's voice.

'It's nothing to worry about,' said Milo, soothingly. 'There's a couple of other faces coming in that we don't want you to see, that's all. Did I tell you I was retiring and going legit?'

'Faces my black ass!' screamed Zoo Blue, who had now noticed the polythene beneath his feet and realised the significance. 'Dey's gonna fuckin' pop us!' He had a knife in his hand and was thrusting it at first at Ferris, then at Milo.

Ferris reached out, grabbed Zoo's knife hand then, with an outward twist of his own hand forced the knife from the black man's grip. He then continued to twist Zoo's arm until it was much too far up his back. Zoo Blue screamed in pain. Teargas whimpered in fear when he saw Milo pointing a large handgun at him. Still holding Zoo's arm, Ferris bent down, picked up the knife, rammed it up Zoo Blue's backside, then kicked him to the ground where he screamed and writhed in agony.

Milo handed the gun to Ferris. Teargas was on his knees with his hands together in prayer, only he wasn't praying to God he was praying to Milo for mercy. Ferris put a single bullet through his eye. The shot was still echoing around the walls of the cellar as Teargas fell on top of his screaming associate. Ferris kicked him clear so he could see the Zoo Blue's face.

'I won't talk, man!' Zoo was screaming. 'I never grassed on you to nobody, man!'

'Yer've a lot ter say for a feller with knife up his arse,' remarked Ferris, irritably. 'Keep fuckin' still will yer? I'm trying ter put one through yer eye.'

Zoo Blue threw himself to one side. Ferris fired and took away most of the black man's head. The polythene sheet was collecting blood rapidly. Ferris handed the gun back to Milo.

'There's no such thing as a nigger that can keep his mouth shut, boss. They'd have been flappin' their gums the minute they walked out of the place.'

'You're a racist, do you know that, Tony?' said Milo. 'It's an annoying defect in your character.'

Ferris shrugged. 'I take as I fuckin' find, boss. Nobody likes the sound of his own voice more than a nigger.' He looked at the Rolexes on the dead men's wrists, then at the heavy gold jewellery glinting in the dim light. 'Do I get ter keep the scrap metal?'

'You get to burn it with them and sieve it from the ashes if you're that desperate,' snapped Milo. 'I want no connection between me and them appearing on the streets. I do hope that's clear, Tony.' He looked down at the bejewelled corpses and rubbed his chin, pensively. 'D'you think they'll fit in the furnace without you having to chop them up?'

Ferris shook his head. 'Doubt it, boss. I'll have ter saw the legs off – mebbe the fuckin' heads as well.'

Milo nodded, Ferris was much more of an expert in this sort of thing. 'Quick as you like,' he said, 'before the black bastards start to smell.'

Chapter Four

Sam hadn't yet heard of Ron Crusher, whose death would occupy his life for quite some time to come. He was pre-occupied by the black man with the glinting tooth who gave a loud shout and slapped a triumphant domino down with sufficient vigour as to almost have the flimsy table collapse.

'Fours about, I out!'

Sam, who hated triumphalism in domino players, looked at the double blank he had left in his hand and enquired, 'What?'

The other two players sighed, resignedly. 'He done won again, man.'

The four of them were standing at a rickety table on a street corner in Bridgetown, Barbados. Half an hour earlier Sam had been simply walking past and had been seduced into the game by the gold-toothed man. It was a version of dominoes he'd never played before and after six games he still didn't understand the rules, other than it was costing him five Barbados dollars a game.

In the half hour taxi ride from the airport into town he had decided he liked the island enough for him to want to spend a full week there. It had no volcanic mountains or sweaty rainforest, just pleasant rolling countryside; like the Yorkshire Dales with coconut trees and beautiful brown girls who smiled at him as they swayed past him in the hot streets. And that was before he'd checked out the brown girls swaying up and down the white beaches.

'How come you've won with fours about?' he asked. 'I had fours about in the last game but I didn't win.'

'That's because ya didn't have a one in the hole,' explained Gold Tooth. 'Shuffle the bones, man, maybe ya can bring yo'self some luck, luck, luck.'

Sam nodded, none the wiser. It might help his cause to have a few locals as friends, and if that meant allowing them to screw him out of a few quid, then so be it. Losing at dominoes had to be a legitimate expense, although he might have to word it differently on his expense sheet.

A Christmas float had just gone past, full of red-coated Bajans singing 'Jingle-Bells'. It must have been in the high eighties and none of them looked to be feeling the heat, not even Santa Claus, complete with padded suit and false, flowing beard. At five o'clock that morning Sam had still been in cold and murky Unsworth. It was now four in the afternoon – 8 p.m. Unsworth time.

As he shuffled for the next game, Sam thought it would do no harm to make an initial enquiry. 'Have any of you ever worked on the ships?'

'Ya mean the cruise ships?' said Gold Tooth, picking up a line of seven dominoes in one huge hand.

'Er, yes. There's one in at the moment and I wondered what the procedure was for going on board to visit an old friend.'

'Better for yo' frien' to visit you,' suggested the

oldest of the men. 'Dey won' let ya on without a boardin' card.'

'How would I get hold of a boarding card?' It was his turn again before the oldest man, whose name was Horace, gave an answer.

'I could maybe get ya one for fifty dollars.'

'Barbados dollars?'

'US mister. BB dollars is only good for old guys who waste their days playin' the bones.'

'Like you, you mean?'

'I only help out when they short. Old Horace is a busy, busy boy.'

'Right – shall I come with you?'

'Better ya stay here an' enjoy the game. What ship is it?'

'Caribbean Rose.'

'Sails at seven o'clock,' said Horace, knowledgeably. Cruise ships contributed considerably to the island economy and most of the locals had all the sailing times in their heads.

'In that case I could do with it fairly sharpish.'

'Fairly sharpish,' repeated Gold Tooth with a broad grin. 'I like that, fairly sharpish. Boys, we must add fairly sharpish to our vocaboolary. Where you from, man? You sound kinda Canadian.'

'Yorkshire,' said Sam. 'It's east of Canada, about the same latitude, but we don't have any Mounties, nor any proper mountains for that matter.'

Gold Tooth clicked his fingers. 'I knew you was from that part of the world.' He turned to Horace. 'Ya better get him that card, fairly sharpish.'

The old man set off at a loping run that seemed

to belie his years. Twenty minutes later he was back, much to Sam's relief, as he was another twenty Barbados dollars down. The old man handed him a plastic card in a slim leather wallet with a rose design on the front. The name on the card was Mariella Crusher.

'Er, this is a woman's card,' Sam pointed out.

All three men examined the card and came to the same conclusion. 'It don' make no difference, mister. All ya do is flash 'em the card before ya go up the gangway. Don' even bother ta take it out of the wallet. They all the same, standard issue. Wait until there's a lotta folk goin' on board.'

Sam wasn't convinced but he handed over the fifty dollars anyway. 'Thanks – and thanks for the game.'

'Any time yo' passin' this way,' grinned Gold Tooth.

'Maybe you'll teach me the rules next time.'

'Maybe we will, maybe there ain't no rules... Hey!'

'What?' asked Sam.

'When ya go up the gangway ya should go up fairly sharpish!'

'I'll do that.'

Sam strolled across the river bridge – after which the town had been named. Dozens of small boats bobbed about on the sparkling Careenage. The sun was hot as he looked at the buildings around him; some quite imposing, some garish and flimsy with much corrugated iron and clapboard. The town oozed noise and life and cheerfulness and colour and seemed a million miles from the brown and grey winter of Unsworth whose only dash of colour was provided by the Scarlet Pimple. Sam smiled to himself as he recited the rude rhyme they had composed the other night in the pub.

A crocodile of schoolchildren passed him by; dressed in smart uniforms with dark blue epaulettes and striped ties fastened loosely around the open necks of immaculate, light blue shirts. He smiled at them and they smiled back. People smiled a lot in Barbados, he thought – mind you, they had a lot to smile about.

A smiling young black man stepped out in front of him and asked, 'Taxi to the ships, mister?'

'Er, yeah, why not?'

'Five US dollar okay, mister?'

'That's fine. How did you know I wanted to go to the ships?'

'Because yo' a white guy and there's two ship in today.'

At the harbour gatehouse an attractive, female security guard was in animated discussion with a middle-aged couple. The woman had a deep, incongruous suntan and wore clothes unsuited to her years. Her bare midriff bulged from too tight shorts and was decorated with an assortment of tattoos. The man wore a white Ping golf shirt, khaki shorts, a white flat cap and leather sandals over fawn socks.

The woman was shaking her heavily jewelled fist at the impassive, security guard, whose two male colleagues leaned against a wall, in deep conversation, seemingly oblivious to the problems their colleague was having. 'It's only a piece o' plastic,' she was grumbling, belligerently. 'How can a piece o' plastic stop me gerrin' on me bleedin' ship?' Her voice was shrill and penetrating. Her accent was West Yorkshire and Sam wished it wasn't.

'Just calm down, Mariella,' the man was saying. 'It can be sorted out.'

'Not if she continue to be a ignorant lady,' said the guard, coolly.

'Ignorant? It were one of your lot what pinched it off me,' bellowed Mariella. 'D'yer remember Bernard? That bleedin' darkie feller what bumped into me in that shoppin' arcade?'

'That's right,' confirmed Bernard. 'Everything fell out of her bag and this old chap helped her pick it up. He seemed a nice enough chap to me.'

Mariella glowered and snarled at the woman in uniform. 'He were a darkie, just like you.'

'I assume you mean he was a man who belong to this island – unlike you?' said the guard, pointedly. Her two male colleagues glanced across at her then gave each other knowing looks that said she didn't need any of their help. Sam approved of how her generous chest pushed at her coffee and cream uniform. Perhaps sensing his stare the guard did a sudden double take of him and he hoped he wouldn't become caught up in this altercation.

Mariella glared at her. 'Yer all the same, you lot. Out fer what yer can get. It wouldn't surprise me if it were one o' your darkie mates what nicked it. All right, how much is it gonna cost us?' She took a gold bracelet off her wrist and shook in front the guard's face. 'Here, have this. It's probably worth a month's fuckin' wages ter one o' you lot!'

Sam cringed and hung back, unsure what to do.

Then he suddenly appreciated his good fortune. Had Mariella Crusher been a distressed old lady he'd have felt honour bound to hand the boarding card over to her with some lame story about how he saw it fall from her bag. As it was, he felt no such obligation and was in fact grateful to the woman for being such a pain in the arse. The guard looked across at him and her eyes softened as she called out, politely, 'Could I see your boardin' pass, sir?'

'Er, yes, miss,' said Sam, with more servility than was necessary. 'I've got it somewhere.'

He took Mariella's card from his pocket and held it up. His heart was pounding and he was ready to run if she examined it closely; but she gave him a beautiful smile and waved him through, watching him for a while before returning her attention to the irate Mariella. 'I think we better ring through to customs and let 'em sort it,' she said, with menacing civility.

Sam recognized that tone of voice. Sally Grover had used it against him when he'd tried her patience just a bit too much. At such times he would soften his attitude – grovel even. But this Mariella wasn't the grovelling kind. She was a hard-faced, rough-tongued woman.

'And how long's that gonna take?' she roared. 'Me bastard ship sails in a couple of hours.'

There was an unnerving profanity about her that always led Sam to avoid such women. He edged past and glanced back over his shoulder. It was obvious from the guard's attitude that it was going to take a long time, probably more than two hours.

Safe now, he strolled down the harbour road towards the towering vessel that was the *Caribbean Rose*; more of a floating hotel than a thing of nautical beauty. He passed a steel band playing, 'Oh I'm Goin' To Barbados', and he dropped a handful of change into an upturned hat, earning himself a collection of assorted smiles.

In front of him was a group of obvious passengers and, remembering the domino players' advice, he quickened his step so as to become one of them.

The ship's officers at the bottom of the gangway were only vaguely interested in the boarding card. One took Sam's bag from him and passed it through metal detector, which set off a bleep. A second officer rummaged inside it, and brought out a small, pocket tape recorder. Sam found himself apologizing.

'Sorry – I thought it was all plastic.'

The officer examined it carefully, taking out the batteries and holding the tape up to the light.

'It's a tape recorder,' Sam assured him. 'Honest.'

The officer took long enough over the job for Sam to become detached from the group, who were all at the top of the gangway, boarding the ship. He hurried after them and was confronted by a smiling crew member holding a laser scanner.

'Could you hold up your card please sir?'

'What?'

'Your card, I need to scan it, sir.'

Sam looked at the card in his hand and he just knew his comeuppance had arrived. He had beaten a few casual eyeballs, but now he was up against modern technology that could tell him the price of a tin of beans, his date of birth, post code, bank overdraft, criminal record and sexual preferences with one flash of a laser beam. From his high vantage point he could see Mariella throwing a wild punch at the busty guard who ducked underneath it and now had the frenzied woman in an armlock. With a bit of luck they'd arrest her and he wouldn't have to face her when she found out he was the cause of all her trouble. Helplessly he held the card up for scrutiny and winced as the laser flashed against it. There was a beep and a computerised voice said, 'Welcome on Board'.

Sam walked on, slowly releasing his pent up breath and wondering why the hell he constantly put himself in such ridiculous situations – why didn't he just stick to building? There was a lot more money in it. Once a copper always a copper, was that it? It was as far as he was concerned. What a bloody awful thing to have in your system. He was still shaking his head to himself when he arrived at the lifts.

Half a dozen passengers followed him in. There was a list of buttons, from 1 to 14. He pressed fourteen. A couple of other fingers stabbed out seven and ten and a recorded voice told him that, 'The doors are closing.'

'First day?' asked a small, bronzed woman with bleached hair and a top that exposed too much wrinkled cleavage.

'How did you guess?' said Sam. He examined his pale reflection in the wall mirror.

'I was paler than you when I got on,' she said, reassuringly. 'Still, we're at sea all day tomorrow.

You can get a bit of a tan then.'

'Not too much,' said another, patchily sun-tanned, woman. 'An hour in this sun takes a layer of skin off you. I should know. I must have used a gallon of calamine lotion this last week.'

'I should go on the boat deck,' advised an elderly man in a T-shirt that said he'd fallen in love with Antigua. 'They're packed like sardines on the sun deck.'

'And use factor 20 at least,' said the small, bronzed woman. 'It'll take the edge off, but you won't get too burnt.'

Sam tried to appear grateful for all this sun-bathing advice, but he was more grateful when the lift emptied at deck ten. He couldn't remember when he had felt so out of place. In the space of ten minutes he had gone from being a legitimate member of society to the cruise ship equivalent of an illegal alien. As a cop he'd done his share of undercover work but it had always been in an environment where he'd felt at home. Being an illegal holidaymaker could prove more of a challenge than he'd anticipated. As the lift emptied at deck ten the elderly man thrust a ship's newspaper into his hand. 'Tells yer what's goin' on,' he said. 'I'm off ter me bed meself. I'm knackered.'

'Thanks.'

It was headed *Aboard and Ashore – Your daily guide to what's on ashore and on board in Barbados.* A name on the front page caught his eye. He learned that passengers could delight to the silky sound of Joey Gladstone in The Courtyard on deck seven at 17.00 and again in the Coconut

37

Lounge at 21.00. The lift had stopped at deck fourteen. The door opened, then closed as Sam stabbed button number seven.

The Courtyard turned out to be the central hub of the ship, occupying three decks with bars and reception areas at the bottom and more bars and shops on the higher levels. Beneath the elegant central staircase was a man singing and playing a baby grand piano. People were milling around, some shopping, some drinking and some, mainly women, just admiring Joey Gladstone. Sam watched him from the balcony of the floor above and had to admit that Joey was nothing if not good looking. His voice was okay and his playing quite adequate, but it was obvious that Joey's job on this ship had been secured by his face rather than his voice. It was also obvious that Joey's father-in-law had good reason to be suspicious.

At a table not far from the piano a young woman was sitting on her own. She was blatantly attractive and Joey smiled at her from time to time. The young woman would smile back and raise her glass to him.

'Is she his latest?' Sam heard a woman's voice coming from a nearby cosmetics counter.

'I don't know, I can't keep track,' replied a red-coated, female staff member. 'He's married, you know. I don't know how he gets away with it. He knows it's not allowed – not with passengers.'

Joey brought his set to an end with 'I Left My Heart In San Francisco' then went to join the young woman, who, by the look of her tan, or lack of it, had just joined the cruise ship which toured the islands, stopping off at Barbados every week to pick up and drop off passengers. An older couple approached and Joey's young admirer stood up, with some reluctance, and left with them. Sam saw his chance. He switched on the tiny tape recorder in his pocket and stepped off the bottom step as Joey was about to go up.

'Joey Gladstone. Didn't I once see you in Unsworth Labour Club?'

The bugger's even more handsome close up, Sam thought. His tan suited him and his teeth were white and even.

'Now, that's very possible,' Joey said, amiably. 'With a bit of luck yer won't see me in there again. You from round there?'

Sam stuck out his hand. 'Sam Carew,' he said. 'I've got a building firm in Unsworth.'

Joey furrowed his brow as he looked at Sam. 'Bloody hell, that's right, you are!' he exclaimed. 'I read about you in the paper – something to do with a builder bumping women off?'

'Actually he wasn't a builder,' corrected Sam, not wishing to give builders a worse name than they already had.

'Wasn't he? He was a bad bugger, whatever he was. Bad do, all round, from what I remember. Mind you, yer put Unsworth on the map for a few days. What happened to him?'

'He got life.'

'Better than he deserved. Bloody hell, fancy meeting you out here. Are yer with the trip?'

'Er, no.'

'I thought not. They've all been on a week, you look as if yer've just arrived.'

Sam knew all about the Unsworth Observer

Holiday Club trip. One of the group, who knew both Joey and his father-in-law, had rung Philip Sims from the ship to tell him all about Joey's antics with the women. This had prompted Sims to enlist Sam's expertise.

'I'm here on my own,' Sam said. 'Found a cheap, last-minute offer. I imagine it's a pretty good life working on here.'

'Couldn't be better, mate. It's better than scraping a living round the bloody clubs. Fancy a jar?'

'Why not?'

Joey bought them each a pint of lifeless Boddingtons that tasted nothing like the Boddingtons at home, but it was wet and cold and just drinkable. 'You could get blind drunk on this for a couple of hundred dollars,' Joey commented. If it was any flatter they could serve it in an envelope, 'but it's either this or local lager.'

Sam almost said he'd have preferred the local lager but that seemed a bit ungracious. 'Saw you chatting the young bird up.' He mentioned it casually. 'I suppose that's one of the perks of your game.'

'One of 'em?' laughed Joey. 'It's the best one. The money's crap but the rest of it's okay. Sunshine, swimming and shaggin', that's what I'm here for, as much of it as I can get before I go blind.'

'I suppose it's a good life for a single man.'

'Single? I wish I was single. I've gorra a wife and kiddie back in Unsworth. Don't get me wrong, I treat 'em right. Send half me money home. I'm best off out here though. Her old man hates me.

We only got married cos o' the kiddie.'

'Doesn't stop you pulling the birds over here, then?' encouraged Sam.

'I once went ten nights without sleeping in me own cabin,' grinned Joey, incriminating himself on the silently spinning tape. 'Ten nights, ten different women. I tell yer, I were well knackered after that. Packed it in for a full week. There were a lot of women disappointed, I can tell yer that. But I'm not a bloody machine. You need a break ter let the sap rise again.'

'I wouldn't know,' Sam told him, truthfully. He put his hand into the bag, as though looking for something, and switched off the tape. Joey was okay, which made him feel guilty. In any event he already had enough recorded evidence – *if* he decided to use it. There was clapping from all around at a troupe of acrobats who were performing on the floor behind them. Joey's face went serious.

'If I had anything about me I'd go back and do the right thing by her.'

'By who?'

'The wife. I really ought to divorce her so she knows where she stands. She's a not a bad lass, just a bit spoilt that's all. Mind you, she'd bore the balls off a buffalo.'

'Why *don't* you divorce her?'

'Her dad'd shoot me.'

'He can't be that bad.'

'You don't know him. I came out here because of him. Always on me bloody back, never good enough for his darlin' daughter.' Joey went quiet and stared at Sam from the edge of his eyes,

41

thinking, as though something was troubling him. 'So, yer on yer own?'

'That's right.'

'And yer've nowt to do with the Unsworth trip?'

'Like I said, I got a cheap deal,' he said. 'Last minute.'

Joey suddenly banged his glass down on the bar and swivelled in his seat to face Sam.

'Hang on a minute! I've just remembered something about you. Yer not just a builder, are yer? Yer a bloody private detective. Yer used to be cop or something. It was all over the papers for ages.'

The singer's eyes searched Sam's face for evidence of guilt. 'It's a bit of a coincidence,' he went on, 'two lads from Unsworth, bumping into each other all this way from home.'

'I suppose it is,' agreed Sam.

'But not such a coincidence when one's a private detective? This last minute deal yer got – it wasn't from a feller called Sims was it?'

There was no point denying it. Sam gave a guilty shrug of his shoulders.

'Aw, bloody hell, I don't believe this. He sent you all this way to check on me? Jesus Christ, what sort of a prat are you?' Joey turned away and shook his head as though he couldn't bear to look at this betrayer of his fellow man.

It was the moment when Sam made up his mind never ever to take on cases like this again. 'Sorry, mate,' he said, lamely. Joey spun round on his stool; there was anger on his face. Sam held up his hands apologetically. 'To be honest,' he said. 'I wouldn't have taken the job if it hadn't been out here. I came for a winter break in the sun. I don't usually do jobs like this.'

'How did he know I were playin' around?'

'Someone on the Unsworth trip recognized you. They rang Sims to tell him what you were up to.'

'Bloody hell! Yer not safe anywhere.'

'Look,' said Sam. 'If you like I'll go back and tell him I couldn't get anything on you – I get paid either way.'

Joey's anger abated as quickly as it had come. He thought about this offer for quite a long time. 'But yer get more money if yer can get something on me, right?' he said.

'An extra grand,' Sam admitted. 'I honestly got the impression that he wanted to split you and your wife up, which is something you seem to have in common with him.'

Joey returned his attention to his drink. 'True,' he said. 'So, what sort of thing would yer need ter take back?'

Sam opened the neck of his shirt and revealed a small microphone clipped to the inside of his collar, then he unplugged the tape recorder in his pocket, laid it on the bar, and pushed it over to Joey. 'You've just given me everything I need. Take it if you want.'

Joey turned the tape recorder over in his hands. 'Simple as that eh? Just a few words out of place and I'm stuffed.' He thought back to what he'd been saying and gave a wry grin. 'I reckon what's on here should do the trick.' Then he pressed the play/record button and spoke into the end with the built-in microphone.

'Sorry Carly, this private detective feller took me by surprise. Yer dad sent him because he thinks I'm no good and I suppose this has just proved him right. Personally I think he's a sad old tosser.' He clicked it off and gave it back to Sam. 'Do what yer've got ter do, mate. It's probably for the best.'

'You're sure?'

'Why not? What's the worst that can happen? My wife divorces me, which is what I want. No, you take the tape and yer extra thousand. Now then, Bernard. Where's the Führer?'

'She's locked up.'

'What?'

Sam turned round in his seat and stared at Bernard Crusher, who held Sam's gaze as a knowing smile crept across his face.

'Locked up?' said Joey.

'Locked up,' confirmed Bernard, with no sign of anguish for his wife. 'You can't go round kicking coppers and expect to get away with it.'

'Kicking coppers?'

'She were like a Tasmanian devil. They were only trying to talk to her but she fails to see reason. She's her own worst enemy at times.'

'Well, why aren't yer with her?'

Bernard turned his smile on Joey. 'Talk sense, lad. A week without the Führer? Opportunities like that don't come round every day.' He looked back at Sam. 'And I reckon I've got this feller to thank for it.'

'Me?' Sam said, with as much innocence as he could muster.

'You nicked her cruise card, didn't you?' said Bernard. 'Don't say you didn't because I recognized it as soon as you showed it to that security bird.'

Sam paused before replying. Was there any point denying the truth? Not really. This man had somehow seen him with his wife's card. 'But you were four or five yards away at least. You must have damn good eyesight to read the name on a card from that distance.'

'I didn't have to read the name. I only had to look at the case. You see, they gave us all nice pink plastic cases, but Mariella had her own that she got from Leeds market. Bought it specially for this cruise. A proper leather one with a rose design on the front. There won't be anyone else with one like it.'

'Ah.' Sam took the wallet from his pocket. 'I was told the wallets were all the same.' He handed it to Bernard. 'Sorry. I bought it from a bloke in Bridgetown. I needed to get on board.'

'Did you now?' said Bernard. There was no condemnation in his voice. An awkward silence followed, broken by Joey.

'This is Sam,' he said. 'He's a private detective from Unsworth. Sam, this is Bernard. He's from Unsworth as well.'

'I assume you're on the club trip?' Sam guessed.

'Right first time, lad.'

'How come you never said anything when you saw I had her card?'

'Because she'd been giving bloody earache all day. I wasn't in the mood to help her.'

Joey looked at Bernard. 'You've maybe heard of

Sam – Sam Carew. He solved that big murder case in Unsworth last year. He's a builder as well.'

'What're you doing on here?' Bernard enquired, with a grin. 'Murder at sea, is it? There'll be a bloody murder if the Führer catches you.'

'He's been sent ter get the goods on me,' said Joey, cheerfully. 'Someone rang the wife's father and told him I were playin' around.'

'I just came for the free trip,' said Sam, who was becoming increasingly embarrassed by his role in all this.

Bernard went quiet for a while, then said, almost guiltily. 'I, er, I think I know who the bloody culprit might be.' Joey looked at him, realising who he meant.

'What – Mariella?'

Bernard winced and nodded. 'I think it's just jealousy – with her bein' past it. She's been watching you carry on all week, grumbling like buggery. Sims is her dentist, she'll have his number in her book.'

Joey suddenly laughed out loud. 'And the bloke he sent's just got the Führer locked up.'

Bernard saw the funny side and let out a bellow that had heads turning their way. Sam joined in because it kind of let him off the hook. The laughter subsided and Bernard studied Sam.

'Mad Carew, isn't that what they called you?'

'It's an obvious nickname,' said Sam. 'It comes from an old music hall monologue.'

'Didn't yer dad have something to do with it?' asked Joey.

'My dad was killed as well.'

'Oh, that's right. Sorry to hear that.'

'A builder who does murders, eh?' said Bernard. 'That rings a bell.'

'I don't *do* them,' said Sam, just in case Bernard was offering his wife up for a victim. 'I try and solve them if I can. I used to be in the police.'

'No, when I said, "rings a bell", I meant it rings a bell insofar as our kid's concerned.'

'Your brother?'

'Aye, lad, me brother. He were a builder and he got murdered.'

'Small world,' said Joey.

'So, would you work for me?' asked Bernard.

'For you? What is it you want?'

'What do I want? I want you to find a murderer for me. The coppers reckon it was suicide, but I know better. Our kid wouldn't top himself while he had a hole in his arse. How much do you charge?'

'Er–' Sam was taken aback by this strange turn of events, 'two hundred a day plus expenses.'

Bernard stuck out a large hand. 'You're on. Are you in the book?'

'Yellow Pages – Sam Carew Investigations Bureau.'

'I'll look you up when I get back. Like I say, it's me brother who were murdered. I reckon the coppers who investigated it didn't know their arses from their elbows. They only put a sergeant on it – feller called Bassey.'

'We used to call him Shirley when I was in the job. He's not the sharpest tool in the box.'

'They've got no nose for crime anymore,' Bernard went on. 'If it's not written down on a piece of paper and printed off in bloody triplicate they don't want to know.'

'Right,' said Sam, at a loss what to do next. He picked up the tape recorder, put it in his pocket, then slid off the stool. 'I'd better make myself scarce. Sorry about your wife and all that.'

'Sorry be buggered, lad,' roared Bernard, happily. 'This ship sails in an hour and I've gorra week to meself. What is it you call it, Joey? Sunshine, swimming and shagging?'

'Well, I have to do a bit of singing as well,' laughed Joey. He looked at Sam. 'Best o' luck then, Sam.'

'Oh,' remembered Bernard. 'You'll need more than luck. I mentioned to that security lass that I reckoned you'd got Mariella's card – I felt it me bounden duty.'

'Oh, thanks very much,' said Sam.

'They're on the lookout for you, lad. I shouldn't try leaving down the gangway.'

'If they arrest you they'll lock you up and start asking questions in a month or two,' warned Joey. 'They're very laid back in many ways round these parts.'

'Can you swim?' enquired Bernard.

'Swim?'

'Aye, lad. A private detective should be able to swim. That *Magnum PI* feller could swim like a fish.'

'Well, I can do few strokes,' said Sam, 'but I'm not what you'd call amphibious – anyway, Unsworth's not exactly Hawaii.' At the far side of the room he saw the female security guard appear, in the company of two ship's officers. 'Which deck's the lowest for jumping off?' he asked Joey, with some urgency.

'Boat deck, through that door, next floor up.'

There was a shout from the other side of the room as the busty guard spotted him. He ran out of the door and into an open lift. The doors closed just in time for him to catch a shrinking glimpse of the guard's frustrated face. He got out on the next deck and raced down a long narrow corridor with cabins on either side. An attendant with an armful of towels squashed herself against the wall as he flew past her until he came to a wide, staircase landing, the full width of the ship, with doors on either side. There was a shout from behind him, indicating that his pursuers were hot on his trail. He opened the door to his immediate left and stepped out on to the lifeboat deck, beyond which was the harbour. Pausing only to kick off his shoes, Sam vaulted over the side.

The sea was thirty feet below which gave him time to curse his stupidity before he hit the quiet water in the arse-tearing sitting position. He couldn't howl because he was underwater, tumbling around, disoriented, scared, not knowing up from down. The sky above the water was quite dark now. He knew he had to kick to the surface but he didn't know which way was up. Kicking himself deeper into the water would be bad. His lungs were soon bursting but he had the presence of mind to know that as long as held his breath his body's natural buoyancy would bring him to the surface; what he didn't know was how long this would take. He took a sharp, involuntary gulp as a large fish flicked its tail against his face. He inhaled no more than an eggcup full of water but it was enough to have drowned him. He was choking and sinking and he realised with absolute certainty that he was about to die. Drowned. Just about his worst nightmare. Then he spotted the ship's lights shining on the surface and with the very last of his energy he kicked towards them. Within seconds his head broke clear of the water. His lungs gulped, greedily at the air. He threw up seawater, mucus and flat beer in a series of retching, spluttering coughs that would have been heard all around the harbour but for the sound of revelry coming from above.

He had been under for maybe thirty seconds but it had seemed like a lifetime, or maybe the end of a lifetime – it still could be. All this leg kicking and coughing up water was sapping his strength with a worrying rapidity. He knew that, very shortly, he would be sinking again through sheer exhaustion, this time with no hope of coming back up. There was the sound of something hitting the sea near his head – half splash, half thump. He looked up and saw a circular lifebuoy floating almost above the surface. It was only about ten feet away but it took his exhausted body half a dozen flailing strokes to reach it, to hang on to it for dear life, a dear life that had just been saved, and not for the first time.

This is just so ridiculous, he thought. A man of my age not being able to swim properly. He held on to the lifebuoy for ten minutes until some strength returned to his muscles. Then he kicked out with his feet and managed, after a while, to acquire a rhythm of sorts that propelled him along the side of the ship. He kept as near to the vessel as he could, obscured from shipboard eyes by the inward curve of the hull. There were no shouts from above. Why wasn't the person who had thrown him the lifebuoy shouting at him? It certainly hadn't fallen in on its own. Someone knew he was in the water.

Any minute now he expected a police launch to come tearing across the harbour with a search-light picking him out and a voice from a loud hailer instructing him to give himself up or they'd shoot. *Did they have guns in Barbados?* He was asking himself this as he arrived at the bow of the ship and cautiously peered round to look for the enemy. The short stretch of water between him and the shore was clear, and there was no one about who seemed to be looking for him. A hundred yards away from the ship he could see a ladder attached to the low, sea wall. He headed in that direction.

He was making good progress and after a while he began to feel quite pleased with himself. The only nagging doubt he had was the identity of the person who had thrown him the lifebuoy. The person who had saved his life.

It took him just a few minutes to arrive at the ladder. To his left he could see that the ship's gangways had been taken up and men were un-fastening the massive mooring ropes. He pushed away the lifebuoy, grabbed the bottom rung and heaved himself out of the water.

A hand reached down to help him up. 'Welcome to Barbados,' said the guard with the generous bosom.

Chapter Five

Sam sat down on an iron mooring post and collected his energy and his thoughts. The guard had folded her arms across her ample front as she waited for the explanation she'd just asked for.

'I'm still waitin'.'

'I'm still thinking,' replied Sam, disappointed at this unexpected end to his evening. He took the tape recorder from his pocket and pressed the play button. Nothing.

'Well that just great, that is.'

'Give it to me.'

She took it from him and removed the cassette. 'The tape seems to have survived,' she said. 'Maybe I should hang on to it for evidence of wrong doing.'

He looked up at her, with what he hoped was appeal in his eyes. 'Wrong doing? I nearly drowned back there, you know.'

'Did you now?'

'Yes, as a matter of fact I did.'

It sometimes worked, to play on a woman's sympathy, to show her he'd already suffered enough for his sins. Was this the way out of it? She seemed a reasonable sort, very nice looking too.

'What are you planning to do with me?' That sometimes worked as well. To remind her that she had power over him, power she mustn't abuse –

with him being a decent chap and undeserving of any further punishment.

'Well now, let me see.' She considered the options. 'You stole a cruise card and illegally boarded a ship. What I should do is hand you over to the police.'

But you're not going to, are you? He kept this thought to himself and asked, 'Are there any alternatives?'

'Have you any suggestions?'

'Well, I know you're not open to bribery. When Mrs Crusher tried to bribe you she ended up in jail.'

'She ended up in jail because she was a ignorant lady. If she'd been polite we could have helped her. As it is she'll prob'ly be locked up until she cool off. Overnight, prob'ly.'

'You could have helped her anyway,' said Sam. 'You knew I had her card.' There was a polite challenge in his voice but he tried not to make it sound like blackmail. 'Her husband told you – I know this because he told me he told you.' He watched her eyes and they briefly registered surprise. 'I gave him the card,' he added. 'So, all's well that ends well eh?'

'Except that she's still in jail.'

'She assaulted a police officer,' Sam pointed out. 'And she insulted you.'

'You seem to know a lot.'

'I think you turned a blind eye to me because she was insulting you and you didn't want her to get away with it. Can't say I blame you.'

'You don't blame me? Well that's very nice of you.'

'Look, we don't want to get each other in trouble do we?'

'Who are you, mister?'

Sam gave her a broad smile and stuck out a hand. 'Sam Carew, private investigator. I had some business on board which will be concluded as soon as you give me my tape back, and you are?' He noted from her ring finger that she wasn't married. She hesitated before shaking his hand and replying, 'My name is Francine le Bon.'

'Beautiful name for a beautiful lady. What time do you finish, Miss le Bon?'

'I'm finished now. How do I know you are who you say you are?'

He took his wallet out of his back pocket and produced a damp driving licence. 'If you need further identification you'll have to accompany me back to my hotel where I left my passport, from where we might as well go for something to eat.'

'That won't be necess'ry. You'll accompany me from this harbour and take me home to get changed into something suitable for the Plant-ation Restaurant where you will buy me dinner and tell me exac'ly what you been up to.'

'It will be my pleasure. You don't really need to keep that tape, do you? You can keep the recorder.'

She gave them both back to him. 'By the way,' he said, 'thanks for throwing me that lifebuoy. You saved my life.'

'What lifebuoy?'

'So, it wasn't you?'

'No.'

Then it was probably Bernard or Joey – decent of them, he thought. He got to his feet and walked with her along the harbour road. Behind them the *Caribbean Rose* gave Barbados a farewell hoot and moved sideways from its mooring as the passengers on the sun deck lined the rails and gave an intoxicated cheer to no one in particular. From the gatehouse emerged an unmistakable figure, running towards down the moonlit harbour-side with whirling arms and high stepping legs, waving and cursing volubly at the departing ship.

'Oh, no,' groaned Francine. 'I guess word must have got through that her card turned up.' She turned her face away from Mariella, who hurtled past without sparing them a glance and stood at the dockside bursting with volcanic rage and shaking her fist at the ship. The happy passengers waved back and cheered all the louder at this funny woman who had come to wave them off. In almost military unison, Sam and Francine quickened their step to something just short of running.

'How long you stayin' in Barbados, Mr Carew?'

'Haven't made up my mind. I'm either going back tomorrow or I'm staying another week. Maybe you can persuade me to stay on, eh?'

'Let's just see what tonight brings, Mr Carew.'

Sam was enjoying the Plantation restaurant, especially as Joey Gladstone's father-in-law was picking up the tab. The lively band had just left the stage and a limbo dancer was snaking his willowy body under a flaming pole set not much

55

more than a foot above the floor.

'Don't take this the wrong way,' Sam said, 'but how come a classy looking woman like you works as a security guard?'

'Maybe I'm on the lookout for a rich husband. I get to frisk all the likely candidates.'

'Well you're looking in the wrong direction if you're looking at me,' said Sam, in between mouthfuls of creole fish. There was a clapping and cheering from the audience as the dancer got under the pole unscathed. Sam joined in. Francine placed a hand on his.

'You see,' she said, 'Barbados is a beautiful island, but it's also a very small island and I'd like to see more of the world. Maybe me live in England or America for a while.'

Sam's plate was clean and he picked up the menu. 'This Bajan grub's excellent. Fancy a pudding?' He read from the menu: 'Rositas Cassava Pone; Bajan Bread Pudding; Orange Cake...'

'D'you like what you see?' Francine was wearing a low cut dress that left little to Sam's imagination.

'Very much indeed.'

'Well I don' keep me figure like this by eatin' Bajan puddings. This is the first proper meal I've had in a month. I been stickin' rigidly to a peanut and melon diet that I read about in *Cosmopolitan*.'

Sam's eyes strayed down to her bosom. 'I'm not sure about the peanuts – but the melons seem to be doing the trick.'

She slapped his hand, playfully, then, with a great effort of will she put on a straight face. 'Norm'lly I'd have reported you to the police and let 'em pick you up,' she said. 'But I felt a magnetism when our eyes met and I jus' knew – what's more I knew you could feel it too. It was somethin' – somethin' spiritual. Tell me you felt it, Sam.'

He was watching the stage as she spoke to him and it took him a while to run what she'd just said back through his brain. Was she serious, or was she teasing – or had she had too much to drink? Could be that a blunt rebuttal might offend her and who knows what she might do? She did have a certain authority, and was probably in a position to have him locked up. The old proverb which began, 'Hell hath no fury...' came to his mind.

'I definitely felt something,' he told her, with as much conviction as he could muster. 'But maybe I'm not quite as spiritual as you. We Yorkshire lads tend not to be very spiritual.'

'I could pleasure you, Sam Carew. Pleasure you like you've never been pleasured before.' Her fingers crept up his arm and a sensuous smile played on her lips.

'Well, er, I'm easily pleasured,' admitted Sam, nervously. 'Everybody says that.' He didn't see the mischievous grin she was hiding behind her hand.

'I don' want to be disillusioned, Sam,' she said earnestly.

'Don't you?'

'No, and I know I wouldn't be if I went to England on the arm of a good man like yourself.'

Come to England with me? The limbo dancer was snaking under the lowest pole of his career;

flames were burning the fine hairs off his chest; the audience was shouting and clapping encouragement; Sam's mind was elsewhere.

'Francine Carew,' she sighed. 'It has a beautiful ring to it, don' you think?'

More of a ring than you'll ever get. He was panicking more than he had when he was on the verge of drowning. Suddenly he wasn't hungry any more.

'Look, Francine, this has been a fairly full day for me. I've travelled four thousand miles; I've been half-drowned; I'm jet-lagged and dog tired – and now meeting a wonderful woman like you is too much for a man to take in one day. I wonder if we could skip the pudding and I went to bed – to sleep?'

There was a loud burst of cheering as the dancer took a bow, having broken his personal best. Francine continued with her game and kissed Sam on his cheek. 'You're a thorough gentleman, Sam Carew. I've chosen well. You could have taken advantage of me, you know that don' you?'

He enfolded her hand in both of his and looked into her eyes. 'Francine, I wouldn't dream of taking advantage of you. What we've got is too special.'

He was at the airport at eight o'clock the following morning and back in Unsworth twelve hours later.

Chapter Six

'I didn't expect you back for another week.'

'Got the job done,' said Sam. 'No point stopping. I picked up my fee, with a bonus, last night.'

'I thought you'd have spun it out.' Sally spun a pencil around in her recently manicured fingers. 'Barbados in the middle of winter? You're losing your touch.' She shook her head at him and returned her attention to her calculator as she ran a pencil up a column of numbers. He twisted his head to look over her shoulder.

'What are you doing? I hope you're not moonlighting, young lady.'

'I am, actually. Alec asked me to do his weekly accounts. There was nothing to do here, so I said I would.'

'That's good,' said Sam. 'Divide your time between the two businesses. Make full use of your time – makes sense.'

'Makes sense to me as well. Alec said he'd pay me extra.'

'Did he now?'

'Yes. You could do with more work to keep this side of things alive.'

'I know,' Sam said, casually. 'I picked up another job out in Barbados.'

'Will you be commuting?'

'The job's in Unsworth. At least the brother of

the bloke who was murdered's from Unsworth. Could be anywhere I suppose, I didn't have time to check further details.'

'We've got a murder?'

'We? It was "you" a minute ago. Now it's a murder you're suddenly part of the firm.'

She ignored him. 'Who was murdered?'

'Bernard Crusher's brother.'

'Who's Bernard Crusher?'

'I pinched his wife's boarding card. She missed the boat. His brother was murdered.'

'And that's the full story, is it?'

'Pretty much – oh, the police think it was suicide.'

'It's not much to go on.'

'He'll be contacting me when he gets back next week.'

'Do you want me to do some checking in the meantime, so I can impress him when he gets in touch?'

'It's *me* you're supposed impress. *I'll* impress the clients.'

Sally threw him a Benny Hill salute. 'Yes, sir. Sue rang, by the way.'

'What did she want?'

'How should I know? She's your ex-wife, not mine.'

'Sal, what did she want? I know you two will have been gassing for at least half an hour.'

'I think she might be wanting you to have the boys over Christmas.'

The boys were Sam's twin, but non-identical, sons.

'When, and how long for?'

'Christmas Eve. Three days.'

'Tell her yes.'

'I'd prefer you told her.'

'So would she. Fraternising with ex-wives is a bad idea. It should be banned by law. It's the biggest cause of earache known to man.'

'Don't you want to know why she wants you to look after them?'

'No.'

'Her fiancé's taking her to New York for Christmas.'

Sam demonstrated his disinterest by looking at his watch – half past nine. 'I told Alec I'd put some time in on the Dalby Parade job if there was nothing urgent here. *Is* there anything urgent here?' he asked hopefully. Laying bricks on a cold December day held little appeal for him, but Alec was short handed and the job was running behind schedule.

'Nothing I can't handle,' Sally said. 'I had a woman in yesterday wanting us to track down her long lost boyfriend. Her husband died recently and she wanted to make up for lost time. She hadn't seen the boyfriend since they went out together in Leeds back in the late forties.'

'Is she stinking rich?'

'Doubt it, she lives in sheltered housing on the Robertstown estate.'

'I hope you told her we don't do misspers?'

Sally ignored this. 'Well he sounded a bit foreign, his name's Horatio Flangebaum, so I rang up directory enquiries and they came up with a chap of that name living in Brighouse. Believe it or not he was the very same Horatio

Flangebaum. Stroke of luck when you come to think of it.'

'What, out of all the Horatio Flangebaums in Yorkshire your nose led you to the right one straight away? You should buy a lottery ticket.'

Sally ignored this as well. 'Well, she was ever so pleased.'

'How much did you charge her?'

'Sam, how could I charge a bereaved widow for something that only cost us a phone call?'

'She doesn't sound very bereaved, chasing after Horatio Flangebaum the minute her husband falls off his perch. She'll be telling her friends and before you know it they'll be queuing up for our free services. Sally this is a business, we don't work for nothing, not for anyone.'

'Do you want me to check on Bernard Crusher's brother or not?' she asked.

'If you can find the time. My information is that he was murdered and that the police think it was suicide.'

'So, you don't know his first name, or how old he was or what he did for a living or was he married or where and when this happened?'

'No.'

'So, if I came up with anything it would be a miracle.'

'It would be unnecessary. His brother will fill me in on all that when he gets in touch.'

'But wouldn't it impress the hell out of him if you knew this stuff already?'

This forced a grin from him. Sally was probably the most resourceful person he could have employed to run his detective agency for him.

The trouble was, that given half a chance, she would run his life for him. He thought a lot about Sally and she frequently shared his bed, but she couldn't fill the aching void that Kathy Sturridge had left in his heart. Kathy had died rescuing him from a fire started by a man trying to silence him. That, and the fact that he had worshipped her, would be hard to top.

'Sally, my client will be back next week. I can't start the case until then. There's no point spending days trying to get information he can give us in a few minutes.'

Her face dropped, she fancied a bit of detective work to break the boredom. Anyway, she thought, just because he said she shouldn't didn't mean to say she couldn't. Her face brightened. 'Owen rang,' she said. 'He's got a problem he hopes you might be able to help him with.'

'Owen's a walking problem. Tell him I'll meet him in the Clog and Shovel at five.'

Although Alec Brownlow was Sam's nearly equal partner the fact that Sam had pretty much given him half the firm in exchange for Alec's building and business expertise, meant that Alec never complained about Sam's frequent absences. It was a partnership founded on friendship and trust – which are the worst kind of business partnerships – but this one was bound by a crafty contractual clause. Sam still owned fifty-one per cent and had tied Alec to the firm with a clause that said that Alec could only leave and take his forty-nine per cent share of the firm out with Sam's agreement, otherwise the shares reverted to Sam. Alec agreed because he had nothing to lose and he knew he could trust Sam to do the right thing in the end. Sam wasn't entirely without a business head on his shoulders and Alec did pretty well out of the deal. On site he exerted plenty of authority over Sam the bricklayer.

'I need that wall brought up to wallplate tonight.'

'Nay, Alec! It's ten o'clock now, it gets dark at four.'

'It's not my fault you turned up late. You can work through your dinner hour. There's about a thousand bricks, you can have Jimmy all to yourself. I bet you fifty you can't do it.'

'Sod that! If I do it I want a hundred quid bonus.'

'You're on.'

'Alec, just remind me who's the boss of this firm.'

'When you're on site, I am.'

'Just thought I'd check.'

Sam slung his bag of tools over his shoulder and climbed the scaffold where Jimmy, the best of the labourers, was stacking bricks. The string line was already set up for the next course; not many labourers would bother to do that.

'We're working through dinner, Jimmy. We've a hundred quid bonus to split if we get the wallplate on tonight.'

'I've spent it already,' said Jimmy. 'I'll follow yer up wi' the pointing. Have yer brought any snap?'

'No, I was planning on going to the café until this cropped up.'

'Yer can share me sarnies. Cold sausage and

beetroot, wi' a fair size cookin' apple for pudding. I think there's a maggot in your side but it's all good protein.'

'Jimmy, lad,' said Sam – he called him lad despite Jimmy being over sixty – 'they should give you a Michelin Star for site catering.' He scooped a trowel full of compo from a ligger board and spread it on the bricks. 'Right, the clock's running. Let's get motoring.'

By half past four the work was done, the wooden wallplate, on which the roof trusses would be fixed, had been set in mortar and the freshly laid bricks covered with polythene to protect them from the night's elements. Sam and Jimmy were the last men on the site.

'Good job done,' said Sam, standing on the ground and appraising the work through the descending gloom. The courses were level, the joints even and the brickwork clean. 'The old man would have just about approved. I'll make sure there's an extra fifty in your packet on Thursday.'

'Cheers, boss. When I first started work down t' pits it took two months for me to earn fifty quid. Mug's game workin' down there. I reckon bloody Scargill did me a favour.'

'Don't you mean bloody Maggie?'

'I know who I bloody mean.'

'I'm meeting Owen in the Clog. Fancy one on the way home?'

'Not me, boss. I know you – one drink'll turn into a session. Me an' my missis are saving ter go to see our Mandy in Australia.'

'Australia! What sort of a firm am I running when brickie's labourers can afford to go to

Australia? You're supposed to go to Blackpool and sit on the beach with your trouser legs rolled up and a knotted hanky on your head. If my dad were still alive he'd turn in his grave.'

'I think you're turning Irish, boss.'

'Talking of Irish, where's Mick and Curly, I wonder if they fancy a jar? I don't want to be stuck with that gloomy Welsh bugger all night. He's gone even more miserable since he got transferred to CID. Evidently he's got a problem and there's nothing more depressing than a Welsh bobby with a problem.'

'Just seen them going home, boss, which is where I'm headed – g'night.'

It crossed Sam's mind to pick Sally up from the office and take her with him but he suspected that Owen's problem might be one he didn't want to share with a woman. In his younger days Owen had been possessed of a certain wayward charm which cost him dearly once the CSA caught up with him. He now lived with the local post mistress, upon whom he bestowed his sexual favours twice a week in lieu of rent. Her husband approved of this as it relieved him of a task he was no longer up to. On top of which the post-master and Owen were soul mates – united in pessimism. Sam suspected that Owen's unusual love-life was catching up with him, but he was wrong.

'I think I made a mistake taking this plain clothes job, Sam. Don't feel like a proper copper without a uniform, see.'

Sam glanced at Owen's current uniform. He

suspected that Owen went to charity shops and swapped his dropping-to-bits clothes for something not quite as tatty. The Welshman wore a geography teacher's jacket and rhinoceros-arse shaped trousers; both items had been made to measure for someone six inches fatter and two inches shorter than he was. Sam shook his head.

'I can see you haven't given up grave robbing. How on earth did a scruffy sod like you get so many women? Here's me, oozing charm and sophistication, with trousers without holes in and you get all the birds. How did that work out?'

'I appeal to their maternal instinct,' explained Owen. 'It's called "lost boy" charm. Women find it irresistible. I was born with it, see. I found that the uniform didn't do any harm, either.'

'Owen, you were made for plain clothes work. I never met a copper who looked less like a copper than you. Me, I couldn't wait to get out of uniform.' Sam was sampling his first pint of the evening. He held it up to the light to check for cloudiness then smiled at Dave who was watching this action with some disapproval. 'Good as ever,' Sam called out.

'Then they plonk this car-nicking case on me,' grumbled Owen. He swilled a full half pint down in one gulp, emptying his glass before continuing: 'I've got to solve it all on my own. Inspector bloody Bowman hates my guts, see, and it's all because of you.'

'He hates you because you made him look a fool solving those burglaries on your own, thus getting your transfer to CID,' Sam pointed out.

'It was you that solved that case, boyo. You

67

know it, I know it and bloody Bowman knows it. I think I've soared too high moving up to CID.'

'God, you're such a misery.'

'Misery is very much underrated,' said Owen. 'Happiness can be an annoying trait, especially in a policeman.'

'Anyway,' said Sam, 'you haven't moved up, you've moved along the corridor. Apart from a plain clothes allowance you don't get any more money. You're a detective constable not a chief bloody superintendent.'

'No bird soars too high if he soars with his own wings,' mused Owen, studying his empty glass.

'What?'

'I was quoting my dear old dad – a fount of knowledge. Trouble is I didn't use my own wings, I used yours. Still, there is an upside.'

'What – an upside? You've found an upside to something? And I came along here thinking you'd got postwoman Pat pregnant.'

'It gets me out of Sergeant Bassey's jurisdiction, see.'

'Biggest arsehole in the nick is Shirley,' remarked Sam, 'in more ways than one. So, what about these car thieves? Incidentally, have you ever heard of a chap called Crusher who topped himself?'

'When?'

'Don't know.'

'Where?'

'Don't know.'

'What's his first name?'

'No idea.'

'How did he kill himself?'

'Owen, you're a detective now. You're supposed

to be helping me.'

'Is that what detectives do, perform magic tricks?' said Owen. 'As it happens the name does ring a bell. I once nicked a chap called Ron Crusher for GBH. Got eighteen months. He was a well-behaved lad so I imagine he served a year. Did a bit of allsorts as I remember. Club singer, nightclub bouncer – he was working the door at the Queen of Clubs when I tugged him.'

'Milo Morrell's place,' mused Sam. 'Now there's a villain if ever there was one – and this Ron Crusher was a bouncer, was he?'

'He was in those days, mind you by all accounts he didn't bounce very high when he threw himself off Ridings House.'

'I think I might have heard about that,' remembered Sam. 'It was some jump.'

'Roof to pavement. Does that sound like your man?'

'The bloke I'm talking about was a builder, apparently.'

'That's the fellow,' said Owen. 'He went into building after he came out. He learned a trade inside.'

'I always thought that was a prison skive,' said Sam. 'Don't tell me the prisons are actually producing tradesmen.'

'He came out as a plasterer.'

'Ah, that sort of tradesman.'

'I'm told he was pretty good. Set himself up as a builder.'

'Hmmm.'

'I don't think he was ever of the calibre of Carew and Sons, though. More of your cowboy builder so I believe.'

'Sounds like my man. I'm working for his brother who thinks he was murdered. Haven't quite got all the details yet. When did he die?'

'Few months ago – about June I think. He wasn't a bad chap wasn't Big Ron. It was the name that stuck in my mind. Good name for a bouncer, Ron Crusher.'

'So, it was definitely suicide was it?'

Owen nodded and rubbed his long chin, remembering. 'All the witnesses said it was. Screamed like a banshee all the way down. I must admit, I thought it was all very odd when I heard.'

'When you heard what?'

'When I heard he'd topped himself. Didn't seem the type. Very amiable man when he wasn't bashing people about. Very likeable, look you. Popular with the ladies, although I believe he was married.'

'So, it might not have been suicide?' said Sam, hopefully. He could see a prolonged investigation here. A month at least at two hundred a day plus expenses.

'And the other thing I thought sounded odd,' Owen went on, 'was the scream.'

'The scream?'

'Yes, the scream. I've had experience of a couple of jumpers in my time, look you, and neither of them screamed. If *they* didn't, I wouldn't have thought Ron Crusher would either, not if he'd decided to top himself. In my experience suicides seldom scream.'

'Not much point,' agreed Sam. 'Unless you change your mind halfway down.'

'From what I hear, Ron didn't change his mind. He screamed from top to bottom – and he had a good pair of lungs on him did Ron. Probably had some Welsh blood in him. When he sang in the clubs he called himself Ronnie Crush, silly sod.'

'When did you start speaking ill of the dead?' asked Sam.

'Since I became a detective. I now speak ill of everyone, mainly you.'

'You always spoke ill of me.'

'Only behind your back,' said Owen. 'I've now decided to speak ill of you to your face. You're a selfish bastard, you know that, don't you, look you?'

'Don't you, look you? What sort of talk's that?'

'It's my native vernacular. I'm very proud of my mother tongue.'

'Mother tongue? You were talking English.'

'Don't split hairs, boyo.'

'Anyway, what have I done that's selfish? It's not even my round.'

'I'll tell you why you're selfish. I get you here to discuss my problems,' said Owen, 'and all you can talk about are your problems.'

'I just asked a casual question, that's all. Anyway, what *is* your problem?'

'Bloody car thieves, isn't it. I've got to round up a gang of car thieves single handed because CID have got more important things to deal with, according to Bowman. I reckon he just wants me to fail so he can kick me down the corridor back to uniform.'

'Can't have that, see, look you,' said Sam.

'You're much more useful to me in CID.'

'I didn't join CID just to be of service to you. I did it to serve the community. And don't take the piss out of my vernacular.'

'So, you're saying I'm not part of the community now, are you?'

Owen finished his drink and got to his feet. 'I'll get the drinks in,' he said, 'while you're thinking.'

'I'll need more than you telling me someone's nicking cars.'

'Why? It's as much as you gave me about Ron Crusher – and I've practically solved that case for you.'

Chapter Seven

'No need ter mention this ter the Führer,' said Bernard. 'She'd do her nut if she thought I were throwing money away on what she'd call a wild goose chase.' He was sitting in Sam's office. Sally was at her own desk, ostensibly taking notes.

'So, she doesn't think it was murder?'

'No, lad. She believes the police.'

'Did the police know about Ron screaming all the way to the ground?' enquired Sam, casually.

Bernard was taken aback, as was Sally who had her information about Ron Crusher at the ready, intending to impress both her boss and his client.

'You've been doin' your homework, lad. What else do you know?'

'I know he was married and that he was a night-club bouncer who did time for GBH and that he once sang in the clubs under the name Ronnie Crush.'

Bernard gave a small laugh. 'Aye, daft bugger. He had a good voice on him, though. Better than all them young kids you see on *Pop Idol*.'

'And I also know he fell off the top of Ridings House last summer and screamed all the way down.'

'I think I'd scream if I fell off the top of Ridings House,' commented Sally as she put away her notes on Ron Crusher. Sam's information was better.

'Ah, but would you scream if you were committing suicide?' Sam asked her. He looked at Bernard and stole Owen's line. 'Suicides seldom scream, Mr Crusher – and why would Ron top himself? He was cheerful and very popular, especially with the women. Did he, er, did he put it about much?'

'More than most,' conceded Bernard. 'He was happily married but he liked to play away whenever he could.'

'I don't suppose his wife was too pleased,' said Sally.

'Not sure she ever knew.'

'Any idea where she was when he died,' Sam enquired, 'just as a matter of interest?'

'I know exactly where she was. She were in Blackpool gerrin' bladdered with my missis and a busload of other women. It was a two day trip. The Führer had just come out of hospital – only a twopence ha'penny bloody operation but yer'd have thought she'd had a leg off. She were sat round the house with a face like a smacked arse – Ken bloody Dodd couldn't have cheered her up, so I had no chance. Anyroad, as soon as I heard this Blackpool jaunt were on I talked her into goin' – anythin' for a bit o' peace and quiet.'

'So, Mariella could give Eileen an alibi if she needed one?' concluded Sam, mentally crossing Ron's wife off his list of suspects.

'She'd never need an alibi,' commented Bernard. 'She's like a mouse is Eileen. Soft as they come. She lost everything when she lost our Ron. We've been worried about her committing suicide.'

Sam tapped a pencil on his desk. 'Suicide –

that's the theory we have to discredit. The trouble is, apart from the scream there's nothing to suggest Ron didn't commit suicide.'

'Oh yes there is.'

'What?' asked Sam, apprehensively.

'Me – I'm suggesting it. And I'm backing my suggestion up with hard cash. You've impressed me, so far, lad.' He took out his cheque book, wrote out a cheque for £3,000 and pushed it across the desk to Sam.

'Two hundred a day's the agreed figure. I don't expect to be paying for days you're not working on my case, so there's trust involved here. That should keep yer going for a while. When it's run out, let me know, but I want proper receipts for expenses.'

'I'll make sure you do, Mr Crusher,' Sally assured him. 'And you can trust Sam. How is Mrs Crusher by the way?'

'Still not talking to me – which is the way I like it, love. She thinks I had something to do with her cruise card going missing.'

'So, you didn't tell her it was Sam who took it.'

'Oh, he told you that, did he? Well, no, I'll not be telling her, not yet anyroad. I want him alive until he solves this murder.'

'You're a man after my own heart, Mr Crusher.'

'I wish I were, love. I'd get shot of my missis in a minute, if you'd run away with me. Very quarrelsome woman is Mariella – *and* she's let herself go over the years. Used to be a bit of a looker, face like an angel some said. Not now though, not any more – face like a robber's dog.' He beamed at Sally, displaying two rows of gleaming teeth that were too even to be his own. 'You've only to say the word and me an' you'll be off to paradise.'

'Paradise, eh? I'll have to give it some thought,' laughed Sally, with one eye on Sam to gauge his reaction to this flirting. He seemed miles away. Sally said, 'Damn,' to herself.

'I need to organise a plan of campaign,' Sam decided, coming out of his thoughts. 'So I'll contact you in two days to get as much information I can from you. In the meantime if you can make a list of his friends, his enemies, what work he was doing, was he into any dodgy dealing, did he owe anyone any money, any girlfriends – in fact any stuff I might be interested in. Even if you don't think it's got anything to do with his death.'

Bernard got to his feet and stuck out a hand. 'Strikes me I've come to the right man, Sam. I've heard you're a mad bugger but happen it'll take a mad bugger to get to the bottom of this.'

'I try to be as professional as I can,' said Sam, who didn't like his Mad Carew label.

'You weren't very professional when you were flapping about in that water,' grinned Bernard. 'Me and Joey had a right laugh, watching you.'

'So, it was you who threw me the lifebelt?'

'It were Joey actually. He reckoned you were drownin'. I couldn't tell from where I were standin'.'

'Joey was right. He saved my life.'

'He's a good lad is Joey. Bugger for the women but a good lad.'

'I'll write and thank him. Send him the money his father-in-law paid me,' Sam decided. 'It's the least I can do.'

'I know what I'd do,' remarked Bernard.

76

'What?'

'I'd get meself down to the local swimming baths and take a few lessons. One less way of dyin'. Handy for a feller in your trade.'

'What? Can't you swim?' said Sally, not even trying to hide the amusement in her voice. 'What about riding a bike? Can you ride a bike?'

Sam scowled. 'Don't you start.'

'Go on. What did you find out?' he said, after Bernard had left.

'Me? You told me not to bother.'

'I know what I told you, which is why I know you bothered.'

She took out her notes. 'Well, Bernard Crusher's got at least twenty dry cleaning shops all over Yorkshire, so he's not short of a bob or two. He's been married twice. First wife ran off with a Polish ice cream man from Bradford. He married Mariella about three years ago. He's fifty-six and she's forty-six. No kids. She used to be a club singer as well. Apparently she was quite pretty in her time.'

'The years haven't been kind to her, then. You look a good twenty years younger than her.'

Sally tried to work out if he was complimenting her or insulting Mariella. 'Let's hope she never finds out it was you who nicked her cruise card.'

Sam shuddered at the thought, then looked at Sally through narrowed eyes. 'Don't even think about trying to blackmail me with that.'

'Never crossed my mind,' lied Sally.

'What did you find out about brother Ron?'

'They say he committed suicide.'

'Now you see why you're the worker and I'm the boss. How did you get all this information, anyway?'

'I rang all the Crushers in the book and asked for Mariella. When I found one I told her I was doing a market research on perfumes and that she'd get a free bottle of Chanel No.5 if she answered a few questions about her family life. It's amazing what a woman will tell you for a bottle of Chanel.'

'You didn't get much on brother Ron.'

'That seemed a bit intrusive. I did ask if she'd got any sisters or sisters-in-law who might be interested. She told me she'd got a sister-in-law but she wouldn't be interested as she'd just lost her husband. I said how terrible it was for one's husband to die young and she said it's even worse when they commit suicide. At least I knew I'd got the right Mariella Crusher.'

'You'd better send her a bottle of Chanel. Conjure up some bogus compliment slip on the computer. I don't want her getting suspicious. The less I see of Mariella Crusher the better.'

'I've already bought a bottle,' said Sally. 'Where did you get your information?'

Sam tapped his temple with a forefinger. 'Good detective work,' he told her, 'is not all about picking up the telephone. It's about legwork and knowing the right people to talk to, and good old fashioned common sense.' He picked up Bernard Crusher's cheque. 'Tell you what, let's have a night on the town tonight, courtesy of Mr Crusher. His late brother worked the door at the Queen of Clubs. We should check the place out, if only as a token effort.'

'What – Milo Morrell's place?' said Sally. 'I used to go there when I was young and fancy free. I gather it's changed a lot since then. They say it's full of pushers, pimps and smack-heads now. Hey! I must have met this Ron Crusher.' She screwed up her face, trying to remember. 'Do you know, I think there *was* a doorman there called Crusher. That's right, there was. I always thought Crusher was a nickname. Big feller, nice smile, he used to try it on with all the girls.'

'Did he try it on with you?'

'Probably, but I was saving myself for you.'

'You didn't know me then.'

'No, but I had a mental picture of the man of my dreams and Crusher didn't fit the bill.'

'And I do, eh?' preened Sam.

'By the time I met you I'd learned not to be so fussy.' She was always more than a match for him in the repartee department.

'Tell you what,' he decided. 'I'll ring Owen and see what else he knows about Crusher when he was a doorman. Then we can skip the Queen of Clubs and go into Leeds. There's this great new Indian opened – you like Indian, don't you?"

'Owen knew Ron Crusher?'

Sam winced as Sally tapped her temple with a forefinger. 'I see,' she said. 'So he's where you got your information from. What happened to the legwork and good old-fashioned common sense?'

He stood in front of her as she got to her feet. Then he placed a hand on each of her shoulders. 'Sally, how come I never get away with anything with you?'

'Why'd you want to get away with anything?'

'Because it's what men do. They get away with stuff. Women weave their wily spells and men get away with stuff.'

'Only until the stuff catches up with them, like it did with Ron Crusher.'

'You smell nice. Are you weaving a wily spell?'

'It's the Chanel I bought for Mariella.'

He kissed on her lips and for a few minutes their night out was forgotten. Then Owen burst in. He was eating a Mars Bar and was halfway through a bite when he realised what he'd walked in on. Sam's jacket was on the floor, his shirt was out of his trousers and Sally's blouse was unbuttoned to the waist. Without saying a word the Welshman went out as quickly as he had come in, but his impatient outline hovered outside the frosted glass door. They made themselves respectable, then called him in.

'Owen,' said Sam. 'those big bony things on the end of your arm are called fists. You use them for hitting villains and knocking on doors.'

'Oh, I was in a hurry, see,' said Owen chewing and swallowing the last of the chocolate. 'There's another three cars been nicked and Bowman's doing his nut. You'd think I was pinching the things myself. I wondered if you'd come up with an idea, with you having had a week to think about it.'

'The problem is, Owen, I've got a murder to solve. Ron Crusher's brother doesn't think he topped himself and I've got the job of proving it. I'd love to catch your car thieves for you but I've got a living to make.'

'I thought you made a decent enough living from

your building firm,' grumbled Owen. 'I thought you and me helped each other out. I'm taking some leave just after Christmas, see, and I'd like to have this thing wrapped up before then. If I go away without solving it I've no doubt Bowman'll pull out all the stops to find the villains while I'm away, just to make me look incompetent.'

'Leave? You didn't tell me you were taking leave.'

'I don't tell you everything, why should I?'

'Because you could spend your leave helping me. If we catch a murderer you get the glory as far as the police are concerned and I'll pick up my wages from Mr Crusher.' He put an arm around Owen's shoulder and described the situation with his free hand. 'Imagine the headlines in the *Unsworth Observer*. OFF DUTY COP, OWEN PRICE, SOLVES MURDER MYSTERY DURING HIS HOLIDAY. That'd be one in the eye for Bowman.'

Owen looked interested. 'I was planning on going skiing,' he said, with enough lack of conviction to convince Sam that his recruitment drive had succeeded.

'Skiing?' he howled. 'Owen, since when did you take up skiing? You're Welsh – Welshmen don't ski. They play rugby and sing songs and eat leeks but they don't ski.'

'Will I get paid?'

'Course you will. A hundred a day and all the Mars Bars you can eat.'

Owen gave this some careful thought then came to a decision. 'You find my car thieves and I'll cancel my holiday and give you a fortnight of my valuable time, but I only work a five day week, look you.'

'Good as done, Owen. Now can we have some privacy?'

'Oh – right. I'll give you a ring tomorrow to check on progress.' Owen looked at Sally and gave her one of his singular smiles that displayed a full array of gleaming teeth. 'You could do a lot better than him, you know. We Welshmen are renowned for our sexual magnetism.'

'He's got written proof of that from the CSA,' confirmed Sam.

'Wow!' said Sally, 'two good offers in the space often minutes. It's got to be the perfume. Can I keep it, Sam? I'll send Mariella a bottle of lavender water. This would be wasted on her.'

Sam's hired Subaru Imprezza was in the car park behind the Humming Bird café on Ragley Road. Sam had been assured by his sons that such a car had much street cred and would be high on a car thief's wanted list.

Inside the café the air would be thick with cannabis fumes, small packages would be exchanged for large notes and various items would be bought and sold for only a fraction of their true value. On Bowman's instructions the Humming Bird was given special dispensation for its nefarious trading, as it placed most of the Unsworth villains where the police could pick them up without too much running around. Oddly, this never occurred to the villains. The car had been there since lunchtime, as had Sam and Owen. It was now getting dark and Sam was confident that the temptation to take it would prove too much for someone, hopefully one of Owen's car thieves. Owen wasn't as convinced as he sucked on a Werther's Original.

'Even if it gets nicked how are we going to keep up in this thing? We might as well be on push bikes for all the chance we've got of catching them. And how do we know it's the same car thieves? It might be just a joyrider.'

They were in Owen's rusting Ford Sierra which was parked in a side street with a clear view of the car park exit.

'Joyriders don't nick modern cars with sophisticated locks because they don't know how to do it,' Sam pointed out. 'Joy riders are just thick lads who think there's something clever about driving fast. From what you tell me we're up against someone with a bit more know-how than your joyrider. And we'll keep up all right – the last thing they want is to get caught speeding.'

'Well I just hope we don't have to travel too far, this car's on its last legs. I thought I might have been given a car but oh, no–'

Sam interrupted him. 'I think we're in business.' The Subaru was standing in the car park entrance, its indicator flashing as it waited for passing traffic to clear. Owen started up his Sierra. He followed the Subaru along Ragley Road, down Cenotaph Hill and across Ackersfield Bridge until they were south of the canal and into an industrial area.

'I thought so,' said Sam. 'They'll have a holding place around here where they can doctor the cars with false plates and engine numbers before they send them on their way.'

'I imagine they'll respray them as well,' commented Owen who was becoming pleased with their day's work.

'No, too expensive to get it just right,' said Sam. 'They'll just move them at night under street lights – it's hard to tell the colour of a car under street lights. Then it's on to a ferry and out of the country. Here we go, he's turning. Drive straight past, we'll follow them on foot.'

The Subaru was signalling a right turn into an industrial estate. Owen drove fifty yards past then parked up. He and Sam ran back to the estate entrance and arrived in time to see the Subaru flashing its lights, and a roller shutter door opening to allow it inside. Within a minute the car was in, the doors rolled back down and the building returned to innocent darkness, just like all the buildings surrounding it.

'I'll ring for help,' Owen decided.

'Not if you want to claim the collar you won't,' warned Sam. 'If you ring for help the first man to cuff the ring-leader will be given the collar. It wouldn't surprise me if Bowman makes sure he gets in first. He's stuffed me once or twice in the past.'

'But–?'

It was going through Owen's mind what would they do if they were outnumbered? What if the villains were armed? It was also going through his head that Sam's nickname had little to do with any old music hall monologue.

'Have you got an ASP?' Sam was asking, taking out an expandable police baton from within his coat.

'Where did you get that? That's police issue that is. You're not supposed to have that.'

'Oh, shut up moaning,' said Sam. 'Have you brought one?'

'It's in the car.'

'Well go and get it. And a spare pair of hand-cuffs if you've got some. I came without mine.'

'You're not supposed to have handcuffs... Oh never bloody mind!'

'I'll be taking a look. Put your mobile on vibrate.'

Owen hesitated for a second then ran back to the car. By the time he returned, Sam was nowhere in sight. Owen made himself as small as he could and ran towards the building into which the car had been driven. There was no sign of Sam. 'Carew, you bloody madman,' he muttered. 'Where the hell are you?' His phone vibrated in his pocket.

'Hello?'

'I'm at the top of the fire escape.'

Owen looked up and saw a shadowy figure.

'I'll keep this switched on so you can hear what's happening,' Sam told him.

'What do you want me to do?'

'Play it by ear.'

'What sort of plan's that – play it by ear? Play what by ear?'

Sam had a large bunch of keys in his hand which he was trying in the padlocked door. 'It's open,' he reported to Owen. 'I'm going in. If anyone runs out the front, you nab them, pretend there's a lot of you.'

This plan alarmed Owen but Sam was inside now so it was a fait-accompli. At the side of the roller door was a personal door. Owen stood in the shadows at the side of it. His nervousness, as usual, affected his bladder.

Sam entered the building and found himself on the top of a two storey mezzanine that occupied about a third of the length of the building. Below him were approximately a dozen top of the range cars: Jaguar, Mercedes, BMW, Lexus, Audi, and now, a Subaru. The main lights were out and the only illumination came from a couple of powerful inspection lamps on the ground floor. As far as Sam could tell there were only two men down there. He figured they were just part of a bigger organisation, but nicking them would be good enough. In his experience there'd probably be enough information lying around to get the rest of the gang. Paperwork, fingerprints, forensics, DNA, maybe even the odd address in the offices at the side of him; when villains become complacent they get poor at covering their tracks. He crept down a flight of stairs on to the lower mezzanine, on which were many racks of tyres. Below him, the bonnet of the Subaru was up and the two men were poring over the engine. In the dark, Sam kicked into something metallic that fell ten feet to the concrete floor with a loud clang. It was too late for him to take cover. The men looked out from under the bonnet and pointed a lamp at him, frozen in self recrimination, the last syllable of a swearword still on his lips.

'What the fuck?' said one.

Sam decided that his best method was to defend his position at the top of the stairs. He flicked out his ASP and waited for them. They recognised the weapon. 'Ow, bollocks! It's a copper.' But they didn't halt in their stride.

'Owen!' bellowed Sam, his voice echoed off the breeze block walls. 'Bring the troops in. Go, go, GO!'

The two men hesitated now, wondering what might happen. Nothing did. Owen was taking a pee. They returned their attention to Sam. One of them walked to the wall and flicked on several switches. One by one, strip lights flickered into life until the whole building was brightly illuminated. They looked all around to see if he had any accomplices.

'He's on his own. I bet he's not even a copper. If yer a copper show us yer warrant card.'

Even if Sam had a warrant card he wouldn't have shown it to them. He'd got more chance as a fellow villain than as a copper. He held up two hands as if in surrender. 'Okay, I'm not a copper. I'm just trying me luck, that's all. No harm done, eh lads? Owen!'

'Who the fuck's Owen?'

'He's me mate. Thick as two short planks, never there when you need him, probably buggered off. OWEN!'

The men advanced up the stairs. Outside, Owen was desperately trying to finish peeing. Sam's voice was coming through his mobile. He freed one hand, held the phone to his ear, then squeezed it between ear and shoulder as he gave a couple of quick shakes and zipped himself up.

Sam was holding his position at the top of the stairs by threatening the men with his ASP, cutting the air with it as a swordsman would with his foil. 'Stay back, lads. No need for any of us to get hurt.'

The larger of the two made a grab for his legs. Sam brought the weapon down on his shoulder, hurting but not disabling him. The man screamed in pain and rage. 'I'll do yer for that, yer bastard!' Sam continued to wave the ASP about, keeping them at bay.

'OWEN!'

The uninjured one dived at Sam's legs and grabbed one from under him, pulling him down the stairs on his back. He threw the ASP away with all his might and heard it clattering among the cars. If he couldn't use it, neither could they. A heavy blow to the side of his head stunned him. He kicked upwards; more of a blind reaction than an aimed kick. His shoe hit something soft and earned him a rewarding grunt of pain, and a bit of time to regroup. The larger man was holding his right shoulder with his left hand and the other was clutching his testicles. Sam was still on the floor trying to get up. The larger man began kicking him in his ribs. He grabbed the man's feet to stop a third kick and brought him to the floor. Blood was obscuring his vision. The first blow had opened a gaping cut in his head and he was really beginning to wish he hadn't bothered to help Owen.

'Owen!' he screamed. 'Where the bloody hell are you when I need you?'

He heard a flurry of thumps and none of the blows seemed to be hitting him, which was how he knew it had to be Owen. At long last.

'You took your time. What kept you?'

'I was having a pee. I've told you my bladder can't stand stress.'

'My head can't stand stress either. They were trying to kill me. These aren't your normal car thieves.'

'Well, I'm here now, look you. Why did you try and tackle them on your own? Just look at the state of you. All this could have been avoided with a bit of careful planning.'

Sam pushed himself to his feet and appraised the situation. Both men were unconscious; one was just stirring, the other dead to the world. Owen took out two pairs of cuffs, dragged the men so they were back to back and handcuffed them together.

'Is it all right if I call for back up now?' he enquired taking out a handkerchief and handing it to Sam to stop the flow of blood. He examined the head wound closely. 'Nasty – I'd better ring for an ambulance first.'

'Not for me.' Sam inclined his bleeding head towards the two car thieves. 'They might need one. I'll take the Subaru and get myself to hospital. I'm not sure what Unsworth Car Hire will think if they find out I had it stolen on purpose. You stay here and take all the credit. It'll not do me any good.'

'You can't drive in that state,' protested Owen who, otherwise, liked the sound of this idea.

'I'm okay. It looks worse than it is.'

'This isn't my usual bed,' said Sam to the nurse as he looked around the large accident ward. He was in Unsworth General. 'What's the damage?'

'Two broken ribs, ten stitches in your head and some bruising. Good night out was it?'

'I wasn't drunk, I was pursuing my lawful occupation.'

'What's that – suicide pilot?'

'Private detective. Can't I get an upgrade to a better ward? I need my privacy.'

'You'll get what you're given.'

'But I'm a regular customer and I'm no trouble – you ask anyone.'

'You're giving me trouble now.'

The two arrested men were surprised not to have been charged with assault on Sam but, in their interview, no mention was made of him, so there was no point in them opening a can of worms and asking silly questions about the mysterious absence of the man whom they had assaulted. They had no option but to plead guilty to car theft. Four others were arrested over the next few days, going on evidence found at the scene, and Owen basked in glory. A most reluctant Inspector Bowman was instructed by the chief superintendent to put the irritatingly jubilant Welshman up for a commendation. Owen's flashing teeth gleamed from the front page of the *Unsworth Observer* for three days on the trot. On the down side Owen knew he owed Sam very big time indeed, and he also knew that Sam wouldn't let him forget it. There was a suspicious suicide to investigate – Owen's holiday job.

By the time Sally arrived at the hospital Sam had been X-rayed stitched and plastered and was making a nuisance of himself on the ward. The nurse had already told her he was in no danger and she had on her unsympathetic face when she walked up to his bed. He detected something else behind her lack of sympathy. An imminent explosion.

'Owen told me what happened.'

'Did he now? I told him to keep my part in it to himself. It won't do him any good if Bowman finds out I helped him.'

His words seemed to fall on deaf ears. 'According to Owen,' she said, her lip quivering, 'one of the men in the garage was a killer.'

'What?'

'Out on life licence, which will now be revoked – so I understand from Owen. He had a reputation of being something of a psychopath – a real nutter. Killed a man in a fight just for the pure hell of it. Served twelve years, most of it in segregation. He wouldn't have thought twice about killing you, and from what Owen tells me he wasn't so far off.' There were tears in her eyes. 'If Kathy had still been alive she'd have given you hell for putting yourself in that position.'

'How was I to know he was a killer?'

'You knew there were thieves inside that building – and thieves come in different shapes and sizes. Some of them like hurting people. You were a copper, you know that.'

Sam tried to make light of things. 'Sal, I know what I'm doing. I plan things and I had no plans to die today. Honest, I'm okay.'

'*You're* okay? You selfish bastard! What about the rest of us?'

'Us?'

'The people who love you.' She hesitated before adding: 'Your sons. Did you think about them when you were blundering into that bloody building, trying to get yourself killed just so that Owen would help you out?' Her fists were clenched and she looked to be on the verge of hitting him.

'Sally, I'm sorry.'

She didn't hear him. She had gone. A nurse came by and clipped a heart monitor onto his fingertip.

'Your wife seemed upset.'

'She's not my wife, she's...' His voice tailed off. Despite him once dumping her for Kathy, Sally was still very fond of him – he wasn't so blind as not to know that. But what right had she to be so upset at him? – none whatsoever. His thoughts quickly turned to the job in hand, the alleged murder of Ron Crusher. He would have to start digging, talking to people who knew Ron; piece together the links in the chain that led to his death. If Ron's death was planned there would definitely be links. There would be events, situations, circumstances and people; not all directly connected with Ron Crusher. Some of them would just be connected to the next link. There could well be people involved who had never heard of Ron Crusher, nor he of them. People such as Derek Fleming and his sister, Jeannie, who, back in 1967, were found by the police in a reeking council flat in Leeds. Derek was seven and his sister was nine.

Chapter Eight

Leeds: 1967

The police had been alerted by a neighbour who had heard the children crying on and off for five days. There had been no sign of the mother who was, more often than not, off her head with drink and drugs. The mother went to prison for a while and didn't fight the custody order that deprived her of the children she hadn't wanted in the first place; neither of the fathers had lifted a finger to help so why should she? She went back to her life of prostitution and drugs while her son and daughter ended up in different children's homes in different towns.

Derek actually cried for his mother, although in later years he could never understand why. His sister, so he was to learn, didn't shed a single tear – not for their mother anyway. A few prospective adoptive parents came to look at him but he wasn't what they wanted. Too old, too plain, too emaciated and far too shifty looking. He was ten when he went to the Paddock House Home for boys in Leeds, and twelve when he was first raped by Mr Forbuoys, one of the carers. Mr Forbuoys didn't call it rape, he called it loving. He said it was natural for a boy to want to give pleasure to the man who was looking after him. All boys wanted to do that, said Mr Forbuoys. This made

Derek feel quite odd because he didn't want to do it, not one bit. It hurt him and made him cry at night and none of the other boys asked him why. It was as if by allowing him to confide in them they would be adding his sorrows to their own, and they already had enough of them, mostly of a similar nature to Derek's. Mr Forbuoys had made him promise to keep it to himself or bad things would happen.

With her being the pretty one it was on the cards that Jeannie would suffer a similar fate to Derek. In her case it was a one eyed house parent at Beaulieu Park Home for Girls in Sheffield – Mr Frampton. He was known as Popeye by those who only knew him as a house parent, and Hampton Frampton by the girls who'd had more intimate experience of him.

Frampton was careful in his selection of victims. He chose the meek and the known liars, Jeannie came under the second category. The first time he assaulted her she had gone straight to the police station to report what had happened. But she had a reputation as a liar and a thief and her word counted for nothing. Frampton was interviewed as a matter of course and no action taken. After that he stepped up his abuse of her and constantly threatened to send her to a girls' reformatory if she went to the police again.

'All part of growing up in an institution like this,' he would say. 'Men such as me have needs and you should be damn well grateful enough to supply them needs.'

He was a big man in all senses of the word and

he always hurt her. She even had to suffer the indignity of putting a contraceptive on him rather than him have to do it himself.

'All part of the pleasure,' he'd tell her. 'You'll have a man of your own to do this for one day. You'll thank me then for all the tuition I've given you.'

The only thing Jeannie looked forward to was stabbing him to death one day. It had to be stabbing. She needed to stick something horrible in him the way he stuck something horrible in her. Over the months her abhorrence of this man had mounted until it was total. If she got locked up for murder then so be it. But she figured that if she did it while he was actually raping her she might well get away with it. She would stab him once and disable him. Then she would kill him slowly, letting him know he was dying and why. She would tell him how she'd leave his penis out with its contraceptive on, so that people would know what a foul pervert he had been in life and they would vilify him long after his death. In fact she would wait until he had ejaculated so that there would be no doubt about his vileness. With this in mind she stole a sharp knife from the kitchen and hid it in her cardigan pocket in preparation for the next time she was summoned to his room, 'For one of our little talks,' as he would put it.

The summons duly came and her heart was pounding as she walked along the corridor and tapped, lightly on his door. There was no answer. She checked in her pocket for the knife, which she would slide under the mattress and bring out when the time came. She knocked again – still no answer.

She felt a mixture of relief and disappointment, having built up her courage thus far. If he wasn't in he'd surely call her back some other time, very shortly, and she'd have to prepare herself all over again. She tried the handle. The door was unlocked. She opened it slightly and called in.

'Mr Frampton?'

No answer.

She pushed the door fully open and entered the room. Frampton was sitting in a chair with a *Daily Mirror* on his knee. His head lolled to one side. His good eye was half closed and his glass eye wide open and glaring, blankly at the headlines: *Four Killed in Belfast Bombing*. Jeannie took a couple of steps towards him and listened for breathing. Nothing. She took another couple of steps and touched his face. It was soft and cold and devoid of life. Frampton was dead.

She sat in the chair opposite and stared at him for several minutes. This was the first time she'd seen a dead person. Then she remembered all he had done to her. All the pain and fear and humiliation and self loathing he had inflicted on her. Her face crumpled and tears began to pour down her cheeks. The lousy bastard! He had died on his own and she'd wanted to kill him. He had died before she had time to take her revenge. He had died before she could take away his power and taunt him and terrify him with it. She had wanted him to scream for mercy and know just *why* he was dying. She wanted him to feel wretched remorse for what he had done to her. She had wanted to wield power over him – the power of life and death. And she would have chosen death because that was what he deserved. But he had denied her that. And she had so desperately needed it. The bastard had won.

She took the knife from her pocket and plunged it into his chest, where his black heart would be, if he had a heart. Then she sat back in the chair to test her feelings. To see if this satisfied her need for vengeance. Had he bled just a little it might have helped. But dead men don't bleed.

Footsteps sounded outside. They stopped at the open door and a voice from behind her said, 'Is everything all right?' It was Miss Adams, who was a bit dopey, but otherwise okay.

'Not really, Miss. He's dead.'

Miss Adams took a nervous step forward. When she spotted the knife she let out a scream that made Jeannie jump.

'It's okay, Miss. He was dead before I stabbed him.'

Miss Adams backed away, out of the door, and ran down the corridor, screaming once again. Jeannie made her way back to her dormitory. She knew she'd be in some kind of trouble, but anything was better than being constantly raped by Hampton Frampton. Some of the other girls would be relieved when she told them, so that was something. It didn't stop her feeling cheated though.

She stared, belligerently, at the detective inspector sitting opposite. Also in the room was the solicitor representing her, and a detective sergeant. Jeannie had spent the night in a cell. There seemed to be a lot of confusion as to what to do with her. She had told them about the abuse and given the names of five other girls whom she knew had been definitely raped by Frampton. Now he was dead most of them would confirm her story.

'You might as well let me go,' she said. 'All I did was stick a knife in a lump o' shit. It wasn't even live shit. Where's the harm in that?'

'According to your statement,' said the inspector, 'you went there with the intention of killing him.'

'That's right – and he ordered me to go there with the intention of raping me. What did the other girls say? Did they tell you we all called him Hampton Frampton?'

The change of expression on the sergeant's face told her the answer to that was, *yes*.

Jeannie picked up on it and grinned. 'They did, didn't they?'

The inspector sighed and looked at the sergeant. People couldn't just get away with sticking knives in dead bodies, but pursuing this case would open a real can of worms. Officers he couldn't spare would be tied up investigating the girls' home; interviewing past residents and staff, and as far as he could tell from the statements given by the other abused girls, Frampton wasn't the only one at it. With this revelation looming over it the home would have no option but to clean up its act. If the girls made a complaint it would be the home in the dock and not Frampton. His instructions from above were to let this girl off with a reprimand. He leaned across the table and glared at her. She met his gaze, defiantly.

'Young lady,' he said, sternly, 'you've committed a very serious crime. Under other circumstances you'd be looking at a custodial sentence. In the eyes of the law the body in which you stuck the knife was that of an innocent man who'd died of a heart attack. If you had a complaint you should have come to the police and we'd have investigated the matt–'

Jeannie cut in. 'I did,' she said. 'I came to you for help the first time he raped me. And you believed him, not me. No one ever believes kids. It were you lot what let the fuckin' pervert get away with it. So why should I take a bollocking from you?'

She stood up and walked to the door. The policemen were at a loss what to do. The solicitor got to his feet.

'My client seems to have a point,' he said. 'Do I take it this matter is closed?'

The inspector nodded his head. Jeannie had already left the room.

Paddock House Boys' Home, Leeds: 1974

Derek was fourteen when Johnnie O'Brien came into his dormitory after lights out. Johnnie was a big lad, two years older than Derek and someone to be avoided because of his bouts of unpredictable violence. He'd spent a lot of his life in reform school and no one ever dared ask what he was doing in Paddock House. He woke Derek up with a thump on his back and whispered in his ear.

99

'Gerrup, Fleming.'

'What?' Derek didn't know who it was in the dark. Johnnie shone a torch on his own face, lighting it up from underneath, so he looked spooky.

'Who are you?' Derek asked. Johnnie gave him another thump. 'Y'ask too many questions, our kid. Jus' gerrup an' get dressed an' do as yer fuckin' told.'

Derek got out of bed and took his clothes from his cupboard. Other boys looked over their bedclothes to see what was happening. Someone asked what was going on and Johnnie snarled at him. 'Get back ter fuckin' sleep, dickhead!'

Derek got dressed, gloomily. Whatever was in store he knew he wouldn't like it. 'Where are we going?'

Johnnie sniggered. 'Yer goin' to have a good time – a right good fuckin' time.'

'I'm tired, I just want to go back to bed.'

The youth struck Derek with the flat of his hand, sending him staggering to the floor. 'Yer do as yer told, our kid, or yer'll get a lot more o' this.'

They left the home via a window and over a wall where a van was awaiting them. Johnnie got into the front and sat next to the driver while Derek was bundled into the back.

After a journey lasting about ten minutes Derek was led into a large, terrace house and into a smoky, raucous room full of foulmouthed men who were laughing and drinking. Many seemed to have drunk too much. The noise quietened when he entered and he felt that all the eyes were on him. They were sitting in a variety of chairs arranged in a semi-circle around a large, sheepskin rug in front of an open fire. Derek was made to stand on the rug. The room was airless with a fug of stale cigarette smoke, and stank of alcohol, body odour and stale farts. Someone said he was a bit too young and skinny and Derek wondered too young and skinny for what? Johnnie gave him a glass of whisky and told him to drink it. Derek took too big a mouthful and spat most of it out, Johnnie cuffed him around the side of his head and snapped. 'D'yer know how much that fuckin' stuff costs? Gerrit bloody drunk!'

Derek took another sip and felt it burning his throat as it went down. Some of the men laughed. 'First time eh, lad? Yer'll get used to it. Good stuff dunt come easy.'

'Hear that?' said Johnnie. 'We're here ter do yer a favour, Derek. Best favour yer'll ever fuckin' have – eh, fellers?'

More laughter. 'I wish someone had done me a favour like this when I were a lad,' one called out. 'Happen I wouldn't o' done so much wanking.'

A young woman came in to the room, not much more than a girl, probably late teens. She went straight up to Johnnie and asked, 'Have yer got me money?'

He handed her a wad of pound notes. 'Fifteen quid,' he said, 'Two quid each, less a fiver fer me.'

The girl counted first the men in the room, then the money, which she put it in her handbag. Then she looked at Derek and asked, 'Is this him?'

'Zola, this is Derek,' said Johnnie. 'He's not much ter look at but he's a cock virgin.'

The girl gave Derek a cross between a smile and a sneer. 'Well, Derek. I haven't got all night. Let's get on with it.' She took her clothes off without ceremony or embarrassment and stood in front of an amazed and worried Derek, who wasn't sure where to look. She was a good-looking girl with a body to match. Some of the men made noises of approval.

'What d'yer think of me tits, Derek?' she said, thrusting out her breasts, which were pert, but a long way off voluptuous.

He didn't know what to think. She reached out and unzipped his trousers. He tried to stop her but Johnnie grabbed his hand. 'Don't be rude ter Zola Gee, Derek, lad. Get yer clothes off.'

'What?'

'Sorry gents.' Johnnie gave an apologetic smile to the assembled group, then his face turned ugly and he swung his arm in a vicious arc that sent Derek staggering, almost into the fire. He banged his head against a marble mantelpiece and fell to the floor.

'He's not quite up ter scratch, isn't my boy,' Johnnie sniggered.

'Yer mean he hasn't a clue why he's here, more like,' remarked Zola. She held out a hand to help Derek up and said, almost kindly, 'Are you all right, love?'

Derek nodded, bleakly.

'Just take 'em off,' she advised. 'I'm not gonna bite yer.'

Derek felt blood coming from his ear, where Johnnie had struck him and from his eye where he had fallen against the mantelpiece. He let the naked girl pull him to his feet. Then he un-buttoned his shirt and shivered with embarrass-ment at the thought of having to show off his scrawny body and private parts to these awful men who were laughing and making crude comments that he didn't quite understand. 'She might give yer a dose, lad but she'll not bite yer. Why d'yer think none of us'll shag her?'

'Stop scaring him,' she scolded. 'I promise you, Derek. I'm clear at the moment – and I only get it because of mucky buggers like this lot.'

Derek, under Johnnie's threatening gaze, was almost undressed. Eventually he stood there, naked and weeping, with his hands covering his privates. 'Let her see it,' ordered Johnnie, harshly.

Derek took his hands away and the men laughed. So did Zola.

'Didn't yer check his credentials before yer brought him?' she asked Johnnie. 'Last time I saw one like that it had a hook in it.'

Derek went crimson. She reached down and took hold of him, working her hand back and forward until he could feel the same sensation as he had many a time under the blankets in his bed. 'Not bad,' she was saying as he got bigger. 'Not too bad at all.' She winked at Derek. 'Not the smallest in this room by a long way. Okay, I think I'll go on top.' She pressed her hands on his shoulders and pushed him to the floor, where she straddled him, took hold of him, and guided him inside her.

Derek was sobbing. Partly through the shame of what was happening to him and partly because it was giving him pleasure and he knew it was wrong to take pleasure from something as dirty and humiliating as this. Zola was moving up and down rapidly. Through the edge of his vision he could see that some of the men were openly masturbating. One of them told her to, 'Slow down, lass, we want a proper show for our money.' The girl was looking down at Derek and laughing. Laughing at his shame and his indignity and his helplessness and he hated her. He hated her and wanted her at the same time. He reached his climax with a series of tearful yelps that quickly died down to a whimper – a weeping, sobbing whimper. Zola kept moving until there was nothing left to work with, then she got to her feet, picked up her clothes and left the room. Derek didn't see her again until the following week.

Chapter Nine

Ron's wife wasn't quite what Sam expected. He'd been told by Bernard that she was a mouse who wouldn't say boo to a goose but the first thing Sam saw in her eyes, when she opened the door, was anger.

'Mrs Crusher?'

'Who are you?'

'My name's Sam Carew. I'm working for Bernard Crusher.'

'That useless twat!'

He was taken aback by her language. He assumed that, at the mention of Bernard's name, she would have made him welcome and given him access to any information she might have.

'I take it you don't get on with him.'

'Neither him nor his cow of a wife. She's worse. What is it you want?'

'He's hired me to try and prove that your husband didn't commit suicide.'

She heaved so heavy a sigh that Sam thought tears were imminent. If they had been, she held them back. 'You'd best come in,' she said.

He followed her inside. It was a comfortable, semi-detached house in Norton Bywater, a pleasant village on the Leeds side of Unsworth. Certainly not the kind of house Sam would readily associate with a cowboy builder-cum-nightclub bouncer.

'Nice house,' he commented, looking round at the comfortable furnishings.

'Thank you.' She motioned for him to sit down and sat down opposite. 'Mind you, it'll not be mine for much longer.'

'Really?'

'It's being repossessed.'

'Oh, I am sorry.'

She gave a hopeless shrug and ran her fingers through her hair, which was greying and unkempt. 'A month before Ron died he owned the place, lock stock and barrel. But I found out, afterwards, that he'd taken a loan out, using this as security.' She waved a descriptive arm around the room. 'It wouldn't be so bad if I could find out what he did with the money. A hundred and fifty grand. I didn't know the house was worth that much.'

'It's probably worth quite a bit more,' commented Sam, 'The way prices are going up at the moment.'

'What goes up, must come down,' she said, dismally. 'My Ron could tell you that. Ah, well, it's to be hoped it is worth more – he took out a high interest mortgage. I haven't made a single payment and they've applied for a possession order.'

'Get a solicitor on Legal Aid,' Sam advised. 'I can put you on to one who'll give them the run around for months. Courts hate kicking people out of their homes. Didn't he have life insurance?'

'Half a million – and that's not including the mortgage cover. I'd have been well placed if he'd died accidentally. But he wasn't covered for

106

suicide on either policy.'

'No one ever is,' said Sam, 'which adds to my list of reasons for him not wanting to kill himself.'

Her shoulders slumped. The anger he'd seen wasn't really her. She was a woman who could manage the occasional skirmish but she knew the battle was lost. 'Well, I won't deny it'd make my life easier if you could prove that,' she said. 'A whole lot easier. In fact if you can prove my Ron was murdered, whatever that prat of a brother-in-law of mine's paying you, I'll pay the same.'

'There won't be any need for that. Do you mind telling me why you don't like Bernard?' He offered her a cigarette which she accepted and lit as she thought of an answer.

'It's mainly *her*,' she said. 'Have you met her?'

'Er, sort of,' admitted Sam, awkwardly.

'Never got on with her,' said Eileen. 'Up until Ron died me and Bernard got on all right, but she's such a complete shit. They know I need money but I haven't had so much as a bloody bean off them, and I know it's her. She's ready to fork out for fancy holidays and private detectives, but when it comes to family she doesn't want to know.'

'It's Bernard who hired me, not his wife,' Sam pointed out. 'It sounded to me as though he and Ron were quite close.'

'I can't figure that one out,' she said. 'They weren't all that close. Chalk and cheese, Bernard and Ron. Anyway it's all her money.' She blew out a savage lungful of smoke as if it contained all her wretchedness. 'She's got the money in that marriage. Bernard didn't have a pot to piss in

107

when he met her.'

'But, I thought Bernard owned a chain of dry cleaning businesses.'

She gave a short laugh. 'Owns them? He owns bugger all does Bernard. He *used* to be the successful brother – managed a big furniture warehouse – but he gave it all to the bookies. Good head on his shoulders but he liked the horses did Bernard. It was one thing him and my Ron had in common – only Bernard had it bad. My Ron always knew when he'd had enough, not Bernard, though. When he met Mariella he'd just got the push from his job. He owned the suit he stood up in and a clapped out motorbike.'

'So, where did the dry cleaning businesses come from?'

'She owns them – Bernard runs them. Her first husband left them to her in his will. I blame him because I reckon he should be a man and stand up to her. My Ron'd have had her fer breakfast. He might have had his faults but he took no shit from no one.'

'Ah,' said Sam. 'I see.'

He studied her as she got to her feet and walked to the window. She gazed outside with her left arm wrapped around her stomach, supporting her right elbow as she drew heavily on her cigarette. He wondered how many years these last few months had put on her. She was middle-aged, plump, care-worn and defeated. Maybe once she'd been pretty, but right now, without any money or property she had a bleak future, unless...

'Do you have a job?'

'No job no kids.' Her voice was distant. 'If we'd

had kids they'd have rallied round. Helped their old mum. But we couldn't have any. My fault as it turned out.' She added the last sentence as if to exonerate her late husband from any blame. 'He never blamed me, you know. He'd have made a brilliant dad, but he never once blamed me.' She turned to face Sam and gave him a bleak smile. 'You'd have liked him,' she said, with confidence. 'Most blokes liked him. He was a bugger. I know he played around, but that's who he was. I could take it or leave it. So I took it. It was only right if I couldn't give him kids.'

Sam failed to see the logic in this but he didn't argue. 'And you've no idea where the money went – the money he borrowed?'

She shook her head. 'Not a clue. He drew it out in cash. I've searched the house high and low. And if he bought something with it there's no sign of that either.'

'What do you think he might have bought?'

'With a hundred and fifty grand? I thought about it a lot. It could be anything really. The only things I can think of is a bit of building land or another house – or maybe a property abroad somewhere. It could have been that he was planning a big surprise for me. But I've checked with the solicitor and everyone who knows him.'

'No joy?'

'None at all.'

Sam was as baffled as she was, except that he was fairly certain that the missing money had something to do with Ron's death. This was the link he would have to follow. Find the money and find the killer. 'I need to know as much as I can

109

about Ron,' he said. 'About his friends, his enemies–'

'He had a few of them and no mistake, but none that'd kill him.'

'Right – and anyone he worked with, did business with, his acquaintances? Did he play cards? Did he like a bet?'

'He played cards and he liked a bet but, like I said, he never got in deep. It won't have been that. He never walked away from a table without settling up and he never owed the bookies a penny. Ask anyone they'll all tell you the same.'

'What about drugs?'

'Never touched drugs. He called it a mug's game. He liked a good drink but he could hold his liquor could my Ron.'

'Did he ever get up to anything dodgy?'

'How do you mean?'

Sam tried to phrase this carefully. 'Any business dealings he wouldn't want the police to know about?'

She gave short laugh. 'What do you think? He was in the building trade.'

'So am I,' said Sam. 'I've never done a dodgy deal in my life, nor my dad before me.'

'Well Ron wasn't quite the angel you are then, was he?' she retorted, sharply. 'Anyway, I thought you were a private detective?'

'I'm both.'

'Oh.'

He decided she deserved an explanation. 'I inherited the firm when my dad died. I'm a qualified brickie, but I'm also an ex-copper. I've got a partner who runs it while I'm not there, which looks like being most of the time for the foreseeable future – so?'

'So, what?'

'So, did he get up to any dodgy deals?'

Eileen pulled a face, as though she felt it wrong to tell him her dead husband's secrets. 'Some of it was dodgy,' she conceded, 'some of it legit. He was never a big time villain or anything.' She smiled at a memory. 'He called himself an opportunist and, do you know, that just about describes him.'

'Would you write down anything that might be of help?' Sam asked. 'Anything at all, no matter how daft or insignificant. It's amazing how something stupid can unlock a case.'

'I'll do what I can.'

'Any names as well. Ron's dead and you owe allegiance to none of his friends.'

'Are you asking me to get his pals into trouble?'

He shrugged. 'You tell me. How many of them have helped you since he died?'

'None. Haven't seen any of them since the funeral.'

'Well, there you go, then. Could be that one of his friends was the cause of his death.'

'Murdered him, you mean?'

'It's possible. I'll call back in, say, a couple of days and see what you've come up with.'

'As I say, I'll do what I can.'

As he got to his feet she took his hand in hers. 'From a money point of view,' she said, 'it'd make life so much easier if you proved he'd been murdered. But it's not just about the money. I don't like thinking he was so unhappy as to kill himself. He was a bugger was my Ron but I did love him. I loved him so bloody much it hurts just thinking about him. My life were shit before I met him.'

'Had it rough, did you?' probed Sam. People's past lives often had a bearing on a case.

'You could say that ... and I could say it's nothing to do with you, and nothing to do with what happened to Ron.'

'Fair enough.'

'He made me laugh,' she said, 'and I loved him.'

'I'll do my best for you,' promised Sam. He gave her a kiss on her cheek because he thought she needed it. He suspected it might have been the first show of affection she'd had since Ron died. He now felt better about himself knowing there was an altruistic dimension to this case. Sally would appreciate that. It might even give Owen some encouragement.

'There's a cheque gone out for three grand, what's that for? Bernard, if yer've started throwing my money away on horses, I'll–'

'I haven't.'

Bernard then cursed under his breath. She only looked at the books once a blue moon, mostly she just took out what she needed and trusted the accountant to confirm he hadn't been fiddling the books. Just his bloody luck. Still, might as well come clean. Without him running the business it would have gone to the wall by now. He knew full well it was the only reason she'd married him. It certainly wasn't his sex appeal or good looks. He'd married her for her money and she'd married him because of his business brain.

'I gave it to a detective agency,' he said, firmly. 'If the police won't prove that Ron was killed I owe it to him to do it myself.'

'Bernard, have yer gone off yer fuckin' trolley? Your Ron topped himself. He did the high dive in front of a big crowd, including a couple o' coppers.'

'Well, I don't think he did.'

'Well I do – I mean, you and your Ron didn't even get on all that well. What's it all about?'

'I always looked up to our Ron. He never did me any harm. In fact he got me out of a couple o' scrapes when I was a kid.'

'He were a wrong un was Ron. If someone did kill him he happen had it coming.'

Anyway,' said Bernard, stubbornly. 'I've laid the money out, now.'

'My money you mean.'

'*Our* money,' he insisted. 'If it wasn't for me you wouldn't have a business and you know it. The way you were running it into the ground before I came along was criminal.'

Mariella snapped back. 'I'm telling the bank that, in future, all our cheques have to be signed by me – and with me ownin' ninety-nine per cent of the shares they'll do as I say. That's how much of the money is yours. God knows why I married a useless pillock like you.'

'You know very well why you married me.'

'Do I? Well, I'll tell yer one thing for nothing Bernard bloody Crusher – you don't deserve me.'

'I don't deserve piles but I've got 'em,' muttered Bernard.

'In future I'll pay all the bills – that's company

bills an' private bills.'

'Are you saying you don't want me to do this?'

She suddenly softened, which wasn't like her. 'I'm sayin' I think yer wrong about this. I think your Ronnie topped himself, and that bitch of a wife of his drove him to it – which is why I won't lift a finger to help her. Do what you have ter do, but that three grand's all yer get. I might not be the world's best businesswoman, but I do know about throwin' good money after bad.'

He gave her a conciliatory kiss, which was just about the only form of affection that ever passed between them since they had grudgingly con- summated their marriage some three years ago.

Chapter Ten

Derek was made to perform with Zola six times in all before contracting gonorrhoea. The doctor who periodically visited Paddock House asked him how he got it and Derek said he didn't know. Mr Forbuoys was informed and he looked suitably aghast at the news. He called Derek a dirty, filthy boy.

'But, sir – you said it was all right for you to do it to me.'

'What's all right?' enquired the doctor.

'For him to do it to me,' said Derek. 'He said it was all right for me to pleasure him because he looked after me and it was only natural.'

Forbuoys blanched. 'I assume you don't believe a word of this nonsense, doctor?'

'Not a word. Are you saying, boy, that Mr Forbuoys gave you this dirty disease?'

'I don't know,' said Derek, sullenly. 'Johnnie O'Brien made me do it with a woman, in front of men.'

'Who's Johnnie O'Brien?'

'Oh dear,' sighed Forbuoys, convincingly. 'I was afraid O'Brien might be mixed up in this.' He was relieved at the introduction of a usefully disreputable name into this true, but unlikely, story. 'O'Brien doesn't really belong in here, he belongs somewhere more secure. Bad influence all round.'

'I think we'd better bring the headmaster in on this,' suggested the doctor.

'Good idea,' agreed Forbuoys, 'I'll fetch him.' He was already planning his condemnation of Derek. How the boy was a fantasist and how puberty must have made his fantasies seem real enough for him to bring these monstrous accusations. However the clap wasn't fantasy. He'd have to have a private check up to make sure he hadn't caught anything off the boy.

What bit of courage Derek found had deserted him when faced with the headmaster, Johnnie O'Brien, Forbuoys and the doctor. Johnnie just sneered and called him a lying loser. This, coupled with Forbuoys' denial, left Derek on his own. Sobbing. He was made to sleep in a room of his own until the antibiotics had done their job.

Forbuoys never came near him again and Johnnie stopped taking him to perform in the sex shows. He did give Derek a serious beating as a punishment for squealing on him, and Derek didn't squeal on him this time. There was nothing to be gained.

The antibiotics did their job on his body but not on his mind. He gradually withdrew into a world of his own, speaking only when spoken to and never using two words where one would do – and never using one word when a nod or a grunt or a shake of the head would do. He felt useless and confused and simply not belonging to this world.

When he was seventeen he was sent to a hostel where he looked after himself with his dole money. He developed no social skills and had neither girlfriends nor boyfriends. All he had for pleasure was his right hand and a machine to play his records on.

When he was nineteen Jeannie tracked him down and came to see him. Derek remembered once having a sister but suspected she might be dead. She was really pretty and he was overjoyed to see her and he poured his heart out to her. She was horrified by his Paddock House story and listened in floods of tears. Then he asked her about her life and she told him how she had been adopted by parents who weren't brilliant but at least they never neglected her like their mother had. Her hatred of Frampton still festered within her and sharing this with Derek wasn't going to help him, so she did what she did best. She lied. One day, when he was strong enough to listen, she might exchange stories. While it was happening she'd survived by planning her revenge on Frampton, but now it was all over she just wanted to forget it and get on with her life. But it wasn't easy.

Being two years older, she remembered their mother better than Derek did. Their mother was a drunken cow, she told him; she was not fit to have children. Then Jeannie left, promising to come back and look after him and make everything better. But she didn't.

Chapter Eleven

Sam flopped down in the chair opposite Sally, who was sitting in his chair at his desk.

'I assume it's all right if I sit down?'

'Be my guest.' She took a file from *his* drawer. 'I've got some information for you about Ron Crusher.'

'I hope it's better than the information you got me about Bernard.'

She frowned. 'What was wrong with that?'

'You told me he owned about twenty dry cleaners around Yorkshire. In fact he doesn't own any.'

'Oh yes he d–'

He didn't let her finish. 'His wife owns them all, he just runs them.'

'Oh – same difference,' she said, dismissively.

'It's not, actually,' commented Sam, without elaborating. 'Right, what have you got for me this time?'

'In 1983 Ron did a year in Armley for GBH.' She looked up at Sam to see if this was news to him, by the expression on his face it wasn't. If his expression didn't change *she'd* be doing time for GBH. 'While he was inside he did a building course and came out as a qualified plasterer. He worked on building sites during the day and as a doorman at night.' She still hadn't told him anything he didn't know and his expression was getting to her. 'In 1992 he'd got a bit of money together and decided to start up his own building business. Took on a chap called Paul Smith to run it.' There was a spark of interest in Sam's eyes now which gave her encouragement to continue. 'Ron just handled the business while Paul did all the technical stuff. Apparently they did all right in a dodgy sort of way. Paul Smith's still running it although he's apparently cleaned up the act.'

Sam knew enough about the veracity of the first part of her report not to doubt the rest. He was impressed. 'Where did you get all this from?'

Sally gave him a cheeky smile and ran her fingers across the desk. 'Sorry, your honour, I did it again,' she said, as though admitting some major crime.

'Did what again?'

She pointed, hesitantly, to the telephone. 'I used the forbidden thing.'

'Who did you ring?'

'Alec. He's been around the trade a long time, mostly in Leeds. I thought there was a fair chance he'd know Ron Crusher. You'd have asked him yourself but you're scared he'd bite your head off.'

She knew Alec liked getting involved in Sam's business even less than Owen did. Sam only involved him if he was stuck, which he frequently was. There was too much of a crossover between the two businesses for Alec's liking, with Sam taking the men off the sites to do odd jobs for him.

'He didn't know too much about Ron's dodgy dealings,' Sally went on, 'but I suspect you could

119

get a lot more out of Mr Smith with your leg work and good old fashioned common sense, not to mention your charm.'

'Have you done something to your hair?'

Her hand went to her hair. '*I* haven't. A hairdresser did all that for me.'

'It looks ... different.'

'Different nice?'

He grinned and nodded. 'In fact you look different nice all over. What have you done to yourself?'

'Well, with me being on double money I've been pampering myself. New clothes, hairdresser, beautician, I've even joined a gym.'

Sam half closed his eyes and said, in an atrocious Chinese accent, 'Confucius say: It is wise employee, especially one on double bubble, who takes out boss now and again, or bubble may burst.'

She threw her head back, sensuously. 'You'll need to scrub up really well to come out with me. And young beauties such as I, don't expect to pay.'

'I'll pick you up at seven.'

'Dinner?' she suggested.

'Why not?'

'I'm not going anywhere where I have to collect my food on a tray. I want a tinkling piano and a waiter with a dodgy french accent. I want a table with a proper tablecloth and a candle, and one of those big linen napkins.'

'I was thinking of fish and chips.'

'I'm thinking of a bill that'll make you hyperventilate and a man on the door with a top hat who'll expect a tip that he can fold in his gloved hand as he flags a taxi down.'

'I'd better have a bath.'

He leaned up on one elbow as she got out of bed and walked, naked, to the bathroom. The evening had gone well, apart from the astronomical bill. 'How long did you say you'd been going to the gym?'

She wiggled her backside. 'Twice, so far. What do you think?'

'Never actually thought you needed it. Still, you'll need to be fit to keep up with me.'

Sally turned to face him; leaned, provocatively, against the bathroom door and said, with a challenge in her eyes, 'Come and have a go, big boy, if you think you're hard enough.'

He lifted up the bedclothes and studied what he saw under there. 'Better leave it another ten minutes, I'm not a machine.'

'We're good together, you and me, Sam. You know it and I know it.' Without waiting for a comment she disappeared into the bathroom.

He grinned as he listened to her singing, loud but way out of tune. Even he could sing better than Sal.

Eileen plonked a cardboard box on Sam's desk. 'All his stuff's in here. There might be some personal stuff but I can't bring myself to go through it. Always meant to. If you see anything I might be interested in, would you let me have it back, please?'

'Of course, Mrs Crusher.'

'There are some accounts, but my Ron kept changing accountants. He reckoned it kept the taxman guessing.' She looked across at Sally who was busy doing Carew and Son's books.

'This is Sally,' said Sam. 'My right hand man.'

'Hello.' Eileen held out a feathery hand. 'I'm Eileen Crusher.'

'Pleased to meet you, Mrs Crusher.'

Eileen returned her attention to Sam and took a folded sheet of paper from her pocket. 'I've made out a list of everyone I can think of who had anything to do with him.'

'That's great,' smiled Sam, taking the list from her. 'Anything else?'

Just for a second a guarded look came into her eyes – enough to make him want to know what it meant. It was a guarded look that might be hiding the key to this whole case. But it would keep. The two names that stood out on the list were Paul Smith and Milo Morrell.

'What business did your husband have with Milo Morrell?'

'He worked for him, on and off. Used to sing in his club, years ago. Then he did door work, then he took on that building work – building Milo's new club in Huddersfield.'

'He built a new club for Morrell? Sounds like a big job.'

'The biggest he'd ever taken on.'

'Did he finish it?'

Eileen gave a dry laugh and shook her head. 'No – my Ron rarely finished anything he started. He'd always take what he called "the meat" out of the job, make sure he got paid up to date, then

122

move on, leaving someone else to do the finishing. He wasn't much of a finisher wasn't my Ron.'

'I don't suppose Morrell will have been pleased with that.'

'Oh, no. That's not why he didn't finish Milo's job.' It didn't escape Sam's notice that she called him Milo. 'He'd only been working on it a month when he died. I reckon that could have been the first job my Ron saw through to the end.'

'Did you know Morrell well?'

'Not really. Met him a couple of times at his club. Never liked him.'

Then why call him Milo? Sam kept this thought to himself. Sally was thinking exactly the same thing. 'What about Paul Smith?' he asked, instead.

'Decent bloke. He came round to see me after Ron died and asked if he could take over Ron's contract. There was no need for him to ask me, he could have just done it. There wouldn't have been much in writing between Ron and Milo. He wasn't big on writing things down if he didn't have to, wasn't Ron. He knew how much he was owed at any given time, that's all he ever needed to know as far as he was concerned. Anyway Smithy gave me a couple of thousand to cover materials on site. It just about paid for the funeral.'

'I don't suppose you've come up with any ideas of what he bought with the money?'

'Honestly, Sam, my mind's been going round in circles. I keep coming back to property, or maybe a share in something.'

'Like a club?' suggested Sally.

Both she and Sam looked at her. Eileen

123

dropped her eyes and shook her head. 'I know what you're thinking. Milo wouldn't do a thing like that. Anyway, my Ron might not have liked paperwork but he wasn't stupid. He wouldn't have handed money like that over without a solicitor and a proper contract being involved.' She tapped her temple. 'He had a good head on his shoulders, did my Ron. Right, if there's nothing else, I'd best be on me way.'

Sam smiled and got to his feet. He shook her hand and held open the door. 'Keep in touch, Mrs Crusher,' he said. 'And if you think of anything else that might help us don't hesitate to contact me.' *Especially that thing you're hiding from me.* 'Everything you tell me will be strictly confidential.'

He stood at the door and watched her as she walked up the street. Sally, who was standing behind him, commented, 'I don't think Mrs Crusher's the shrinking violet she's makes herself out to be.'

'She has more to tell us, that's for sure,' agreed Sam, going back into the office. 'Trouble is, it might be a job prising it out of her.'

'Sounds like a job for your assistant.'

'What, you?'

'No, I mean Owen. If anyone can uncover a woman's dark secrets it's harmless Owen Price.'

'He'll uncover more than her dark secrets if we let him loose on her.'

Bernard rang him up the same day. The sum total of his information was the name Milo Morrell, who was, to quote Bernard, a proper wrong un.

124

'Did you know Ron's house is being re-possessed?' Sam asked him. 'He borrowed money against it just before he died.'

There was a defensive pause. 'What's that got to do with me? I suppose Eileen's been slagging us off for not helping her.'

'You're not her favourite people,' said Sam. 'I don't suppose you've got any idea what he did with the money?'

'Haven't a bloody clue. What Ron did with his money is no business of mine.'

Sam became exasperated. 'Mr Crusher. It's you who employed us. Yet when I ask you questions, you don't sound very enthusiastic. Are you sure you want me to carry on?'

'I'm sorry, lad. To be honest, now I've set you on I'm wondering if I'm not just being daft. My wife thinks I'm throwing money away. Happen she's right.'

'For what it's worth, Mr Crusher, I think Ron was murdered.'

'You do?'

'Yes, I do. I know the where and the when, all I need to find out is the why and the who.'

'Sounds simple when you put it like that.'

'It's not simple, Mr Crusher. That's why I need you to be enthusiastic.'

'It's hard to be enthusiastic when the Führer's breathing down me neck all day long.'

'So, what do you want me to do, Mr Crusher?'

'I want you to carry on, lad. Get to the bottom of it. He was the only brother I had and if someone's killed him I wouldn't like to think they'd got away with it.'

Sam arrived on site as Alec was sitting in the cabin, having a relaxing smoke. It was Christmas Eve.

'Lads like their Christmas bonus?' Sam enquired.

'They didn't grumble, so I suppose they must,' said Alec.

'I thought we'd discuss our own bonus.'

'Suits me.'

'Thousand each?'

It crossed Alec's mind to ask Sam what he'd done to earn his part of the bonus but he already knew the answer. Sam had earned his bonus the day he'd handed over half the company to Alec in exchange for Alec running it. It had settled the joiner's life and left Sam free to do what he liked best – catching villains.

'Fair enough,' said Alec. 'I think we can afford it. We've caught up this last week, and they've asked us to price up another job in Castleford. Fair size as well.'

'Have they now? Have you got the plans?'

Alec tapped his bass. 'Plans and spec in here. I thought we'd have a look in the pub. You are taking me for a Christmas drink I assume. The lads are all waiting for us in the Clog and Shovel.'

Sam looked down at the joiner's bass – a hessian toolbag with rope handles – and laughed. 'Alec, I'm not pricing a job up in the Clog on Christmas Eve. Our competition will be taking that stuff back to their offices in fancy briefcases. Then they'll be bringing in quantity surveyors, accountants and estimators.'

'They can bring in who they like. I know how much stuff costs and how long it takes to do. I'll take it home with me. All you have to do is tell me how much profit we want.'

'Thirty per cent ... tell me about Ron Crusher's firm.'

'I thought you'd never ask.'

'Sally?'

Alec nodded. 'She said you might come bothering me. So, in anticipation, I asked around. I never knew the feller meself but I know a couple of lads who've worked for him.'

'And?' asked Sam, as he took Alec's tab-end and lit his own cigarette. Rain was hammering on the cabin roof and one of the men had left a radio on, playing Christmas carols.

'And he were a good bloke if you didn't cross him. He dealt mainly in cash, never bothered with sub-contract tickets or VAT or nowt. In fact I don't think he bothered much with builders merchants. Most of his stuff arrived on site on unmarked wagons, without delivery notes. Used a fair amount of immigrant labour, although by all accounts, he paid them a decent enough wage.'

'Villain with a heart of gold eh? That's what I keep hearing about him.'

'Everybody was evidently amazed when he topped himself,' Alec added. 'Still, you never know what goes on inside a bloke's head.'

'What about this chap who's taken over – Paul Smith?'

'I think he's straight,' said Alec. 'Good builder as well, by all accounts. Could do with him here if you've left us permanently.'

'I haven't left – I'm available as and when. If we need him we'll get him. I gather he's working on that Milo Morrell job. He should be glad to leave after that.' Sam opened the cabin door and scowled at the weather. Then he turned up the collar of his coat and said, 'Right, I'll see you in the Clog. I'm just having a couple. My boys are coming tonight. We're going to have a good old fashioned Christmas.'

'Sally joining you?'

'Just for a drink. Then she's coming round tomorrow to cook the dinner.'

'You should snap her up before someone else does.'

'You should mind your own business.'

Chapter Twelve

Derek didn't decide to choose Christmas Eve 1980 as his last day on Earth. It more or less chose him. He had a deep hatred of the world around him. He didn't wish the world any harm, he just didn't want to be part of it. If Jeannie had come back to him, as she had promised, it wouldn't have been so bad. But she had her own life to lead. Good luck to her. He bore her no grudge. Nor did he bear a grudge against Forbuoys or Johnnie O'Brien. In fact the only person he bore a grudge against was the man who shot John Lennon. That was an awful thing to do.

When his mother had walked out on him and his sister the only things she left in the flat to enable them to survive were running tap water and her collection of Beatles records. The two kids played the records incessantly at first, dancing around the small, dirty room to the sound of 'Love Me Do' and 'She Loves You'. There was no radio, no TV, no food, just tap water and The Beatles. After three days something went wrong with the stylus on the record player and both children cried. Being deprived of their mother was bearable, being deprived of food was painful, but being deprived of their friends, The Beatles, was the worst thing.

Throughout his time in Paddock House Derek had no opportunity to buy any records. But the sound of The Beatles coming from any room, any radio, any television, would draw him like a magnet. His favourite was John. He loved the edgy, sour sound of John's voice. It was the voice of someone who didn't give a shit, someone who could stand up for himself. He would probably have stood up for Derek in Paddock House had he known about him. He had even sent a letter to John, telling of his misery but he guessed it just got swallowed up with all the other fan mail. In any event, John didn't write back.

Then, when he was sent out to live on his own, he saved up and bought a second hand Sony tape player. To his delight he found he could buy Beatles music on tape, relatively cheaply.

On December 8th 1980 some pathetic nobody shot John Lennon. It might as well have been Derek whom he shot. How he wished he could have taken John's bullets for him, all four of them. What a noble death that would have been. Derek mourned for sixteen days, then, on the afternoon of Christmas Eve, he went into Leeds City centre and got drunk. It didn't cost him much. He hadn't tasted alcohol since it had been forced on him by Johnnie O'Brien. The bar of the Three Legs was packed with Christmas revellers. Derek was surrounded by laughter and singing as he drank his three whiskies and two pints of Tetley's bitter, and he knew this was a world to which he could never belong. As he stepped out into the street the Christmas lights were shimmering through his drunken haze and the winter drizzle. The town centre was bustling with late shoppers and a heavy lorry was coming up the

Headrow. The driver was hoping to beat the traffic lights at the Briggate junction. He had a home to go to, presents still to buy, and a Christmas drink to have with his wife. Derek put paid to all that. He stepped out into the road, giving the driver no chance at all. Derek was dragged fifty feet under the skidding wheels of the sixteen-tonner. His sad life was over and the driver's Christmas had been ruined.

It was Boxing Day and Zola Gee was on the bus when she read of Derek's death. It was the reference to Paddock House that caught her attention:

The victim was identified as unemployed Derek Fleming, 20. Little is known about him other than he was a former resident of Paddock House home for boys.

She put the paper down and ran the name through her memory. Her association with Johnnie O'Brien from Paddock House wasn't one she remembered with any great pride. What was the name of that lad who'd caught a dose from her? His name was Derek, wasn't it? She'd stopped doing business with Johnnie after that. He'd scared her. Derek, if it was the same lad, was the last in a line of half a dozen boys Johnnie had brought to the "shows". She'd done okay out of them. Regular work. Fifteen quid for fifteen minutes. That's the longest any of them lasted. Some of them seemed to enjoy it. The last one didn't though. He cried a lot and it bothered her. She shouldn't have done it to him but she needed the money. And she was scared of Johnnie, which was nearer the truth.

Zola was now 24 and still on the game. She didn't work the streets though, she worked for an escort agency which, she thought, gave her profession a certain respectability. There was less danger and an element of protection. Her only qualifications were a desperate need for money and stunning good looks. But it was a profession that took its toll on a woman's looks. Most thirty-year-old pros had a ravaged look about them, as if all the energy and life and decency and self-respect had been sucked out of them. Most thirty-year-old pros went on to become forty-year-old-pros, then fifty-year-old has-beens selling themselves for a gin and tonic. That wasn't how Zola saw her future. She got off the bus outside the Fforde Grene pub. There was someone who worked there who had lived in Paddock House during the time Derek was a resident. She often went there to meet clients. Their eyes had met in the past and a look of recognition had passed between them, but nothing had been said. Until now.

'Remember me?'

The young barman nodded, reluctantly. 'Your name's Zola,' he said, than added, 'it's been a long time.'

'Six years since I was mixed up with that scumbag O'Brien.'

'O'Brien, yeah. Johnnie O'Brien. What'll you have?'

'Large brandy please, nothing with it.'

He stuck a glass in an optic of Courvoisier, pressed out two measures then set it down in front of her. 'You remember me, then do you?' he

132

said. 'I'm surprised you remember me.'

'You looked familiar when I first saw you. It took me while to place you.'

He leaned across the bar, and muttered. 'You saw a lot more of me than my face. I was only fourteen.'

'Oh dear. I hope I didn't corrupt you. I wasn't all that old myself.'

'Not on your own you didn't,' he said. 'It was Paddock House that corrupted me. Took me years ter get me head together after I left that place.'

'Are you all right now?'

'As right as I'll ever be. Got engaged last week.'

'Does your fiancée know about...?'

'She knows I was in a home. She doesn't know what happened to me in there. If she did she'd want to talk about it, maybe even nag me into doing something about it. I couldn't handle that.'

Zola didn't know whether to go on. He obviously had bad memories of her. At the time she'd fooled herself into thinking she was doing the boys a favour. At least that's what O'Brien had told her. She took a sip of her brandy and felt uncomfortable under his gaze. Perhaps it had been a mistake coming in here.

'Why did you come over to talk to me?' he enquired. 'I've seen you in here loads of times but you've never bothered to talk to me before.'

'I was just wondering if you knew this chap.'

She laid the newspaper on the bar and pointed to the article on Derek's death. He gave it the cursory glance of someone who already knew about it, and looked back at her. 'Derek Fleming –

yeah, I knew Derek. Not as well as you knew him, but well enough. You remember him, do you?'

'Not sure.'

'Well, he wasn't very memorable wasn't poor old Derek.'

'I assume he was one of ... of O'Brien's boys?'

He nodded. 'He was the one after me. The last in the line as it happens.'

Zola winced. He was the one who had cried, she was afraid he might be.

'Caught a dose of clap. We were never sure whether he got it from you or Forbuoys.' The barman's tone was unforgiving but not threatening.

'Forbuoys?' she said. 'He, er, he worked at the home didn't he?'

'Forbuoys was a nonce. Still at it by all accounts. Between him and O'Brien they did Derek's head in. It wasn't pleasant for any of us, but Derek took it really badly. Some of us reckoned Derek was a woofter which is why it had a bad effect on him – being forced to do it with you in front of all them fellers, wanking away like monkeys in a cage. It was as if we were just getting ready for manhood and then it was snatched away from us.'

'I don't understand. What was snatched away?'

'Our dignity, love. Our dignity, pride, self esteem – call it what you want – went right up the bloody spout. Well, that's how it felt for me. I think it was a bloody sight worse for Derek.'

Zola listened to all this with mounting shock. Tears welled up and poured down her cheeks. Even at the time she knew she might be corrupt-

134

ing the boys but she chose to listen to O'Brien's lies about them all being volunteers. She was now being told that she had been instrumental in making young boys' lives so miserable that one of them eventually killed himself. That wasn't how things were supposed to be. She was supposed to be a professional pleasure giver. She hurried from the pub, and away from her life as a prostitute. The young barman picked up her brandy and drank it, satisfied that he had exacted maybe a morsel of retribution for his suffering.

The DHSS put up the money for the most basic of funerals. Jeannie was the only one there. She knelt in the crematorium chapel and wept copious tears of pity for herself and Derek, and tears of rage against the bastards who had driven him to this. She should have at least written to him, if only to show him she cared and hadn't abandoned him. But she had been too ashamed to tell her baby brother that his big sister had been locked up for theft – yet again. She had been released the day before he died and turned up at his hostel with a card and a Christmas present for him, only to be told of his death by an inebriated hostel warden who gave her the news with a smirk on his face. The news threw her.

'He's dead, lass. Chucked hisself under a wagon yesterday – pissed as a fart. Right bloody mess by all accounts.'

'Derek didn't drink,' was all she could think of to say. She had stood in the doorway completely bereft. Derek must have felt he had no one in the world. No one to turn to. She should have been

135

that person for him. There was now another deep wound inside her. But the people who had inflicted this wound were still alive. She should have helped her brother, there was no doubt about that; she should have helped him but she wasn't responsible for his death. In some ways it was a relief that she now had a couple of live targets for her retribution. In avenging Derek she would purge herself of all the harm Frampton had done to her. Hopefully.

Chapter Thirteen

'Dad, couldn't you have got a bigger Christmas tree?'

'I'm an injured man. You can't expect me to go lugging a ten-foot tree all the way from Unsworth market. I suppose your mum's got a Norwegian pine, bigger that the one in Trafalgar Square.'

'No,' said Tom, sitting back in one of Sam's new chairs and putting his feet on the new coffee table. 'But it's a proper, festive tree. That's just a twig with a few coloured lights. You haven't even got a fairy on top.'

'There's children in Africa who don't have any Christmas trees at all. They don't have presents, they don't have sweets, they don't have telly–'

'You can tell Dad's got no proper argument when he starts waffling,' said Jake to Sally. He was sitting next to her and his dad on Sam's new set-tee, bought with the other furnishings under her guiding eye, from GFS on the Unsworth Trading estate. According to the TV adverts GFS had a permanent sale that was always just about to end.

'Humour him,' she advised. 'It's his age. Would you young gentlemen care for a glass of wine?'

'Sally, what're you doing? They're fourteen years old.'

'Oh, yes, and how old were you when you had your first drink?'

Sam decided it was pointless arguing with her,

137

so he sat back as Sally poured them each a glass of Chardonnay. He proposed the same corny Christmas Eve toast his dad had, ever since Sam could remember. He missed his dad.

'Peace on earth and goodwill to all men.'

The other three raised their glasses and repeated his words. Tom asked, with juvenile innocence: 'Will you two be getting married, soon?'

'Sooner the better,' said Jake, looking at Sally. 'It's your duty to keep Dad out of trouble.'

Sally laughed away her embarrassment. 'Hey, don't lay that burden on me. The United Nations couldn't keep your dad out of trouble.'

There was a moment of peace as the four of them drank their wine and stared at Sam's limp, two feet tall tree with its twelve winking lights that winked their last as they watched.

The silence lasted another three seconds before Tom started giggling. Sam was annoyed at having spent a tenner on lights that only winked for an hour. Jake was giggling now, as was Sally.

'You wouldn't be laughing if you'd just wasted a tenner on dud lights,' grumbled Sam.

'A tenner?' Sally said. 'Where'd you get them from?'

'Called in the Clog on the way home from getting my stitches out – I can take the strapping off my chest next week.'

'I expect we should be thankful you didn't take the stitches out yourself like you usually do.'

'These were a bit tricky,' said Sam, fingering the wound on his head. 'Anyway, this chap in the pub was selling off surplus Christmas stock. Stands to reason they'd be cheap.'

'Sam,' said Sally, 'they were selling those in Unsworth market for five quid a box. He probably bought all the unsold stuff from the market at half price and flogged it off round the pubs.'

'Dad, to say you're supposed to be a brilliant detective,' commented Jake, 'you're a bit gullible.'

'Ah, but he's also brilliant bricklayer,' said Sally. 'Bricklayers are supposed to be gullible.'

'An uncommon combination,' mused Jake, stroking an imaginary beard. Then he raised an inspirational finger. 'I've got it. You should do undercover work as a bricklayer.'

'Is there much call for undercover brickies?' enquired Tom.

'You should buy yourself a deerstalker and call yourself Barratt Holmes,' suggested Sally, happily going along with the boys. Sam was lost in thought, nodding to himself. 'Oh, heck!' she said. 'I think we've put an idea into his head.'

'Owen, lad, me and you are going to do some real detective work.'

They were in the Clog and Shovel. It was Boxing Day afternoon and the pub was full. Sky Sports was showing an FA Cup 2nd round clash between Unsworth Town and Notts County. Owen became immediately suspicious.

'What sort of work?'

'Work that'll earn you money on top of the hundred a day I'm paying you. We're going undercover as a bricklayer and his labourer. I've already checked. Paul Smith's desperate for good brickies– Good grief! That was a mile offside!'

There was a groan of dismay from the tele-

139

vision viewers as Unsworth went one down to a goal that the whole pub agreed was offside.

'I've never done any labouring, look you. Anyway, how you going to work with broken ribs?'

Sam patted his sore ribs. 'Practically as good as new, anyway you'll be doing all the heavy lifting. I'll teach you all you need to know in an hour. It's a good healthy life and you'll be on double bubble.'

'Working with you isn't what I'd call healthy. In fact I'd say you're a walking health hazard.'

Sam slapped him on his back. 'You're a cautious man, Owen. I like that in a partner.'

'Partners is it? Maybe I should be getting half your fee.'

'It was a figure of speech,' said Sam. 'You're one of life's wage earners Owen. Always settle for what you are. That's the secret of happiness– Oh, get rid of the sodding ball. Bloody hell! Did you see that?'

'I could tell you what you are, boyo, but I don't think you'd be very happy about it.' A smile crossed Owen's face as he thought of a snag in Sam's plan. 'Tell me, boyo, how do you propose we get paid for the work we do on this job if we're working under false names?'

Sam thought for a second, then groaned as the Unsworth keeper let in a soft goal. 'I'll buy an off-the-peg limited company, with you and me as directors. It'll be above board, apart from the names on the letter heads. I'll just ask Smith to pay by cheque made out to the company. He won't object to that – I wouldn't. Pass the bloody ball, man!'

Paul Smith Builders (Leeds) Ltd were working on Milo Morrell's new club near Huddersfield. It was a job that had been started by Ron Crusher. At 8 a.m. on a cold Monday morning in early January, Sam and Owen drove on to the site in Owen's Ford Sierra. Sam's Range Rover might have aroused curiosity.

It was Paul Smith's only contract and he'd just agreed to build a squash court and snooker room beside the almost finished club, and had promised Morrell that it would be ready in May. It was proving to have been a rash promise considering the trouble he was having finding decent bricklayers. Sam knocked on his cabin door and Smith opened it. Fresh faced – obviously not a tradesman. Possibly a surveyor or an engineer.

'I'm looking for Mr Smith.'

'That's me.'

'I was wondering if you were setting brickies on.'

'I am if you're a proper brickie, not just a bodger. I've sacked two of them in the past week.'

'Apprentice trained,' Sam assured him. 'I can build in any bond you like; English, Flemish, garden wall–'

'Who did you work for last?'

'Carew's in Unsworth. Do you know them?'

Smith gave a vague nod and looked beyond Sam at the Sierra and the shadowy figure of Owen, eating a Mars Bar. 'What are you – a two and one gang?'

'Er, no – there's only me and a labourer. He's a good lad but to be honest he's got his work cut out keeping me going.'

'You're that good eh?'

141

'I'm pretty good, yes. You can have the two of us for £16 an hour. I'm worth that myself. If you don't think so you can sack me at dinnertime. My name's Sid Charlesworth by the way.'

The young builder thought about it for quite some time and Sam was beginning to wonder if he'd been rumbled. Was there something about him that told the man he wasn't genuine? Had he said something wrong? To his relief, Smith said, 'Right, I'll give you a start, Sid, see how you go on. You can put the footings in. I'll have a scout round for a two and one gang to work on the superstructure with you. There's three month's work here at least, seven days a week if you like.'

'Thanks Mr Smith. Five and a half days is plenty for me.'

'You might as well call me Smithy, everyone else around here does.'

Sam felt guilty at his deception. He'd no intention of staying for three months. If someone had played such a trick on him he wouldn't be so pleased. Builders can't afford to be messed about by the men. Still, while Sam worked there, Smithy would have as good a brickie as he could get for the money. Job number one would be to worm his way into the builder's confidence and find out as much as he could about Milo Morrell and Ron Crusher.

The club itself was almost ready. Inside were a few of the finishing trades. Electricians, a heating engineer, painters and carpenters. Sam and Owen were working on their own some distance away, building the footings to the new squash and snooker club. They had been working there

142

for four days when Smithy came over to Sam, who was just bringing the blockwork up to damp course level. 'You've done well,' he commented. 'The building inspector, chap called Rastrick, is coming out later this morning to do an inspection. I won't be here.'

'I'll handle him,' Sam assured him.

'He's a bastard.'

Sam grinned. 'Aren't they all?'

'No, they're not,' said Smithy. 'You get moaning buggers and some are thick buggers but this bloke's a full weight bastard. The bloke who had this firm before me used to bung him.'

'You mean Ron Crusher?'

'Yeah, did you know him?'

'Heard of him.'

'I don't believe in giving out bungs. You never know what it can lead to.'

'It can lead to trouble,' said Sam. 'Is he actually asking for a bung?'

'Not outright. But he makes it more than obvious that he'll go a lot easier on us if we make it worth his while. He's had me jumping through bloody hoops to get work passed.'

'Ah, I know the type. Do you want us to sort him?'

'Sort him?' said Smithy puzzled. 'How will you do that?'

'I'd sooner keep it to myself.'

Sam was unravelling a roll of pvc damp proofing over the footings when the building inspector arrived.

'New to the game, lad?' he enquired, without

143

introducing himself.

'Who are you?' enquired Sam, without stopping what he was doing. He knew he was talking to the building inspector. The man had an officious air about him. He wore a flat cap, a dark blue fleece and green wellingtons.

'Rastrick, building inspector.'

And what makes you think I'm new to the game, Mr Rastrick?'

'Because you're using the wrong blocks, that's why.'

'No, I'm not,' said Sam. 'These blocks comply with building regs.'

'They don't look right to me. I ought to stop the job and send them away for testing.'

'Come on,' protested Sam. 'You can't do that.'

'I can do what I like,' said Rastrick, lighting a cigarette and flicking the spent match at Sam. 'If you take this wall above damp course without my approval, the lot comes down.'

Sam gave the matter some thought, then he got out of the trench and climbed up to where Rastrick was standing. 'I've heard you're hard to please, Mr Rastrick. But I think I see where you're coming from.'

'I thought you might, lad. What with you being around a long time.'

'If there's one thing I've learned, Mr Rastrick,' went on Sam, 'it's that we've all got to rub along together in this game. You scratch my back, I'll scratch yours. Are we talking the same language?'

'Keep talking, lad. I'm listening.'

'Owen,' called out Sam. He winked at Rastrick and explained, 'We work as a team, me and

144

Owen. He's the one who deals in readies.'

Owen came across, knowing full well why.

'What?' he asked.

'Mr Rastrick needs a sweetener to smooth our path.'

'Ah,' said Owen. 'A smooth path's the path to tread. A rocky road's the one I dread.'

'He's bit of a poet, with him being Welsh,' Sam explained. 'I think fifty should set the ball rolling.'

'Fifty it is,' said Owen. He took out a wad of notes from his pocket and counted out five tens.

The inspector looked, greedily, at the wad. 'I think you might find the path's a lot smoother if you double that. Fifty quid doesn't go far these days. A hundred quid a week and you'll find the job runs like clockwork, at least your part of it.' He jabbed a thumb in the direction of the club. 'I should have a word with your gaffer. Get him to see sense if he wants that place to open on time.'

'I'll do that, Mr Rastrick. A hundred do you say?'

'Aye, lad. Look on it as tipping a waiter for good service.'

'Sounds about right to me, Mr Rastrick. Owen, give the man his tip.'

Owen counted out another fifty. The inspector pocketed the money, glanced at Sam's work and said, 'It'll do. Carry on.'

He turned to go and Sam called out, 'Just a minute, Mr Rastrick – Owen's got something else you might be interested in.'

'Well, be quick about it, I haven't got all day.'

'This won't take a minute, boyo.'

Owen reached into his pocket and took out his

warrant card, which he showed to Rastrick. 'DC Price,' he said, 'Fraud Squad. Mr Rastrick, can you give me any reason why I shouldn't arrest you for obtaining money by corruption?'

The inspector looked at the warrant card and went white.

'We have you bang to rights, Mr Rastrick,' said Owen, convincingly. 'Your reputation precedes you.'

'Look fellers, give me a break. I'm only doing what half the inspectors in the game are doing.'

'No, you're not,' said Sam. 'You're a rotten apple in a barrel.'

Rastrick took the money out of his pocket and threw it at Owen. 'There's your money,' he whined, petulantly. 'I've taken nothing off you. What are you going to do about it?'

'I'm going to arrest you,' said Owen, picking up the money. Sam admired his style. He'd never known Owen bluff anyone –and the bluff was working. Rastrick was visibly shaking.

'Unless,' said Sam, thinking out loud.

Owen and Rastrick looked at him.

'Unless what?' said Rastrick, seeing a lifeline and wanting to clutch at it with both hands.

'We actually have bigger fish than you to fry, Mr Rastrick,' Sam said. 'We might overlook your lapse in honesty if you help us.'

"Help you? In what way.'

'We'll let you know,' said Sam, mysteriously. 'In the meantime we'd be obliged if you kept your mouth shut about who we are and didn't bother us. We'll contact you. It's information we want. Information you'll be party to.'

'I'll help in any way I can,' promised Rastrick.

'This deal only stands if you keep your mouth shut about who we are. You blow our cover and you'll lose your job and your freedom.'

'You can trust me.'

'We'll be in touch,' said Sam. 'Oh, and don't give anyone else on this site a hard time or we'll be down on you like a ton of bricks.'

'We convinced him that Owen's a copper,' said Sam. 'Owen threatened to arrest him for corruption.'

'You're kidding!' exclaimed Smithy. 'Jesus, I wish I'd been there.'

'So if you hear any rumours that there's a couple of coppers working on the site you know where they came from. Personally I don't think Rastrick will be saying anything to anyone.'

Sam was covering himself just in case the worst did happen.

'If he sees you laying bricks he'll know you're not a copper,' said Smithy, who had been admiring the way Sam had brought up the wall six courses above damp course in the space of half a day.

'He won't see me laying bricks,' promised Sam. 'He won't come near this site until I ring him. Strikes me it was your mate Crusher who started all this.'

'He was no mate of mine,' said Smithy. 'I actually quite liked him but he was no builder – more of a chancer.'

'So I've heard. It must have come as a shock when he topped himself.'

'I'll say. Not that type at all. And the way he did

147

it – jumping off that roof. Couldn't do with heights couldn't Ron. He used to throw a wobbly if he stood on a thick carpet.'

'I heard a rumour that it might not have been suicide,' said Sam, as casually as he could.

'Wouldn't surprise me,' agreed Smithy. 'I know Ron's brother's been going round spouting his mouth off. Met him once, don't know what to make of him. Odd bugger, not a bit like Ron.'

Sam scooped up a trowel full of mortar and spread it, expertly on the top course of bricks. 'Takes all sorts,' he said. 'I gather Ron mixed with a rum crowd when he was working on the doors.'

Smithy gave a wry grin. 'Well, he got mixed up with Milo Morrell. He's rum enough for me.'

'What's he like?'

Smithy shrugged. 'He's okay with me but I wouldn't like to cross him. Pays me in cash, but I put it through my books – even if he doesn't put it through his. Imagine, a job this size and getting stage payments in cash. He came round with twenty one grand last week. Plonked it on the table in the cabin and asked for a cash receipt.'

Sam whistled at the amount, then a thought came into his head. He regarded Smithy seriously. 'Smithy, you know it's got to be bent, that much cash. Doesn't it bother you?'

'It bothers me a lot. But I just look at this job as my way of getting the business up and running. Once I'm away from here I'll breathe a lot easier.'

'That's if he doesn't keep finding more jobs for you.'

'How do you mean?'

'He could be laundering cash through you.

148

Next thing you know he'll have you building houses. I could be wrong but you might well have a job getting away from him if he really is bent.'

Smithy sat down on a stack of bricks. 'Something like that has crossed my mind,' he admitted. 'When he came up with this squash courts thing I told him I wouldn't be able to fit it in as I'd got other work lined up. I hadn't really, but by the end of our conversation he made it clear that I had no option. He accepted my price without any argument – it's a good price as well.'

'I'm only warning you of this because it happened to a pal of mine,' said Sam. 'Got mixed up with a dodgy businessman. Things went well at first, the next thing the businessman had taken over the company and my mate's working for him. All the cash he'd been paid was marked as loans. This could be happening to you, Smithy.'

Sam didn't actually have a friend who been such a victim but during his time in the force he'd come across enough similar scams to know what was going on.

'But, if it got to court,' Smithy sounded worried, 'I'd be able to prove I'd only been paid for work done.'

'I suspect Morrell's already thought of that,' said Sam. 'My guess is that he'll be way ahead of you. I should check your contract, if I were you.'

'I don't think I dare,' sighed Smithy. 'Do you think that's what happened to Ron? I know he took out a big loan just before he killed himself. Maybe it was to get Morrell off his back. I knew there was something going on between them. I asked Ron about it but he told me to mind my

149

own business.'

'Why would he kill himself if he'd just got Morrell off his back?' wondered Sam.

'I've no idea. None of it makes sense to me. Maybe I should just take the money he's paid me and do a runner.'

'From what I hear of Morrell you'd have to run a long way very fast.'

Smithy gave a long sigh. Sam felt sorry for him. He was just a young man trying to forge ahead in a tough game – unfortunately he'd got off to a bad start. 'In that case,' Smithy said, 'I'll just have to plod on and see what happens. At least it won't come as a great shock to me, if and when he makes his move. Maybe I can do something to prepare myself.'

It occurred to Sam that it was time Smithy was told the whole truth. Maybe it would help the lad in the long run if they worked together.

'Look, Smithy, there's something else,' he said.

'Oh great, what sort of something?'

'My name isn't Sid Charlesworth.'

'It isn't?'

'No, it's Sam Carew.'

'I don't understand.'

'I'm a private detective working for Bernard Crusher, Ron's brother. He doesn't think Ron was murdered. I've been hired to find out the truth. I thought working here for a while might help. But you're a decent bloke and there's obviously no point lying to you any more.'

'What about Owen?'

'He's a genuine copper on holiday. He's my mate, just here for the ride. Smithy, I think we

150

can help each other here.'

Smithy sat on the bricks with his head in his hands. 'Jesus, I wish I hadn't taken over from Ron. I could have walked away but I saw an opportunity and walked into it with my eyes shut. You're right Sid, or Sam or whatever your name is. What's Owen's real name?'

'Owen Price,' said Sam. 'He's a pedigree Welshman, wouldn't let me change his name.'

Sam had worked, mechanically, all during this conversation. 'You're a damn good brickie for a private detective,' Smithy commented, curiously.

'I'm the son in Carew and Son. Part brickie, part private detective.'

Smithy gave a thin smile. 'Better known as Mad Carew. I remember now. You were in all the papers about a year ago. I should have twigged when you said you'd worked for Carew and Son.'

'I don't see why,' grinned Sam. And I don't see why I should stop working for you just because you know who I am. We could see this thing through together. If I can pin this murder on Morrell and he's banged up, you're home and dry, free and clear, up and running.'

Smithy brightened. 'What do you need from me?'

'As much as you know. All the suspicions you've put to the back of your mind as being none of your business. Stuff which, at the time, you didn't want to know about. Dodgy looking characters, suspicious goings on.'

'So, you don't want me to actually *do* anything?'

'I want you to carry on as normal. Keep pushing the work along, give me a bollocking now and

151

again. Just sit down and have a good think, then keep your eyes and ears open. Morrell's not going to suspect you with you being around since before Ron died. Tell me, is there anyone working on this site that Morrell himself set on?'

'There's Phil, he's a general labourer. One of Morrell's old doormen who took a bit of a hammering. Left him with a bad limp. He's not much use but Morrell pays his wages so it's no skin off my nose.'

'He's worth keeping an eye on. Just assume he's reporting everything you say and do back to Morrell. He might not be but it's not worth the risk.'

Smithy nodded. 'Fair enough. I don't actually have too much contact with Morrell, with his other club being in Unsworth. But he comes over here sometimes with a bloke called Tony. Really hard looking bloke. Some of the Leeds lads on the site reckon he's done time for murder. The only other stuff I know are the rumours.'

'What rumours?'

'Oh the sort you get in any site cabin. About Morrell being a big time drugs dealer, white slave trader, running protection rackets, you name it. All I really know is that up to now he's been okay with me.'

'Apart from bullying you into doing more work for him.'

'Well, yeah. Look, he's as bent as a nine-bob note, I know that. I suppose I've always known that.'

Owen arrived, breathlessly pushing a barrow of mortar. He tipped it on to a ligger board, stuck his hand into his pocket and brought out a Cadbury's mini roll.

'He's knows about us,' Sam said. 'I told him.'

'Oh, does he, look you?' Owen said, peeling back the wrapper and shoving the cake into his mouth.

'He's okay with it,' Sam assured him. 'It's looking more and more like Morrell's our man.'

Owen looked down, distastefully, at the pile of mortar. 'Does this mean I don't have to mix this rubbish any more?'

'Sorry, Owen,' said Sam, 'it means nothing of the sort. It means we're staying here until we get to the bottom of it.'

Owen now looked upon Smithy as he would a fellow Carew sufferer. 'Do you hear that, boyo? I've only got two weeks, see. He's got me doing this drudgery on my holidays. I assume he's told you what my proper job is.'

Smithy nodded.

'That needs to be kept a secret,' said Owen, 'especially from my employers.'

The young builder grinned. 'You can trust me.' He looked down at the mortar. 'Actually, this isn't rubbish, this is very good composition. Most labourers struggle to get it right – either too much sand or too much cement or too much water.'

'You're a natural,' added Sam.

Owen looked down at his glutinous creation through new, somewhat smug, eyes. 'Well, when you do a job...' he said, 'it's with me being from the valleys, see. It's in the blood.'

Chapter Fourteen

August 1981

Johnnie O'Brien lived on the eighth floor of Staincliffe Heights, a block of council flats in Leeds. There was no queue of people desperate to live in them. A decrepit motorbike was parked in the ground floor lobby, chained to the staircase balustrade. The floor was covered in filth and litter and the walls in illiterate graffiti. Jeannie pressed the lift button and was surprised when it arrived. The doors opened and unleashed a stink she didn't want to try and identify, so she opted for the equally malodorous stairs which had the marginal advantage of ventilation. She wore a blonde wig and sunglasses which disguised her face – but her skimpily clothed body left little to the imagination. It earned her the obscene admiration of two passing adolescent boys and a muttered curse from a whiskery old woman who was hanging her washing over a communal balcony. 'Fuckin' whore.'

It was the impression Jeannie wanted to give, although she wasn't a whore by any stretch of the imagination. She carried a large shoulder bag that contained a complete change of clothing, a pair of marigold washing-up gloves and a plastic carrier bag. The door to number 32 was newly painted, bright red, and was graffiti free which might well have spoken of the respect, or fear, that the resident commanded. Jeannie gave a polite knock which got her no response. She gritted her teeth and hoped the courage she'd summoned to get her this far hadn't been wasted. If so she'd have to go through it all again, but she was sure he was in. He never emerged before midday, she knew that much, having watched his movements for several days. Her second knock produced a shout of, 'Who the fuck is it?'

She didn't enlighten him. Shouting through doors was no way to conduct business such as this. She just knocked again. Eventually his blurred outline appeared at the far side of the frosted glass door. He was grumbling and he seemed quite big. She drew in a deep breath and braced herself. He opened the door six inches and peered round. She was wearing no bra and her shoulder bag tugged at one side of her shirt revealing an indecent amount of her right breast. A bolt was drawn, a key turned in the lock and the door was opened to reveal Johnnie O'Brien in his jeans and nothing else. He was more flab than muscle. The flesh that she could see was well decorated with cheap tattoos, including the inevitable spider's web on his neck.

'Mr O'Brien?' she asked, brightly.

'Who wants ter know?' He was unshaven and his bleary eyes were transfixed by her half exposed breasts.

'My name's Dawn, I'm trying to track down my brother Michael. He lived at Paddock House at the same time as you. Would you mind if I came in?'

Her skirt was as revealing as her shirt. She had nice legs and he could see just about every inch of them. O'Brien stood back and allowed her inside without saying a word. She went into the living room, making conversation as she went.

'They're a lot bigger than you think, these flats, aren't they?'

'If you say so, love.'

To him she looked like a prostitute and he figured she must have an ulterior motive. If she was trying to sell herself he wasn't going to stop her. Maybe this was a free introductory offer.

'What is it you want?'

'Oh, like I said, I'm trying to track down my brother. I thought you might be able to help.'

'Your brother? Look I don't know nowt about no brother.' He sat down, heavily, in a chair. 'To be honest I've just got up. I had a late night last night and I'm not even sure I know what day it is, never mind yer brother.'

'Tell you what,' suggested Jeannie. 'Is that your kitchen? Why don't I make you a cup of coffee? Shall I take this dirty cup through?'

With her back to him she bent forward and picked up a cup from the coffee table. It was a deliberate act. The back of her skirt hitched up, revealing her knickers. Red, frilly, brief, and inviting their removal. Whatever she was up to, it was working. Johnnie O'Brien knew that much. She was clattering around in the kitchen now, opening cupboards and drawers.

'What did you say your name was?' he called out.

'Dawn – Dawn Jones. My brother's name was

Michael Jones.'

He scratched his tattooed belly and gave the name some thought. 'Nah, can't say I remember him.'

'Maybe after you've woken up a bit, eh? Could you show me where you keep your coffee?'

'It's in the cupboard next to the sink.'

'I'd much rather you showed me.'

Her voice was dripping with sexual invitation – a "come on" if ever he'd heard one. Johnnie got up from his chair and went into the kitchen. She was wearing the marigolds and had taken off her wig and sunglasses, but he scarcely had time to be surprised at the change in her appearance. He didn't see the large kitchen knife in her hand as she thrust it upwards, under his ribcage, through his liver and into his heart. She pulled it out and stood back, not quick enough to avoid the spray of blood. Johnnie remained in a standing position for several seconds, staring at her in shocked disbelief.

'I actually told you a bit of a fib,' she said, apologetically. 'My name's really Jeannie Fleming – my brother was Derek Fleming. You must remember Derek. He's the one who killed himself because of you.'

She hoped he was taking it all in because that was part of her plan. She not only wanted him to die, but she wanted him to know why she'd killed him.

'You do understand *why* I've killed you, don't you, Johnnie?'

She asked him in the manner of a strict mum who was making sure her child knew why he was being punished. To her satisfaction he nodded, then he dropped to his knees with blood trickling from his mouth as well as pouring down his chest. He rocked backwards, then on to his side. Then he died.

Jeannie waited for a while until she was completely satisfied her job was done and there was no breath coming from his body. Then she stripped off her blood-spattered clothes and stuffed them, along with the bloodied knife and the marigolds, into the plastic carrier bag – she had plans for the knife. Completely naked apart from her shoulder bag, she went to step over him and paused, with her legs astride his body as she noticed her reflection looking back at her from a long mirror hanging on the living room wall. Jeannie liked what she saw. Never had she looked so good. She couldn't resist the temptation to strike an erotic, domineering pose over the bloodied body of her dead victim.

'Pity you're dead, Johnnie, boy. You're missing a treat here.'

She went into his bathroom where she washed herself thoroughly before checking, using the mirror where necessary, for any specks of blood she might have missed.

Jeannie guessed she'd left traces of herself somewhere in the flat but she'd have to be a suspect for them to tie such evidence to her – and why would anyone connect her to him? She had got his new home address by ringing up Paddock House, saying she was from the DHSS investigating a fraudulent claim, and asking if he still lived there. The woman she spoke to remem-

158

bered John O'Brien and had been keen to disclaim any responsibility for him. She told Jeannie that O'Brien had left there several years ago and gave her the address he'd moved on to. It had been that simple. Fortunately he still lived there.

Satisfied with her work, she dressed, leisurely, in jeans, blouse, denim jacket and ankle length boots; completing the ensemble with her blonde wig and sunglasses. Then she put the plastic carrier of bloodstained clothes and knife into her shoulder bag, left the flat, locked the door behind her, went down the stairs and walked to her car that was parked several streets away. Only then did she allow herself a faint smile. Her wound was partially healed, but there was more work to do.

It wasn't until the stink of human putrefaction coming from Johnnie's flat became noticeable above the general stench of the area that his body was discovered two months later. The police found not a single clue as to who had killed him, or why. Nor were they all that bothered.

Chapter Fifteen

Smithy had found another bricklaying gang to work with Sam, whom he knew might be leaving him any time. But Sam promised to continue working for the full fortnight duration of Owen's holiday. This was partly because he felt an obligation to help Smithy out and partly because he figured something of interest might turn up. He had also thought of an additional idea that might produce information. Eileen Crusher was holding something back, something about her past life. It could have a bearing on the case. They had been working there for ten' days and Owen had just struggled up a ladder carrying a hod full of bricks when Sam put his proposition to him.

'Owen, you're a man of some considerable charm when it comes to the opposite sex.'

The Welshman examined the callouses on his hands. 'What is it you want to know?' he said. 'If it's to do with Sally you should snap her up before someone else does.'

'No, it's nothing to do with Sal. I was just wondering how to get some information out of Eileen Crusher. It's the sort of information you'd only get during a fairly intimate conversation.'

'You mean pillow talk?'

'Something like that. It strikes me she's ready to unburden herself on the first decent man who comes her way. I'd take the job on myself but if it got back to Sally that'd be me and her finished.'

'Which would be a shame. Are you engaged to Sally at the moment?'

'I'm not quite sure – I might have said something in the heat of the moment.'

'Throes of passion eh,' said Owen, knowingly. 'Bad time to start making promises. Does she wear your ring?'

'She's got one from the last time we were engaged but she hasn't put it back on. I don't like asking what she did with it.'

'Sold it if she's got any sense,' commented Owen, who was glad of a breather from carrying bricks. He took out a Mars Bar and sat on a pile of lintels. 'What's this Mrs Crusher like?'

'She's what I'd call a fading beauty,' said Sam, building Eileen up somewhat. 'Very pleasant, very sad ... in need of a shoulder to cry on.' He didn't look at Owen as he was talking, he just carried on laying bricks. The Welshman was hooked, Sam could tell without looking at him.

'Well, I do have a certain experience with women in need.'

'You have indeed. And I don't wish to be crude, but she's gone a long time without the other,' added Sam.

'Ah, the ingredient that brings a flush to the jaded woman's face,' said Owen. 'Especially when put there by a man with talent in that field. A sexually satisfied woman is a rejuvenated woman, look you. And I've rejuvenated a few women in my time.'

'I can't argue with that. Would you like to meet her?'

'A casual introduction would do no harm. I can't promise anything but I seem to have been sowing my wild oats in the same field for longer than I usually care to.'

'There's no need for Postwoman Pat to find out.'

'Does Mrs Crusher have a house of her own?'

'She has a very nice house, but if I don't solve this case she'll have it repossessed.'

'In that case it's a matter of common decency that I help you. Does this mean I can resign as a labourer? I'm getting callouses on my hands. Women don't like men with calloused hands.'

'I think we should stick it out 'til the end of the week.'

'After that you want me to stick it in.'

'You're being crude, Owen.'

'I'm just reminding you of what you're asking me to do. Will I still be on your payroll?'

'I suppose so,' said Sam, reluctantly. He shaded his eyes from the glare of the low sun and looked across the site at a new Mercedes pulling up outside the main club building. 'Do you think that might be Morrell?'

'No idea, boyo – never met him.' A second man got out of the driver's side. 'I'll tell you what, though,' Owen added. 'I think I know that fellow with him from my time on the Leeds force. Haven't seen him for oh, twelve years, but if it's him he's a thoroughly bad lot.'

'Who is he?' asked Sam.

Anthony Arthur Ferris. Vicious bastard. Was sent down for murder the last time I heard of him. He'll be out on life licence I expect. Why they should let an animal like that loose on the streets beats me.'

'Smithy said Morrell had a mate called Tony,' remembered Sam. 'Who did he murder?'

'Someone who owed money, as far as I can remember. He was an enforcer was Tony.'

'Maybe he's taken up where he left off,' said Sam. 'Bit of a gamble for a man on life licence. Slightest hint of naughtiness and they can recall him.'

'I don't think he was ever famous for his brains, boyo.'

'Any idea what prisons he was in?'

'I imagine he'll have started out in Wakefield. After that, it depends on how he behaved.'

'Who at the nick's likely to find out for us?'

'I think DS Seager's our best bet. She thought the sun shone from your arse, boyo. Other than that she's a very sane individual.'

'Janet Seager,' mused Sam. 'Yeah, she'll do. Do you think you could give her a bell and ask if she can feed Ferris's name through the computer? Find out where he did his time.'

Half an hour later DS Seager rang back with the information Owen had requested and told him she was doing it for him, not for Sam.

'What makes you think it's Sam who wants this information?' Owen asked her.

'Because I know you're helping him on a case, and before you ask how I know, just remember I'm a detective.'

'And a very good one if I might say so, Sarge.'

'Don't flannel me, Owen. And tell Sam to watch himself if he's dealing with Ferris. He's an ugly customer by all accounts.'

163

Ferris had served his time in several prisons, but latterly in Wealstun, a category C prison north of Leeds. He'd apparently gone inside as a drug addict and come out supposedly clean – an interesting piece of information that Sam thought he might use to his advantage.

During his time in the police Sam had been to Wealstun and knew the place quite well. Fortunately, he had never visited there during Ferris's time inside. Sam strolled across the site and was admiring Morrell's car when the two men came out of the club. Sam gave Ferris a smile of recognition. 'I thought it was you, getting out of that car. Tony, isn't it?'

Ferris scowled at him. 'Do I know you?' He was a tall, heavy, mean-looking, bull-necked man with a shaved head and bad teeth.

'Well,' grinned Sam, 'the last time we met you told me to fuck off. Last year in Wealstun. I tried to sell you some smack. Sid Charlesworth. I don't suppose you remember me.'

Ferris took Sam's proffered hand and shook it. 'Yer right, I don't remember you. Wealstun eh? Fuckin' holiday camp that place.'

'Maybe for you. I thought it was a shithole.'

Ferris roared with laughter. 'They're all shitholes, lad. How long were yer in for?'

'I was doin' the last year of a five. Got parole after three. They moved me around a bit. Armley to start off with, then Durham, then Blundeston then Wealstun.' He named three prisons he knew Ferris hadn't been to. 'I had a beard all the time I was inside.'

'I think I do remember yer,' said Ferris, trying

to picture Sam with a beard. 'Smack eh? Is that what yer were in for?'

Sam shrugged. 'Partly. I was a jack of all trades. Bit of this, bit of that.' He looked at Morrell and added, quickly, 'Straight now, though. Straight as an arrow.'

'You're a good brickie by all accounts,' said Milo Morrell. His face somehow matched his name. He had the heavy features of an Eastern European shot-putter with the ears and broken nose of a Yorkshire rugby league player. He was a big man, running to fat, with a full head of dark hair and a mouthful of expensive dentistry which he showed off to Sam in a false smile. 'How come you got mixed up in all that drugs crap?'

'Well,' said Sam. 'I had a wife who wanted more than I could give her on a brickie's wage. So I tried to make some easy money on the side. She's gone now, good riddance. Got myself a nice girlfriend.'

'Did you know Ron Crusher,' enquired Morrell. 'The bloke Smithy took over from?'

'Vaguely,' said Sam, suspecting this might be a useful answer.

Morrell nodded, thoughtfully. He took a small cigar from his pocket and lit it without taking his eyes off Sam. 'Were you by any chance doing business with him?' he asked, casually. 'The same sort of business that got you locked up?'

Sam once again gave what he thought was a useful answer. 'He'd mentioned something,' he said, without explaining himself further. Morrell was asking him if he was somehow dealing in drugs with Ron Crusher – he really hadn't seen this one coming. Could drugs be the reason Ron

165

Crusher had been killed?

'He mentioned something, did he?' said Morrell. 'I wonder what it was he mentioned?' He and Ferris exchanged a quick glance, then Morrell smiled at Sam. 'You interest me, Sid. Do you know my club in Unsworth – The Queen of Clubs?'

'Never been there. I know it, though.'

'Maybe you'd like to call in one night as my guest. Bring your nice girlfriend with you.'

'I'd like that,' Sam said. He didn't detect the smirk on Ferris's face.

Morrell's smiled broadened. 'That's settled then. Tomorrow night about eight o'clock. Introduce yourself to the man on the door. He'll show you up to my office.'

After Morrell and Ferris had left, Smithy came out of the club building and shouted at him. 'I'm not paying you to stand around chatting to all and bloody sundry. Morrell's not paying your bloody wages, I am!'

He walked right up to Sam and added, quietly. 'Phil's sweeping up just behind me.'

Sam glanced over Smithy's shoulder at the labourer whose brush was moving slowly and deliberately. It could well be, Sam thought, that his ears were the most industrious thing about him. He certainly wasn't worth his wages as a labourer.

'Hey, who d'you think you're talkin' to? I'm not one of your bloody lackeys,' retorted Sam, loud enough to set Phil's ears twitching. He stormed off to where Owen was standing, open-mouthed. The shouting had carried right across the site.

Smithy stormed back into the club building, passing Phil on the way. 'And you can get your bloody finger out as well,' he snapped. 'You don't get paid for pushing muck round in a circle.'

'It's nowt to do wi' you,' muttered Phil. 'Morrell pays me, not you.'

'Well, next time I see him I'll tell him he can pay you to work somewhere else and not get under my bloody feet!'

Phil, suitably chastened, picked up a shovel and swept the rubbish into it.

'What was all that about, boyo?' enquired Owen, as Sam got back to him.

'Just a bit of play acting to keep Morrell's man fooled.'

'You mean Phil? You think he's definitely Morrell's eyes and ears?'

'Well, there's certainly no other reason for Morrell paying his wages,' Sam said. 'He's about as much use as a one-legged man at an arse-kicking contest.'

'I saw you speaking to Ferris and Morrell. Did you glean anything from them?'

'I think Ron Crusher could have been dealing drugs,' Sam said.

'Drugs, is it?'

Sam nodded. 'I told them I'd done time for dealing. Morrell asked me if I was doing business with Ron at the time of his death – I said I might have been. He's invited me to his club tomorrow night. I must say, it's all looking very promising.'

'It's all looking very dangerous,' said Owen. 'Maybe I should come along to keep an eye on you.'

'No need,' said Sam, cheerfully. 'I'll be taking Sally.'

Chapter Sixteen

December 1983

Jeannie ran Forbuoys down with her car but she didn't quite kill him.

The fact that Derek had now been dead three years didn't diminish his sister's need for absolution and retribution. If anything, every passing day with nothing done, added to her guilt. She knew Forbuoys' every movement but had taken care never to talk to anyone who might be later questioned about his death. With him living in Paddock House it would be difficult simply to walk in, kill him, and walk out without being seen. However she did it she must get away with it or true justice wouldn't be served. On top of which she didn't fancy going to jail.

A year after Johnnie's death she had sent Forbuoys a parcel containing a newspaper clipping about Johnnie O'Brien's murder, and the still bloodied kitchen knife and a letter.

Dear Nonce,

I expect you remember Johnnie O'Brien at Paddock House. This is the knife we killed him with for what he did to us. Show it to the coppers if you dare. You were worse then him. Fucking us young lads who needed looking after not abusing. You'll pay for what you did, just like O'Brien did. It might take us weeks, it might take years but we'll get you. Wherever you go we'll track you down.

She rightly believed that Forbuoys wouldn't dare tell the police – it would open too dangerous a can of worms. They would assume O'Brien had been killed by one or more former residents of Paddock House and they would go round asking questions. And too many of the same type of answer could be very bad for Forbuoys. He burned the letter and threw the knife away before leaving Paddock House in a state of terror. He took a job in another children's home in Nottingham, but Jeannie had made it her business to know the right people. She had a boyfriend who worked for the DHSS and another in the police. It took her just a week to track Forbuoys down and send him another letter.

Dear Nonce,
You can't hide from ghosts, we know your every move. You are a dead man.

She left it another two years before she made her move. Two years of agony for Forbuoys. He lost weight, lost his nerve, lost his job and lived on a diet of tranquillisers, alcohol, junk food and nightmares. He had thrown the knife away the day he'd received it but it stayed to haunt him, like a bloodied spectre. Sometimes during his sleep he could actually feel it plunging into his heart and he would wake up screaming.

One night he was shuffling out of his local pub, at his usual time, ten past eleven, when Jeannie ran him down. She'd been waiting a short distance away, with the lights switched off and the engine running. The second he stepped, unsteadily, into the road she put her foot hard down and drove straight at him. The force of the impact threw him high over the roof. Through the mirror she watched him land on the road behind her then she drove back to her home in Leeds without bothering to stop and see if he was alive or dead. A month later she read a sad article in the *Daily Mirror* about a former Nottingham care worker who had been the victim of a hit and run driver and had been left paralysed from the neck down. Jeannie sent a get well card to him at the hospital:

Dear Nonce,

Told you we'd get you.

Her job was done but the pain was still there; the pain she'd suffered at the hands of Frampton. She had avenged Derek, but it hadn't been enough. The need for revenge was still burning and there was no one left. Still, she'd done the job for Derek, and now it was time to join him. Time for Jeannie Fleming to join her brother in the land of oblivion.

Chapter Seventeen

In 1985 Milo Morrell had bought the derelict former toffee factory just outside Unsworth and turned it into the The Queen Of Clubs – a night-club-cum-cabaret bar. His original idea had been to use it as a means of laundering the money he made from drugs and, more recently, human trafficking from Romania, where he had several contacts. In recent years the competition in both these fields had begun to cause him trouble he could do without, and he'd been pleasantly surprised at the fact that his club was making money on its own merits.

And now it was on the cards that the gambling laws, tightened in the late 1960s in the erroneous belief that it might combat crime, were due to be modernised. Some groups, such as the Salvation Army, were worried that this might turn Blackpool into some sort of British Las Vegas, and that addiction to gambling might increase. But it was all music to the ears of Milo Morrell. With the combination of gambling, booze and entertainment he figured he could probably make enough money to go legit – hence his new club in Huddersfield. But first he had to do a bit of tidying up. He needed to know how much Sid Charlesworth knew. And if Sid knew too much, Sid would have to go.

Sam and Sally walked into the picture on the CCTV monitor in Morrell's office, causing him to say, 'Aw shit!' to himself. He'd forgotten he'd asked Sid to bring his girlfriend along; this could complicate things if he decided to pop the man tonight. If it needed doing it should be done straight away. Unfinished business was bad business. He could never settle until a job like this was done. Tony was on hand. Maybe he'd have to pay him double. He flicked a switch on a speaker-phone and his voice was picked up in the earpiece of one of the doormen.

'Be polite to these two and send them up to my office.'

The doorman nodded, then smiled. 'Mr Morrell's expecting you. Through that door, straight up the stairs, it's the door in front of you.'

'Service with a smile,' commented Sally, then to Sam she added, 'I'm as suspicious as hell.'

'That's why we're here,' Sam pointed out as they climbed up the luxuriously carpeted flight of stairs.

'Just don't do or say anything that he might not want to hear,' she warned. 'I'm getting a bad feeling about this.'

'I'm not stupid, Sal.'

'And remember I'm with you. You're not just risking your own neck.'

He put an arm around her shoulder and gave her a reassuring squeeze. 'I'll look after you, Sal, don't worry.' There were framed photographs of famous boxers on the wall and the club music played through muted speakers. 'Like I told you,' he said, 'this is strictly pleasure. If Morrell had anything else in mind he wouldn't have asked me to bring you along. He's just checking me out to

172

see if I'll work for him.'

'Doing what?'

'Dealing, I imagine.'

'What, cards?' she asked, naively.

'Er, no. It's not a casino, Sal.'

'Oh – Sam! You never told m–'

They were at the top of the stairs and the door in front of them opened. Morrell stood there with a welcoming smile on his face, the second false smile they'd seen in the space of two minutes. Sally took an instant dislike to him. It seemed he was trying to conceal an inner brutality behind an all too thin, artificial, veneer. And it didn't work

His hair was unnaturally black, his skin unnaturally brown and his teeth looked as though they might glow in the dark. Her suspicion mounted. Sometimes Sam got it wrong, which was why he spent a lot of his life extricating himself from trouble. She'd be very surprised if this evening was destined to be strictly pleasure.

'Welcome, Sid,' said Morrell, 'and this charming lady is?'

'Sally,' said Sally, holding out her hand for him to shake. He took it and kissed her fingertips and she knew things weren't right. It crossed her mind to come over all dizzy and ill and ask Sam to take her home, but somehow she knew that wouldn't work. There was nothing behind Morrell's smile. No humour, no friendship. As opaque as a lavatory window.

'Sally,' he said, ushering her through the door with a hand cupped under her elbow. 'You look like a lady who's used to fine champagne.'

'I'm a bricklayer's girlfriend,' Sally pointed out.

173

'They don't go much on champagne, don't brick-layers.'

Morrell roared with laughter. A large, hard-looking man with close cropped hair and an ugly scar above his left eye was lounging on a red leather chesterfield. He had been picking at his teeth with what looked like a silver toothpick which he now left protruding from his mouth as though it were some sort of fashion accessory. He didn't get up – another sign that things weren't all they seemed. So, thought Sally, the boss was overly polite, his gorilla wasn't. Bad that.

'This is Tony,' said Morrell. 'Of course Sid's already met him.'

Sally accorded Tony just a nod. She didn't want this brute kissing her hand, he might bite it off. The office was more like the executive suite in five-star hotel, except that it was furnished in sumptuous poor taste, with a well-stocked bar on one wall beneath an ornately framed poster of Mohammed Ali standing over a defeated Sonny Liston. On another wall were framed posters of people who, presumably, were Morrell's heroes: JF Kennedy, Errol Flynn, Elvis, Frank Sinatra and Marlon Brando in his 'Godfather' guise. A porno-graphic nude mural took up most of the space on a third wall, on which was also hung, incongru-ously, the only thing in the room she'd have taken home with her – a painting she suspected was a genuine Lowry, whose matchstick men would have been confused by the company they were keeping. Morrell picked up two glasses of cham-pagne from the bar and handed one each to Sam and Sally.

174

'I just thought I'd have quick word with you, Sid, before you and Sally went down to the club – which won't cost you a penny, by the way. Wine and dine as much as you want, it's all on the house.'

'That's very generous,' said Sam. "What is it you want to talk about?'

Morrell smiled and sat down on a barstool. He wore an expensive looking dinner suit, patent leather black shoes and red socks. He leaned on the bar and with both eyes trained on Sam, who, like Sally, remained standing, clutching his drink.

'I like a man who gets straight to the point, Sid. I can see you're one of those.'

'I just want to get stuck into the wining and dining,' grinned Sam.

Morrell roared once again with insincere laughter. Ferris's face didn't slip. Sally became very nervous. She sipped the Dom Perignon without tasting it.

'You're an unusual sort of bricklayer, Sid.'

'In what way?'

'Well, for a start you seem quite intelligent.'

'Looks can deceive,' put in Sally, with what she hoped was a mischievous grin on her face.

'How do I know he's not a police grass working under cover to fit me up with something or other?'

'Oh yeah, and you can tell that from my crap bricklaying, can you?' said Sam, confidently. 'I'm not like Ron bloody Crusher, y'know. I didn't learn my trade on a six week course in the prison workshops. I'm the genuine article, me.'

'Oh, you're a genuine bricklayer, I'll grant you that,' admitted Morrell. 'It's just that in my job I tend to worry that people aren't quite what they seem.' He smiled at Sally. 'Tell me, do you and Sid enjoy each other's confidence? I'm a great reader of body language and I can see you're comfortable with each other – been together long?'

'Quite a while now,' said Sally, then she looked at Sam, who added, 'Pretty much ever since I got out of Wealstun.'

He had filled Sally in with the fabricated story of their relationship but it wouldn't do for her to sound as though she'd learned it off by heart. 'And yes, we enjoy each other's confidence.' He didn't know why he was saying this, other than it might speed things along a bit.

'So, she knows about you and Ron Crusher?'

'I knew they'd talked about doing some business together,' chipped in Sally, who saw no harm in saying this.

'Did you know what sort of business?'

'Well, it wasn't building business.'

Morrell laughed out loud once again. 'Of course it wasn't. Building's for fools and losers.'

Sam stiffened at such an insult. His occupation was infinitely more worthy than Morrell's and he felt like telling him so. Sally took his hand and smiled at Morrell.

'Like you said, Sid and I enjoy each other's confidence. I can't say I liked him doing *that sort* of business with Ron – with Sid just having come out of prison.'

'Point taken,' said Morrell. Then to Sam he asked, directly. 'Do you know who Ron's supplier was?'

Sally knew this was a step too far and was willing

176

him to say no, but Sam felt like taking a gamble. He hesitated at first, knowing that Sally was part of this gamble and maybe it wasn't fair to involve her. In the end he couldn't help himself.

'Mr Morrell,' he said. 'I think everyone in this room knows who Ron's supplier was.'

Sally saw Ferris look up. He was watching Morrell's face, as if waiting for an instruction. Sam felt the sudden tension he'd created. Maybe he'd said the wrong thing – but he couldn't take it back now. Morrell poured himself a whisky and offered a glass to Sam, who needed one. So did Sally, but it was apparently unladylike to drink whisky. Morrell topped her glass up with champagne. Ferris reached into his pocket, took out a tiny, plastic bag and poured the contents on to the glass top of a coffee table. Sam recognised it as cocaine, Sally suspected the same. Ferris took a credit card from his wallet and used it to arrange the powder into a neat line. Morrell followed their eyes and watched his employee snorting a line of blow.

'Not when you've got work to do, Tony.'

'I were gerrin' bored,' said Ferris, 'with all this talk. Yer'll be tellin' 'em what nice fuckin' teeth they've got next.'

Morrell gave him a fixed smile which he then turned on Sam and Sally. 'Never mind him,' he smiled. 'I've been trying to persuade him to get his teeth fixed.'

Sally was wondering what work Morrell had in mind for his thug. Morrell returned his attention to Ron Crusher. 'Ron had a big mouth, by the sound of it,' he commented. 'I do one deal with him and he blabs.'

177

'I'm sure I was the only one he told,' Sam assured him. 'And I didn't tell anyone.'

'Are you sure?'

'Absolutely. If I'd told anyone it would have got back to the coppers eventually and they'd have lifted you.'

Morrell gave an appreciative nod. 'That's a very good point,' he said. 'And I like people who make good points. Talking of good points, do you know what happened to the 20 kilos of pure quality blow he bought off me?'

Sam, who had spent some time working with the drugs squad, suppressed his surprise at such a large quantity. By the time it reached the streets a single kilo of cocaine, sold in twists, could fetch upwards of £50,000. Even if Ron had only intended trading the powder on to street dealers he could have trebled his investment in a few days. Sam shook his head. 'If I knew, I wouldn't be laying bricks for a living.' He threw back his whisky and said, casually, 'Actually, I thought you had it.'

'You mean you think I screwed him out of his hundred and fifty grand then tossed him off a high building?'

Sam shrugged. 'Whatever happened, it was none of my business.'

'I don't do business like that, do I Tony?'

Ferris gave an almost imperceptible shake of his head. Sam was becoming fascinated by this whole conversation. Sally just wanted to get out of there.

'If I did business like that I wouldn't stay in business long,' said Morrell. 'Have you ever run your own business, Sid?'

Sam shook his head. 'No head for business, me.'

'What you need in business is honour,' Morrell told him. 'Even if the business isn't strictly kosher you must have honour. If you haven't got honour no one will do business with you. And you can't do business with yourself. Am I making sense, Tony?'

This time Ferris gave a slight nod and stuck a cigarette into the opposite side of his mouth from the toothpick.

'It seems to me,' said Morrell, 'that there's 20 kilos of coke lying around somewhere, with a street value of a million quid.'

'Well, I don't know where it is,' Sam assured him.

'I'm sure you don't,' said Morrell. 'Laying bricks is no job for a man with that much cash in his back pocket. Lying on a beach in the South Pacific with a pina colada in one hand and a dusky maiden in the other, that's what the man with a million will be doing, not laying bricks in Huddersfield.'

'You've got that right,' agreed Sam, who couldn't, for the life of him, see where all this was leading. Despite Morrell's admission of drug dealing Sam still didn't know if he had killed Ron. Now was as good a time as any to find out. Maybe if he asked politely enough Morrell might tell him. With a question like this it all depended how he phrased it.

'*Did* Ron top himself?'

'How would I know?'

Sam shrugged, as though it were unimportant. Morrell said, 'You think I killed him?'

'Maybe he deserved it,' Sam said.

'Maybe he did.' Morrell went around the back

179

of the bar and came back wearing a pair of white gloves and carrying a large handgun.

'What's that?' Sam asked, trying to hide his alarm. Sally was on the verge of fainting.

'It's a Smith and Wesson 500,' smiled Morrell. 'The most powerful production revolver in the world today.'

'You sound like Dirty Harry,' said Sam. The gun wasn't pointing at him and there was a fair chance Morrell just wanted to show his toy off.

'Don't I just?' said Morrell. 'Trouble is it only takes five rounds but it'd blow a hole in you and one in the wall behind you. And it makes one hell of a noise, doesn't it, Tony?'

The conversation seemed to have taken a turn in which Ferris was interested. The thug grinned and said, 'Bloody deafening. Not for indoor use – as a rule.'

'I know,' said Morrell. 'A two-two's the indoor shooter. A two-two and a cushion over the face. Tell you what, Tony, I'll ring down to the club and tell them to turn up the bass. Let the boom boom drown out the bang bang. He threw the fifteen inch long gun to Ferris, who was still sitting in the chair. 'The job needs to be done, Tony, and you can't use the basement, the furnace is on the blink and we've got cockroaches.' He turned to Sam. 'I've got the council on to it. I don't know what they use, but you can't fucking breathe down there.'

'Double bubble – two bodies?' asked Ferris.

Morrell gave a reluctant nod, then added a condition: 'Fee to include disposal.' He then explained to Sam, 'Disposal's a bit awkward at the

180

moment, Sid, what with the furnace being knackered. You'll probably end up down at the scrapper. Did you know I had a scrapyard? I have my fingers in many pies. What will you do, Tony, sit 'em in a motor and put it through the crusher?'

Tony pointed the gun at Sam and Sally and grumbled at Morrell. 'I don't know why yer mess about with all this fuckin' chat.'

Sam was trying to think of a way out. Sally was frozen with fear.

'To be honest,' said Morrell to Ferris, 'it wasn't until he fingered me as the supplier that I made up my mind.' Then to Sam he explained, 'It's nothing personal, Sid. You see, I'm going legit and I just can't afford to have a bricklayer knowing I dabbled in drugs. What Ron got was a bargain. Call it a closing down sale if you like. I sold him twenty kilos of pure coke at cost just to get rid of it. I also had to get rid of a couple of dealers who were getting a bit flaky. Now I'm having to get rid of you.'

'You don't have to do that, I could work for you,' said Sam, mesmerised by the gun.

'You know,' said Morrell, 'if you'd come on your own I might have considered it. I'm not blaming you, I blame myself – I shouldn't have asked you to bring her.' He inclined his head towards Sally, 'But taking her on as well is just too much of a risk – women and business don't mix. And there's no point you telling me to let her go. She obviously knows as much as you do. However, if it's any consolation I do believe you when you say you haven't told anyone else.'

Sally was mute with fright. Had she the power of speech she'd have told Sam what she thought of his stupid idea in coming here.

'What are you going to do with us?' enquired Sam. Sally couldn't believe how calm he sounded and how stupid a question he'd just asked. She found her voice from somewhere. 'They're going to bloody well kill us,' she said.

'It's only business,' Morrell assured them. 'Sometimes in business you have to make sacrifices. And I'm sacrificing you two.' His voice changed and he spat out an incredibly harsh command. 'Turn around and face the fucking wall!'

'Run, Sal!'

Sam put his head down and charged at Morrell, catching him full in the throat and sending him, choking, to the floor. Sally ran out of the door with Ferris hard on her heels. Sam had Morrell on the floor, punching him in the face, trying to knock him out so that he could go and help Sally. Then he heard her scream and he froze. With one hand holding Morrell by the scruff of his neck he turned around. Sally was backing, white-faced, into the room followed by Ferris who had the gun pushed right into her mouth. From behind them came the heavy thud of music from the club; music that would disguise even the loudest of bangs.

'Back off,' growled the thug, 'or I'll blow her fuckin' head off. NOW!'

Morrell's bloodied face twisted into a grin. He rolled out from under Sam and began to kick at him in anger. Sam put his hands up to protect himself but he daren't retaliate. Morrell kept kicking until Sam began to lose consciousness. The last thing he heard were Sally's screams.

182

They were still there when he came round. Screams coming from the depths of a very black and painful tunnel. It was an effort for Sam to open his eyes and when he did he was no wiser, and he couldn't understand why only one eye would open. He didn't know where he was, who he was, or to whom the screams belonged. The screams subsided to sobs, then the odd, rhythmic howl of pain, as through the victim had accepted her fate. Now he recognised the voice. He recognised Sally's voice before he knew who he himself was, or where he was. Then he knew who he was because he heard her shout out his name – an anguished shout for help, followed by a harsh curse and a slap. There was a pain in the back of Sam's head. He touched it, tenderly, and felt a lump and matted blood. Then he touched his right eye, the one he couldn't see through, and winced out loud with the pain. His nose felt as if it was broken, his ribs ached and his knuckles were skinned and painful. He remembered Morrell now, and patches of what had happened began to piece themselves together, all accompanied by those noises from beyond the wall. At first he had thought Sally was in the same room, so loud had been her screams, but he was here on his own.

It was a small, empty room, maybe ten feet square, with just one window which was guarded by bars. There was a smell of stale urine which told him he probably wasn't the first person to be locked up in here. He could do with a pee himself but he was bound hand and foot and he had never felt so helpless or defeated. Sobs and squeals and moans came through the wall. Sobs and squeals and moans and sniggers and raucous laughter; each sound like a knife twisting through his heart. What the hell was happening? It had to be Sal who was in there. It was up to him to stop it happening to her. How the hell was he going to manage that?

The awful sounds were coming from behind a freshly plastered wall and Sam's good eye followed the ornate, Victorian skirting that ran around the other three walls before it changed to a more modern, seven inch variety. There was an ornate, plaster cornice around the same three walls and none along the wall with the inferior skirting. This was a new wall, dividing a larger room in two, and he could tell by a couple of linear shrinkage cracks that it was probably a stud wall – plasterboard on timber frame. You can't build masonry walls on a foundation of joists and floorboards.

He tugged at bonds tying his hands behind his back. Just a gentle tug would send a racking pain through his body. So he began to curse in order to numb the pain. Anaesthetic obscenities he used to call them. The worse the pain the worse the obscenity. Then he realised it wasn't all bad. He'd been tied up in a hurry by a man whose mind was on other things, such as Sally. Whoever did the job should have crossed Sam's wrists to allow him minimum movement. He let out a series of agonised yells and looped his hands under his feet, then he rolled on his side to allow the pain to subside. Still muttering his anaesthetic curses he eased himself up and began to pick at the knots with his teeth. As he picked away, he could hear music thudding up through the floor and the sound of Sal's pain and humiliation and despair coming through the wall; and he wept cold tears of rage. The other voice was probably Ferris; Sam closed mind to what he was actually doing to her. Such thoughts wouldn't help him to think straight. Whatever it was it was, it was no doubt a prelude to putting a bullet though her head – then Sam's.

As he loosened his bonds he tried to maintain enough calm to consider his situation. He was imprisoned by three solid walls, a barred window, no doubt a solid, securely locked door – and a couple of layers of half inch plasterboard. Someone hadn't thought this prison out properly. The rope dropped away at last and it was the work of a few seconds to free his feet. He spat out a mouthful of blood and tried to think clearly. To think of a plan.

He tapped on the wall to confirm his suspicions. It sounded suitably hollow. The sickening sounds from the far side continued; and he knew it was all his fault. He'd brought Sally here and caused her to be subjected to this. He stood back from the wall and allowed his rage to mount and send adrenaline induced strength to his aching muscles. It wasn't difficult. Just a few feet away was a man with a gun who was raping Sally. A pathetic sob was followed by a rasping laugh that taunted him as much as it did its intended target – Sally. Sam primed himself with a piercing scream then he hammered at the plasterboard with the sole of his shoe. Half a dozen vicious kicks in quick succession. Ferris didn't even bother to turn around. He figured it was just the cry of the doomed man banging on the wall to be let out. The final kick provided a hole big enough for Sam to force himself through. Sally was on the floor, naked and deeply distressed. Her face was badly bruised, there was blood all around her mouth and streaks of it on her body. Ferris was straddling her. His trousers were off and he was visibly aroused.

When Sam was halfway through the wall the thug looked around; his eyes went from Sam to the gun, which he'd left on top of a chest of drawers, Sam's eyes followed and he knew he had to get to the weapon first.

'Hold on to him, Sal!'

Sally automatically responded by grabbing the thug's shirt. Ferris tried to tear himself away but she clung to him, tenaciously, obeying Sam's instructions. She wanted to obey Sam, not this man who had made her feel so weak and helpless and unimportant. Eventually he tore himself away from her but those few seconds had given Sam enough time to get into the room and dive for the gun. Ferris lunged at him, too late. Sam grabbed the weapon and flung himself out of the thug's reach, pointing the gun, aiming low. Although his blood was boiling, his instinct told him to disable rather than kill. He squeezed the trigger, hoping the safety wasn't on. It wasn't. In the confines of the room the report was ear-splitting. He blew away that part of Ferris's anatomy with which the thug was about to violate Sally. A mess of blood and body tissue sprayed around the room, some went on Sam and Sally. She was grabbing at her clothes and sobbing loudly. Sam knew no comfort

186

or apology for her. Ferris was rolling on the floor in howling convulsions of agony. Sally was now vomiting. Sam waited until she had recovered a bit then took her into his arms and hugged her but she was frozen with shock and didn't respond.

'Did he...?' Sam asked.

She frowned and shook her head, unable to look him in the eye, unable to speak about it. Such was the depth of her shock and humiliation.

'That's good, Sal.'

His words were of no comfort to her. She had resigned herself to being raped. She was about to allow Ferris his way without putting up a fight. In her mind she *had* been raped.

'Can you dress yourself or do you need help?'

'I can ... manage.' She retched again then turned her back to Ferris so she didn't have to look at him.

Sam tried to think. They weren't in the clear yet. Morrell would be expecting two shots. Then he'd expect Ferris to report that the job was done – apart from the disposal bit. Sam tried the door but it was locked. The key was probably in Ferris's pocket, which Sam didn't fancy searching because of all the blood and gore down there. He looked through the window, they were obviously on the top floor. Ferris began to lose consciousness and his howling subsided to a moan.

'Have you got a mobile?' Sam asked her. 'I think they took mine.'

She pointed to her bag.

'Sal, I'm really sorry about all this. I didn't think for one minute–'

'Please, just do what you have to do to get me out of here.' Tears were running freely down her cheeks, mingling with the blood as she struggled to dress herself. 'God, Sam, you look a mess.'

'It's probably worse than it looks.' Sam tried to sound positive.

He took the phone out of her bag and dialled Owen. 'Owen, it's Sam. We're in a fix. Sally's been attacked by Ferris. I've just shot him. We're in The Queen of Clubs, locked in a room on the top floor. If anyone comes knocking who's not the police, I'm going to start shooting.'

'Is Sally okay?'

'Yeah, she's fine.'

Sally looked daggers at him as she fastened her bra.

'Is Ferris dead?'

'Not yet.'

'How do you mean, not yet?'

'I shot low. He's not the man he was.'

'Sam,' said Owen. 'I'm ringing Bowman. Are there any other guns in the building?'

'Possibly,' said Sam. 'I shot Ferris with Morrell's gun. Morrell's downstairs, waiting for Ferris to report back that he's killed us. You need to hurry.'

'I'll tell them to bring an armed response unit. Stay safe.'

The phone went dead and Sam looked down at Ferris to see if he was in a similar state. He didn't look too good. Death didn't seem too far away. Sam wasn't one of life's natural born killers but the memory of what Ferris had done to Sally left him with no feelings of guilt for what he'd done to her attacker. He felt no fear, no pity, shock, guilt, or deranged euphoria – none of the feelings that reluctant killers usually felt. At that moment all he felt for Ferris was loathing. It occurred to him that he should have asked Owen to send an ambulance. Blood was pouring out of the whimpering thug's groin, soaking into the bare floorboards. An ambulance wouldn't go amiss for Sally either.

He dialled 999 and asked for two ambulances to be sent as a man had been shot and a woman assaulted. Yes, the police have been notified. I suppose you'd better hurry, the man appears to be dying.

Sally was almost dressed now. Sam told her to press her hands to her ears as he fired another shot into the ceiling.

'Morrell will be expecting to hear two shots,' he explained.

She nodded her head and wondered how he could think so clearly under such circumstances.

'Will the police be long?' she asked.

The wail of a police siren answered her question. 'There must have been a car in the area,' said Sam. 'I doubt if they'll come in before back-up arrives.'

A minute later there was a banging on the door, which was locked from the inside. 'Tony?' It was Morrell's voice, a bit more nasal then usual. 'The police are outside. What the fuck's going on?'

Sam placed a finger to his lips. Tony gave a loud moan. Morrell unlocked the door to the room where Sam had been held and poked his head through the hole in the wall. Some of his expensive teeth were missing and his face was almost as

189

bloodied and battered as Sam's.

'Come and join the party,' said Sam pointing the gun at him. 'We can all wait for the police together.'

Morrell took a look at Ferris, whose blood was spattered all over Sam, Sally and the four walls. Then he looked at the dreadfully battered face of the man who was pointing the gun at him, then at the shock on Sally's – and he realised Sam meant business. He crawled through the hole. 'What the hell have you done to Tony?'

'He was about to rape Sally.'

'The fucking animal! I didn't tell him to rape her.'

'Oh no,' said Sam. 'You just told him to murder us both.'

'That was just business,' muttered Morrell. 'He let his dick get in the way of my business. I knew he was a racist but I didn't have him down as a rapist – not when there's work to do. I hope the bastard dies. Do you hear that, you stupid bastard? I hope you die.' He gave Ferris a hard kick in the ribs. It was obvious that the thug could hear and feel him but Ferris couldn't give a damn. He had other things to worry about. Such as was he going to live and if so how would he manage without his meat and two veg?

Morrell looked across at Sam and Sally and smirked at the hatred pouring from their eyes. 'Don't look at me like that. What's done's done. I'll deny telling him to fucking kill you.'

'It's your word against the two of us,' Sam pointed out.

'Oh yeah, and did you actually hear me tell him

to kill you?' Morrell asked.

'I'm not interested in your actual words,' snarled Sam, who desperately wanted to wipe the smirk off Morrell's face. 'It's what I'll say in court that counts.'

'When my brief's finished with you it'll be you they send down for murder.'

'Oh, really?' said Sam. 'Is that what you think? Well, in that case I might not bother with the courts.' A deranged look came into his eyes, one of his tricks if Morrell did but know it. 'In that case I might as well put a bullet in your brain right now. I know, I'll tell the police you went for me. All the circumstantial evidence is on my side. I mean, look at the state of me. No one's going to go out of their way to try and convict me of anything.'

'You wouldn't dare,' said Morrell, but there was fear in his voice.

Sam gave a shrill, manic laugh that unsettled Morrell. 'Oh really? If you think I wouldn't dare I suggest you look at your mate on the floor.' Morrell looked down at Ferris then back at the gun being pointing at his head by this blood-spattered madman. 'Do you have any last prayers?' enquired Sam. 'Before I blow your brains out?'

'Don't!' screamed Sally, who wasn't sure if he was acting or not. You could never be sure with Sam.

'Why the hell not?' said Sam, coldly. 'I'll be doing the world a favour.' His face was set like stone, his eyes wild. He pressed the gun against Morrell's forehead. His thumb pulled down the hammer and the trigger cocked with an ominous click. Morrell's face drained of all colour. He held up his hands. 'Okay, okay – you've made your point. I'm scared. That thing could go off without you wanting it to.'

'But I *do* want it to,' said Sam. The image of Sally about to be raped was so clearly in his mind. 'You're going to die, Morrell.'

'Sam,' implored Sally. 'Please, I beg of you. This is murder.'

'Listen to her,' whined Morrell. He got down on his knees. 'Oh, dear God, please don't kill me.'

Sam stepped back, still aiming the gun at Morrell's head. 'You'll excuse me if I don't stand too close,' he explained, wiping blood off his mouth with his sleeve. 'I've got enough blood on me as it is.'

Morrell's eyes were squeezed shut as Sam squeezed the trigger. The bullet went harmlessly through the ceiling. Morrell wet his pants in terror. Sam seized his chance. In an unhinged voice he said, 'The next one's got your name on it, Morrell. Did you kill Ron Crusher?'

'W–what the hell's Crusher got to d–do with anything?'

'Never mind. Did you kill him?'

Morrell was shaking with fear. 'Oh God, p–please don't kill me you mad bastard. Just p–put the gun away and I'll tell you what I know.'

There were more sirens outside now. Shouts, banging car doors, feet running up the stairs.

'Did you kill Ron Crusher?' snarled Sam, stepping forward and bending Morrell's head back with the barrel of the gun. There was a loud knock on the door. A voice he recognised as Bowman's shouted:

192

'This is the police. Open the door. If you have a weapon in there throw it out and come out with your hands on your heads. You as well, Carew.'

Sam waved a relieved Morrell to the door at the point of the gun. 'I'm sending Morrell out first,' he shouted. 'He's responsible for all this. Take him, then I'll throw the gun out.'

'Is Sally okay, Sam?' It was Owen.

'Not really.'

'Sam?' said Morrell, getting to his feet, shakily. 'Hey ... I thought your name was Sid. Are you the fuckin' police?'

'Who else is in there?' Bowman called out.

'Tony Ferris,' replied Sam. 'He's been shot and Morrell's so scared he's pissed his pants. He ordered Ferris to kill us. He'll deny it, but that's what all this is all about. I'm sending him out.' Sam unlocked the door and urged Morrell, at the point of the gun, to walk out into the arms of the waiting police. Morrell immediately began protesting his innocence.

'Sally and I are coming out next,' said Sam. 'She'll tell you just how innocent he is. Treat her gently.'

He threw the gun out, took Sally's arm, and led her outside. 'It's all over now, love,' he assured her.

Sally staggered and fell to the floor in a dead faint.

Chapter Eighteen

She woke up from her sedated sleep to see him watching her, intently. She was in a one bed ward. It was early morning. Bandages encircled his head, there was a patch over his eye, his nose was covered in plaster and he wore a hospital gown. His clothes had been taken away by the police as they contained important bits of Ferris which might be needed in evidence; evidence of what, was never explained to Sam.

'I just thought I'd come to check on you, Sal,' he said. 'The boys called in to see me. Sue brought them. They asked after you. Sue sends her love. They all do, in fact. Sue had a bit of a dig at me for putting you in danger – well, a lot of a dig, actually. I couldn't argue with her. I'm waiting for a doctor to discharge me, then the police want me to go to the station to make a statement.'

She listened to all this with a puzzled frown on her face, as if she didn't know what he was talking about. Her hair had been pulled back off her pale, bruised face and tied with a black velvet scrunchy. A nurse arrived.

'Is she okay?' Sam enquired.

'She's still in shock,' the nurse reported. 'They sent me to look after her because I've had training in these matters.'

'How long before she's okay?'

'She's okay now, aren't you, love?' said the nurse. 'You'll talk to him when you're ready and not before.'

Sally nodded. Sam smiled at her. 'You did well,' he said. 'Because of you we got him.'

'I gather you got there just in time,' said the nurse. 'But what happened to her was still a form of rape, even though he didn't, you know...'

'I know,' Sam said. 'What she went through was horrific.' He knew something about rape victims himself. He knew that a rapist takes things away from a woman that are almost impossible to replace: self worth, dignity, pride... Ferris would have tried to make Sally feel like dirt, but if Sally could be made to feel that she had turned the tables on him and had placed herself in a position of power over him it could repair a lot of the damage. It could make her a survivor rather than a victim. And Sam didn't want his Sal to be anyone's victim. He held her hand.

'Sal, you held on to him long enough for me to get him. He didn't expect that.'

A light came into her eyes as she remembered. He detected a faint nod. 'We beat him, Sal. Me and you together, we beat the bastard. Because of you he won't be hurting any more women. You've hurt him far more than he hurt you.'

'Is he dead?' she whispered.

Sam was relieved to hear her speak. 'He was still alive the last I heard. Do you remember where I shot him?'

Another nod, then she grimaced and asked, 'Did I help do *that* to him?'

'Well, I couldn't have done it without you,

195

could I? – wouldn't have had time. That few seconds you held on to him was the difference between him winning or losing. You made him into a loser, Sal. You beat him in the end, and he's lost big time.'

He caught the nurse's eye. She gave him a look that said, *Carry on, you're doing okay. This is what she needs to hear.* 'He'll rue the day he ever messed with Sally Grover,' was all Sam could think to add.

Sally was crying now. He sat beside her on the bed and held her to him. She put her arms around him and sobbed into his shoulder. Sam cried a little as well. It had been a tough time for him too. The nurse watched with approval, knowing Sally was receiving far better medicine than she could ever give her. After a while her sobs subsided.

'Feeling better?' Sam asked.

'A little... Sam, are you in any trouble?'

'Well, I've some more cracked ribs so don't squeeze too tight, but apart from that I'm fine.'

'I meant in trouble with the police for what ... you know.'

'For shooting the scumbag? Well, I haven't been arrested or anything, but I'm not in the clear.'

'He was an animal.'

'He won't be doing it to anyone again.'

'No,' she said. 'I don't suppose he'll be able to do anything much.'

'He'll be able to sing soprano in the prison choir.'

'Oh ... oh I see.' She wasn't up to appreciating his humour yet. 'Sam, you look a real mess.'

'All superficial,' he assured her. 'They only kept me in because I was concussed. It's standard procedure.'

'Well, you'd know the standard hospital procedure better than most.'

Sam smiled at her sarcasm. She was coming round.

'Thanks for saving my life, Sam. I didn't want to die that way.'

'That's okay,' he said.

'I really thought you were going to kill Morrell,' she whispered. 'You had a look in your eye that I've never seen before.'

'It's just an act I put on to unnerve people. It was how I first got the name Mad Carew.'

'I thought it might be an act – I wasn't sure, though.'

'Maybe it wasn't all an act. I *was* very cross with him.' He was still holding her. 'But I'd no intention of killing him. I just wanted to wipe that smarmy smile off his face.'

'You did that all right. I've never seen anyone so terrified that they peed themselves.'

Sam grinned. 'Owen and the boys marched him straight through his club, complete with wet trousers. They'd no need to. They could have taken him out of a side door. But they wanted to humiliate him. Owen shouted to make way for Mr Morrell, he's had a bit of a fright, as you can tell by his trousers. It's something he'll never live down, Sal.'

'Shouldn't you be scared of what he'll do to you?'

'Not sure. Right at this moment I reckon the

police will be turning over his club and his house, looking for drugs and whatever else they can find. He'll be charged with attempted murder at least. I'll rest easy if he goes down for a few years.'

'I suppose I'll have to make a statement,' she said. 'Re-live the whole nightmare.'

Sam said the wrong thing. 'It's good that he didn't actually...'

'Rape me?' said Sal. 'No, he didn't *actually* rape me. He just beat me, he terrified me into complete submission, he forced me to strip, and all the time I knew he *was* going to rape me – as and when the mood took him – and then he was going to kill me.' She was in tears again now. 'Oh Sam, I was so scared I couldn't even fight him. I just let him do what he wanted to me. Am I a coward, Sam?'

He kissed her forehead. 'No, Sal, you're not a coward. I'll tell you what a coward is. Milo Morrell, he's a coward. He was down on his knees, peeing himself and begging for his life, which is something you didn't do – that makes you braver than him. His courage was tested and he failed the test. 'What you did was act normally. In a situation like that submission was your best option. Sal, if you'd tried to fight Ferris you'd be dead now.'

She gave a weak smile and took his hand. 'You're a smooth talker, Carew.'

'I speak only the truth, Miss Grover.'

'I suppose I know that. God I was mad at you – terrified, but as mad as hell at you.'

'That's good,' he said. 'If you have to take it out on someone, take it out on me. I'm as much to

198

blame as anyone.'

'I couldn't believe it when you came through that wall. One minute I'm dying in the most horrible way possible and the next minute you're bursting through the wall like the Incredible Hulk.'

'I try to please.'

She was crying again, still in his arms.

'She'll probably do that a lot,' said the nurse. 'It's good that you're with her, Mr Carew. You can stay as long as you want.'

'I think the police might need me shortly.'

'I'll tell them they can't have you.'

Sally looked at her from over Sam's shoulder. 'You have the man in here who did this to me.'

'So I believe.'

'He was going to kill us both but Sam got to him first. You should tell everyone that, especially the nurses who are looking after him. I think they should know.'

'Most people already know,' said the nurse. 'And I think you should know that the famous Mr Mad Carew is about to hit the newspapers again. We've been turning reporters away all morning. They're saying he's a very brave man.'

Sally tapped Sam's head with her finger. 'Where there's no sense there's no fear.'

The nurse laughed. 'You seem to lead a very public life for a private investigator, Mr Carew.'

'It's a special gift he has,' said Sally, who now had a very special hold on Sam.

And Sam knew it.

He had been sitting in the interview room for

199

almost half an hour before Inspector Bowman and Sergeant Bassey appeared. Sam switched on the tape recorder and spoke into it:

'Detective Inspector Bowman and Sergeant Bassey have entered the room. Sam Carew has been waiting here for half a bloody hour, very badly injured and wondering what took them so long. How come I always get you two when I'm being interviewed – a uniform and a suit. You haven't got some hidden agenda have you?'

'You do not have to say anything,' said Bassey, sitting down opposite Sam, 'but it may harm your defence if you do not mention, when questioned, anything you may later rely on in court. Anything you do say may be used in evidence.'

'You've shot and seriously injured a man,' said Bowman. 'I don't need to tell you that we need to take a formal statement.'

'I was just about to leave,' Sam said, still irritated at having been kept waiting when all he felt like doing was going home to bed, 'as is my right.'

'It would be wrong to exercise your rights right now,' said Bassey. 'With you just having shot a man's genitalia off.'

'He's not a man, he's a rapist,' Sam pointed out.

'Which is why you deliberately aimed the weapon at his genitalia,' said Bowman.

Sam glared at him with his only available eye. 'I aimed low so as to stop him rather than kill him,' he retorted. 'If it had been you he'd probably be dead by now – or you would.'

'So, you had your wits about you when you pulled the trigger – you had time to consider the options?'

'I had about a tenth of a tenth of a second to weigh up all the pros and cons,' said Sam, who knew just where this was leading. 'It was instinctive. If I hadn't got to the gun first, Sally and I would have been dead.'

'What were you doing there?' Bassey enquired.

'Sally and I had been invited there.'

Bowman leaned across the desk. 'According to Morrell he thought you were a bricklayer called Sid Charlesworth.'

'I was pursuing my lawful occupation as a private investigator.'

'Investigating what, exactly?' asked Bowman.

'The murder of Ron Crusher.'

'Would that be the same Ron Crusher that was seen by two policemen and about fifty witnesses jump off the Ridings Building last year,' said Bassey sarcastically.

'They saw him *fall*,' corrected Sam. 'No one saw what caused the fall. You lot did your usual half-arsed investigation and came up with a result that caused you the least bother – suicide.'

'It *was* suicide,' said Bowman, 'I looked into it myself.'

'Did he leave a note?' Sam asked. 'Did he show suicidal tendencies beforehand? Could you find any reason for him to top himself? Did you know he'd just bought twenty kilos of coke from Morrell just before he died?'

The two policemen went quiet. Bowman cleared his throat and said, 'We're here to take a statement about the events leading up to you shooting Anthony Ferris. Yours and other statements will be sent to the Crown Prosecution Service for them to

201

make a decision whether or not to prosecute you.'

'Will you be reopening the Ron Crusher case?' enquired Sam, provocatively.

'It would be in your best interest not to meddle in police business, Carew,' snapped Bowman. 'If you know anything which may be of interest you should inform us and not go blundering in on your own.'

'I should have thought a million quid's worth of coke floating around your patch might be of interest.'

'Just make the statement, Carew. After which we will decide whether or not to place you in custody.'

Owen took him home from Unsworth Police Station. 'How's Sally?' was his first concern, despite Sam's obvious condition.

Sam shook his head. 'When I left her she was okay, but she comes and goes. It was a right bloody ordeal I put her through – I'll never do it again.' He held his forefinger and thumb a fraction apart. 'She was that close to being murdered.'

'So were you, by all accounts.'

'That would have been my own stupid fault.'

'How did your interview go?'

'Quite well, considering it was Bowman and Shirley. They treated me like I'd just burned down the local orphanage, but they didn't hold me. I think Bowman likes me really.'

'If he finds out I've been helping you he'll have my guts for garters. You've been treading on his toes.'

'I didn't get anywhere near his toes. He wasn't

even investigating Morrell. He'll have to now, though.'

'And I suppose you told them that, did you, you tactless bastard?'

'I told them I was investigating Ron Crusher's death on behalf of his brother. They told me if I knew anything worth knowing I should pass it on to them – usual crap. I told them that Morrell had told me he'd sold Ron twenty kilos of coke for a hundred and fifty grand.'

'Why on Earth would Morrell tell you that?'

'I gave him the impression I knew all Ron's business, so he thought I already knew.'

'Not a very smart move,' Owen commented.

'It seemed a good idea at the time.'

'But it'll have been why he decided to have you and Sally killed,' concluded Owen, 'so it wasn't one of your better ideas.'

'No – Bowman didn't think so, either.'

'You're lucky they didn't charge you.'

'What with?'

'First Degree Stupidity.'

'It wasn't through lack of trying. Bassey asked why I'd gone tooled up, silly sod.'

'I do believe he's a big fan of *Miami Vice*,' Owen explained.

'I told him I'd left my own tools in the car and anyway what good's a brickie's trowel against a Smith and Wesson.'

'Depends,' said Owen.

'On what?'

'On whether you're shooting people or laying bricks. You can't lay bricks with a Smith and Wesson.'

'You're being humorous Owen. That's an unfortunate trait that you should guard against.'

'When in Rome,' said Owen. 'Ferris has woken up, did you know?'

'Is he singing soprano?'

'You could say that. Soft bugger thinks he's dying. He's singing like a bloody canary – grassing Morrell up good and proper, see. He's already told us about three contract killings he did for Morrell. Frankie Baker, Zoo Blue and Teargas.'

'Teargas,' recalled Sam, his mind going back to his CID days. 'I remember Mr Teargas – very unsavoury character in every way. Nearly had him for murder once – the witnesses were all scared off. Tugged him myself once for possession.'

'Where the devil did he get a damned stupid name like that?'

'He liked onions and beans, apparently,' Sam said.

'A bit smelly was he?'

'A bit? I reckon he made his own hole in the ozone layer. If we wanted to soften a villain up we'd stick him in a cell with Teargas. Worked a treat. It was bad enough having to share a police station with him.'

'Well, according to Ferris,' said Owen, 'Zoo Blue shared a furnace with him. Morrell seems to have upset Ferris, I don't know how.'

'I think I do,' said Sam. 'When a man's lying on the floor with his bollocks shot off the last thing he needs is a bollocking, which is what he got from Morrell. He booted him in the ribs and told him he hoped he died.'

'He's from London,' said Owen, as if it

explained Morrell's behaviour.

An odd thought struck Sam. 'You know, if Ferris had done as he was told and not wasted time by going for Sally we'd have both been dead and Morrell would have been in the clear.'

'So Sally did you both a favour by being attacked?'

Sam nodded. 'Weird, isn't it? I might mention that to Sal. I was only around to save her life because she saved mine by delaying Ferris. I'll take her away for a while when she's up to it, by way of thanks.'

'By way of apology, more like.'

Sam ignored him. 'Weekend in London,' he decided, 'something like that. Decent hotel with a trouser press and an en-suite bathroom. Take a ride on that big wheel thing, see a show, nice meal afterwards. She likes being spoiled, does Sal.'

'Very racy place, London,' commented Owen. 'My favourite show's *Les Miserables*.'

'I'd never have guessed.'

'Mrs Crusher and I got along very well on our first date.'

'First date? Owen you randy old dog! I only mentioned it to you yesterday.'

'I called in around teatime and introduced myself as your associate. She seems quite taken with me. We ended up going to the pictures to see *The Passion Of The Christ*.'

'Sounds like you had a laugh a minute,' said Sam. 'What did you do afterwards – go for a stroll round Unsworth cemetery to brighten the mood?'

'We're going line dancing at Unsworth Working Men's Club next week. I understand it's a very sociable evening.'

'Line dancing? You'll get thrown out of the Eisteddfod if they find out you've been line dancing.'

'I've already bought my Stetson.'

'If I'd known she was going to do this to you I'd never have let you anywhere near her. She sounds highly unsuitable if you ask me.'

'Well, I'm not asking you, and she's a very accommodating lady if you must know,' said Owen.

'Oh, Owen, you didn't. Not on your first date?'

'I never reveal the secrets of the boudoir,' Owen said, 'which is all part of my Celtic allure. I must say, I'm very taken with the lady.'

'Hey! I'm only paying a hundred a day for you to get information out of her. Anything else and you're on your own time.'

'Can you think of any reason why Tony Ferris should hold a grudge against Milo Morrell?' enquired Detective Inspector Bowman.

'A grudge?' said Sally.

'I'm just curious, that's all. He's dropped Morrell right in it. Told us all we need to know and a lot more besides. I think he wanted to get it all off his chest before he died.'

'So, he's dead then.'

For a moment she felt a guilty relief that Ferris was dead. It meant there was no one left alive who had ever violated her. Her relief was short-lived.

'No, he's going to live, as it happens. It's just that nobody chose to tell him the good news – what with him being so helpful. He was really annoyed when they finally told him, but it was too late then.'

The rest of Sally's story had pretty much tallied with both Sam's and Ferris's. With such evidence against him the thug would be recalled to prison after he got out of hospital. Ferris would be charged with attempted rape, attempted murder and various other crimes. He would be an old man, if and when he got out.

Sally sipped her tea and tried to think. It would be better if she could blot out the whole nightmare. Ferris had admitted to the assault, which would save her an ordeal in court.

'Morrell was angry with him,' she remembered. 'I think he was angry because he should have killed us both and not wasted time on me. He told Ferris he hoped he died. I suppose that got his back up.'

The woman detective, accompanying Bowman, said, 'If it's any consolation, Sally, the ordeal he put you though saved both your lives, insofar as it bought you time.'

'Sam saved our lives,' Sally told her, emphatically. 'What happened to me just bought him some time.'

'And how do you feel about that?' enquired Bowman, with genuine curiosity.

'You mean do I think it was worth the sacrifice? – I suppose I do. The main thing that makes it easier is the poetic justice that Sam handed out to the man.'

'You mean Carew shot him, down there, in the ... there on purpose?' The two detectives glanced at each other.

Sally spotted her mistake immediately. 'I think he shot low to avoid killing the man. Sam only had a split second to make up his mind.' She detected a brief look of disappointment on both their faces, so she asked, 'Will he be getting a bravery award?'

'I think he should get a stupidity award for putting both your lives in danger.'

'I'm forced to agree with you, Inspector,' said Sally.

Sam sat back in Sally's chair and lit a cigarette. He'd been cutting down until recently, but now he was back to twenty a day. On her desk was a brochure from her gym and he was wondering whether or not to join. At his age it would do no harm. It had a swimming pool, sauna, steam room and squash courts – all for forty five pounds a month. The swimming pool alone might be worth that – if they taught him how to swim. First he'd have to give up smoking, which he would, as soon as he'd finished this packet. It was Friday and he'd generously given Sally a week off to convalesce, Owen was due back at work on Monday and Smithy was in a state of confusion with his employer being locked up and the police swarming all over the site. There was a knock on the door and Bernard walked in.

'You look a picture,' he said. 'Is the hooter broken?'

'It is,' said Sam, fingering his swollen nose. His

eye had reopened but his face was still black and blue. 'Excuse me if I don't get up, I've got my ribs strapped up.'

'So, was it Morrell? I read about you in the papers.'

'Was what Morrell?'

'Who killed our Ron?'

'I don't know. The police turned up just as he was about to tell me.'

'So, he knows how he died, then.'

'That's just it, I don't know. If you read the papers you'd know I was in a tricky situation. It wasn't ideal for questioning him.'

'So, we're no wiser, then?'

Sam shook his head in a non-committal sort of way. Bernard sat down in the other chair and folded his arms, waiting. Sam was drawing on his cigarette, wondering whether to tell all he knew. The police wouldn't thank him.

Bernard detected his reluctance. 'I'm paying two hundred a day for information about our kid's death,' he reminded Sam, who nodded.

'According to Morrell,' Sam said, 'and I happen to believe this – Ron bought twenty kilos of cocaine off him for a hundred and fifty grand just before he died.'

Bernard whistled. 'Cocaine? Jesus, Ron! You stupid bugger.'

'I'm guessing Ron had never got mixed up in drugs before,' said Sam. 'Morrell was unloading the stuff at cost so he could go legit. I reckon he made Ron an offer he couldn't refuse. Twenty kilos of coke is worth a million on the streets.'

Bernard sat there, rubbing the back of his neck

and weighing up the implications. 'Well, it's a right beggar is this. Are you saying the police will be reopening the file on our kid's death?'

'I got the impression that it's pretty much on the cards,' said Sam, 'but it's not something they'd share with me – I'm not their favourite person. If they do reopen the case, you won't need me.'

'Right, I'll, er, I'll leave it to them, then.' Bernard decided this on economic grounds, with Mariella not being forthcoming with any more cash. 'I reckon me and you are just about square wi' money with you being due a bit of bonus for your troubles.'

'That's very generous of you, Mr Crusher.'

'It's my way of saying I'm not sacking you because I'm not satisfied, it's just that–'

'I understand, Mr Crusher. The police have got the resources to deal with this,' said Sam, '– and the authority.'

'Aye, lad, that's right. But having said all that I did like your methods. You're a winner.'

'I don't feel like a winner.'

'No, mark my words, you're a winner. It's something I've always envied in a man. I wouldn't know a winner if it trotted up and bit me on me arse. Been my downfall that. Marrying Mariella was a gamble. I don't think she'll stay the bloody course.'

'I gather you like a flutter on the horses,' said Sam.

'Like it? No, I wouldn't say I liked it,' grumbled Bernard, 'backing losers is in me blood. The last horse I backed kept looking round to see if its plough were running straight.' He held out a hand for Sam to shake. 'I think it were money well spent, lad. You gave the bobbies a kick up the arse, that's all what were needed.'

Half an hour later, Sam was toying with the idea of ringing Alec to see if he had any work for him of a supervisory nature, when Sally came in.

'Carew,' she said, 'you're in my chair.'

Sam got up, painfully, and sat in his own chair.

'How do I look?' She presented her face for his inspection. Her bruises were still quite colourful and she hadn't chosen to hide them behind make-up.

'Not at your best.'

'Well, I feel a million dollars. Do you know why?'

'I can't think of any good reason off hand.'

'Because I'm still alive,' she told him. 'I should have been dead, but I'm alive.'

'That's a good reason.'

'Owen tells me you're taking me for a luxury trip to London.'

'I wondered why you'd come in. You were supposed to take a week off.'

'And do what? Sit around in front of the telly and paint my toenails. Have you ever watched daytime telly?'

'Not really. I've never painted my toenails either. By the way, Bernard Crusher's just been in to tell me he doesn't want me on the case any more. He's going to leave it up to the police.'

'Oh dear, what a shame. I was just beginning to enjoy working on that case.'

Sam looked at her battered face. He raised his

eyebrows and began to chuckle. Maybe she didn't occupy the place in his heart that Kathy had, but she was a damn good substitute. Sally laughed as well, her first for a while.

'Ow!' she yelled. 'Don't – it hurts when I laugh.'

'I know,' agreed Sam, holding his ribs. He laughed even louder then stopped as he saw tears streaming down her crumpled face. She was sobbing. He found her a hanky.

'Sorry, I can't help it,' she said, wiping her eyes. 'It's like men farting. They can feel it coming and they think, "Ah well, better out than in".'

He smiled at her crude analogy and wondered how many times she'd made him laugh and smile over the years. She smiled back and asked, 'Shall I book the hotel, or will you? Don't answer, I'll do it. I want to wake up to the sound of room service tapping politely on the bedroom door, not the sound of a toothless landlady scraping the toast. I'll try the Savoy and work up from there. Shall we fly down or slum it on the train?'

'The train's actually quicker in the long run.'

'First class, then.'

'What else? Sal, don't you want to wait until your bruises go?'

'You're worse then I am.'

'I'm used to walking around looking like this.'

Sally gave him a smile. 'Sam, no one can see my real bruises. The real bruises are buried in here.' She tapped her breast.

Chapter Nineteen

Morrell was in an environment he could handle. He was being threatened by the law and not by a lunatic. Up until then he had exercised his right to remain silent. He knew such a silence might be used against him in court but he had weighed up the pros and cons and on balance thought it better to wait and see what evidence was stacked against him before he opened his mouth.

Statements from Sam, Sally and Ferris had been enough to arrest him for murder and conspiracy to murder. His silence had been instrumental in him being held on remand in Armley prison, Leeds, and he had decided it was time to tell his side of the story and apply for release on bail. He was accompanied by his barrister when interviewed by Bowman and DS Janet Seager.

'And how is Tony?' he enquired.

'Well, he won't make father of the year,' said the inspector.

'He won't make father of *any* year,' added DS Seager.

Morrell laughed. 'He's a fairly flaky witness all the same. Convicted murderer, self-confessed sex beast, brainless thug.'

'The other two witnesses are solid,' said the inspector. 'Their evidence will stand up in court. There's also the matter of Messrs Zoo Blue and Teargas,' Bowman added. 'I understand from Mr

Ferris that you gave them a nice, warm send off. He'll be telling us all about it in court.'

Morrell's face didn't flicker. His barrister spoke.

'I understand one of your witnesses has the nickname Mad Carew. Got thrown out of the police force for causing humiliation and injury to a certain inspector, who's not a million miles away at this moment. That will really impress the judge.'

Morrell smirked, Bowman's face hardened. It was at times like this that he hated Sam the most.

'So,' said Morrell. 'I'm basically being held here on the evidence of a brainless thug, a nutter and an hysterical woman. Are you really going to oppose bail, Inspector?'

'We are,' said DS Seager, 'on the grounds that there are other serious charges to follow.'

'What charges?' enquired the barrister.

'The little matter of 20 kilos of cocaine you sold to Ron Crusher for a hundred and fifty thousand pounds.'

'And you know this on the evidence of three unreliable witnesses?'

'That's for a judge to decide.'

The barrister looked at Morrell. 'There's not enough here to hold you on remand.' Then to Bowman and Seager he added, 'We won't wait for a court hearing, if that's all right by you. I'll apply to a judge in chambers and arrange for my client to be released straight away.'

Bowman got up to leave. 'That's entirely up to you. Well, we've got your statement, we'll show it to the CPS and take it from there.'

'You might have been on stronger ground had you found my client's fingerprints on the gun,' said the barrister.

'Seeing as how everyone was lying and I never touched the gun, there won't be any,' added Morrell.

'Quite,' said the barrister.

'There's also the matter of Mr Crusher's death soon after the transaction took place,' Janet Seager reminded them.

'The *alleged* transaction, Sergeant,' said the barrister. 'Your evidence is anecdotal and flimsy.'

Morrell smirked again.

Inspector Bowman stared, with some distaste, at this clever bastard who had an answer for everything. 'Evidence has a habit of coming together, Mr Morrell,' he said, mysteriously. 'And I'm very confident it will in this case. So I wouldn't hold out too much hope if I were you, despite the eloquence of your very expensive legal representative.' He and Janet Seager left before Morrell could ask him what it meant.

'What was all that stuff about evidence having a habit of coming together, boss?' she enquired as they drove back to the station.

'No idea, Janet, but it wiped the smile off his face – which told me he's as guilty as hell. I just wish Carew wasn't involved. He'll muddy the waters sure as hell.'

'I know how to handle Carew, boss,' said Janet. 'Suppose I take the case?'

Bowman thought about this and nodded. 'Okay, but the first time he gets in your way I want him arrested for obstructing the police in their enquiries, perverting the course of justice and being a general pain in the arse. Why he can't just stick to laying bricks God only knows? Still, when he and his girlfriend testify in court it may be enough to have Morrell locked up.'

'It's a big maybe, boss. And I think it'll mean putting both Sam and Sally in safe houses.'

Bowman frowned. 'Do you think that's necessary, Sergeant? It's a very big expense. I doubt if Carew will want a safe house. I'll arrange one for the woman.'

'It might be as well to stick a copper outside Ferris's ward,' suggested Janet.

The constable sitting outside Tony Ferris's one bed ward had only been on duty a few hours when a doctor approached wearing a surgical mask. He took a bundle of such masks from his pocket and handed them to the young policeman.

'I don't want anyone going in to see Mr Ferris without wearing one of these,' he said, 'and that includes you. We've had an MRSA scare on one of the other wards and Mr Ferris is particularly vulnerable.'

The constable said he'd do this and placed the masks on the chair beside him. He'd read about how the super bug was killing 5,000 people a year in NHS hospitals and he didn't want to become part of that statistic. The doctor slipped into Ferris's ward just as the policeman was donning one of the masks.

Ferris was existing on reducing doses of local anaesthetic administered to his nether regions. His future looked bleak. The only satisfaction he got was from the knowledge that he'd tucked up Morrell good and proper. He didn't know that Morrell had just been bailed. He glanced up at the doctor.

'Come ter give me a new set o' balls?'

'I've just come to do a few checks, Mr Ferris,' said the doctor from behind his mask. 'Could you lie back and close your eyes, please?'

Ferris did as he was instructed – there was no point doing anything other in this place. The doctor took a small towel from his coat pocket and placed it, gently, over the thug's face. Then from his other pocket he took a four pound lump hammer, with which he struck Ferris a single, powerful blow between where his eyes would be unsuspectingly closed beneath the towel, which soaked up the resulting spurt of blood.

The doctor left as quickly as he had arrived and was never seen again.

Chapter Twenty

Sam was back on site. The break in London had done him a power of good. Sally had vented her spleen on his credit card, treating herself to what vengeful women like to call 'retail therapy'. Sam took his punishment like a man and figured a few weeks overtime on site might make a useful dent in the bill. The bruises and scars on his face had more or less healed, his nose had returned to its original size – if not shape – and most of the strapping had come off his chest. He was building a nine inch boundary wall in double Flemish bond. The face would show each course with alternate headers and stretchers.

'I don't know where they train brickies nowadays,' Alec had moaned to him in the Clog the night before. 'They can do stretcher bond and bugger-all else. I asked young Mark if he knew what a queen closer was – he looked at me daft and told me not ter talk mucky.'

'Modern building methods,' said Sam. 'On houses, stretcher bond's all that's needed. It's taken all the beauty out of brickwork, at least that's what my dad used to say.'

Mark, a young brickie, was helping him build the wall. Watching, learning and labouring. Sam picked up a brick and struck with it the chisel end of his brick hammer, expertly cutting it in two along its length. He threw away the worst half, which had cracked in two pieces and showed the other half to Mark.

'Queen Closer. It goes next to the end brick to maintain the bond around the corner.' He demonstrated by laying it in place, then laying the corner brick beside it.

'I remember now,' said Mark. 'We did it in building college.'

'In one ear out the other eh?'

'I s'pose so. Never built in Flemish bond since.'

'No one ever does,' said Sam. 'That's why so many garden walls fall down. Best bond you can use for a nine inch wall. Right, now you remember what a queen closer is, you can cut me some.'

'Right boss,' grinned Mark. 'Hey, did they name it after you?'

'Name what after me?'

'Queen closer. It's what you did.'

'Mark – what the hell you talking about?'

'The police closed the Queen o' Clubs. Some of us went there last night. There were a sign on the door what said it'd been closed by order of the police until further notice. I bet that Morrell bloke's spitting chips. My mate works on security in the court house. Word is that Morrell's gonna get bail today. I wouldn't like ter be in your shoes if gets out.'

'Wouldn't you now!' snapped Sam. 'Well, I wouldn't like to be in your shoes if this wall's not finished tonight. I've shown you how it's done – you finish it.' He wiped his trowel, threw it in his toolbag and walked off to the site hut, leaving a gob-smacked Mark staring at his back.

'I can see why they call yer Mad bloody Carew,'

he muttered, not loud enough for Sam to hear.

Sam didn't know about the bail hearing – no one had thought to tell him; the prospect of Morrell being let out on bail wasn't one he relished. He knew that influential villains could work their evil from inside prison but, on balance, they weren't as dangerous when locked up. It wasn't just his own skin he was worried about, it was Sally's as well. He rang Owen. It was all he could think of.

'He got bail from a judge in chambers this morning. I was tied up in court or I'd have rung you sooner.'

Sam scowled, 'How the hell did he manage that?'

'Good barrister, I expect. I'm on the case with DS Seager. I assume you'll co-operate, Sam. She's a good copper is Janet.'

'I gather they closed his club,' said Sam non-committally.

'Past tense, boyo. It'll be open tonight, business as usual.'

'He has a funny way of doing business.'

'By the way, this other thing that cropped up...' Owen sounded nervous.

'What?'

'Ferris is dead.'

'Oh.'

Sam felt his stomach lurch. For the second time in his life he'd killed a man. Despite Ferris being a poor example of the species he had still been a person, somebody's son. It wasn't a good feeling. Then came the even worse news. Owen's voice came over the phone, interrupting his thoughts.

'It wasn't you who killed him, see. He was

220

bludgeoned in his hospital bed by some bogus doctor about ten minutes after Morrell was released. Not long enough for him to have got to Ferris himself, but long enough for him to have authorised the killing. Sam, it was a real professional hit – you and Sally might need to go into witness protection.'

There was a long silence as Sam weighed up the implications.

'Sam? Are you still there?'

'I'm thinking.'

If Morrell decided to go the whole hog and take them all out he'd probably go for the easiest target first – Sally. Police protection probably meant a safe house. He'd spent some time in one of those and it had been a worrying, boring, mind-numbing experience. He couldn't put Sally through that, not after all she'd just been through.

'We won't need witness protection,' he said. 'We won't be testifying.'

'The court could issue you with a summons.'

'Sally and I will be withdrawing our statements. It won't get to court. I don't even trust the court to nail him. With Ferris dead they can't touch Morrell on the Zoo Blue and Teargas killings. Let's face it, the coppers only had Ferris's word that they're actually dead.'

'Well, boyo, he's a slippery customer, all right.' It sounded as though Owen didn't disagree with Sam's decision.

'Owen, I need to get hold of him fairly sharpish. Could you get me his mobile number or something.'

'Sam, I've been on the case two bloody minutes

221

and you're compromising me.'

'Owen, I've got to think of Sally. There's only me who can do this.'

There was a silence as Owen thought it over. 'Okay, but it goes without saying that you didn't get his number from me.'

They met the following day on the steps of Unsworth Town Hall. Morrell was dropped off from a Mercedes which he told to go round the block. He wore an expensive looking, black Crombie overcoat. His tan was still intact although it must have come out of a bottle, as had his jet black hair. His lips curled back from his teeth as he strolled up to Sam. Somehow he'd had them fixed, they looked brighter than ever.

He smirked at Sam. 'Shit scared eh? I thought you might be.'

On one finger was a heavy gold sovereign ring, the type worn by gypsy horse dealers. He also had large, diamond stud in one of his ears, the type worn by middle-aged women on the make. To Sam's mind Morrell was a cross between the two.

'Well, I'm not pissing my pants,' Sam said, 'like some I could mention.'

The smirk dropped from Morrell's face. Sam mentally kicked himself for saying it. He was here to do a deal and he'd already got the man's back up.

'I'm prepared to withdraw my statement,' he said. 'So is Sally.'

'And for that you think I'll leave you alone?'

'You'd be stupid not to, and you know it. You

took a risk having Ferris killed. Killing three of us would be just too risky. So you killed him and assumed we'd cave in. Morrell, this is the west end of Yorkshire not the East End of London. Anyone who fancies himself as some sort of a Mafia Godfather up here's going to stand out like the bollocks on a starving dog.' Morrell leaned towards him and spoke to Sam's chest. 'For the benefit of whoever's listening,' he said, 'I didn't have anything to do with Tony Ferris's death. You must think I'm a fucking idiot.'

'I'm not wired,' said Sam.

'Prove it.'

'What?

'Prove it.'

'Come on, this is ridiculous. It's freezing out here.'

'Prove it.'

Sam gave an exasperated sigh; he took off his fleece jacket and stripped himself to the waist, showing he was not wearing any electronic listening devices. 'Satisfied? If you want me to take anything else off, forget it.' Passers by gave him curious glances as he quickly put his shirt and coat back on.

Morrell grinned at Sam's embarrassment. 'It's a very public place to strip off. Couldn't you have chosen somewhere more private for a meet?'

'And got a bullet in my back?'

'You've got a nasty, suspicious mind, Mr Sam Carew.'

'So, do we have a deal?' Sam was loathing every second he had to be in this vile man's company. He hated having to be scared of him. It wasn't

Morrell's physical presence he was scared of, it was his amorality; his coldness; his total lack of decency and conscience; and his capability of killing innocent people without turning a hair. It was simply part of his business. To Morrell, death was just a living. He rattled out his terms:

'If I hear from my brief within the next twenty-four hours that you and your lady friend have withdrawn your statements I won't need to do any further business with you. Simple as that. Our friend Tony, on the other hand wouldn't listen to reason. Still I imagine it's hard to be reasonable when you've just lost the crown fucking jewels. Prided himself on his orb and sceptre did our Tony. You blew away the full set, did you know that? They found his bollocks stuck to the skirting board.'

'And you finished him off.'

Morrell's teeth flashed but his smile didn't reach his eyes. 'I was still in the courthouse when he passed away.'

'I'm not saying you did it personally.'

'Oh, is that what you're not saying? I'd say you're fishing.'

'Hardly fishing,' said Sam. 'If I didn't think you'd had Ferris killed I wouldn't be here.'

'Lucky for me you've got a suspicious mind, eh?'

Sam waited a moment then said, 'So, you'll leave us alone?'

Morrell shrugged. 'Unless you begin to get in the way of my legitimate business – yes. And as for the Ron Crusher business, which I under-stand started you off on this–'

'What about Ron Crusher?' Sam asked, a little too quickly.

'The Ron Crusher business,' continued Morrell, 'should be a lesson to you not to mess with legitimate businessmen. Still, I think you've learned that lesson today.'

The Mercedes came round the block. Morrell turned and left. Sam stood there feeling a mixture of relief and frustration. He'd had no option but to do what he did. He cursed under his breath and walked round the corner to where a dark blue Transit van was parked. He tapped on the door. It slid open. DS Seager, Owen and a specialist sound engineer were inside. Janet Seager had headphones around her neck. Sam apologised.

'Sorry, it was all I could do. I thought at one point he was going to admit to having Ferris killed but I don't reckon he said enough.'

'He didn't,' confirmed Janet. 'We'll get him, though. He'll slip up. He's crafty but he's not clever. There's a lot going on around him. Ron Crusher, the drugs and now Ferris. His luck won't hold forever.'

'I hope not.' Sam unfastened his belt and unclipped a tiny microphone that was attached to it. A wire ran down his trousers to a black plastic box containing a battery and transmitter.

'I thought he had you rumbled for a minute,' said Owen.

Sam reached into his trousers and brought out the listening equipment. 'I'm not sure he didn't,' he said. 'But if he'd tried to frisk me down there I'd have had to stop him, on decency grounds.'

'I don't think he knows the meaning of the

225

word, boyo.'

Sam smiled. 'Sorry I can't be of more help. It's as far as I go. We'll be withdrawing our statements.'

'I understand, Sam,' said Janet. 'Just don't get in the way of our investigations.'

'Scouts honour,' promised Sam, who had never been in the scouts. And Owen knew it.

'I feel bad about it,' said Sally. 'Isn't it our civic duty or something?'

'Not with something as tenuous as this. If it was a cast-iron case and they were going to lock him up and throw the key away, I'd say go for it; live in a safe house for a while until the case is over. But there's nothing cast-iron about this.'

'Would you have withdrawn your statement if I hadn't been involved?'

'I'd like to think I would. It's definitely the sensible thing to do. I might be a bit irresponsible at times but I'm not a martyr to my cause.'

They were in the office. The phone had rung, intermittently, all morning, while Sam had been out. His story not only been in the *Unsworth Observer* and the *Yorkshire Post*, but he'd also made the nationals. If nothing else, it had been good for business. Sally ran her pencil up the list of callers, all of whom had been told that Mr Carew wasn't in the office but would call as soon as he got back.

'Missing wife,' she read, 'missing dog; unfaithful husband; thieving employees at a sanitary ware manufacturer; three insurance companies – they might be worth following up. Good money

226

that. Safe money as well.'

'Sal, if I just wanted to make money I'd stick to building.'

'Blimey, you've changed your tune.'

'No, I haven't. You wanted to do jobs for nothing, I want to pick and choose. That's different.'

'Oh, and Paul Smith called. Sounded a bit worried.'

'I'm not surprised. Did he say what he wanted?'

'Advice, by the sound of it.'

Sam picked up the photo of his two boys that he kept on his desk, and he vowed to himself to be around as they grew up. His general disregard for his own safety wasn't fair on them. They looked upon him as a hero, which he knew he wasn't. Heroes are sensible men who go into danger fully aware of the risks they're taking. Sam never stopped to think about risk and it was high time he did.

'Okay, get more details about the insurance jobs. You know what I'm capable of. Get me something that sounds interesting. Did you get Paul's number?'

Sally got up and took a piece of paper over to him. 'This is his mobile number.' She sat on his desk, facing him. Her skirt was hitched up above her knees, which he had always considered very shapely. 'By the way,' she said. 'I'm still thinking it over.'

'Thinking what over?' he asked.

'Your proposal, what did you think I meant?'

'Proposal–?'

'It *was* a genuine proposal, wasn't it?'

It seemed a bad time to be denying knowledge

of a proposal, which he had probably made in the heat of some moment. He pulled her on to his knee. 'Yes,' he said, 'it was.'

They kissed then Sally asked him, 'Do you still think it's the wrong thing to do – us getting married?'

He grasped at the straw she was offering. 'I'd prefer us just to live together.'

'You know why I don't like that idea.'

'Ah yes, the shame that *living over t' brush* brought upon your ancestors up in the hills of Barnoldswick – the land of whores and comic singers, where respectable folk used to put their marriage licence in the window to show the world how decent they were, unlike your loose living ancestors.'

'They weren't my ancestors, they were my grandparents. My mother vowed never to inflict such shame on her own children.'

'Sal, this is the twenty-first century. Half the parents in the country aren't married.'

'Are you withdrawing your proposal, Sam Carew?'

'No, the only thing I've withdrawn today is my statement to the police. Do you have an answer for me, Miss Grover?'

'I'm giving it due consideration.'

'You appear to be giving due consideration to my shirt buttons. Is the door locked?'

'You should know, Sam. You locked it when you came in.'

'Ah, observant. We need observant people in this business. At the moment I'm observing that you've inherited some of the raciness from your

228

hill-billy ancestors. I'll do my belt, you do your bra – and take the phone off the hook.'

Their love-making was passionate, vigorous and uncomfortable. The carpet was more industrial than boudoir and Sally manoeuvred herself on top to save wear and tear on her backside.

'You'll have to get some decent Axminster down if you want any more of this,' she told him.

'I'll get a sheepskin rug.' He gazed up at Sally who was completely naked and in fine form for a woman well into her thirties. 'Have you thought of an answer yet?'

'I've decided I want a sincere proposal,' she said, getting up and gathering her clothes. She went to the small kitchenette just off the office and ran the tap as Sam pulled on his trousers. He put the phone back on the hook and it rang almost straight away. 'Saved by the blasted bell,' she murmured to herself.

'Eileen,' said Sam, 'what can I do for you?... No, he's taken me off the case, it's up to the police now... Really?... Look Eileen, I'm not sure what I can do. In fact I'm not sure I want to get involved. It all got very heavy.' There was a long moment while Sam listened to what Eileen had to say. Sally was dressed by the time he spoke again. 'Okay, I'll come round this evening, take care ... bye.'

'What did she want?' said Sally.

'She wants to hire me. She wants to take over from Bernard.'

'I thought she had no money.'

'She has a half million pound life insurance policy on Ron, that won't pay out on a suicide.

229

She offered me twenty per cent – a hundred grand – if I can prove it wasn't suicide. Apparently she heard about the case against Morrell being dropped. I guess Owen must have told her.'

Sally whistled. 'A hundred grand?'

'Or nothing, if I can't prove it.'

'We should take it.'

'We?'

'I have a vested interest in this,' said Sally. 'Withdrawing my statement against Morrell really hurt. A small share in a hundred grand would assuage the pain.'

'A share, eh?' He grinned at her cheek. 'I guess you've earned a share.'

'Ten per cent?' she ventured, planning to settle for five.

'Fifty,' said Sam, buttoning up his shirt and tucking it into his trousers, 'and not a penny more. I'm not made of money, woman. And that's after expenses.'

'Sam, there's no need–'

He held up a hand to stop her protest. 'There's every need, Sal. I want you to get on to the solicitors and get them to draw up a contract that ties her down to paying. I don't mind taking a hundred grand off a woman with half a million.'

'Right, what about the other jobs?'

'Tell them we'd love to help them but we're absolutely flooded out with work. Tell the same to anyone else who rings up, and Sal–'

'What?'

'You're strictly an office worker. You don't come with me anywhere where there might be trouble.'

'I don't want you to wrap me up in cotton

wool, Sam.'

Smithy came over to see Sam in the Clog and Shovel. His face was drawn. Sam had never seen him smoke before but he said 'thanks' when Sam, purely out of politeness, offered him one. 'He reckons I owe him a hundred and sixty thousand pounds.'

Sam didn't need to hear the name Morrell to know who Smithy was talking about. The sum didn't surprise him. Morrell wasn't the kind of man who dealt in peanuts.

'How does he work that out?'

'He's got cash receipts.'

'You've got work done for that amount. He'd lose if it went to court.'

Smithy's shoulders sagged. 'You know when you said I should check my contract?'

'Go on.' Sam feared the worst.

'He says the cash was a loan, and payment on the work isn't due until it's been given a final certificate of approval from his architect.'

'Which is in your contract.'

'Yes, but it's just a standard clause. It's usual for work to be approved by an architect prior to payment. You must know that yourself.'

Sam nodded that he did know that. 'You said, *his* architect. Is it a specific, named architect?'

'Yes – Gordon Beresford. He's not a proper architect, he's some sort of architectural technician.'

'So, you've signed an agreement to say that the money isn't due until this Gordon Beresford issues a final certificate. Is there anything in the agreement to say what happens if Gordon Beresford proves unreasonable or isn't physically capable of approving the work? I mean, what happens if Gordon Beresford dies or just tells you to piss off?'

'I've read the contract and there's no clause to cover that. Why do you ask?'

'Because someone did a similar thing to my dad. It wasn't for a fortune but it was enough to hurt.'

'What happened.'

'Dad went to court and lost – and I know the law hasn't been changed. Taught him a lesson never to use a named architect. It's a kind of legal scam where crooks can use a ridiculous point of contract law not to pay out money they owe. In court all Gordon Beresford has to say is that he isn't satisfied with your work. He doesn't even have to say why. He'll probably come up with something, but he doesn't have to. The contract won't oblige him to be reasonable, neither does the law.'

'So, couldn't I get another architect to approve it? Or the council?'

'It has to be him. The work could be approved by the council, the queen, the pope, the club could be up and running, but if Gordon Beresford doesn't sign a certificate of final approval you won't get paid. It's his signature that triggers that part of the contract concerning the release of the money. No signature, no trigger, no money. If you bump Gordon Beresford off it would go to a judicial review and the court might appoint an architect. I don't suppose you fancy doing that, though?'

232

'I've never actually met Gordon Beresford.'

'Why doesn't that surprise me,' said Sam.

'I can't believe the law can be so obviously unfair.'

'In civil cases the law has no conscience. The wording of a contract takes precedence over what you and I like to call justice. The lawyers will say you shouldn't have signed such a contract. He's legally entitled to sue you for the money he's given you, but he won't.'

'He won't,' pointed out Smithy, 'because I don't possess his bloody money. I spent it on his club.'

'Wrong,' said Sam. 'He won't because he looks upon himself as a businessman – and business-men don't waste time in court. He just wants you and your building skills. He wants you on his team and he wants you to work for a wage until you pay off his hundred and sixty grand, which you never will because he'll be always adding interest to it. To him that's sound business.'

'And if I refuse to work for him?' asked Smithy. 'I mean, I know he's out on bail but surely when it gets to court–'

'Tony Ferris went against him and he got killed,' said Sam. 'It scared the shit out of me. I withdrew my statement. He won't be going to court. Sorry.'

Smithy drained his pint and shook his head. 'Jesus, Sam. I can't work for him, not under these conditions.'

'The trouble is,' said Sam. 'Morrell will have convinced himself that you owe him either a hundred and sixty grand or your services for life.

233

It's the way his warped mind works. He genuinely believes he's a good businessman.'

'And what will he do?'

'I think if you don't go along with him, your life will be in serious danger. The man is twisted. You could go to the police, although I'm not sure what they can do until he actually harms you. They're gunning for him over the Ferris killing. Hoping he'll make a mistake.'

'Do you have *any* helpful advice?' There was a measure of desperate sarcasm his voice.

'Well, I'm pulling all the stops out to nail him for killing Ron Crusher. If I'm successful you'll be out of his clutches.'

'I suppose that's something. So, what do you suggest I do?'

'I suggest you stay safe and go along with him until I do my job. You never know, if you don't give him any hassle he might pay you a decent wage.'

'Great,' said Smithy, miserably. 'Anything else to cheer me up?'

'You could keep your eyes and ears open for me,' said Sam. 'I'm getting well paid for my work. If I'm successful I'm prepared to shove a bit your way.'

'What do you think your chances are?'

'Fair to middling. All I can really do is keep an eye on him and hope he slips up. That's where you'd come in handy.'

Smithy got up to go. He hadn't heard anything that gave him cause for optimism. 'I'll do what I can,' he said, 'and thanks – I think.'

Chapter Twenty-One

'Where would Ron hide 20 kilos of cocaine?'
Sam couldn't think of a tactful way of asking her
the question so he just came straight out with it.

Eileen screwed up her face and said, 'No idea,'
without much enthusiasm. 'What would it look
like?'

'Well, it's just a fine, white powder. Probably
split up into twenty bags – plastic probably –
about the same size and weight as your average
bag of sugar. Only the price is different.'

'I don't know. I don't think he had any secret
hiding places – the boot of his car, maybe. You
know, it's really hard to take in that he was dealing in drugs. He hated drugs. Are you sure about
it?'

'Not a hundred per cent. I think it was a
situation he was forced into. Morrell made him
an offer he couldn't refuse, as they say. The
trouble is I don't know what help it would be if I
found the stuff. I'd have to hand it over to the
police straight away. Maybe they'd be able to tie
it in to Morrell. One step nearer to proving that
Morrell had him killed. I'm actually clutching at
straws. Where's his car?'

'Repossessed – it was a lease car.'

'I suppose I could pop round to the lease
company and ask them if they noticed a million
quid's worth of cocaine in the boot.'

'The police found the car for me and brought it back, I imagine they'd have looked in the boot, with the circumstance of his death being a bit suspicious.'

'I wouldn't bank on it. Have they been to see you, recently?'

'Not since they brought the car back. Why?'

'I thought they might have come round asking the same questions as I'm asking.'

'Why would they? All charges against Morrell have been dropped.' Her eyes added, *because you withdrew your statement*, but she didn't say it.

What neither of them knew at the time was that the drugs had already been found that day by a cleaner at Bernard Crusher's house. They were in a black plastic bin liner in his cellar; it contained twenty clear plastic bags. The woman had looked inside because she knew she hadn't put it there, and she'd been cleaning the house for three years. At first she just shrugged her shoulders and went on with her work. Then, a few weeks later, when she heard about Morrell being arrested and drugs being involved and Mrs Crusher's dead brother-in-law being mentioned she began to get suspicious about the contents of the bag. She told her husband and he said don't be daft it could be weed killer or anything. But it didn't look much like weed killer to her. A few days later she was watching *The Bill* on TV. It had a storyline involving cocaine that showed packets of stuff very similar to the stuff in the cellar.

The next day she'd told Mariella that she'd found some bags of what looked like either weed killer or cocaine. Mariella asked her how on earth she knew what cocaine looked like and the woman said she seen the stuff on telly last night. Mariella took one look in the bag and called the police without first telling Bernard. Within an hour Bernard had been arrested on suspicion of dealing in class A drugs. Sam was completely baffled by the whole business. Nothing made sense. He went to see Bernard, on remand, in Armley prison.

'I didn't put the bloody stuff there,' Bernard said. He'd been in a week and had already acquired a prison pallor. The shock of being locked up does that to a man's complexion.

'I believe you,' said Sam.

'Thank God for that. Have a word with Mariella will you? She doesn't believe me. I thought she'd have given me the benefit of the doubt and asked me before she told the bloody coppers. She hasn't been to see me, you know. The old bag!'

'Had you two had an argument?' enquired Sam.

'I wouldn't call it an argument. More a blazing row. Nothing out of the ordinary, though. It's hard to live with someone like her without having fights every two minutes. But there was no need for this, no need at all. God knows what she's told the coppers. Do *you* know?'

'Sorry. I'm just a prison visitor. Any idea how the stuff got in your cellar? Could Ron have left it there?'

'God knows, anything's possible. He rarely came round to ours.'

'Did he have a key?'

'Well I didn't give him one and I'm damn sure

Mariella didn't.' He thought for a while than said, 'I suppose it's possible, though. One of his lads fitted us a new front door, complete with lock. It wouldn't have been difficult for him to have had a spare key cut just for himself.'

'And is that something he might have done?'

'It is,' conceded Bernard, after some thought. 'Bloody hell, Ron, between you and the bloody Führer, you've dropped me right in it. Have a word with her, will you, Sam? Make her see what damage she's doing with her big mouth.'

'I'll see what I can do.'

It was the first time Sam had seen Mariella since that day in Barbados. She opened the door and glared at him, suspiciously.

'What d'yer want?'

'Mrs Crusher?' He wasn't supposed to know who she was.

'Who wants ter know.'

'My name is Carew – of Carew Private Investigatio–.'

'I thought me husband made it clear he didn't need you any more.'

'It's your husband who sent me to talk to you, Mrs Crusher.'

'Did he now? Well he's got a bloody cheek after what he did. I could have got done for it meself yer know. In fact I still might fer all I know. I blame their Ron. It were bad enough him gettin' mixed up in all that drug stuff without dragging Bernard into it.'

'Can I come in, Mrs Crusher? I don't think we should talk on the doorstep.'

238

'I'm not sure what we've got ter talk about, but go on, wipe yer feet.'

He followed her through to a very comfortable living room. Expensively carpeted, with a leather chesterfield and matching chairs. *Coronation Street* was showing on the massive television which sat above an array of fancy-looking equipment that told Sam she'd be able to receive every television station in the known universe and play music and films to a professional standard. How his boys would love a set-up like this. Mariella sat down on the chesterfield and Sam assumed that it would be okay for him to sit down on one of the chairs, although he hadn't been invited.

'Your husband swears he knew nothing about the drugs.'

'Well, he's hardly going to say any different, is he?'

Sam sat back and studied her. Her face was as hard as he remembered; her tan had been regularly topped up by a sun lamp and it showed, as it always does. She showed little sign of a bereft woman whose law abiding husband had just been locked up for drug dealing.

'I believe him,' Sam said.

'I don't.'

'Why not? Has he given you cause to suspect something like this has been going on?'

She replied in the same harsh voice he'd last heard talking to Francine le Bon. 'That's between me and the police. I've given a statement ter them and I'm not going to fuckin' discuss it with you.'

Sam held up his hands. 'Quite right. I'm not here to step on police toes. I'm here because your

239

husband asked me to talk to you. If you don't want to talk, that's fair enough.' He got up to go.

'I never said I wouldn't talk ter you.'

Sam remained on his feet and looked around the room. On the wall was a studio photograph of a young woman; good looking in a hard-faced sort of way, and who looked vaguely familiar. He took a step towards it.

'This you?' he asked.

'In a different life,' she said. 'I used ter be a club singer.'

'Were you good?'

'Yes, I were very good. A bloody sight better than Ronnie bloody Crush.'

'So, you knew him when he sang in the clubs did you?'

'I did. Known him on and off for twenty odd years. It was him what introduced me to his brother, just after me last husband died.'

'Sorry to hear about that – was it an accident?' He wasn't actually fishing, but it came out like that. She gave a raucous laugh.

'Hey! Mebbe yer think I'm in the business of bumpin' people off, eh? Like rich husbands and arseholes like Ron Crusher?'

'I didn't mean that,' said Sam quickly.

'He died of prostate cancer,' she said. 'Got to his bones before he knew he had it. His doctor told him were just run down. It's the bloody doctor as wants bloody runnin' down. National Health Service? I wouldn't pay 'em in fuckin' washers. He were a proper man as well. Self made. Not like that useless bugger I married next.'

'I understand Bernard ran your business very

well,' said Sam, not quite knowing why he was defending Bernard, other than that he didn't like this woman one bit.

'That's all he did. He were no good fer nowt else – if yer know what I mean.' She added the last bit with a distasteful leer, then laid back on the settee and crossed her legs in a manner that might have seemed seductive in another woman. Sam was pleased she was wearing slacks. He'd done his duty by Bernard. There was nothing to be gained by staying in the company of this revolting person. He made to leave and was stopped by her next remark.

'I know what yer thinking.'

Sam doubted it. 'What am I thinking?'

'Yer thinin' me and Ron had it off, just because we worked in the same business. Well if we did, it's none o' your bleedin' business.'

'I wasn't actually thinking that,' said Sam, truthfully. 'If I'm thinking anything I'm wondering why you're so sure Bernard was mixed up in Ron's drug dealing.'

'I didn't at the time,' she admitted. 'It's just that it explains a lot of things ter me. A lot of odd things he were doing. Secretive like. I didn't think much of it at the time because he could be an odd bugger when he wanted. I mean, why did he hire you to prove that Ron didn't top himself when it were bloody obvious that he did? I always thought there were summat funny about that. They were never that close. Very odd that.'

'And you told all that to the police?'

She nodded, so did Sam. 'Well, if you're right,' he said, 'you've sure stuffed him.'

241

'He stuffed himself, Mr Carew.'

His initial instincts about Mariella had been spot on. He detested her and felt like telling her. 'Do you know what I think, Mrs Crusher?'

'What's that?'

'I think you just want to punish Bernard, and you've found a convenient way to do it. I think Ron had a key to this house and left the drugs in the cellar. I don't think Bernard had anything to do with it, and I think you know it.'

She gave another laugh – one that set Sam's teeth on edge. 'Yer might be right, Sam bloody Carew. But why would I want the daft bugger out of the way, eh? I haven't got another feller. If nowt else Bernard's good at runnin' the business. I'd be daft ter get rid of him.'

'I don't know why, Mrs Crusher. In fact this whole business doesn't make a scrap of sense to me.'

'I'll tell yer what doesn't make sense,' she said. 'It doesn't make sense why you're still botherin'. It's not as though yer gonna get paid any more money.'

'I'm actually working for the other Mrs Crusher.' Sam saw no reason not to tell her, she'd find out soon enough anyway.

'Her?' He'd never heard so much withering scorn injected into one short word. 'She hasn't got two bloody ha'pennies ter scratch her arse – ah, I see. Insurance, that's it, innit?'

Sam said nothing. He was fascinated by the mask of pure hatred on Mariella's face. 'Why do you hate her so much, Mrs Crusher?'

'Because I bloody do, that's why! Because she

drove him to it. Ron'd be still alive had it not been fer that bitch.'

'Care to elaborate?'

'No, I wouldn't fuckin' care to elaborate! But I can tell yer one thing. If yer tryin' ter prove it weren't suicide yer've got a job on yer hands. Ron topped himself as sure as I'm standin' here. And he didn't deserve ter fuckin' die! That bitch of a woman's tryin' ter get insurance money where she's not entitled. As far as I'm concerned she can stew in her own shit!'

There were tears of rage dripping down her cheeks and Sam knew it was time to go. A few minutes ago she'd referred to Ron as an arsehole and here she was, crying tears for him. What was that all about? At that moment it seemed he was a million miles from collecting twenty per cent of Eileen's insurance money. Eileen – the same woman who had referred to Morrell as Milo. Things like that didn't slip his mind, but nor did they make any sense either. This whole thing was just too complicated to unravel. Anyone sane would give up, he thought. Then he smiled when he remembered that he wasn't completely sane. How fortunate an asset that was in this line of work. The one thing he knew for certain was that Ron Crusher had not committed suicide. But he wasn't going to tell that to the volcanic Mariella. She looked to pack a mean punch, and there was a limit to the depth of his insanity.

Chapter Twenty-Two

Five weeks had gone by and Sam had made no progress. Bernard had been allowed out on bail and had gone back to the marital home, mainly, because it was a condition of his bail. Sam had successfully taken on one of the insurance fraud jobs and been well paid for it. He'd also spent a week on the tools at Alec's behest. Smithy was working for Morrell for the same wage as Carew and Sons paid their labourers and he wasn't at all happy. He called into Sam's office whenever he could get away from the Huddersfield site.

'He's using me as a bloody lackey, Sam.' He sat down without being asked. 'Did I ever tell you I was engaged to a really beautiful girl?'

'No, you didn't – congratulations,' said Sam. 'When's the big day?'

'You see, that's the other thing I didn't tell you. The engagement's off. My devoted fiancée wasn't happy with my financial downturn. I couldn't tell her the real reason behind it all. I mean, what would I have said to her? I'm working for peanuts because if I don't the boss'll have me killed?'

'Yes, you couldn't have told her that,' agreed Sam. 'Women can do unpredictable things. They don't think things through like us men.'

Sally let out a hoot of derision. Sam hadn't realised she was there. 'Hey, Miss Clever Clogs, I thought you'd gone out to get some sandwiches.'

'Got 'em,' she said. 'Got back just in time to hear your latest little pearl about how you men think things through. By the way, Smithy, she wasn't worth hanging on to if she leaves you because of money.' She looked at Sam. 'A good woman will stick to a man through thick and thin, for richer or for poorer, for better or for worse, in sickness and in hea–'

'We get the picture, thank you,' said Sam. 'What did you get me?'

'Ham and tomato, and a custard tart. Would you like me to nip out and get you anything, Smithy?'

'No thanks. I'm supposed to be organising some proper heating for Morrell's office in The Queen Of Clubs.'

Sally went cold at the sound of the place. She looked at Sam, but he was deep in thought. 'You mean new radiators and piping?' he said.

'Stuff like that, yeah. The radiators he's got in now must have been there since Dick's days.'

'Heated by a furnace that uses human fuel.'

'Don't go there, Sam,' warned Sally, who had been dealing with her trauma in the same way that men coming from the two worlds wars had – she didn't talk about it and she tried not to think about it.

Sam held up a hand in apology, then to Smithy he said, 'I assume he'll be expecting you to use a sub-contractor?'

'I'm thinking of using the firm I use in Huddersfield.'

'I'd like to suggest another firm – Carew and Son. Well, we might have to use another name

245

but that won't be a problem.'

'And do what?' asked Smithy suspiciously.

'And do what we always do – a good job,' said Sam. 'We'll fit the best central heating his crooked money can buy and throw in a couple of well-hidden cameras and a few microphones free of charge. I can't be fairer than that.'

'And do you know someone who can do all that?' asked Smithy. 'Someone you can really trust?'

'Billy Timmis,' said Sam. 'Plumber and electrical contractor. I was talking to him only this morning. He's been working for us, on and off, for ten years.'

'Will he know about modern day surveillance cameras and listening equipment?' Smithy asked.

'What he doesn't know he'll find out,' said Sam. 'But I think this'll be a piece of cake to him. He's a real gadget freak is Billy. In the eighties he worked as a sound engineer for quite a few big rock bands. Knows his stuff – good plumber as well. He'd be tickled pink to do a job like that. No doubt I'll have to pay him extra. Very careful man with a shilling is Billy. He's working out on one of our sites now. Do you want me to give him a bell and get him to go with you to work out what's needed?'

Smithy looked at Sally. 'What am I getting myself into?'

'Anyone's guess, Smithy. Where will Morrell be while all this is going on?'

'He's gone off for week in Paris.'

'That's good,' said Sam. 'He won't be sniffing round, then.'

'I suppose not. He wants it done for when he gets back. He only told me yesterday. That's the sort of thing I'm having to put up with.'

Sam grinned. 'Then it'd be a shame to disappoint such a nice man. I'll ring Billy. You can pick him up from site. He'll need a hand – I suggest you be a plumber's mate for a couple of days.'

'After what I've been doing it'll be a step up,' said Smithy. He managed a rueful smile. 'Anything to get me out of this fix I'm in. I'll be glad to get back to earning some real money.' He got up to go. Sam opened a drawer and took out a cheque book.

'I guess you'll work better if you're not worrying about money all the time.' He glanced across at Sally. 'Is it okay if I give him a thousand?'

'Of course, why ask me, you're the boss?'

'Because it's part of *our* expenses.'

'Ah. I'll put it in the book.'

He turned to Smithy. 'It's a special deal Sal and I have got going. If we can prove Ron Crusher didn't commit suicide we get a nice share of an insurance payment.'

'Well, thanks. I must admit, it'll help keep the wolf from the door.'

'There'll be more for you, as and when.'

'You sound very sure of yourself,' said Smithy.

'He does tend to come up smelling of roses,' said Sally, '...among other things.'

The driver of a black Mercedes which had followed Smithy from Huddersfield to Unsworth watched the young builder emerge from Sam's

247

office. He unclipped the car phone, dialled in a number and spoke for a half a minute before putting the phone back and driving off.

Sam was in the Clog and Shovel with Owen when Billy came in, carrying a smart leather case. Sam was glad to see him, with Owen being in one of his more morose moods. He signalled to Dave to pull three more pints and asked Billy: 'Did everything go okay?'

'All done and dusted. Four new radiators, one of them a double.' Billy looked at Owen whom he'd never met before. 'Plus various ancillary works which I'll explain to you when you've got a minute.'

'You can explain in front of Owen,' said Sam. 'He knows what's going on.'

'It doesn't mean I approve of it,' said Owen.

'He's a copper,' explained Sam. 'Owen, this is Billy.'

'Pleased to meet you, boyo.'

'He's Welsh,' added Sam, unnecessarily.

The two men shook hands.

'Right,' said Billy. 'Well, what I've done is I've stuck a couple of wireless web cameras in. One's in a wall clock, the other's in his TV. He'll never spot them unless he thinks he's being bugged and does a search – and even then he'd have his work cut out.' He put the case on the table and took out a laptop computer. 'The web-cams are calibrated to this laptop. You take this to within say a mile of the cameras and you'll pick up sound and vision clear as day. The beauty is that you don't have to sit outside in a van, watching a screen all day. This

248

has got an internal DVD writer. It's an expensive piece of kit but it'll record for up to seven hours.'

'The wonders of modern technology,' marvelled Sam, who wasn't quite sure what Billy was talking about. 'What with all this and DNA, it's a wonder there's any villains walking the streets.'

'Ah, but just suppose Billy was a villain,' said Owen. 'Imagine the problems he could cause you.'

'That's right,' said Billy. And I'm only an amateur compared to some of the real whiz-kids. It's a different world, mate. Different police force as well, I imagine.'

Owen nodded, gloomily. 'Oh, you can say that again, boyo. It's all paperwork, computers, spy cameras and forensic bloody psychologists nowadays. We could save a lot of police time, look you, if they'd let us give the villains a swift kick up the arse now and again. A size eleven inserted up the sphincter can have a very civilising effect on the recidivist.'

'There'll always be plenty of old fashioned baddies around,' said Sam. 'I reckon Morrell's very much your old school. He might have his phones checked for bugs but it'll never occur to him that there's web cameras lurking in his office. Good work that, Billy.'

'We'd have had to jump through bloody hoops to fix all that up,' grumbled Owen. 'Then done it at the dead of night. Breaking in, covering our tracks, hoping no one sees us.'

'We didn't even have to do any breaking and entering,' pointed out Sam with a grin. 'Broad daylight, banging and clattering. That's the advantage of being a trustworthy builder.'

Owen pulled a face. 'It's the advantage of you being a privateer.'

Sam took a sip of one of the pints that Dave had brought over. 'Privateer?' he said. 'I thought I was a private eye.'

Owen gave a slow, wintry smile as the joke unravelled in his mind. 'Now there's ad lib humour at its finest,' he said, 'although there are those who would call it ad nauseam humour at its worst.'

'That was your round,' said Sam. 'Dave's waiting for his money.'

Billy drank his pint, gave Sam the bill for his work, and left Sam and Owen on their own. Owen returned to his thoughts. Sam got hold of the wrong end of the stick.

'I won't drop you in it, Owen, if that's what worried about.'

'What?'

'You can spy on Morrell whenever you want. Pick up info on him – that's bound to impress Bowman.'

'I'm in love with Eileen.'

'What?' said Sam.

'I'm in love, see. Which is a bit of a bugger.'

'Bit of a bugger? – it's supposed to be a many splendoured thing.'

'I've fallen head over heels in love with her.'

'That's what line dancing does to you. Head over heels? Does she know?'

'I declared my devotion last night. She was quite taken aback. I'm afraid I might have made a bit of a fool of myself. There's no fool like an old fool, isn't that what they say?'

'Well I don't see why she should be so taken aback. You've been living with her for a while now.'

'Ah, you knew that, did you?'

'Well I knew Postwoman Pat had kicked you out and you haven't been grumbling about conditions at the police house. I kind of put two and two together.'

'Well, what do you think?'

'What do I think about what?'

'About me being in love with Mrs Crusher.'

Sam gave it some thought. 'To be honest. I don't think she's got over Ron's death yet. Are you sure you're not just a shoulder to cry on?'

'I'm not sure about much at all, except that I'm in love with her.'

'Weren't you once in love with Postwoman Pat?'

'That was a union of convenience.'

'No,' said Sam. 'You definitely once told me you loved her. You're easily besotted Owen. I remember you once telling me that you loved Janet Seager.'

'That was before I found out she batted for the other side, which I still think is a great shame, incidentally.'

'True, I fancied her myself at one stage – still do as a matter of fact.' Sam studied Owen's dejected face. Like a bloodhound having a bad day. 'Dare I ask if your relationship has been fruitful as far as my investigation's concerned? Have you dug out any dark secrets from her past?'

'You never fail to sink to the occasion, do you, Carew. I'm pouring out my heart and all you can

251

think about is your investigation.'

'Well, have you?'

'No, I bloody haven't.'

'I don't think you've tried.'

'I seem to remember being dropped from your payroll after you found out I was having a good time with Eileen.'

'Ah, I did that for your benefit,' said Sam. 'Just think how bad you'd feel if she found out I was paying you to be friendly with her. Tell you what, why don't I test the water for you?'

'If I wanted my water testing you'd be the last person I'd come to.'

'No, I'll find out how Eileen feels about you. Then you'll know.'

Owen mulled over the proposition, then drank the remaining half pint in his glass in one swallow. 'Then I'll know eh?' he mused. 'I'm not sure I want to know. Maybe I've been too forward – frightened her off, boyo.'

'Then I'll smooth things over for you.'

That day events weren't running smoothly for Eileen. Owen's declaration had unnerved her. She'd been given a court date for the house possession hearing and she'd had a phone call from Mariella.

'Slag!'

'Who is this?'

'Who d'yer think it is, yer fuckin' slag?'

'Ah, Mariella, how nice to hear from you.'

'Don't you bloody Mariella me. I know your bloody game. I know yer've had another feller in yer bed before Ron's gone cold. No wonder he bleedin' topped hisself. What happened? Did he find out yer'd been on the game? Did yer go back to it? Slags like you can't leave it alone. Once a slag allus a slag.'

Eileen knew she couldn't compete with Mariella in a slanging match. 'For your information, unlike you I've never been on the game. Anyway, what's it got to do with you?' she enquired, almost politely.

Mariella exploded at such a accusation. 'You fuckin' lyin' bitch! I've never sold it in me life.'

'By the way,' said Eileen, cooler than ever, feeling she had the upper hand. 'Ron didn't kill himself. The police have admitted to me they're not sure it was suicide. There was even an article in the *Yorkshire Post* about it, entitled *Did he jump or was he pushed?* You must have read it. Sam Carew's on the job. He reckons Milo Morrell did it. He's fairly confident he can prove it. And by the way, I know you were one of the tarts Ron was screwing. He told me. He said he did it because you handed it to him on a plate which was something he could never resist. He also told me you made him feel sick afterwards.' She was fishing because she couldn't understand why Mariella was so angry.

The phone went dead, Eileen looked at it and hoped she'd been wrong with her accusation. She didn't want to think that Marietta had been one of Ron's women. An hour later Sam knocked on her door. She opened it and managed a smile.

'Please tell me you've got good news.'

Sam returned her smile. 'Mixed,' he said. 'We're pretty near getting Morrell to trip himself

253

up – but that's not what I came about.'

'Owen?' she guessed.

Sam nodded, and accepted her invitation to go inside. He glanced around. 'Still keeping the wolves at bay?'

She showed him the court summons. He studied it and rubbed his chin in thought.

'I'll give you a letter to say that we're very near proving Ron didn't commit suicide and that it's just a question of tying up our information with what the police know. Give it to your solicitor and ask him to seek an adjournment for as long a period as possible. While ever there's a possibility that you can pay the money, there's a good chance of holding the court at bay.'

'Thanks,' she said. 'On the subject of Owen – I've had Mariella on the phone not long since, calling me a slag.'

'Isn't that one her terms of endearment?'

This brought a smile to her lips. 'For some reason she objects to Owen living here.'

'Do *you* object to Owen living here?' asked Sam, bluntly. Her eyebrows enquired as to why he was asking this question. 'He's worried,' Sam explained. 'Worried he might have been too er ... too presumptuous.'

'Too presumptuous?' repeated Eileen. 'Well, he did get a bit sincere last night. He's a good man, but he doesn't come without a reputation. I had his previous girlfriend on the phone a few days ago, giving me advice I didn't need.'

'Ah, Postwoman Pat.'

Eileen gave a grin. 'I knew her name and that she ran a post office ... thanks.' She took a cigar-

254

ette that Sam offered her. He put one in his own mouth and lit the two. 'But I'm not ready for a serious relationship.' She tapped her heart. 'Ron's still very much in here, despite all the grief he's giving me. I like having Owen live with me. He makes me feel safe and he's good company. We also satisfy each other's needs.'

'They don't go away forever when someone dies.'

She looked at him, wondering how he knew, but chose not to ask. 'If you're acting as his emissary you can tell him I want him back, but tell him not to be so bloody serious.'

'That'd be like telling Mariella not to be so bad tempered.' He snapped his fingers. 'I know what I was going to ask you – would you mind if I went through Ron's private paper's – if he has any?'

'Such as...?'

'Such as anything. From his birth certificate down to his gas bills. Business letters, private letters, anything.'

She gave a slight smile. 'Ah, this will be your ulterior motive for coming to see me.'

'What?'

'Owen tells me you always have an ulterior motive.'

'He does have a cynical side to him.'

'Don't worry, I'll go along with your ulterior motive. It sounds as though it might benefit me in the long run.'

Sam went back to his office to see Sally before she went home – to make sure she was okay. There was no reason why she shouldn't be okay but he needed to be sure. There was a guilt hanging around his shoulders that he couldn't shake off. He kissed her on the cheek and sat down in his chair.

'Well?' she said. 'Anything you want me to do – people to ring, bills to pay?'

'Ah, glad you reminded me.' He took Bill Timmis's bill from his pocket and opened it. His eyes widened. 'Wow! Four thousand seven hundred quid!'

'What for?'

'Four radiators at Morrell's club.'

'Plus a few items he hasn't mentioned. How are we going to put that through the books?'

'Not sure,' said Sam. He rubbed the back of his neck as he gave the bill some thought. 'We'll have to pay him out of Carew and Sons and sort it out later.'

'Alec won't be pleased,' she said. 'It might present a cash-flow problem.'

'Are things that tight?'

'You can well afford it in the long term, but you're waiting for a couple of overdue stage payments. I'm having to do a juggling act with money at the moment.'

'Alec never mentioned it. I was working on site all last week.'

'He doesn't like you to think he can't handle things. The payments were due the week you and I were in hospital. Alec was supposed to handle all the business affairs, but he didn't.'

'He runs the sites like clockwork,' said Sam.

'He's pretty good at the business as well. But he's useless at chasing money up.'

'I assume it's Barraclough's Mill and the Dalby Parade job?'

'Correct.'

'Dig me the contracts out, would you?'

He rang the Dalby Parade Developers first. 'Mr Evershed? Sam Carew – Carew and Sons ... fine, thank you. Mr Evershed, this is just a courtesy call to let you know I'm pulling our men off your site. You see this other job's cropped up that I'd be an idiot to turn down. It'll only take about a month or so and, well, we have to go where the money is. We'll be back on your site five weeks tops...What?... Actually I think you'll find it's *you* who are in breach of the contract, Mr Evershed by being late with your payments, there's a stage payment one month overdue, and another due yesterday that we haven't received. If you have a cash flow problem it wouldn't make any sense for us to get in any deeper... Oh, I see ... tomorrow it is then. Can you arrange a bank transfer straight into our account?'

After a few farewell platitudes Sam put the phone down. 'Job done,' he said to Sally. 'Rule number one in building. When you're good at your work you've got the upper hand. A crap builder gets crap treatment. That man's scared to death we'll walk off the job. The money should be in our bank tomorrow. Do you think you can do the same with the Barraclough's Mill job?'

'Same story?'

'I've got one or two others up my sleeve, but that'll stand another airing.'

Chapter Twenty-Three

The picture on the laptop was amazingly clear. Sam could move from one web cam to another with the press of a key or he could have both pictures running on a split screen. He was sitting in his Range Rover in the Pear Tree car park just a hundred yards from The Queen Of Clubs. Morrell was sitting at his desk, unaware of his every move being watched.

Sam stubbed a cigarette butt out in his ashtray and took out the DVD that had been recording the last six hours, during some of the time he had been in the pub playing darts. He put in another disk. Sally would be picking him up at midnight and he'd leave the machine recording events until Morrell left the club. He could run them through at his leisure on fast forward until he saw or heard something interesting. It was boring work but it could well be worth it in the end. Worth it in two ways. A hundred grand from Eileen Crusher and satisfaction that he'd got back at Milo Morrell. Sam hated unfinished business.

He watched it for quarter of an hour and was just about to go back in the pub for a last pint when both he and Morrell heard a knock on the office door. Morrell called out, 'Come in.'

Sam's eyes widened when Smithy was pushed into the room, followed by a huge black man who would have dwarfed even Ferris. There was blood on Smithy's face and he looked terrified. Morrell got up from his chair, walked across the room and punched the young builder, viciously, in the stomach, causing him to double up in pain. Sam grimaced in sympathy. He could almost feel the blow himself.

'I expect loyalty from my employees,' Morrell said, evenly. 'Do you know the meaning of the word, Paul?'

Smithy grunted and nodded through his pain and tried to straighten up. Morrell signalled the thug with a slight wave of his hand. A heavy fist hit Smithy in the side of his head, knocking him to the floor.

'What were you doing at Carew's office?' There was menace now in Morrell's voice. 'I can't let people get away with consorting with the enemy. That bastard's trying to get me locked up. Are you in cahoots with him, you piece of shit?' Morrell nodded to the black man, who kicked Smithy in the ribs hard enough to break them. Sam was dialling 999.

'Emergency, which service please?'

'Police.'

'Putting you through.'

'Unsworth police.'

Both the thug and Morrell were laying into to Smithy now. Sam got out of the car. He spoke as he ran. 'There's a murder going on at the Queen of Clubs. Milo Morrell and one of his gorillas is beating up a man called Smith.'

'Who's calling?'

'Sam Carew. Tell Bowman. He'll know it's kosher.'

Sam put the phone back in his pocket and ran around to the front door of the club where he was stopped by a large bouncer in an evening suit.

'I need to get in,' pleaded Sam. 'There's a murder going on in there.'

'I know who you are, pal,' sneered the bouncer. 'There'll be murder goin' on out here if yer don't fuck off.' He pushed Sam away with such force that he fell, backwards, to the pavement. He got to his feet and ran around the back of the club where he knew there was a fire escape. Morrell's office was on the first floor and the fire door only opened from the inside. He grabbed the fire escape rails and kicked at a window. Then he leaned across, undid the catch, slid it open and climbed inside. His mobile phone rang. It was Bowman.

'Carew? What's all this about?'

Sam kept his voice to a whisper. 'There's no time for this. Smithy's being murdered in Morrell's office in the Queen of Clubs. Get some men down here NOW!' Bowman wanted to talk more, but Sam turned his phone off. Smithy was still taking a beating in the next room. Sam switched on the light and looked round for a weapon. Nothing obvious, just a table and a few heavy looking wooden chairs. He picked one up, worked out the best way of using it, and took it with him out into the corridor. Outside Morrell's office he took a deep breath, then kicked open the door. No sign of Morrell. Just the black thug and Smithy, who was on the floor in a pool of blood, worryingly silent. The thug turned to face

Sam and thrust his arms forwards, wrestler style and began to circle the room as Sam threatened him with the chair. With a casual sweep of one hand the thug knocked the chair away. Sam went forward and got in a few straight lefts before the black man wrapped his arms around him and began to squeeze, with a big grin on his face.

'This is what they call the last waltz,' he sniggered. 'It'll be your last fuckin' waltz, Carew.'

Sam hated how everyone seemed to know who he was. Having a well known face was a draw-back in his business. But right now it wasn't the biggest drawback.

'I've rung the police,' gasped, trying to pull himself clear.

The thug's face twitched in anger. He squeezed harder, as if trying to get the job done before the police arrived. Sam felt his already delicate ribs beginning to crack and it crossed his mind that mentioning the police might have been a bad idea. The thug adjusted his position so that he could finish the job with one almighty squeeze. For a split second it gave Sam the space he needed to draw his head back and deliver an eye-watering head-butt to the thug's nose. The crushing arms relaxed. Sam took a step back and kicked hard at the black man's crotch, sending him to his knees in agony.

Smithy lay, motionless on the floor. Sam knelt beside him and felt his neck for a pulse. None. He turned the young builder face up and attempted CPR. Two breaths into the mouth then fifteen strong presses on the chest between the nipples, one hand on top of the other. Stop to listen for signs of breathing, then repeat. Time and time again. He'd once brought a half-drowned man back to life by doing this. But not Smithy.

After five futile minutes Sam sat back on his haunches. 'Oh, Jesus, Smithy!' he murmured. 'What the hell have I done to you?'

'That's what I'd like to know.'

Sam turned round and looked up at Bowman. Behind the inspector was Morrell, with a concerned look on his face. He rushed past Bowman and pushed Sam to one side as he leaned over Smithy. Then he hit Sam full in the face.

'You bastard, Carew. If you had to take it out on someone why not pick on me instead of one of my men!'

'What?'

Sam rubbed his bruised cheek and looked from Morrell to Bowman. 'Come on, Inspector. You don't think I did this.'

Bowman said nothing, but knelt beside Smithy and checked for signs of life, concluding with, 'This man's dead'. He then looked at Sam. 'What I know is what I see. And what I see is you leaning over the body of a dead man.'

He looked at Sam's hands, grazed from the blows he'd landed on the thug, and at the bruise on his forehead where he delivered the life saving head butt. Sam looked around for the thug but there was no sign of him.

'There was a man in here.' He glared at Morrell. 'One of his men. A big black feller. They did this to Smithy.'

'I haven't been in here all evening, Inspector,' said Morrell. 'Nor has any of my men – apart from young Paul, who I'd sent up to check on the new heating system that's been playing up.'

Sam was about to blurt out how he'd recorded the murder on DVD, but thought better of it. Owen walked into the room behind Bowman.

'Smithy was a good pal of mine,' Sam said to Bowman. 'If you don't believe me ask your own officer.' Then to Owen he said, 'Smithy's dead, Owen. Morrell and one of his gorilla's killed him.'

'He's lying!' snorted Morrell. He's the one with blood all over him. He's the one you caught red-handed.'

Bowman looked at Sam with some distaste. 'I've no reason not to believe you and the victim weren't friends,' he said, sourly. 'But friends fall out and I know you to be a hothead. I can also smell alcohol on your breath.' He turned to Morrell. 'I'd keep your mouth shut if I were you, Morrell. Your word counts for nothing with me.' Then to Owen he said, 'DC Price, read Mr Carew his rights. I want him arrested and brought down to the station for questioning.'

Sam let Owen read him his rights then he whispered in the Welshman's ear. 'It's all on DVD. The laptop's in my car in the Pear Tree car park. Tell Sally to record everything that goes on after we've left, then bring it down to the station.'

He knew he'd got Morrell for murdering Smithy but, in doing so, had he blown his chances of proving that he'd also had Ron Crusher murdered? Recording any conversation that went on after tonight's drama might be Sam's only hope. With a bit of luck, before the night was out, Morrell might convict himself of two murders.

One of which would earn Sam a hundred grand. He was desperately sad for what had happened, but Smithy wouldn't want sentiment getting in the way of Morrell getting his just desserts.

It was turned five o'clock the following morning when Sam heard his cell being unlocked. He rolled off his bed on which he'd had no sleep. Sally had obviously turned up with the incriminating recording. But would it show Morrell owning up to the killing of Ron Crusher? It was the only question on his mind when he saw Owen standing there, with a solemn look on his face. It obviously hadn't worked. He'd allowed himself to be arrested and locked up for nothing. Still, they'd be able to arrest Morrell for Smithy's murder. Maybe Morrell would feel it a wise move to have Ron's killing taken into consideration when it came to sentencing.

'Your car's been stolen,' said Owen. DS Janet Seager was with him.

'Oh, no – you've got to be kidding!'

'Sorry, boyo. I went with Sally to pick it up and it wasn't there. We've had a good look round. I've even reported it missing on your behalf, but we've had no luck so far.'

Sam sat back down on the bed and rubbed the back of his neck. 'Jesus, Owen! I'm in deep trouble if we don't find that laptop.'

'I know that, boyo.'

'Have you mentioned it to Bowman?'

'Owen mentioned it to me,' said Janet. 'I'll be telling Bowman when he comes back on shift. You've had us doing overtime, Sam.'

'Thanks.'

'Unfortunately it's thanks for nothing,' said Janet. 'Why the hell did you go in like that – trying to do our job for us?'

Sam shrugged. 'There wasn't any time to wait. They'd already started on Smithy. I thought I might just get to him in time.'

'Bowman won't be on your side,' said Janet. 'If the CPS recommend prosecution I can see him opposing bail. This, on top of you shooting Ferris, is getting a bit much.'

'Well, I can prove the existence of the webcams,' said Sam. 'Ask Billy Timmis to link them up with another laptop.'

Janet thought about the legal implications. 'Hmm, I don't see why we can't do that,' she concluded.

Sam tried to collect his thoughts. 'Surely forensic will show that it wasn't me who killed Smithy.' He looked at his grazed fists, as did Owen.

'The other feller never turned up,' Owen said. 'The feller you reckoned beat Smithy up. No sign of him. Morrell says there was no one else in the room but you and Smithy.'

'Reckoned?' said Sam. 'How do you mean, reckoned? Don't you believe me?'

'As a matter of fact I do, see. But it's not what I believe that counts.'

'We both believe you, Sam,' said Janet. 'Which means we have to find this other man. What did he look like?'

'He was big,' remembered Sam. 'Bigger than Ferris.' He tried to picture the man who had tried to crush the life out of him. 'Very tall, taller than

265

me. About fortyish... Jesus, what did he look like?' Sam closed his eyes and tried to picture the man. 'Short hair – close-cropped ... and he had tattoos on his neck. No idea what. Some design or other. Definitely more than one. Big rough bugger. Six three, eighteen, twenty stone. He tried to crush me to death but I managed to nut him and kick him in the goolies.'

Owen was writing it all down. 'So, we're looking for a big black man with very sore goolies. Might your kick in the goolies have needed hospital treatment? You do tend to summon up unusual strength when you're in a tight corner.'

'It's possible,' conceded Sam.

'At least he's got some goolies left,' said Owen, remembering Ferris. Sam made no comment but thought the remark was in bad taste considering the circumstances.

'Have Smithy's relatives been told?'

Janet shook here head. 'Not yet. I'm going to see his parents as soon as I've finished here.'

Sam looked at them both. 'You will tell them you don't believe I had anything to do with it?'

'It'll probably get us into trouble,' said Janet. 'They'll start asking Bowman all sorts of questions he doesn't want to hear.'

'But you'll do it?'

Janet looked at Owen and spoke for both of them. 'We will.'

'Thanks for that,' said Sam. 'Look, the most important thing is to find my lap-top. Who do you think took the car? It can't have been Morrell. He didn't know what I was up to.'

'He wasn't supposed to know what Smithy was

up to,' Owen pointed out. 'I'm not ruling him out. Although local scallies is my bet.'

'Let's hope so,' said Sam. He sat with his head in his hands for a while as the gravity of his predicament hit him. Then he looked up. 'If we don't find the laptop this might not be an easy one to get out of.'

'We'll do our best for you, Sam,' promised Janet, 'but I'm not sure you deserve it. You're a walking disaster at times.'

'Are you blaming me for Smithy's death?'

'No,' she said, quickly. 'That's not what I meant.'

'Maybe it's enough that I blame myself,' said Sam.

After they had left, and the cell door had clunked shut behind them, he began to wonder why the hell he'd allowed himself to get into this predicament. All this and he was no nearer proving that Ron Crusher hadn't topped himself. And what if he *had* committed suicide. There had been plenty of witnesses, including two coppers.

Marjorie Mutch, a cleaner at Ridings House, presented herself at the counter of the West Yorkshire Police in Unsworth. 'I want ter report seeing a suicide,' she told the duty sergeant.

'A suicide? When did this happen?'

'Last summer. A feller called Crusher chucked himself off a building. It was in the papers. It's just that I read in the *Yorkshire Post* that some people think it might not have been suicide. They reckon he might have been pushed. But I'm here ter tell yer he wasn't pushed, he jumped. I were on the same roof having a smoke. I saw it all.'

The sergeant took her into an interview room to make statement about a death that had already been written off as a suicide, witnessed by many, including two of his officers. However she was right about the newspaper article which, in effect, said the police had got it wrong. Her statement would do no harm at all.

She told of how she hadn't come forward at the time because she wasn't supposed to be on the roof, only where else could she go for a smoke? She was only a cleaner and didn't get paid enough to be one of them snobby non-smokers. It was her only enjoyment.

'So, you actually saw him jump?'

'I did, clear as day. He were standin' right on the edge when I got up there. Next thing I knew he'd gone. Jumped. Everybody below were screamin' blue murder. I just buggered off before I got into trouble. Shock o' my life I can tell yer. Anyroad, I feel better now I've told yer. They can sack me if they like. If they do I get unfair dismissal accordin' ter me husband, so why should I care?'

'Thank you very much, Mrs Mutch. There was a bit of doubt creeping in. With your statement we can put it all to bed. I imagine our detective inspector will be pleased.'

'Put it ter bed, is that what yer call it?' she cackled. 'I must tell me husband that one. He thinks yer all twats. Mind you, he's a bit of a twat hisself.'

Bowman had insisted that Sam was given no

favours, with him being an ex-cop. He was non-committal when Janet asked him if he believed Sam was guilty.

'The evidence says he is. Two men alone in a room. One of them ends up beaten to death. The other man an ex-copper who is known to be handy with his fists. The CPS says there's enough evidence to prosecute.'

'What about the cameras in Morrell's club?'

'You didn't tell me about any cameras in Morrell's club.'

'Didn't I? Right.'

'Nor do I want you to tell me, unless they turn up something useful. If the cameras cause a problem it's your arse that's on the line, not mine. Are we clear about that?'

'Perfectly,' said Janet, not knowing whether to thank him or not.

Chapter Twenty-Four

Being an ex-cop in jail was going to be no picnic. Sam found that out in the holding cell as he waited to be called to reception to be given his prison kit.

There were eighteen men in the cell, all on remand. The one standing next to Sam asked him, 'Are you the copper in for murder?'

'I'm a bricklayer,' said Sam. 'Who says I'm a copper?'

'He did.' The man nodded towards a large prison officer standing outside the cell door.

'Well I'm not a copper I'm a bricklayer.'

'Carew?' called out the PO, opening the door.

'That's me,' said Sam. 'Carew the bricklayer.'

'You takin' the piss, Carew? When you speak ter me you address me properly. You say, "Yes, Mr Gratton".'

Sam said nothing as he stepped out of the cell. He felt a heavy blow in his back that propelled him towards the reception desk. The PO behind the desk gave him a form with a number on it.

'From now on you're 794002,' he said. 'Empty your pockets and take off your watch and any jewellery.'

Dumbly, Sam did as he was told. He was given a pillow case in which he put his prison issue kit: a tracksuit bottom, three T-shirts, three pairs of socks, a pair of cheap trainers, two bed sheets, two blankets, a pillow, a cup, a tin plate and a plastic knife, fork and spoon.

He was then escorted by Gratton and another officer down to the hospital wing where a doctor gave him a very cursory medical check which consisted of:

'Are you a practising homosexual?'

'No.'

'Do you take drugs?'

'No.'

'Do you have a medical condition that requires medication?'

'No.'

'I'm pronouncing you A1. Change into your prison issue and leave your clothes here. They'll be returned to you on your release. During your time on remand you'll be placed on a ward.'

'A ward, what about a cell?'

'You're on a capital charge. We need to keep an eye on you.'

'I'm not going to top myself, if that's what you think,' said Sam.

'Please don't argue with me.'

'You heard the doctor,' snapped Gratton. 'Shut yer mouth and get changed!'

He was taken to what looked like an ordinary hospital ward containing twenty beds. Half were occupied by men reading, or talking to each other or just staring, blankly into space. Other men mooched around, in some sort of a daze. Gratton, who turned out to be a ward PO, walked up to one of the beds.

'This is your bed, Carew. Keep it clean and tidy. Piss the bed, yer get three days segregation.

271

Shit the bed, yer get four days segregation. Wank in bed, yer get five days segregation. Climb into another man's bed, yer get one month in segregation. Do you understand, Carew?'

Sam nodded, although he couldn't stand this ignorant, arrogant idiot.

'I said, do you understand?'

'Yes,' hissed Sam. 'I'm not bloody deaf!'

Most of the inmates were now looking at this newcomer, who was talking back to Gratton.

'I don't think anyone else in here's deaf, either, yer piece o' shit!' snarled Gratton. 'Just because yer used ter be in the police doesn't get you any favours in here. I've been twenty five years in this job and I know better than ter do any favours.'

Sam saw no point in denying anything. Gratton was telling the truth and in prison a man's past had a way of coming out. He knew there were many men in the prison system whom he'd put there – quite a few in this very prison. That should be fun, he thought. How the hell was he going to get out of this? As Janet had forecast, Bowman had successfully opposed bail. First job would be to contact his solicitor to get him another bail hearing. 'When can I use the telephone?' he asked Gratton.

'When yer issued with a phone card.'

'When will that be?'

'Given yer behaviour, never. Make yer fucking bed, Carew, and lie on it.'

Half an hour later Sam was lying on his bed, alone with his thoughts for the first time since Smithy had been murdered. Whatever troubles Sam had, they were nothing compared to poor

Smithy's. Smithy was dead, and he would be alive were it not for him helping Sam Carew – the walking disaster area. Sally seriously assaulted and Smithy dead, all because they had helped him. And they weren't the only ones. His lovely Kathy had tried to help him and she had died. Last year a beautiful young prostitute had been murdered because of him. If he got out of this mess he'd stick to building. It wasn't fair on those around him. Someone called out.

'Is that right, yer used ter be a filth?'

'What?'

'Were yer a copper?'

The low buzz of conversation on the ward stopped, as if turned off by a switch. Sam knew that to appear weak at this point would do him no favours in the future. He put down the paper and walked over to the questioner.

'What's it got to do with you?' he asked, with as much artificial belligerence as he could muster.

The man backed down, as most men would when faced with such anger. This act had served Sam well in the past. He might have to use it a lot while he was in here. He might have to back it up as well.

There was a dog-eared library book in his locker, *A Stone For Danny Fisher*, which presumably hadn't been returned by the bed's previous occupant. Sam sat in his chair and began to read it. He became conscious of the man in the next bed looking at him. Sam glanced up. The man gave a nervous smile. He wore a short, greying beard and glasses.

'Evening,' said Sam as pleasantly as he could,

273

'Sam Carew. I'm in for a murder I didn't do.' He felt he had to establish his credentials right from the start.

'Likewise,' said the man. 'I killed my wife, but it wasn't murder.'

Sam made no comment. The man offered no explanation, he just said, 'It looks like that new screw's got it in for you, Sam Carew.'

'What new screw?'

'Gratton. He only came on to the ward this morning, I've never seen him before and I've been here three months. I heard him talking. By the sound of it he got himself transferred from one of the wings. He knew you were coming.'

'Did he now?' said Sam, puzzled.

At eight o'clock that night, a ward orderly came round with the dispensary trolley. He was accompanied by Gratton, who was evidently doing a double shift to pick up the overtime. The orderly took two tablets from a bottle and handed them to Sam, along with a small beaker of water.

'What are these?'

'They'll help you sleep.'

'They'll sedate me, you mean,' said Sam. 'I don't need the chemical cosh, thanks very much.'

'We're not askin' yer, Carew,' growled Gratton, 'we're tellin' yer. Get these down yer gob and don't give us any trouble.'

'You force that stuff down my throat and it's assault,' snapped Sam. 'Maybe I can't do much about it while I'm in here but I sure as hell can kick up a fuss when I get out, which won't be long.'

Gratton sneered at him. 'Now where have I

heard that before? Do yer know, we haven't got one guilty man on this fuckin' wing.'

'You've got at least one,' retorted Sam, 'and I'm looking at him. Just do your job and leave me alone.'

'Oh, I'll leave you alone all right, Carew. Think yer a cut above the others do yer?'

'I'm a cut above you, that's all.'

Gratton raised his voice so that every inmate on the ward could hear. 'Did yer hear that, lads? This is Sam Carew an ex-copper who thinks he's better than all you fuckin' scum.'

There was no instant reaction, but Sam knew the damage had been done.

'I'll check with the doctor,' said Gratton. 'See if he thinks yer need summat ter settle yer down.'

The lights had gone out and Sam was dozing when two pairs of hands grabbed him from his bed and dragged him along a corridor to a cell where he was forcibly held down as a third PO injected him with a syringe. He was asleep before they got him back to his bed.

The effects on him were so severe that he struggled to wake up the following morning. An officer was shouting in his face, telling him to get of bed and get himself to the showers if he wanted any breakfast.

He was in a daze until the following afternoon. His head didn't clear until he was allowed outside for exercise. Mostly the men stood in groups, smoking and talking and laughing. On seeing him the laughter turned to scowls and muttered curses. One man detached himself from the nearest group and strolled in Sam's direction. As he

275

passed by he jabbed an elbow, viciously, into Sam's side, sending him to his knees in pain. The man walked on without a backward glance. Sam stayed down until the pain had passed. His eyes were shut when someone thumped him at the back of head, sending him sprawling. As he lay on the ground a man's shadow came over him. Sam tensed, expecting another blow. Probably a kicking this time. At some stage he knew he'd have to make a stand – show them he wasn't there to be pushed around, but not today. Today he felt as weak as a kitten. He had no fight in him.

'I think you should know, Gratton's in Milo Morrell's pocket.'

Sam looked up. It was a cultured voice and belonged to a middle-aged man with an intelligent face who spoke without looking down.

'I shared a cell with Morrell when he was in recently. He was treated like royalty – so was I for the week he was in. I must say I found Morrell quite an agreeable chap, but I do read the papers and I gather you and he don't get on.'

'You gather correctly.' Sam sat up and rubbed his sore head, 'And Morrell's a real monster, believe me.'

'Oh, I do believe you. Agreeable chaps don't usually command the respect Mr Morrell did when he was in here. I'm in for embezzlement, by the way. I don't command a morsel of respect, but that doesn't matter. I'm being transferred to a D category prison tomorrow. Goodbye.'

That evening he was due another dose of medication. The animosity of some of the ward inmates towards him was becoming unnerving. Gratton had been talking to them and laughing openly in his direction. Sam was reading his book when he heard the dispensary trolley approach and Gratton's rough tongue enquire: 'What's it ter be, Carew – the pills or the needle?'

'Give me the pills,' said Sam, 'I've only just woken up from the needle.'

'Good lad, I need ter keep an orderly ward.'

Sam had a sleight of hand trick that had served him well in the past, as well as entertaining his pals in the pub. He took the pills in one hand, appeared to transfer them to the other hand and pop them into his mouth. Then he took the water and drank as both Gratton's and the orderly's eyes were fixed on his mouth, making sure he wasn't tricking them. As Sam swallowed he dropped the pills under his bed sheet. Gratton grabbed him by the jaw.

'Not hiding the pills under yer tongue are yer, Carew? Tryin' ter trick us?'

Sam opened his mouth wide for examination and wiggled his tongue around.'

'He's swallowed 'em,' confirmed the orderly and moved on the next bed.

Gratton leaned over Sam and whispered in his ear. 'Sleep well. Some o' the scum in here asked me not ter sedate 'em ternight. They want ter give yer a proper welcome. Trouble is, yer'll be asleep, so yer'll miss it all. Sleep well, and let's hope yer wake up.'

Sam felt an irresistible urge to wipe the smirk off Gratton's face but he knew it wouldn't be wise, even if he could summon up the strength to manage it. He lay awake that night fearing the worst and it wasn't long before his fears were realised. Heavy breathing alerted him to their presence. Two figures were silhouetted against the windows, looming over him. He rolled out of bed away from them. One of them made a grab for him and Sam hit out. There was a grunt, more anger than pain. The second attacker rushed forward, snarling and cursing, his fists windmilling into Sam, knocking him on to the bed of an alleged sex offender who thought he was under attack and leapt out of bed, screaming.

Sam kicked out at his attacker and squared up to what he could see of him in the dim light. He punched the man three times in the face then let go with full bloodied right that drained all his reserves of strength. His assailant went down just as the lights went on. Sam was supporting himself on a table and breathing heavily. Gratton and another officer came rushing down the ward. One man was on Sam's bed nursing a bloodied nose; the second man was on the floor trying to get to his feet. Gratton threw a punch at Sam, who ducked and instinctively swung a weak punch that caught the PO in the eye. Within seconds, prison officers began pouring in from all directions, thumping him and tearing off his T-shirt and shorts. Sam was then dragged, completely naked, along a landing and down a flight of steel stairs to the segregation unit, where he was thrown into a cell and the door slammed on him.

Still dazed by his beating and the speed of events, he lay there for several minutes, then checked his body for injuries, particularly his ribs, which had taken a lot of punishment over the past few months. It was hard to tell the extent of the damage. In Sam's experience, bruises were often as painful as breakages.

He sat up and examined his new home. It measured about ten feet by eight and contained a bed that was bolted to the floor, a table and chair made of cardboard, a sink and a lavatory. He lay on the bed, wishing he still had the tablets. At least he'd have been able to sleep through this nightmare. Maybe tomorrow he'd take them if they were offered.

Ever since Sam's arrest Owen had been more morose than usual. This upset Eileen. Sam was locked up into the bargain. She felt bad about that as well, but nowhere near as bad as Owen felt. She was quite taken with this sad Welshman; which was why she decided throw caution to the winds and do what she could to help Sam. They were in bed when she came up with the idea.

'This laptop computer thing – will it get Sam out of jail if you find it?'

'Probably,' muttered Owen, more to his pillow than to Eileen.

'And where's it likely to be?'

'Now there's a question, isn't it?' Owen turned over and looked up at the ceiling as he sorted out the events in his mind. 'Well, his car was found burned out in Leeds, so I reckon that's where the scallies came from. Car stolen in Unsworth, found in Leeds. Which division is responsible? Both and neither, which means apathy. That's what the scallies bank on. They'll most likely hang

279

on to the laptop for a couple of weeks then try and flog it.'

'Whereabouts in Leeds was the car found?'

'Temple Newsam golf course. Seventeenth fairway. Common occurrence around that neck of the woods. I believe they have a local rule that you get a free drop when your ball lands near a burned-out vehicle. Very resourceful people, golfers. Might take it up myself one day.'

'I know a few people in Temple Newsam,' said Eileen. 'Maybe I can help.'

'Sam needs all the help he can get,' said Owen. 'Ex-coppers have a hard time in jail.'

Eileen ran her hand down his body. 'Would you like me to give you a hard time, Mr Policeman?'

Chapter Twenty-Five

At seven the next morning Sam was awakened from a restless sleep by his cell door rattling open.

'Breakfast's on the hotplate,' called out an officer.

'I need my clothes,' Sam told him. It was warm enough, but he wanted his dignity. He ached all over.

The PO eyed Sam's bruising with something bordering on compassion. 'I'll bring them down while you eat,' he said. 'What happened to you?'

Sam was about to tell him, to maybe enlist his sympathy, but he realised the futility of it. 'I fell out of bed,' he said. 'Woke up in this cell. What's for breakfast?'

'I'll give you three guesses.'

Sam wrapped the bed-sheet around his waist and walked out of his cell over to the hotplate. He opened one of the doors. 'Great, I hate porridge.'

The officer gave a grin and opened another door. 'There's scrambled eggs and toast in here.' He handed Sam a cloth. 'You'd better use this, it's hot. My name's Elliot by the way.'

'But I call you *Mr* Elliot, I suppose.'

'You suppose right.'

Using the cloth, Sam took out the plate and picked up a tin cup of tea. As he was about to go back in his cell he turned to the officer who was in his mid-twenties and wore a single badge on his epaulette. This made him a Senior PO, a rank above Gratton, who looked to be in his late forties.

'You're a human being, Mr Elliot – are there any more like you in here?'

The PO laughed and followed him to the door. 'I've read about you in the papers – Mad Carew, isn't it?'

Sam sat down and ate, hungrily. He hadn't eaten much the day before, due to his heavy sedation. 'I *must* be mad,' he said, miserably, 'to get myself into this damned fix. I'm supposed to have beaten a pal of mine to death. Do I look like someone who beats his pals to death?'

Elliot had no answer. 'I'll get your clothes,' he said. 'You get an hour's exercise each day at one o'clock. There'll be three others taking exercise at the same time. You don't talk to them or try and communicate in any way or you'll all be brought back inside.'

'What are they in for?'

'All convicted murderers. One's a very nasty rapist as well.'

'What, and I'm denied the pleasure of talking to them?'

'You have a sense of humour. It's a great asset in here.'

'How long am I in here for?'

'That's up to the wing governor. You're due to attend a disciplinary hearing in his office at ten o'clock tomorrow morning. In the meantime you're staying in here out of harm's way.'

'Everyone's so thoughtful.'

'You're going to be charged with three counts of assault. I'll bring your charge sheet down to you later so you can work out what to say in your defence. You're allowed to bring in witnesses to speak up for you.'

'Lucky me. I suppose there's a queue of eager witnesses just waiting to help me.'

'I know one thing,' said Elliot. 'You're better off in here than up on the ward, with you being an ex-copper.'

'I'd worked that one out for myself. Am I allowed any creature comforts – telly, radio?'

'Six library books a week and writing materials.'

'What about a phone card?'

'I'll arrange for you to make a couple of phone calls.'

'Thanks.'

It was something. He felt totally cut off from the outside world. Someone needed to know his predicament. What they were doing to him in here. Two calls. One should be to the solicitor. Sod that – he'd ring Sally and Owen. They'd pester the solicitor, day in day out. He couldn't do that from in here.

Sally fervently promised to move mountains to get him out. Owen mentioned something about Eileen saying she might be able to find the laptop, but Owen didn't know how, so it was of no real comfort to Sam.

'Have a word with Bowman and persuade him not to oppose my bail hearing,' Sam pleaded. 'He knows full well I didn't do it. How are you doing tracking down the gorilla who actually did kill Smithy?'

He spoke loud enough for listening prison officers to hear. He wanted them to know the injustice he was suffering at their hands. Owen promised to have a word with the detective inspector, but there had been no sightings of the real murderer.

Later that day Sam measured out the cage with his feet; there was little else to do during his exercise hour. It was fifteen feet by sixteen, one of eight cages. Three other inmates were outside in the same cold air – an empty cage between each one of them, to prevent fraternising. Sam doubted if he could ever summon up any fraternal feelings for any of them. He had recognised one of the prisoners from the media publicity he had received on being found guilty of raping and murdering a prostitute. He had glued her eyes and mouth shut with superglue and had raped her continually until she eventually died – and for some time after that, apparently. In the eyes of the law Sam was down at this man's level – being treated the same.

The bruises caused by his beating the night before were beginning to get sore. After ten minutes he'd had enough exercise and went back inside. Elliot was waiting for him.

'I need to see a doctor,' Sam said. 'I think your mates broke my ribs last night. That bastard Gratton was the worst. He's got it in for me.'

'He rang in sick today,' said Elliot.

'Milo Morrell's paying him wages to give me grief,' Sam told him. 'That's why he got himself transferred to my ward the day I arrived.'

'I remember Morrell,' said Elliot, who didn't seem surprised by Sam's revelation. 'He seemed a decent enough sort.'

'I'm told Saddam Hussein can be quite pleasant when it suits him.'

'Gratton's charging you with causing him physical and mental injury.'

'I only caught him a powder puff blow,' Sam said. 'He went down like a sack of spuds.'

'Knowing Gratton,' said Elliot, 'he'll milk this and be off for weeks. He moonlights as a painter and decorator – wouldn't surprise me if he's slapping on some wallpaper right now, silly sod. If he got found out claiming sick leave and doing another job he'd be booted out of the service and lose his pension.'

'Would he now?' remarked Sam.

'I didn't tell you this, though.'

'No – what's this wing governor like?'

'Mr McNichol? Normally he'll take his officer's side against a prisoner any day of the week. His only purpose in here is to have GOD on his wing.'

'What – is he religious or something?'

Elliot grinned. 'It stands for Good Order and Discipline – to be maintained at all costs. And it often comes at a cost – usually to the prisoners. The officers can go on strike, the inmates can't.'

'Which is why the screws get away with mistreating prisoners.'

Elliot shrugged. 'I suppose McNichol likes to make his job as easy as possible. Most of the staff are the same. It's human nature.'

'Are you telling me that Gratton's human?'

Elliot smiled. 'No comment. Mind you, if any of us is actually proved to be doing wrong, McNichol will come down like a ton of bricks. He got a principal PO kicked out last year for bringing alcohol into the prison and giving it to one of our big time villains in exchange for a parcel of cash being dropped through the officer's letterbox. It happens in all prisons – perk of the job. Most wing governors would've turned a blind eye or just given him a warning.'

'But not McNichol?'

'No, he's an oddball. Cross him and he's goes ballistic. Lives on his own. Just moved into a big new house in the next street to me.'

'Sounds as if I'm in for another spot of rough justice.'

'I shouldn't worry about it,' Elliot said. 'Whatever punishment he gives you will be deferred until after your trial. If you're found not guilty it'll count for nothing.'

'If,' muttered Sam, who was rapidly losing faith in British justice.

'Just don't try and be clever in there,' advised the officer. 'You're up against the system and it'll beat you in the end.'

The wing governor looked up from Sam's file. Sitting beside him was a Principal PO taking notes. There was no hint of sympathy on either face, despite the fact that Sam was badly bruised.

'You've created a poor first impression, Carew. Three charges of assault. One of my officers off sick indefinitely.'

'I assume you're talking about Gratton.'

'Mr Gratton,' corrected McNichol, sharply.

'Look, I hardly touched him,' Sam said. 'He's no more sick than you are. Whereas I've got this to show for it all.' He lifted up his T-shirt and displayed the livid bruising to his upper body.'

A vein in McNichol's neck began to twitch. He fixed Sam with a glassy stare. 'The only thing I know is that you're a threat to the good order and discipline of this prison.'

'It's Gratton who's the threat,' protested Sam. 'He caused all this. He told everyone on the ward that I was an ex-copper who thought all the other prisoners were scum. Because of him I've been attacked both outside and in my bed.'

'I will not have you impugn the integrity of one of my officers,' snapped McNichol, angrily. 'Mr Gratton says you attacked him when he came to the aid of the two inmates you were assaulting.'

'He's lying,' said Sam, wearily. 'He attacked me. I was defending myself. He attacked me because he's being paid wages by Milo Morrell who's got a big grievance against me.' It had already occurred to Sam that Gratton might not be the only one in Morrell's pocket. Villains liked to employ higher ranking officers as well. Such as wing governors.

'How do you know that?' enquired McNichol.

Sam noticed that the governor didn't have to ask who Milo Morrell was.

'It seems to be common knowledge inside this place.'

'Common knowledge is it? Well, it's not common knowledge to me.'

Sam said nothing, there was no point. He was trying to be clever, against PO Elliot's advice. You can't beat the system. McNichol clenched his fist, then sat back and tried to regain his composure. He wasn't used to inmates standing up to him. Most of them knew better.

'Carew,' he said, 'if one of my officers told me that you'd been riding naked around the landing on a motorbike I would ask you why you weren't wearing a helmet. Do you get my drift, Carew?'

'Yes,' said Sam, miserably.

'This hearing is adjourned,' snapped McNichol. 'Take this prisoner back down to segregation. It will be my recommendation, Carew, that you remain there until your trial.'

March 1984

Zola had been off the game since the day she heard about Derek Fleming's suicide. She signed on with a theatrical agency and picked up work as a television extra and photographic model, plus some lucrative work on TV commercials. It was while working as an extra on *Emmerdale Farm* that she met her husband-to-be, a television sound engineer. He knew nothing of her past and she saw no reason to tell him. That had been a different but necessary world. She had now reverted to her real name – the name on her birth certificate, given to her by the parents she could barely remember; parents who had kept her until she was beyond the ideal adoption age before splitting up and sending her into a children's home.

She had often cursed them for not giving her up for adoption as a baby. The selfish bastards had denied her any chance in life; especially the chance to be brought up by a loving family. But now she had John. He was there now, turning and smiling at her; amazed at how stunning she looked – as were many others. She allowed her smile to dazzle the church. Her beauty was her only valuable asset and she had used it well. John was a good man. A good, Catholic man. She had converted to Catholicism to please him. Baptised and confirmed all in the space of the two years she had known him. She had made her first confession and unloaded all her sins on to a bemused old priest who had given her two Hail Marys and two Our Fathers as a penance for nine solid years of prostitution. Zola had considered this too lenient and had done a dozen of each just to be sure of absolution.

The organist was playing Mendelssohn's 'Wedding March' as she walked down the aisle on the arm of one of John's two brothers. The other brother was the best man. She hadn't even considered tracing her own parents. As she arrived at the end of the aisle her consort moved in front of her, lifted her veil and stepped away. John smiled, adoringly at her. The priest welcomed them and they knelt in prayer. All had been rehearsed. All was going well. They stood up as the priest made the traditional appeal to the congregation:

'Does anyone know of any reason why these two should not be joined together in Holy Matrimony?'

The priest smiled down at the happy couple. He didn't expect any response. A voice called out:

'Zola?'

She instinctively turned round.

'It is you, isn't it?'

Zola said nothing. She couldn't believe this was happening.

'Does our John know you were on the game?'

Had she recognised the voice she'd have known it was Neville, one of John's less devout cousins who had used her services on several occasions in the past.

'Shut up Neville!' hissed Neville's mother, John's aunt.

'I'm only sayin' what I know. And I'm thinkin' our John hasn't a clue by the look of him. She were a prostitute, John,' he called out. 'She used ter call herself Zola Gee.'

'How would you know if she was a prostitute?' called out a female family member.

'That's right. How would you know, Neville?' enquired Neville's mother.

Zola's erstwhile happy heart sank like a lump of lead to the pit of her stomach. John was staring at her with the big question in his eyes. It was a question she couldn't answer. To have denied such an accusation would have required thought, preparation, false indignation and a good deal of acting talent. All she could summon was a look of guilt. For the benefit of those who hadn't heard – or didn't know what was going on – whispered explanations buzzed around the church, amplified by the its natural acoustics, until it seemed deafening to Zola.

She lowered her eyes, now misted over with tears, turned and walked back up the aisle, slowly at first, then quickening her pace as she increasingly wanted to get out from under the hundred reproachful stares she could feel burning into her.

As she passed the baptismal font, in complete silence, apart from her own sobbing, she gathered up the train of her wedding gown and ran from church, and out of John's life.

Denis Doogan had once been a pimp, or a "Pleasure Agent" as he sometimes referred to himself. He was now in his late sixties and lived in solitary retirement in his council house in the Halton Moor area of Leeds. A knock on the door aroused him from his snooze in front of an afternoon television show, *Oprah*.

His caller wasn't instantly recognisable to him. Twenty-five years older now and dressed like school mistress, there wasn't a hint of the sexuality she had once oozed. He looked at her ancient Nissan parked in the street and then at her.

'If it's about me council tax I've already made arrangements,' he said.

'You don't remember me, do you?'

'No, I don't love. Am I supposed ter?'

'I used to be called Zola Gee.'

He remembered the name, if not the face. 'Zola ... bloody hell! Zola, is it really you?'

She nodded her head, contritely, as if making a guilty admission. 'I'm afraid so. Have I changed that much?'

'Well, I'd never have recognised yer, I have ter say that ... but now I come ter study.' He peered at her, almost lasciviously. 'Yeah, it's you all right. I'd have recognised yer anywhere.'

'You still talk out of your arse, Denis.'

He cackled, displaying an assortment of unsavoury teeth. 'Allus did, lass. What do yer call yerself now?'

'Eileen.'

'And what can I do yer for?'

'You can invite me in for a start.'

'Aye, right. Come in, lass. I'm not still in business yer know. Irene, did yer say?'

'Eileen.'

'Eileen – right. I did eighteen months fer pimpin' – did yer know that?'

'I didn't, no.'

'Never did anyone any harm and I got banged up fer eighteen bloody months. Nowadays there's fellers runnin' bloody brothels full of illegals what don't see the light o' bloody day, nor any brass neither and there's bugger all done about 'em. Bastards is what they are. I might have been a pimp but I were good ter me girls. Never took bloody advantage. Twenty five per cent plus rent of room that's all I ever took. There were no back seat screwin' fer my girls.'

She followed him through to the living room. It matched its owner, unlovely and unsavoury. 'I gave it up myself,' she told him, 'over twenty years ago.'

'So, why are yer here?'

Eileen sat down in an imitation leather chair that gave a flatulent squeak under her weight. 'To pick your brains,' she said.

He gave another cackle, louder this time. 'Yer'll need an electric bloody drill ter pick my brains lass, plus a bloody search party. If I'd had any brains I'd have been a plumber.'

She smiled at his joke. 'I'm looking for someone who nicked a car the week before last,' she told him. 'It was left burnt out on Temple Newsam golf course.'

'And yer think I know who nicked it, do yer?'

'You used to know everything that went on round here. Are you telling me you've lost your touch?'

'Nay, lass. I know as much as I ever knew, which is everythin' an' fuck all.'

'What's that supposed to mean?'

'It means I know everything what goes on, but fuck all as far as the coppers are concerned. I reckon yer lookin' fer Lee Bateson.'

'Lee Bateson?'

'Aye, lass. Fifteen years old. Been nickin' cars since he were thirteen. The bloody bobbies can't catch him. Do yer smoke?'

'Yes, I do.'

'Than yer'll be able ter give us a fag. I smoked me last one this mornin'. It's a bugger tryin' ter live off me pension.'

Eileen produced a packet of Benson and Hedges, took one out for herself and gave the packet to him. He removed one and put the packet into his pocket. She decided not to protest.

'Could you take me to him?'

He lit up and held out the lighted match for her to use. 'Not if yer gonna get him into bother, lass. Me life wouldn't be worth livin' round here if it were known I got scallies into bother. They leave me alone because they think I'm one o' them.'

'There was something in that car that I want.'

'What sort of thing?'

'A laptop computer.'

'Know nowt about 'em.'

'Neither do I. Can you take me to him – for old time's sake? I might want to buy it off him.'

293

'I'll take yer to him fer old time's sake and twenty quid.'

'You always had a heart of gold, Denis.'

Lee Bateson seemed small for his age and Eileen wondered how on earth he could see over the steering wheel to drive a car. She let Denis do the talking. They were a few streets away from where her ex-pimp lived. The youth was alone in a house that had newspapers at most windows and a vicious-looking pit bull terrier imprisoned in a tiny kennel beside the back door, upon which Denis had knocked.

'Is yer mam in, lad?'

'No, she's workin'.'

Lee had a mean face and fair hair the same length and texture of the fuzz on a tennis ball. He had several rings in both ears, and a recent black eye – it seemed unwise to ask what sort of work his mother did. Denis got straight to the point. 'D'yer want ter make yerself a few quid, lad?'

The youth shrugged. 'Depends.'

'Good answer,' said Denis. 'Very commendable. Never commit yerself. Allus been my motto. Smart lad. I've heard that said about you. That Lee Bateson's a very smart lad.'

Eileen saw a gleam of smug pride light up the boy's eyes. Had he been a smart lad he'd have known Denis was buttering him up to gain his confidence.

'Yer see, lad, I've heard about this car what were burnt out on Temple Newsam golf course.'

'Nowt ter fuckin' do wi' me,' said Lee, defensively. He had one hand on the door and was

294

about to close it in their faces. Denis took a step inside. 'Never thought for a minute it was, lad. But there were summat inside it that I reckon might have come your way – what with you bein' a smart lad and all that.'

'Yer mean like a laptop?'

'That's exactly what I mean, lad.' Denis turned to Eileen. 'I told yer he were smart.'

'You did,' smiled Eileen. 'Have you got it by any chance, Lee?'

'Might have.'

Denis gave one of his grins. 'Non-committal to the end – I like that in a lad. Now, yer know me, Lee lad. I'm not the law nor nowt ter do wi' the bastards. This lady's willin' ter give yer good money fer that computer, providin' it's still in workin' order.'

'How much?'

'A hundred,' said Eileen.

'Two hundred,' bargained Lee, who sensed it was a seller's market. 'I were gonna keep it fer meself – it's a fuckin' good un.'

'Yer talkin' silly money, lad,' said Denis.

'Did it have a disk in it?' asked Eileen.

Lee nodded. 'There's a DVD – borin'. I watched it fer about five minutes. Some twat sittin' at a desk. Thrill a fuckin' minute ... not.'

'Can you play it to me? I just want to make sure it's the right one.'

The youth shrugged. 'Yer might as well come in.'

There was an incongruity about the interior of the house. Gleaming modern electrical equipment set against general squalor and a vaguely fetid odour. Lee ran upstairs and came down with a laptop computer. He opened it, pressed a few keys and within seconds the interior of Milo Morrell's office came up on the screen.

'Milo Morrell,' exclaimed Denis, 'as I live an' fuckin' breathe!'

'You know him, do you?' said Eileen.

'I've had dealings with him. Cockney bastard. Dangerous man. Are you mixed up with him?'

Eileen looked at Lee, who looked a bit too interested in her answer for her liking. 'Never met him,' she said, taking two hundred pounds from her purse. Owen had funded her for up to five hundred. She gave him the money and took the computer before he could change his mind.

'You drive a hard bargain, young man.'

'You drive a crap car, missis.'

'Smart lad,' said Denis, who wished he'd charged more than twenty pounds for his services.

Bowman looked up from his writing to see who had tapped on his door and entered without his say so. He hated minor insubordinations such as this. It was Janet Seager, that prat Price was with her.

'Excuse me, boss, but DC Price has found evidence that should prove Sam Carew didn't murder Smith.'

'Has he now?' Bowman gave Owen a sour look. 'How come I keep hearing the names Price and Carew spoken in the same breath?'

'Like Holmes and Watson?' ventured Owen, hopefully.

'Like sickness and diarrhoea,' said Bowman.

296

Owen responded with a toothy smile. Bowman growled, 'It had better be good. The CPS are not only charging him with murder but on my advice they're having another look at the Ferris shooting.'

Owen took a video cassette from one of his voluminous pockets and asked, 'Would you mind if I put this in your machine, boss?'

Bowman threw his pen on the desk in exasperation. 'I do hope you're not wasting my time again, Price.'

'It's worth a look, boss,' Janet assured him.

The three of them watched as Morrell and his thug beat Paul Smith to a painful death. They saw Morrell leave through a side door just before Sam entered the office, holding a chair and tackling the black man. A few minutes later Bowman saw himself appear on the screen arresting Sam for a murder he'd tried to prevent. The inspector winced. Owen and Janet could almost feel their boss's deep embarrassment. Owen saw no reason not to add to it.

'I made a couple of tapes from the original DVD and dropped one off at Sam's solicitor,' he said cheerfully. 'I expect you'll be hearing from him.'

Sam was toying with his lunch. Barely a waking minute had gone by without him contemplating his chances of being found guilty of murder. The fact that he was innocent didn't make his acquittal a certainty. There were many innocent people serving out time in Britain's prisons, and Sam didn't want to become one of them. In the 1970s it wasn't unusual for the police to fit up a known villain with a murder they couldn't otherwise solve just to get him off the streets. Sam had heard older officers talk about it, some with guilt, some with relish. Many innocent prisoners had served out their sentences and were out on life licence. He knew of at least two who had died inside and subsequently had their convictions quashed. The stand Sam had made against the wing governor was just his way of trying to balance the injustice meted out to him. Innocent men in jail can become very bolshie, and bolshie prisoners tend not to get early release on parole. If he was convicted, but never admitted to it, he would be classified as IDOM – In Denial Of Murder. Such people are always viewed un-favourably by parole boards. Would he end up admitting to a murder he hadn't committed just to get early release? Or would he find such an admission impossible? Admission Impossible – it sounded like that Tom Cruise film. Robert Brown had found such an admission impossible and had ended up doing twenty five years before his conviction was quashed. Locked up at the age of nineteen after having a confession beaten out of him by the Manchester police, then released after twenty five years of hell, with an apology and a few quid in his pocket.

And now this was happening to Sam. How the hell could he ever admit to such a thing? Jesus! – there was a fair chance he'd be locked up until he was old and useless. He'd miss watching his boys growing into men. He'd miss the odd life he'd made for himself. He'd miss laying bricks, he'd miss Owen, and he'd miss Sally more than he had ever cared to admit to himself. Not for the first time he felt a sickness in the pit of his stomach. He spat out a potato on to his plate, then tried to compose himself.

An hour later when the cell door rattled open his face was grey, his eyes were damp and his hands were shaking.

'You okay?'

Sam shook his head and looked down at the cold food on his plate. He didn't see the broad grin creep across PO Elliot's face.

'Your solicitor's here.'

Sam cleared his throat and tried to hide his distress. 'Right, er, do you know if he's got me a bail hearing?'

'You won't be getting bail, Mr Carew.'

Sam's heart returned to his stomach, then he looked up at Elliot. It was the first time anyone inside had addressed him by his full title.

'What?'

Elliot's grin was still in place. 'You won't need bail.'

'Why not?'

'Because you're a free man, Mr Carew. The charges against you have been dropped.'

A flood of relief thawed out the misery that had been choking him. Sam wiped his eyes with the back of his hand, then he got to his feet and hugged the young officer, who hugged him back.

'When can I go?'

'Right now, mate – you're as free as I am. I'll take you to reception to collect your stuff.'

Chapter Twenty-Six

After he had heaped his profuse thanks on to Eileen he had gone back to his flat, where Sally had spent the night with him; catering to all his urgent needs until dawn broke.

'What was it like inside?' she had asked him.

'I ended up with a room to myself with an en-suite toilet – I've stayed in worse places.'

Sally didn't think he had. The bruises on his body had shocked her and she insisted that he go ahead and charge those responsible with assault. But it wasn't the bruises that troubled Sam, it was the fact that he hadn't been able to fight back. These people had used the system against him and he knew he wouldn't rest until he'd settled the score. He woke up with his mind ticking over with ideas as Sally slept beside him. A plan formed. Sam began to smile. He got out of bed and went to the telephone to ring the jail.

'I'd like to speak to PO Elliot if he's on duty... I'm a relative and it's quite urgent... Thank you.'

When Sally awoke Sam was gone, leaving a note saying, *Take the day off*, *love Sam*. That same afternoon Gratton arrived at a house to give the customer a price for painting the exterior. The man was waiting in the drive.

'Mr Worthington?' said Gratton.

'Yes – Mr Gratton?'

The men shook hands. The customer waved a

hand in the direction of the house which had hardwood windows and doors and a cement rendered wall at the front.

'This is it.'

'Do you want me to supply the paint?' Gratton asked.

'No, I'll supply that. The thing is, I want it doing tomorrow. Just the front, the rest can wait. It's a birthday surprise for my wife.'

'Nice idea,' said Gratton, who had never given his wife a surprise all the time they'd been married. 'What colours?'

'I want the walls done in yellow and the wood-work blue, apart from the door which I want pink.

Gratton frowned, 'Blue, yellow and pink – are yer sure? It sounds a bit vivid.'

The man laughed. 'You haven't met my wife. Blue and yellow are Leeds United's colours, she's a big Leeds United fan, she'll love it.'

'I thought they played in white.'

'They used to play in blue and yellow – which is their away strip. She never wears the home strip. Hates white. She reckons it's too plain. Very colourful woman, my wife.'

'I never known 'em play in pink.'

'No, that's my idea. It's what I call her. Before we got married her name was Pinkney, I called her Pinky, it sort of stuck.'

'You're the boss,' said Gratton. He scratched his chin as he worked out a price. 'I'll be working flat out without a break to get it done in a day. The woodwork'll need a quick-dryin' undercoat if I'm going ter do it all in a day. How does a two hundred sound?'

'A hundred and fifty sounds better ... cash in hand.'

'One seventy five,' said Gratton.

'Okay – one seventy five.' They shook hands again.

'I normally leave early, so I'll probably be gone before you arrive so I'll leave the paint at the back of the garage. I'll be locking the house up, but there's a tap under the kitchen window if you need water.'

'What time will yer be home?'

'Around five, bringing my wife with me. I hope you manage to finish by then.'

'I'll have it done if it kills me,' promised Gratton.

Sam was waiting for Alec when he arrived back on site. 'How did it go?' he asked.

'It went okay... Sam, I only did this because of what they did to you.'

'What they did to me was bad, Alec.'

'I can see that, Sam. But don't start thinking I'm some sort of part time secret bloody agent. I know you – you take advantage. This is the last time.'

'So he fell for it?'

Alec managed a broad grin. 'Only hook, line and sinker.'

The light was fading and Gratton was at the top of his ladder putting the finishing touches to the gable. His work had elicited many uncomplimentary remarks from passing neighbours, but Gratton had been working so hard that he'd been oblivious to them; he'd also been oblivious to the

302

man taking photographs of him at work. The white, cement rendered wall had once matched all the others in the street but now it was an intense yellow. The expensive hardwood door was now bright pink, and the window frames and barge-board a piercing blue. He heard a car pull turn into the drive and he looked at his watch. Half past four, they were early. He didn't turn around, as he wanted to look industrious. He had worked flat out for eight and a half hours and he figured the job was well worth the money he was being been paid. Maybe, if the little wife was pleased, he might get a bonus.

'What the hell are you doing!'

Gratton's brush froze mid-stroke. He turned and looked down at whoever was speaking. Then his whole body froze. McNichol was standing in the drive. The governor's jaw dropped open when he identified the man up the ladder.

'Mr Gratton, is that you?'

Gratton could hardly deny who he was. 'Er, yes, sir.' He climbed, slowly, down the ladder, hoping he'd have an excuse ready by the time he reached the bottom. At that point in time he didn't realise it was McNichol's house. He stepped off the bottom rung with the beginning of an excuse in mind. His boss's face was puce with rage.

'You've ruined my house. Look what you've done to my house?'

'Your house?' said Gratton, his excuse forgotten.

'My house. You've ruined my house. Why have you done this, you twat?'

'But – I didn't know it was your house. I

303

thought it was Mr Worthington's house.'

McNichol had him by the scruff of his neck and was pushing him backwards. Gratton was a good fifty pounds heavier but McNichol's rage made up the deficit.

'You bastard, why have you done this to me?'

'I didn't do anything to you, sir, honest. I was working for Mr Worthington.'

'Worthington? How do you mean, working for Mr Worthington? You work as a prison officer. You mean you've been working while on sick leave. Is that what you're saying?'

'That's exactly what he's saying,' called out Sam. He had brought Sally along. There was another man with him as well. McNichol spun round. At first he didn't recognise Sam. Gratton did.

'Carew,' he growled. 'Why aren't you inside?'

'You haven't been keeping up,' said Sam, cheerfully. 'The charges against me were dropped. I was released two days ago. By the way, you did well getting it finished in a day – don't you think so, Mr McNichol?'

McNichol recognised him now. He let go of Gratton's collar and turned his attention to Sam.

'Have you got anything to do with this?'

'I've got everything to do with this,' Sam admitted. 'I set him up. He's moonlighting while on sick leave. He thinks he's being paid a hundred and seventy-five quid for painting your house.'

'I'll get the police,' screamed the governor. 'You've vandalised my fucking house!'

'Actually, your man Mr Gratton did the vandalising,' Sam pointed out. 'I just organised him. Anyway, the police already know. They won't take any action unless you make an allegation against me.'

'Oh, I'll do that, don't you worry, mister. You'll be back inside before you know it.'

'In that case, Sam will be making far more serious allegations against you,' shouted Sally, angrily, 'for allowing him to be badly beaten and allowing him to be injected with drugs against his will.' Sam had told her the whole story in order to justify what he had planned. For a change, Sally fully approved of his actions.

'Take no notice of her,' snarled Gratton. 'She doesn't know what she's talking about.'

'You keep out of this you brainless shithouse!' screamed McNichol. 'You're out of a job and you can say goodbye to your fucking pension!'

'Yer can't do that!' protested Gratton.

'Oh yes I fucking can!'

'He's right, you know,' confirmed Sam. 'You're taking tax-payers money under false pretences. When it gets in the papers it stops being an internal matter. They won't be able to let you off with just a bollocking. They'll have to throw the book at you, otherwise how will it look?'

'You're a lunatic, Carew!' howled McNichol. 'A complete fucking lunatic!'

Gratton was ashen-faced. 'What papers?' he said. 'How will this get in the papers?'

Ah – I hope you don't mind,' said Sam, to McNichol, 'but I gave the *Unsworth Observer* a bit of a scoop. They're running the whole story – the way I was treated inside. I told them about how Morrell used to pay Gratton wages to give me grief – the lot. They've already photographed Michelangelo here, painting away like a good un – and I let 'em take a few snaps of my bruises.' He inclined his head towards the man standing beside him. 'This is Simon, he's the reporter. He's already interviewed some of your neighbours. I understand the nationals are showing an interest, which is where Gratton's job goes up the spout – and I don't suppose you'll end up smelling of roses either, Mr McNichol.'

'Good afternoon,' said Simon, stepping forward. 'I want to write a fair account of what went on, so if you'd like to give me your side of the sto–'

'My side?' McNichol was quivering with hysteria. He bared his teeth as he spat out the words. 'Oh, you want my side, do you? Well I'll give you my side, mister. My side of the story is that Carew isn't right in his head, he's off his trolley, he's a madman, he's a complete and utter fucking lunatic. That's my side of the story!'

Simon took his quote down, verbatim, in just a few squiggles of shorthand.

'Mr McNichol's right, you know,' added Sally. 'But he's *my* complete and utter fucking lunatic.'

'Sally Grover!' remonstrated Sam. 'I've never heard you use that word before. I wouldn't have brought you here if I'd known you were going to pick up words like that.'

'It wasn't my word, it was his,' said Sally, pointing an accusing finger at a severely distraught McNichol.

'Are you two together?' enquired Simon.

'You could say that,' said Sally

'We're partners,' said Sam.

306

Chapter Twenty-Seven

Owen walked into Sam's office. He stood in the doorway and shook his head. 'Bowman's told me to stay clear of you in case I'm infected with the Carew brain disorder.'

'Bowman's always telling you to stay away from me.'

'Maybe Bowman's not a bad judge. I hope you're not thinking of starting a painting and decorating business. I just drove past the poor man's house. It's like something out of Disneyland.'

'The poor man deserved what he got and a lot more,' said Sam. 'And Gratton wants locking up. I'd press charges if I thought I'd get anywhere. Still, the papers made a meal out of it.'

'I heard on the grapevine,' said Owen, 'that PO Gratton's been suspended and he'll most likely lose his job and his pension.'

The prospect brought a smile to Sam's face. 'It's always best to wash your enemy's dirty linen in public,' he said. 'That way they can't sweep it under the carpet.'

'I see we're having a mixed metaphor morning.' Owen looked at Sally. 'Any chance of a brew, Sally?'

'Every chance,' she said, with a bright smile. 'The kettle's in the kitchen. You might as well make us all a cup while you're at it. Coffee for me, please.'

Owen did as he was told. 'You shouldn't stand for this insubordination,' he said to Sam. 'She's undermining your authority.'

'Tell me about it. I'll have coffee as well. What's happening with Morrell?'

'Well, no one's seen Morrell since the day Eileen brought me that disk. Bowman said to pick him up without making a fuss because he's such a slippery character. We've had his home and his club watched, but there's been no sign. I think he's done a runner.'

'Someone could have tipped him off about the disk,' said Sam. 'Do you think it was one of your lot?'

'There was only Bowman, me and Janet Seager knew about it.'

'That narrows it down,' Sam said, 'and Bowman isn't past fraternising with the major villains on a quid pro quo basis.'

Owen gave this some thought, then shook his head. 'No, Bowman wouldn't risk going to jail. He wouldn't go that far.' He plonked a pile of DVDs on Sam's desk.

'What are these?'

'I got Billy Timmis to tune another computer into the web-cameras, see. After they locked you up I recorded four solid days of life in Morrell's office.

'Owen, you're a diamond!'

'During which time,' continued Owen, 'he appeared for only five hours – half of which he spent in the company of three young ladies. I felt like a Peeping bloody Tom.'

'Has Janet seen them?'

308

'Yes. We've got him talking on the phone to someone about Smithy's killing – someone called Roscoe. Morrell was laughing about it – especially with you being fingered for it. But he didn't actually say it was them who did the killing. Otherwise we'd have had you out of prison like a shot. He's very cautious man is Milo Morrell, even over the phone.'

'That's why he's clean,' said Sam. 'Roscoe? I bet he's the big, black guy.'

'I imagine so. The disk Eileen brought will send them both down for life.'

Sam picked up one of the DVDs. 'Is there anything on these where he talked about Ron Crusher?'

'Sorry, boyo, not a sausage. Apart from the telephone conversation with Roscoe it's half business, half rudeness – and plenty of cocaine sniffing. Never tried it myself. Thought about snuff once or twice. Very medicinal is snuff. I'm told it clears out the tubes.'

Sam sat back in his chair and squeezed his eyes shut, massaging them with his fingertips. 'All in all,' he concluded, 'it's been a complete waste of time. All this trouble – what happened to Sally, Smithy being murdered, me getting locked up, and for what? I'm not an inch nearer proving that Ron Crusher didn't commit suicide.'

'Ah, there's something you should know,' said Owen. 'I only found out myself, this morning.'

'Found out what? asked Sam.

'A woman went into Unsworth nick and said she'd been standing behind Ron Crusher when he committed suicide – she signed a statement to

309

that effect.'

Owen sat down and twiddled an itchy ear with his finger. 'Bit of a bugger all round, isn't it?' he commented. The three of them fell into a silence which was broken by the kettle boiling. Owen went into the kitchen and came out after a few minutes with cups of coffee for Sam and Sally, then went back for his own.

'Thanks, Owen.' Sam picked up his cup and thought back to his time in jail. 'You know, I made myself a promise while I was inside – I promised myself that if I got out I'd give up this private detective nonsense and stick to building. Let's face it, I'm no bloody good at it, and I do far more harm than good.'

The three of them sat in silence once again, sipping their coffee. Sam and Sally were both smoking.

'If you're going to give anything up,' commented Owen, 'it should be that filthy habit.'

'Never smoked in prison,' remembered Sam. 'Didn't realise I hadn't till I got out – funny that. I think I *will* give up this detective stuff. It's what my dad would have wanted.'

Neither Sally nor Owen tried to argue with him. Then Owen said: 'I suppose I'd better tell you, because it may well come out sooner or later.'

'Tell us what?' asked Sally.

Owen looked embarrassed. 'Eileen made a bit of a confession to me the day she brought me the computer,' he said. 'She evidently found it because of her connections with ... with the lower reaches of society.'

'Well, I don't know what these connections are,'

310

said Sam, 'but I'm damned glad she had them. She saved my life. Three cheers for the lower reaches, that's what I say.'

'If you feel like that about Eileen, maybe you shouldn't give up on the job just yet,' remarked Sally. 'It'll be like giving up on her.'

Sam seemed grateful she'd suggested it. 'She dug me out some more of Ron's stuff,' he said. 'Photos, army records, stuff from his schooldays, cuttings from a newspaper about his amateur boxing days, prison records, every scrap of paper she could find. Even a swimming certificate.'

'Anything of any use?' Sally asked.

'Not that I know of – it depends what turns up. Something might connect. I must admit, I feel bad about letting Eileen down.'

'She used to be a prostitute,' said Owen.

Sam and Sally stared at him. Neither knew what to say. Owen continued, in a voice clouded with melancholy. 'She called herself Zola Gee. She was only young. Very difficult childhood. She had to do it to survive, see.' He seemed miles away as he spoke, staring into the distance. His great hands were wrapped around the coffee cup, as if for warmth. 'She gave it up because a young man committed suicide. It wasn't really her fault but she blamed herself. He was being abused, see, and she was part of it. She didn't realise it was abuse – not until it was too late.'

'Did Ron know this?' asked Sam.

'What?'

'Did Ron know she'd been a prostitute?'

'No, she didn't tell him. I'm the only one she told. But she apparently met a man when she went looking for the computer. He knew who she was – and he knows who she is now. She thought it only fair that I should know. She's a very fair-minded woman is Eileen.'

Sally was watching Sam's face. 'You think there's a connection, don't you?'

Sam shrugged. 'I think there might be a connection between Ron's death and Eileen's past – suicide or not.'

'Eileen won't have had anything to do with it,' protested Owen.

'I'm not thinking of anything specific,' said Sam. 'But this suicide witness coming right out of the blue sounds very dodgy to me. What did she say, exactly?'

'Not much, only that she saw him jump. She didn't come forward at the time because she thought she might get into trouble with her boss for smoking on the roof.'

'Sounds plausible,' said Sally.

'I've always been suspicious of very plausible stories,' Sam said. 'In my experience the most believable witnesses sound a bit – unsatisfactory, if you get my drift. As if they wished they'd taken more notice of what was happening right under their noses. To my mind this has got Morrell written all over it. Anyway, I'd like to have a chat with Eileen. I knew she was holding something back, which is why I suggested you get close to her.'

'Sam Carew!' exclaimed Sally. 'That was an awful thing to do. Playing with a woman's emotions just to get information.'

'Hey! I didn't tell him to fall in love with her,'

protested Sam. 'Anyway, it seems I did them both a favour. Owen, do you think she'll talk to me about it?'

'I asked her if I should tell you, and she said it's okay. Maybe she wants you to talk to her. I'll ask her anyway.'

'Owen, love – how do you feel about it?' Sally asked him.

'About her being a prostitute?'

She nodded.

He thought for a while. 'I feel quite sad, really,' he said, 'that a young girl should be so desperate as to have to do that to make ends meet. Sex is such a pleasurable thing under the proper circumstances. I find it all so very sad. Doesn't stop me loving her, mind. I've been a bit of a bugger myself in the past. Never had to sell my body though.' Sam was looking him up and down, with an eyebrow raised and a wisecrack ready on his lips. Owen got in first. 'And you can keep your clever remarks to yourself, Carew!'

'So,' said Sally. 'Carew Private Investigations is still in business is it?'

'For the time being,' Sam decided. 'Like you said, I owe it to Eileen.'

Or to Zola, thought Sally, whose interest in the case had been seriously rekindled.

Eileen had already heard about the witness to Ron's suicide before Sam arrived that evening – Owen thought it as well to prepare her. She was suitably miserable.

'I can't see a way of getting round this,' she muttered as she opened the door to him. 'Come in.'

313

As Sam sat down he noticed various items missing from the room. There were no photographs or ornaments, or pictures on the walls. All that was left were the basic requirements of a living room – table, chairs and television. In one corner he saw a stack of three cardboard boxes with writing on them in felt-tip marker pen, indicating their contents. The top one contained videos and CDs. What had looked like a home didn't anymore. She saw him looking.

'Thought I'd make a start,' she explained. 'The building society is getting heavy.'

'Where would you go?'

She shrugged. 'Owen's made me an offer I might not be able to refuse.'

'I'm sure Owen will help you without any strings attached,' said Sam.

Eileen gave a short laugh. 'Oh, he hasn't asked me to marry him or anything. He just wants us to live together. It makes sense economically, it's just that I feel awkward about it.'

'Awkward?'

'Considering my past,' she explained. 'I gather you've heard about my past – it would feel like I'm selling myself in exchange for board and lodging.'

That sort of thing never bothered Owen, thought Sam. Then he asked, 'Is that what you'd be doing, or do you really have feelings for him?'

'I really have feelings for him.'

'I think he feels the same way about you.' This made her smile. Sam lit two cigarettes and gave one to Eileen. She was 48, six years older than Owen. There was evidence of former beauty in there somewhere, he guessed she'd aged a lot in recent months.

'You've known him a long time,' she said. 'Tell me about him.'

'What – spill the beans on a mate?' said Sam. 'He wouldn't thank me for that – I'd sooner he spilled his own beans.'

'I'm not talking about his track record, I'm talking about him. For a man who's been around a bit he seems so...' she searched for the word, '...naïve.'

This made Sam laugh. 'Naïve? – nail on the head I'd say. There's no other side to him if that's what you're wondering. With Owen what you see is what you get. He's a big, daft miserable bugger, but I wouldn't have him any other way.'

'He thinks the world of you.'

'Better not tell him you said that,' Sam said. He sat back, drew on his cigarette and looked up at the ceiling. 'That woman who says she saw Ron commit suicide – I've never met her so I've no reason to doubt her – but in my experience when convenient witnesses turn up late in the day their story's always worth double checking.'

The light of hope lit up Eileen's eyes. 'So, you think she's lying?'

'I think I'd like to have a word with her. The police won't have given her much of a grilling – her story justifies their findings very nicely thank you.'

'The coroner recorded an open verdict,' she said. 'So he wasn't going to commit himself.'

'Very cautious men, coroners.' Sam smiled at her and leaned forward. 'So,' he said, gently, 'tell

315

me about this young man who committed suicide. If you're up to it I probably need to know all about the part you played in his life.'

'What? everything?'

'Not the sticky details. You obviously carry some sense of guilt for his death; I just want to know why.'

She stubbed her cigarette out as she cast her mind back, Sam was only halfway through his.

'I'm actually trying to stop,' she told him.

Sam, knowing how hard it was, stubbed his out automatically. 'Sorry, I shouldn't have offered you one.'

'Don't be silly.' She closed her eyes for a second, frowned, then opened them. 'I was kidding myself that he was up for it, I suppose,' she said. 'If I'd allowed myself the luxury of a conscience it would have cost me money – and I needed money just to get by. Most working girls just get by, you know.'

'I know.'

'It was 1974, I was eighteen, I guess he was around fourteen. His name was Derek Fleming. I didn't know much about him. I thought he was just a kid who wanted to lose his virginity. At least that's what they said.'

'That's what who said?'

'The men. Look do you have another ciggie? I promise I'll quit later.'

Sam gave her another cigarette but didn't take one himself just in case she decided to stop halfway through this one.

'It was a sex show in Leeds – some back street house. A bunch of dirty old men paying money to watch a girl and a boy having sex. I was the girl,

Derek was the boy. I was being paid, he was being made to do it.'

'Who by?'

'Johnnie O'Brien – one of my clients. He told me he could arrange a weekly sex show if he could keep some of the proceeds. Nasty piece of work was Johnnie. He lived in a boy's home called Paddock House.' She looked at Sam to see if the name rang a bell. He was nodding.

'I remember something about that. Big scandal. Ten, fifteen years ago. Weren't some people locked up for abusing the kids?'

'Three,' confirmed Eileen, '–two men and a woman.'

'Isn't it a wonderful world.'

'Anyway,' she went on, 'I did it for about six months; regular income; in and out in fifteen minutes; with them all being young boys it didn't last long. I learned not to look at the watch-and-wank brigade all around the room. I just did the job, collected my money and went – Derek was the last one I did it with.' Tears mounted in her eyes. 'I did it with him quite a few times, he cried every time.'

'Is that why you stopped?'

She shook her head. 'God, I wish I could say it was. The whole thing stopped – I'd given him a dose of the clap.' She lowered her head. 'You can see why I kept it a secret. God knows what Owen will think when he finds out.'

'I don't think Owen will want to know the details,' Sam said. 'How long after this did the boy commit suicide?'

'Six years.'

'That's a long time. Why do you blame yourself?'

She nodded, miserably. 'A couple of days after he killed himself I met a bloke in a pub. He'd been in Paddock House at the same time – he'd even performed with me but I didn't remember him. He told me the effect it all had on them. It took years for them to get over it all. Not only the sex shows but there was all the abuse going on in the home – mainly a bloke called Forbuoys. Derek had been getting it from all ends. According to this bloke, Derek was gay – imagine how that made me feel?'

'If it hadn't been you it would have been some other girl,' said Sam.

'But it wasn't some other girl, it was me – and anyway I don't know whether O'Brien would have managed to persuade another girl to do such a wicked thing.' Her tears were running freely now, Sam took her hand.

'Eileen, you didn't kill him. You were part of a sequence of events that led to his death. It happens to lots of people. It's happened to me a few times but there's no point letting it eat away at you. Can you think of anything, any connection between Derek and Ron – apart from them both apparently committing suicide?'

She shrugged. 'Never tried to make a connection. I never told Ron about me being a working girl.'

'Could he have found out?'

Eileen shook her head. 'I'm sure I'd have known. Couldn't keep his feelings to himself, couldn't Ron. I only told Owen because he might have found out for himself one day, with him being a copper.'

Sam thought for a while. Something told him that Eileen's past and Ron's death were connected. 'What about Milo Morrell?'

'What about him?'

'I don't know yet, but he's a piece in the jigsaw. There's Ron, there's you, there's Derek Fleming, there's Milo Morrell – and there's twenty kilos of cocaine that turned up in Bernard's cellar.' He got to his feet, having made a decision. 'I've got to talk to Mrs Mutch.'

'Who's she?'

'The woman who says she saw Ron jump. Owen got her name. She's a cleaner at Ridings House.'

Sam stood on the flagged pavement and looked up at Ridings House. He pictured the scene in his mind. Ron standing on the parapet, then jumping down on to the concrete flags. It would take a seriously disturbed man to do that, and there was no evidence that Ron Crusher had been seriously disturbed. Inside the doorway was a man at a desk. His uniform indicated that he was of an official capacity so Sam accorded him the respect such officials love. He took out a piece of paper from his pocket.

'Ah, I wonder if you could help me. I'm looking for a lady who's employed here. A Mrs–' He looked at the paper, which was in fact a gas bill, '–Mrs Mutch?'

'Marjorie Mutch? She's a cleaner.' The man said it as though cleaners were below having

319

people come and ask for them by name.

'That'll be her,' confirmed Sam.

The man looked at his watch. 'She'll most likely be on a break right now. She's allus on a break is that one.'

'Where would I find her?'

'Why, is she in bother?' asked the man, hopefully.

'No, I just need to tell her something.'

'Oh.' He looked disappointed. 'She'll be down in the caretaker's room. Thick as thieves them two. Mind you, he's not in, so she'll be on her own. It's down them steps, first door on yer right.'

Sam tapped on the door and pushed it open. She was sitting with her feet up on a formica table, drinking tea and reading *The Sun*.

'Mrs Mutch?' Sam enquired, pleasantly.

She returned his smile. 'That's me.' Marjorie Mutch was around sixty with yellow tinted hair and a dark blue overall that bulged at the belly.

'I wonder if I might have a quick word about the suicide you witnessed last year.

'You from the papers?'

Sam gave her a rueful grin. 'Does it show?'

'I've been expectin' someone like you,' she said. 'Them coppers can't keep nowt ter themselves.'

'We all have a job to do, Mrs Mutch, including you. You do a good job from what I've seen so far. They could do with someone like you at the *Mirror*.'

'*Mirror*, you're from the *Mirror*?'

'I'm freelance actually.' He took out a reporter's notebook.

'Haven't I seen your photo in the paper?'

Sam inwardly cursed his notoriety. 'You're not mistaking me for Brad Pitt are you? It's a common mistake.'

She gave a raucous laugh. 'Gerron wi' yer. What d'yer want ter know, yer cheeky beggar.'

'Nothing much. I just want to write a piece about how a man's suicide looked through a lone onlooker's eyes. Did he see you? Did you talk to him? Do you think you could have stopped him? – stuff like that.'

The smile dropped from her face and was replaced by something a lot more stubborn – unhelpful. 'It's worth a couple of hundred,' he said, 'and I won't give your name if you don't want me to.'

'Two hundred?'

'Cash,' he said. 'Here and now.' He took out his wallet and placed a tempting wad of twenties on the table.'

She looked at it, then at him, then she picked it up and stuffed it in her purse. 'I walked out on to the roof for sly drag. He were standin' on the edge, large as life. Next thing I knew he'd jumped. I ran back inside – end of story.'

'How long did you watch him standing there?'

'Just a few seconds.'

'Did you say anything to him?'

'No – I shouldn't have been there. I didn't want anyone ter know I were there.'

'I gather he was a big man.'

'Very big.'

Sam was writing all this down in pretend shorthand. 'What erm ... oh, I don't know, what was he wearing?'

'A suit, I think.'

'What colour?'

'Just a dark suit.'

'A dark suit ... sounds like a business suit.'

'Couldn't tell yer. Like I said, it all happened so quickly.'

'Hmm... I could do with some sort of description or I can't sell this story. Oh yes, his hair. He had really long hair, apparently, you must have noticed his hair, even if you didn't really notice his clothes. I need something to hang this story on. Was it blowing in the wind? What colour was it?'

'Never really noticed – except that it were long.'

'I gather that he sometimes wore it in a pony-tail. I don't suppose you spotted that, did you?'

'Now I come ter think of it, yeah. I think he did. It all happened that quick, but I remember thinkin' ter meself, "He's got a bloody silly hair-cut," then he'd gone.'

Sam closed his notebook. 'Just one last question, Mrs Mutch.'

'What's that, love?'

'Why have you told me and the police a pack of lies?'

'Eh?'

'You say you saw a long-haired man in a dark suit. Had you been telling the truth you'd have seen a completely bald man wearing a white leather jacket.'

She glared at him with guilt written all over her face.

'Who paid you to tell lies?'

'Nobody paid me. I saw what I saw.'

322

'We both know you're telling lies. It was Milo Morrell, wasn't it?'

Was that fear he saw in her eyes? If it was, there was no point pursuing this conversation. 'I just wish yer'd bugger off an' leave me alone,' she grumbled.

'Okay,' he said. 'Best not to tell any more lies about this, Mrs Mutch. You might end up having to tell your lies in court.'

There was real fear in here eyes now. 'I'll not be sayin' nothin' about it ever again,' she muttered. 'Not ter you nor ter nobody. It's more trouble than it's worth. So just piss off!'

Sam went away, satisfied that his money was well spent. He was more convinced than ever that Ron had been murdered and that Milo Morrell was at the back of it. Marjorie Mutch hadn't seen Ron jump, but it wasn't fair on her to try and make her grass on Morrell. He didn't want to be part of a sequence of events that would lead to her death.

Chapter Twenty-Eight

There was no Paddock House in the phone book. Sam tried Thomson's and Yellow pages with zero success. Sally asked him what he was doing and brought it up on the internet within a minute.

'What does it say?' Sam asked, trying to hide his irritation at the way she tracked things down so easily without getting out of her chair.

'It says plenty. There's a lot of ex-residents getting stuff off their chests.'

'Such as?'

'Such as sexual abuse by the staff. The place was investigated in 1988 and closed down in '89.'

'Let's have a look.'

He leaned over Sally's shoulder as she scrolled down the pages. There were several sites for Paddock House Boys Home Leeds. More than a dozen former residents had stories to tell. The name Forbuoys cropped up regularly. Sam spoke the name out loud.

'Have you heard of him?' Sally asked.

'Eileen mentioned him – this chap Derek Fleming was apparently abused by him. Keep going, see if it mentions a Johnnie O'Brien.'

'Here,' said Sally, almost immediately, as she flicked over on to the second page. 'He sounds a real charmer. Good grief, Sam, what an awful place for a boy to have to grow up.'

'Look at the bottom of the page,' Sam said.

'O'Brien was murdered in 1981, stabbed to death. I wonder if the police got anyone. Does it say?'

Sally kept scrolling. More abuse, more names – three former staff members jailed in 1991; two for rape, one for assault.

'Took them a long time,' she commented.

'It takes a long time for abused kids to grow up,' said Sam. 'Mostly they try to forget about it. Someone must have had the guts to speak up. It only takes one to set the ball rolling.'

Forbuoys' name came up again. This time he was given a first name – Alan. Someone had read how he'd been knocked down in 1983 in Nottingham by a hit and run driver. That someone reckoned the driver had done the world a favour. Nothing more about O'Brien.

'See if Milo Morrell gets a mention,' suggested Sam. 'I'll make us a cup of tea.'

He had a mental block as far as computers were concerned. Sally said it was just laziness. Sam knew he'd have to learn more about them one day if he was to survive in this business. Sally was keen for him to survive as well, which was why she had signed him up for two sets of lessons, one for computers, one for swimming.

'Can't find anything on Morrell,' she reported as he came back with the tea. She took her cup from him. 'Thanks – do we know what's happened to him, by the way?'

'Vanished,' said Sam. 'The only thing we do know is that before he did a runner he spotted one of the web-cams. My guess is that someone definitely told him about the disk – which means he'll know he's up on a murder charge he won't get out of.'

'Who do you think tipped him off?'

'That's what I keep asking myself.'

'You suspect Bowman, don't you?'

Sam gave this some thought. 'Not really,' he said. 'But Bowman was one of the very few people who knew, and he's not beyond befriending one villain to catch another. Do you think you could use your genius to track down this Forbuoys chap – or have you already done it, while I was making the tea?'

'It sounds to me that I deserve a raise,' she said, typing the name "Nottingham Hospitals" into a search engine. Nottingham County Hospital seemed a likely place to start. Two minutes later she was speaking to their records department.

'I wonder if you could help me. My name is Forbuoys and I'm trying to trace an uncle of mine who was apparently knocked down by a car in 1983. I believe he was taken to your hospital. I know you're not allowed to give out such information but I wonder if you could advise me on how to go about tracking him down.'

'I don't know nothin' about not giving information out.' He sounded quite young, 'I'm only working in this department to cover for a bloke who's sufferin' from work related stress. He's been off sick for three weeks.'

'I see,' sympathised Sally, 'and *is* the job stressful?'

The young man gave a short laugh. 'Not so's you'd notice. Nab, he's just a tosser. He's twice my age, he's got more degrees than a thermometer and it takes him all his time to switch the computer on. Complete tosser. There's more life in me granddad's vest. I wouldn't care, he's on a higher grade than me.'

'In that case I'm glad he's off sick, he doesn't sound as if he'd have been much help to me.'

'You're not wrong there, missis. What's your uncle's name?'

'Alan Forbuoys. He was taken to your hospital in 1983.'

She could hear him rapidly pressing keys on his computer. After about half a minute he asked, 'Alan David Forbuoys, born July 1935, admitted in December 1983. RTA victim. Does that sound like him?'

Sally said it sounded very much like him.

'He was in here from December 1983 to April 1984 – then he was moved to Sherwood Paraplegic Clinic. Sounds like he was in a very bad way – sorry.'

'Do you know if he's still alive?'

'Hang on – here we are. I've got him at Larkfield Nursing Home, 45 Nunnington Crescent, Nottingham. He was living there in 2002. Is that any good?'

'That's brilliant.' She was grateful, but curious. 'Are you sure you're allowed to give this information?'

He laughed again. 'Do me a favour, missis – this is the NHS. You've got to commit mass murder to get fired from this place.'

'Thanks, you've been a tremendous help.'

Sally put the phone down and glanced at her watch. It had taken her three minutes to track down Forbuoys. She could sense Sam was staring at her.

'Well?' he asked, eventually.

'Larkfield Nursing Home, 45 Nunnington Crescent in Nottingham – you make nice tea.' She mentioned the address as casually as she could whilst fighting back a smug smile.

He shook his head. 'Is everything so easy – or is it me who makes life hard?'

'It's just simple information technology,' she said. 'Knowing how to use the information – that's the hard bit.'

A middle-aged Irish woman in a blue uniform opened the door. She smiled at him and turned away without asking him who he was; she just called out to him not to forget to sign the visitor's book. Sam looked around for it and spotted it on a table by the door. Above the table was a group photograph of all the residents, taken in fine weather in the garden and entitled 'The Larkfield Gang'. There were twenty two altogether, excluding uniformed staff and a youngish woman sitting smugly in the middle like the manager of an aged football team. Some were smiling, some looked bemused, only five of them were men, one of whom was in a wheelchair. He was scowling.

Along the corridor was a door marked simply, "Office". Sam gave it a polite tap and opened it. The youngish woman in the middle of the photograph was talking to someone on the phone, she waved him to sit down and smiled a greeting at him. She was attractive in an efficient sort of way, with even features, even teeth, shining hair and manicured nails. She put down the phone and held out her hand to him. 'Liz Greening, I'm the manager, how can I help you?'

It occurred to Sam that he perhaps looked like a potential client, or at least was there on behalf of one. 'I've come to talk to one of your residents.'

The smile on her face diminished slightly. 'Oh, who?'

'Alan Forbuoys.'

'And you are?'

'Sam Carew. I'm investigating certain crimes committed in the nineteen eighties and I think Mr Forbuoys might be the victim of one of them.'

To his surprise she didn't ask if he was a policeman. 'You mean the hit and run driver?' she enquired.

'Yes – but I've reason to believe there was more to it than that.'

She nodded, pressed a few keys on her desk computer, ran the mouse across the screen, stabbed another two keys and sat back, looking at Forbuoys' file. 'He has a chequered history has our Mr Forbuoys which, as far as I'm concerned, remains locked inside this computer.' She accompanied her last statement with a threatening smile. 'We strive for an untroubled atmosphere in Larkfield.'

'I know his history,' said Sam, then to prove it, he added, 'I know about Paddock House. I want to talk to him and to no one else.'

'Do you work for an insurance company, Mr Carew?'

'I'm freelance, but this job is connected with an

329

insurance claim. It's purely information I want. Mr Forbuoys' history will stay inside your computer. I promise you that.'

'In that case it's up to him.' She got up from her chair. 'I have to tell you, though, he's not our most popular resident.'

Forbuoys was surprisingly forthcoming about his past life. It was as though he felt he'd done little wrong in abusing the boys in his care and that what had subsequently happened to him was a million times worse. He and Sam were in the empty dining room.

'I never really hurt any of them. All I was doing was satisfying a need. I'm sure you have needs, Mr Carew.'

'I've never forced myself on anyone.' Sam didn't much want to pursue this line of conversation. 'This accident you had – do you think it an accident?'

Forbuoys shook his head slowly, it was about as much as he could manage. From his neck down he was paralysed, apart from some limited movement in his left arm and hand, which was just enough to work the controls on his electric wheelchair. His body looked wasted beneath his drab dressing gown. The skin on his face stretched over his skull like pale parchment. What was left of his hair was closely cropped and he wore thick spectacles that magnified his eyes. From the neck up everything worked more or less normally.

'It was someone from Paddock House. They sent me a letter when I lived in Leeds. They told me how they'd killed Johnnie O'Brien. Do you know about that?'

330

'Not in any great detail. You said "they" – you mean there was more than one of them?'

'According to the letter. It might have been just one person trying to fool either me or the police. O'Brien was stabbed, they said I was next. The police never found who did it.'

'Did you show them the letter?'

Forbuoys shook his head again. 'What do you think? The little bastards knew I daren't show the letter to the police. I'd have been investigated and ended up in jail. As things turned I'd have been better off in jail. I'd rather be an able-bodied convict than a paralysed free man.'

'So, what did you do?'

'What did I do? I ran away here – to Nottingham.'

'And they caught up with you?'

'I'd only been here a week before I got another letter from them. They had some way of knowing where I was. It struck me that one of them might have become a copper. It was two years before they tried to kill me.'

'You're sure it was them?'

'After my accident I got a final letter. It just said, "Told you we'd get you" – that was over twenty years ago.'

'I don't suppose you've still got any of these letters?'

Forbuoys shuddered. 'Burned the first two. A nurse had to read the last one for me. She showed it to the police. I said I didn't know who it was from and they decided it was a crank.' He looked up at Sam, and despite his despicable crimes, Sam felt pity for him. 'The least they could have done,' Forbuoys said, 'was to come back and finish me off. If I could, I'd do it myself. Surely I didn't deserve this?'

'One of the boys you abused committed suicide,' said Sam. 'His name was Derek Fleming. Do you remember him?'

Forbuoys closed his eyes. He nodded before he opened them again. 'Yes, I remember him. I didn't know he'd killed himself. In fact I thought he might be one of them.' There was no remorse in his eyes for the young man he'd driven to take his own life, so Sam's pity for him subsided.

'Exactly why are you here?' Forbuoys asked. 'The manager told me you were doing an investigation or something.'

'I think there might be a connection between the attack on you and a possible murder committed last year.'

'Murder – who was murdered?'

Sam chose not to answer this, instead he asked a question of his own. 'Did you ever meet a girl called Zola Gee?'

Once again Forbuoys closed his eyes. 'Was she a prostitute?'

'Yes.'

'Never met her but I knew about her. One of O'Brien's tarts. If I remember rightly she gave the Fleming kid the clap. I wouldn't touch him after that. Dirty little bastard!'

Sam's loathing of this crippled pervert increased, but there was no point becoming embroiled in an argument with someone who had been punished so heavily for his crimes.

'Did the police ever catch up with you?'

A humourless smile split Forbuoys face. 'Indeed they did. In 1987 I told them everything they wanted to know. Got the place closed down and three people locked up. Surprised there weren't two more – probably had good lawyers. Was it one of them who was murdered?'

Sam shook his head, then asked, 'I assume you told the police about the letters then?'

'I did, but they never got back to me. They'd already decided I wasn't fit to prosecute so I guess they decided not to chase the bastards who did this to me. It's the way their minds work. Anyway, if you're not going to tell me who was murdered I've had enough.'

He pressed a button on the arm of his wheelchair. It spun around until he was facing away from Sam. The chair set off, then stopped. 'I always picture a woman driving the car that knocked me down,' he said, over his shoulder. 'It might be my imagination playing tricks but I have a memory of the car coming towards me and a split second memory of a woman at the wheel. At the time I told the police I didn't remember seeing who was driving – this came to me afterwards. I did tell them later, though. Was it a woman who was murdered?'

'No, it was a man called Ron Crusher. He was married to Zola.' Sam stared at the back of Forbuoys' head, wondering if this was would produce a reaction.

'Never heard of him.'

The chair set off again with a low whine. It was halfway through the door when it stopped a second time. 'Oh, and another thing. When the police questioned me about Paddock House they brought up the subject of O'Brien's murder and asked me if he went with prostitutes. I said I thought he did but I didn't know any names.'

'What about Zola?'

'I'd forgotten about her until you brought her name up, anyway, I didn't want to get involved.'

'Why were the police asking about prostitutes?'

'Apparently a woman who could well have been a whore was seen leaving O'Brien's flat around the time he was murdered. That's when I told the coppers about the woman in the car. They made a note of it, but never came back to me.'

'What did this woman look like?'

'Blonde hair, skirt up to her arse, tits more out than in – a whore.'

Sam was speaking to the back of Forbuoys' head. 'What about the woman who ran you down, what did she look like?'

'She looked like a woman, that's all I can remember. I'd had a bit to drink that night. I was walking out of the pub – correction – staggering out, I heard this engine, looked round, there she was, bang, woke up two days later in hospital. Quick as that.'

'The headlights can't have been on, or you'd have been too dazzled to see who was in the car,' Sam mentioned, half to himself.

'I don't think she had *any* lights on,' said Forbuoys. 'I must have picked her face out from the light in the pub car park. Or it could have been a drunken mirage.'

'If she'd switched her lights off it meant she wanted to give you as little warning as possible.

Do you think it was the same woman who killed O'Brien?'

'I don't know what to think. There weren't any women in Paddock House, not residents anyway.'

'Maybe an aggrieved relative?'

'Maybe. Women can be such violent creatures, don't you think so, Mr Carew?'

'Or a bereaved relative?'

'Or this Zola woman,' said Forbuoys. 'Have you spoken to her?'

Sam didn't want a discussion with him, only answers. 'Have you ever heard the name Milo Morrell?'

Forbuoys seemed to give it some thought. Sam made to walk around him and gauge his reaction, but the chair spun on its axis and he looked up at Sam with an expressionless face.

'No.'

'Did Derek Fleming have any family?'

Forbuoys gave the same scowl Sam had seen in the photo. 'You've already asked more questions than the police,' he said. 'What's all this about?'

'I'm investigating an insurance claim. It's what I do for a living.'

'You're lucky you have a living, Mr Carew. I'm not interested in helping you with an insurance claim.' The chair whined through 180 degrees and transported its occupant through the doorway and down a corridor. Sam never saw Forbuoys again, nor did he want to.

He was back in his office two hours later. Bernard was there, talking to Sally.

'How are things, Bernard?' Sam asked him.

'Couldn't be worse.'

'You've got a swimming lesson this afternoon,' Sally reminded him.

'Anything I can help you with?' Sam asked Bernard. 'Have you got a court date yet?'

'April 2nd – I was hoping it wouldn't get that far. Where's the sense in trying to lock me up for drug pushing? I wouldn't know cocaine from bloody codeine.'

'What about Mariella, what does she think?'

'Well, to be fair to her, I think she's come round to believing our Ron put the stuff there. He'll have had a spare key made when he fitted our new door.'

'If you could find that key it'd go in your favour.'

'Apparently, when he died,' said Bernard, 'he didn't have any keys with him, which was odd because his car was parked not so far away but his keys were never found. The police asked Eileen, but she couldn't enlighten them. Did you know that?'

'No, I didn't,' admitted Sam. 'I don't suppose anyone thought it important at the time.'

'Well it's bloody important now.'

'Is that why you're here – do you want me to look for the keys?'

'It's not why I've come – but it'd do no harm. I'll have to pay you when I can, the Führer's watching every penny I spend.'

'Surely she wouldn't begrudge you spending money to keep yourself out of jail?'

'She bloody would.' He took a large envelope from his pocket. 'Anyroad, this is why I've come.

I've been summoned to court over a bloody parking ticket – going over the time on a meter. I wonder if your mates down at the nick could fix it for me.'

'Why don't you just pay it?' Sam asked.

'Because it's nearly four hundred quid. It dates back to last summer. I don't even remember getting a ticket. It's all been adding up, apparently. It were in and out of court while I were in jail. Mariella did nowt, silly cow, and now she won't give me the brass to pay it. As soon as all this is over I'm leaving her, one way or the other. She can fend for herself which means the business'll go down the pan.'

Sam took the summons, read it, and shook his head. 'There's nothing I can do,' he said. Then he looked at it again, more closely this time. 'I'll pay the fine for you, if you like. I'll add it to my bill. At least it's one worry off your back. I might as well keep this.'

'You're a sound man, Sam,' said Bernard, getting up to go. 'I'll pay you every last penny if I have to sell off a few of me vital organs.'

'You're a free man with the firm's money,' commented Sally after Bernard had gone. 'If his own wife wouldn't lend him the money, why should you?'

Sam handed her the summons. 'Take a look at the date when the parking ticket was issued. 1.05 pm, June 16th last year in George Street, Unsworth.'

'So?'

'So an hour after this ticket was issued Ron Crusher either jumped, or was pushed, off the top of Ridings House, about five minutes walk away.'

'Are, you saying Bernard killed his own brother?'

Sam sat down in his chair. 'I think whoever was driving the car might well have had something to do with it.'

They both dropped into a contemplative silence. 'What about Mariella?' asked Sally, around the time that Sam was thinking the same thing.

'It's a thought – no it isn't – she was in Blackpool that day with a bunch of women. Eileen was there as well.' He gave a short laugh. 'They detest each other, but they can give each other alibis.'

'I wonder if they would – if push came to shove?' wondered Sally.

'Doesn't bear thinking about. In any case – and I don't wish to appear sexist – but if a big, rough, bloke like Ron Crusher was pushed off that roof, I doubt it was a woman who did it. I reckon it was another big, rough bloke. The mystery is, if someone came up behind him, surely the people below would have seen him. The parapet's only about eighteen inches high, it wouldn't hide anyone.'

'Maybe he wasn't pushed, maybe he was just tripped?' Sally suggested. 'Maybe someone crept up behind him on their hands and knees and tripped him up.'

'So, why was he standing on the parapet in the first place?' Sam wondered, then he answered his own question. 'A gun at his back?'

'And a woman can hold a gun just as easily as a man,' said Sally.

'And a woman could have tripped Ron up just as easily as a man could.'

'So,' wondered Sally, 'who was driving Bernard's car? Morrell, one of his men, or our mystery woman?'

'Or someone we haven't thought about,' said Sam. 'But we can't rule Bernard out – which is why I didn't mention the date on the ticket to him. He either didn't notice its significance, or he hopes *I* won't notice it.'

'He didn't seem concerned when you took it off him,' Sally pointed out. 'He just seemed relieved that you were going to pay it.'

'That's what he seemed, all right,' agreed Sam. 'If he's got anything to hide he'll want it paying before someone else over at the court notices the date and the name Crusher – and puts two and two together. Oh, by the way, Forbuoys thinks it might have been a woman who ran him down and killed Johnnie O'Brien.'

'A woman?' Sally was impressed by this. 'Did he tell you anything else?'

'Nothing worth a damn. He's an awful man. What happened to him is terrible but he really is an unpleasant person.'

'So, are we any nearer finding out who killed Ron Crusher?'

'Fifty per cent nearer,' said Sam. 'We've narrowed it down to a man or a woman.'

'Right ... before I forget, it's at half past four.'

'What's at half past four?'

'Your swimming lesson.'

Chapter Twenty-Nine

'According to Forbuoys, the police think a prostitute had something to do with Johnnie O'Brien's death.'

Eileen's expression went from interest to protest. Sam had gone to visit her at home. 'Really? – Hey! I hope you don't think I had anything to do with it. He was murdered *after* I gave the game up.'

Sam studied her for a while, then shook his head. 'No, I don't think it was you – never did. Forbuoys also thinks it was a woman who ran him down.'

'Is any of this connected with Ron?'

Sam wasn't listening. 'One thing puzzles me,' he said, 'at the time of Ron's death you were in Blackpool – with Mariella. I didn't realise you two were ever so pally.'

'Not just with Mariella, there was a full coach load of us – always is, you've got to get your name down early, it's a very popular trip. We go every year for two days – apart from last year. Everyone came home when they heard about my Ron. I hardly saw Mariella. We were all fund raisers for St Joseph's Hospice.'

'I don't see Bernard's wife as a fund raiser,' Sam said.

'She didn't do much,' said Eileen, 'apart from allowing collection boxes in their dry cleaning shops. The rest of us put ourselves about a lot. Organising events, rattling tins, collecting clothes for charity shops – I used to really enjoy it.'

'Used to?'

'I've stopped doing it. At the moment I've all on keeping body and soul together.'

'That's understandable,' sympathised Sam.

'It'd been a good day,' remembered Eileen. 'It was about half past six. We'd just got back to the hotel to get ready to go out for the night and there was a police car outside. We all made jokes about them coming to pick Mariella up. She was never popular.'

'I can imagine.'

'They took me outside and sat me in the car. They were ever so nice. I wouldn't like to do their job, telling people their husband's dead. I just sat there in tears. Mariella tapped on the window and asked me if everything was all right. I told her Ron was dead. She looked ever so shocked.'

'So, she has got a heart.'

'Not so's you'd notice,' said Eileen, sourly. 'When I needed friends she never lifted a finger to help me. Bernard did a bit, but not much.'

Sam had his feet up on the desk. His eyes were on the *Yorkshire Post* but his mind was elsewhere.

'What's she got to do with anything?'

Sally looked from doing the weekly wages. 'Who are you talking about, Sam?'

'Mrs Mutch. Everybody else has connections: Milo, Bernard, Mariella, Eileen, Forbuoys, O'Brien, Ferris, Derek Fleming – Old Uncle Tom Cobbleigh and all. What's Mrs Mutch got to do with anything? We know she was lying, which means she's connected. But who to? What's her connection?

'Morrell?' Sally suggested.

Sam nodded and put down his paper. 'Probably, but the truth is we don't know for sure. What we do know is that Mrs Mutch is the key to it all. Maybe with Milo on the run she'll be bit more forthcoming with the truth.'

'You could tell the police,' said Sally, 'let them talk to her. Tell them about the parking ticket as well.'

Sam gave it a few seconds thought then shook his head. 'The police are nowhere near as convinced as I am that Ron was murdered. They've written it off as suicide and they don't like making work for themselves – they've got enough on their plate as it is.'

'But,' concluded Sally, 'if we can tie a statement from Mrs Mutch admitting she was told to lie about Ron's suicide by Morrell, to the fact that Bernard's car was parked... Hmm, how does Bernard's car come into the picture if Morrell had Ron killed?'

'No idea. That's why I need to talk to Mrs Mutch.'

'I'll come with you, maybe she'll find a woman easier to confide in.'

'Are you saying I haven't got a feminine side?'

'There are many sides to you, Sam Carew, but none of them are feminine.'

Mrs Mutch had been pretty much cleaned up off the pavement by the time Sam and Sally arrived at Ridings House at half past one. With her being much smaller she hadn't made quite the mess that Ron had, although she had plunged from more or less the same spot. The cordon around the area was being taken down; photographs and witness statements had been taken and the police had come to the conclusion that she'd been suffering from some sort of guilt complex at not being able to stop Ron Crusher from jumping.

'People do funny things,' said the caretaker to Sam and Sally who had introduced themselves as insurance investigators. 'I never realised she'd seen the other feller jump off – not till the coppers told me. Shook me that did.'

'Just after she jumped, did you see anyone coming out of the building you didn't recognise?' Sam asked.

'There's folk comin' in and out all the time. We'll have it all on camera. I can let you have a look if you want.'

'Please,' said Sally.

For the next two hours they ran the tape on fast forward, slowing down every time someone entered the building. The camera was situated in the lobby, looking back at the main entrance door. Between 8.30 a.m., when the tape started, and 9.15 over two hundred people entered the building. From then until the tape finished, the people traffic, as the caretaker referred them, slowed down to no more than fifty coming and going an hour.

'This is Marjorie comin' in now,' said the care-taker when the clock on the bottom right of the screen showed 09:57 hrs. 'We have day cleaners

343

and night cleaners. She's on the day shift, ten till four. The night shift's six till twelve.'

The picture showed a scattered procession of women walking up the small flight of steps that led to the front door. All the faces were slightly out of focus, most of them were looking down at the steps.

'I counted five,' said Sam. 'Should there be five?'

'Varies. They don't clock-in any more. There's six altogether, but it's very rare we get a full team in. That's Marjorie second from the back.'

The three of them watched Marjorie Mutch make her final, fateful entrance into Ridings House. 'Do you recognise all the others?' Sam asked.

'They change from week to week. There's only Marjorie and a couple of others who've stuck it out.'

'Sam, it could have been anyone who went in during the last hour and a half,' pointed out Sally.

'Who could?' enquired the caretaker, curiously.

Sam avoided his query with one of his own. 'Do you know the exact time Marjorie jumped?'

'Eleven fourteen. I heard screaming and I looked me watch. Whenever there's a commotion I always look at me watch.'

Sam ran the tape forward to the time Mrs Mutch had died. The on-screen clock said 11.14 when a woman ran in through the door and gesticulated at the security officer. He followed the woman outside. A few seconds later he returned and picked up the telephone on his desk. People were milling around the door. A man entered and pushed his way through the crowd. Sally stabbed her finger at the screen. 'Look, look who that is.' The man was carrying a suitcase and wearing a baseball cap. He walked, casually, towards the camera, as if unconcerned by the tragedy he must have just passed by. Many people were running out now. Just for a second the man glanced up at the camera. Long enough for Sam and Sally to identify him as Milo Morrell.

'We should ring the police,' said Sally. 'He's probably still in the building.'

'Do you know that man?' asked Sam.

'Mr Robertson?' said the caretaker, picking at his ear with a pencil. 'I'm probably the only one left in this place who does. They come and go, yer see. Mr Robertson's had an office here for years. Top floor, room 1217. Hardly ever see him, bit of a mystery man, pleasant enough. He doesn't use the office cleaning service.' He removed the pencil from his ear and examined a blob of wax with some satisfaction. Sally grimaced. Sam pressed the fast forward until the on-screen clock said 11.36. Morrell appeared again, walking away from the camera, carrying the same suitcase, only this time it was obviously heavier.

'Mr Robertson eh?' said Sam. He glanced at a rack of key hooks on the wall. One of them was plainly marked *Master*. 'I suppose you've been in his office, have you, with your master key?'

'I show the fire officers round, that's about all. We have to give tenant's notice, of course.'

'Of course,' said Sam. 'People like their privacy – Mr Robertson more than most, by the sound of him.' He leaned towards the caretaker. 'Can I let you into a confidence?'

'Course yer can.'

Sam looked at Sally, as if to get her permission to reveal his secret. She nodded her assent. Sam went on: 'It's actually Mr Robertson we're interested in. He's er, he's not everything he seems to be.'

'Is he not – what is he then?'

'You really don't want to know. But it'd help us a lot to have a quick look in his office. Of course I wouldn't dream of asking you such a thing – more than your job's worth I should imagine.'

The caretaker started on his other ear, shrugged and said, 'Mebbe.'

'However,' Sam said, 'It'd be worth a lot to me to have a quiet word with my colleague – in the privacy of this room.' He took out his wallet and counted out two hundred pounds, under the caretaker's interested gaze. 'Two minutes for two hundred pounds.'

The caretaker put down his ear-picking pencil and picked up the money. 'I've got me rounds to do,' he said. 'Shut the door behind yer – and put it back on the hook when yer've done.'

Three minutes later Sam was knocking on the door to room 1217. Sally was apprehensive as he had no plan in mind if one of Morrell's men opened it. No one answered. Sam put the master key in the lock and opened it. The room was orderly but covered with a layer of recently disturbed dust. It was just a single room, about fifteen feet by twelve, with a desk, a telephone, four chairs and a filing cabinet.

'You check the desk, I'll do the filing cabinet,' he said. It was completely empty as he guessed it would be.

'Empty.'

'So's the desk,' said Sally. She walked over to the filing cabinet and pulled open the top drawer. 'Have you checked the bottom of the drawers? Sometimes if you file stuff wrongly it falls straight through. I'm always losing things that way.' She lifted out the file holders and found two large, wallet files in the bottom of the middle drawer, and various assorted papers in the bottoms of the other two drawers. 'Very slack filing,' she commented, browsing through the papers.

Sam began going through the wallet files. One of them was full of passports, identical insofar as none of them had the photograph or details of the passport holder. The other was full of passport-type photographs. The faces all looked eastern European. He glanced at Sally.

'What have you got?'

'All this stuff's foreign,' she said. 'Don't recognise the language.'

'He's into people trafficking,' Sam concluded. 'What a charmer.'

'I wonder if he has any redeeming features?' said Sally.

Sam wasn't interested in Morrell's redeeming features; he was searching for a clue that would connect Morrell to Ron Crusher's murder. But Morrell had removed everything else from the room. Sam sighed and sat down.

'Better put the stuff back where we found it. I'll tell Owen. He can put the wheels in motion to get the coppers here.'

'What about the tape?'

'I'll make a copy and give Owen one. All in all I don't think we've achieved much, apart from nailing Morrell with people trafficking on top of everything else.'

'It's something,' said Sally.

Outside, they watched a couple of council workmen washing the concrete flags with a pressure hose.

'There's one thing I know for certain,' Sam said as Sally linked his arm. 'Mrs Mutch no more committed suicide than Ron Crusher did.'

'Who do you think killed her? – I mean, do you think Morrell had something to do with it – or was he just there to clean out his office?'

Sam gave this some thought. 'Well, it was a hell of a coincidence him turning up at a time like that.'

'*After* she'd jumped,' Sally pointed out. 'He can't have pushed her off.'

'He doesn't do his own dirty work,' said Sam. 'But why have her killed at all? If he knows the police have got him bang to rights on Smithy's murder, what has he got to gain?'

'*If* he knows,' said Sally. 'It might have been him finding the webcam that scared him off– nothing more.'

'What, you think I'm jumping to conclusions that he knows about the disk?'

'Well, you do jump to a lot of conclusions.'

'Mrs Mutch jumped to a conclusion,' said Sam, clicking the remote to open his car. 'We know

Morrell likes to get rid of loose ends. If he was the one who persuaded Mrs Mutch to lie to the police, she'll have been a very loose end. Am I making sense?'

'As much sense as you normally do.' Sally got in the passenger seat. 'Maybe you need a break,' she suggested. 'Two or three days away. Come back with a fresh mind.'

Sam fastened his seat belt and started the engine. The idea suddenly sounded irresistibly attractive. Their short time in London seemed a thousand years ago, so much had happened since.

'Would you come with me?'

'I thought you'd never ask.'

Chapter Thirty

Sam had never been shot at before and he found it an unnerving experience, particularly with him being at the wheel of his Mondeo. There was a sharp, cracking sound as the bullet passed within an inch of his left arm and smashed into his radio, cutting Ken Bruce off as he introduced the next record. For a few seconds he hadn't a clue what had happened. It was Sally who realised first.

'Jesus, Sam – someone's just shot at us!'

Sam glanced in the mirror at the black 4-wheel-drive Chevrolet that had been following him for the past few minutes. It was now obscured by the halo of shattered glass surrounding the bullet hole in the back window. Instinctively he began to weave the car from side to side. They were driving along a country road high in the Yorkshire Dales, in search of a pub where they could stop for lunch. They heard another shot but the bullet didn't hit them. Sam put his foot down. The road was winding, and precipitous in places.

'Get your head down, Sal!'

Her head was already down. The chasing vehicle had bull-bars on the front and made its presence felt with a vengeance. The Chevrolet rammed the Mondeo and almost pushed it into the path of an oncoming car, which gave a prolonged blast on its horn as it passed. The angry sound died away in the distance as Sam tried to shake off his pursuer, who seemed to be playing with him.

In the Chevrolet, Milo Morrell was laughing maniacally as he rammed into Sam's car once again.

'D'yer want me ter keep shootin'?' asked the large, black man sitting beside him.

'Not just yet, Roscoe, boy – I want to have a bit of fun with Mr Mad Carew.' Milo laughed again. 'He'll be ever so fucking mad when I've finished with him – no he won't, he'll be ever so fucking dead. No one crosses me and gets way with it.'

They both burst out laughing as Sam almost ran his own car off the road in an attempt to escape Milo's deadly pursuit.

'It's Morrell,' said Sam, as calmly as he could. There was enough clear vision left in his back window for him to make out who was in the chasing vehicle. 'He's got a black guy with him. If it's the man who killed Smithy, he's called Roscoe.'

Sally was dialling *999* on her mobile. Sam was amazed at the calmness with which she described their situation and location. She concluded by saying: 'If you think I'm a crank, ring DC Owen Price of Unsworth CID. Tell him Sam and Sally are being chased by Milo Morrell. He's shooting at us and trying to run us off the road.'

In the distance Sam spotted a sign indicating a turn off to the left. At the very last second he pulled hard on the handbrake, whipped the steering wheel round, released the brake and put his foot down hard. With a loud screech of protesting rubber the car spun on its axis and flew up the new road. A glance in his mirror told Sam that his pursuer hadn't made it. This would give him a few valuable seconds of thinking time.

'Hold on tight, Sal.'

She didn't reply. Her mouth was too dry and her heart hammering too hard. Dialling 999 had used up all her resources. She was in Sam's hands now. The road sloped steeply upwards and was barely one car's width. There were passing-places every so often but Sam sincerely hoped that no cars were coming his way – he was going much too fast. On either side were high hedges that eventually, as they climbed higher, gave way to dry-stone walls, and then nothing. Just a steep upward slope on his left and an even steeper one dropping away to his right. A tractor approached and Sam had no option but to slow down and move into a passing space as the vehicle lumbered past.

'It'll slow Morrell down as well,' he told Sally as he accelerated away. From behind him he heard an angry blast on a car horn. Sam allowed himself a grim smile as this seemed to prove his theory, then his smile froze as a lamb strayed into his path.

'Oh shit, I'm going to have to run it down!' A sheep, presumably the mother, followed in her infant's path, another lamb scampered out. Sam cursed and slowed down and nudged his way through. In his mirror the Chevrolet appeared around a corner about a two hundred yards behind. Sam sped away, one eye on the road the other on his mirror. The 4-wheel-drive mowed straight through the sheep without slowing down.

352

Its lights were now blazing, menacingly.

Morrell had never forgotten the terror Sam had subjected him to when he had held the gun to his head and caused him to piss himself with fear; nor the indignity of having to walk through his own club, past his own customers and employees with soaked trousers. No one had mentioned it to him since, but he knew what they'd been thinking. Sam Carew had damaged his hard-man reputation. Morrell could have lived with that for the sake of business. Revenge and business are poor bedfellows. Killing Ferris had helped restore some of his respect. But now there was a DVD around that would convict him of murder for sure. He'd spotted one of the webcams but hadn't known about the disks until the Bateson kid rang to tell him he'd sold it to a woman for two hundred quid. The kid didn't know who the woman was but Morrell was damn sure it had something to do with Carew.

The meddling builder could ruin his business – and his life. The only thing on Morrell's mind was to kill Carew and terrify him on the way. Once he'd done that he'd be able to think straight. Maybe even dig himself out of the mess Carew had put him in. He was driving with a recklessness that had Roscoe shouting for him to slow down.

'Just shut the fuck up and be ready to shoot when I say so!'

The next thing Sam knew was the Chevrolet looming in his mirror. Through a clear part of the rear window he could see Roscoe aiming a gun at them. Sam weaved the car from side to side. A

353

shot rang out and he saw a puff of dust as a bullet ricocheted off a rock in the hillside up ahead. He kept the car weaving. A second shot missed Sam's left ear by a millimetre and smashed through the windscreen. It was the third shot that had Sally screaming in agony.

'Sal! Are you okay?'

Tears were streaming down her face. Her mouth was opening and closing in dumb agony and she slumped forward. Blood was staining the bottom of her back and Sam was sure she was dead. He flew into a blind rage that anyone could do this to Sal. He stamped on the brakes, causing the Chevrolet to ram into him, but Sam kept his foot hard down and pulled on the handbrake. The weight of his car and the slope was too much for the 4 wheel drive pursuer. The Chevrolet slewed to a halt. Sam jumped out, picked up a large stone from the roadside and, screaming with rage, ran towards Morrell's driver's door and yanked it open. Morrell was sitting there open-mouthed, gaping at this madman with a rock. He tried to grab the gun from Roscoe, but Sam was on him, attacking him with a screaming frenzy, hammering the stone at his head. At this point neither Morrell nor his crony had full control of the weapon.

'Shoot him,' Morrell yelled.

The black man took the gun back from his boss and aimed it at Sam, who threw himself out of the vehicle. The bullet went over his head. As he hit the ground he hurled the rock into the Chevrolet just as Roscoe was taking a second shot. It hit the black man's shoulder as he fired, causing his gun-hand to jerk upwards. Morrell didn't have time to scream. The bullet went clean through his brain and out through the open door, leaving Roscoe shocked and covered in his boss's blood. He leaped from the vehicle and ran off down the road, still holding the gun. Sam, also drenched in Morrell's blood, ran back to his car, back to Sally. The lower half of her body was stained dark red. She was deathly pale, she was still, *but she was crying*. He listened for breathing and to his immense relief he found a faint pulse.

'You're alive, Sal!' he shouted at her. 'Don't lose it, Sal, you're alive!'

'What the bloody hell's been happening?'

Sam was too shocked to hear the tractor driver, who had appeared behind him, talking ten to the dozen. 'I saw a big black feller runnin' like buggery down the side of the valley. I shouted at him but he pointed a gun at me. Scared me half to bloody death he did.' He looked at Sally. 'Oh heck! We'll have ter get her to a hospital. I heard yon gun shots and I knew it weren't just some bugger shootin' rabbits.'

All this was falling on deaf ears. As the man spoke, Sam was checking Sally's pulse. It was weak but she was definitely alive. He turned and was surprised to see anyone there. He gave a start and held up his fists defensively. 'Who are you?' he asked.

The man backed off. 'Hey, I came back to help. Is she still alive?'

'Just.'

He looked at the blood on Sam, then back at the Chevrolet. There was blood on the windscreen but Morrell wasn't in sight. 'It were that stupid bastard weren't it? He tried to run me off the road. What about you, are you okay?'

'I'm fine.'

'You don't look fine. Do you have one o' them mobile telephones?'

'Of course.

Sam took one from his pocket and dumbly handed it to the man, who eventually got through to the ambulance service.

'My name's James Bacup of Bacup's farm in High Tollerton. Everybody knows me round here ... yes, I think we definitely need an ambulance.'

It was all taking too long. Sam snatched the phone from him. 'A woman's been shot in the back,' he shouted. 'We're out in the bloody wilds, we need a helicopter, never mind an ambulance... What? You're not listening to me – you send an ordinary ambulance and she'll die. I know what I'm talking about – I'm an ex-policeman. My name's Sam Carew. The injured woman made a 999 call not long ago telling you we were being shot at... Yes, that was her. It's a hell of lot more serious now. There's one man dead and another on the loose with a gun...' Sam listened for a few more seconds, nodding his head this time. '...I'll ask him.' He turned to the farmer. 'Is there somewhere on this road where a helicopter can land?'

Chapter Thirty-One

Sam had driven the car, oh so gently, the half mile to the landing field, with the farmer sitting behind Sally, holding her shoulders. Sam had held her hand and whispered words of encouragement for the thirty-five minutes it took for the air ambulance to arrive; during which time she had remained unconscious. He didn't know how to stem the flow of blood, with the wound being where it was, and he could only hope it would coagulate and stop of its own accord.

As he watched the helicopter soar, noisily, into the sky he thought about Kathy, whose life had been snuffed out with no hope of survival. Sally was alive, and where there was life there was hope. It saddened him deeply to think that Kathy hadn't been given such a chance. But he also knew that he would be devastated if Sally didn't make it.

The helicopter disappeared behind the veil of tears misting Sam's eyes. He felt an arm around his shoulder.

'She'll pull through will yon,' said James Bacup, confidently.

Sam sniffed and looked at him. 'Do you really think so?'

'When yer live on the land yer watch life and death all the time, lad. Yer get a feelin' about such things. She were nowhere near ready for the knackers yard weren't that lass.'

'My god, I hope you're right.'

He drove, almost in a state of shock, to Harrogate hospital. Owen's mobile had been on answer which meant he was probably in court or something and the only other person he could think of ringing was Sue. Her fiancé, Jonathan had answered.

'Is Sue there? – it's Sam.' There was a moment's unhelpful hesitation – for some reason Jonathan still thought of Sam as a rival for Sue's affection. 'It's an emergency, Sally's been taken to hospital.'

'Oh, right, I'll get her.'

'Sam, what's happened?' She was concerned. Sue and Sally had always got on.

'Sue... Sal's been shot. Please don't ask me for details, it'll no doubt be on the news. She's being taken by helicopter to Harrogate hospital. I'm following by car. Her parents need to be told. They live in Bournemouth.'

'Do you know the address?'

'Her dad's called James, her mother's called Rachel. Owen should be able to track them down. I can't get through to him at the moment.'

'Don't worry, Sam, I'll sort it. Are you okay?'

'I'm fine. Sue, I've got to go.'

Ten hours later, Sam had been joined in Harrogate hospital by Owen, Sally's parents – who had flown up from Bournemouth and whom Sam had never met before, and two uniformed police.

Sue and the boys had been and gone – once

they were satisfied that Sam was okay. While they were there a staff nurse came to tell them that Sally had been stabilised and taken to theatre.

'It's good news that she's stable, Dad,' Jake had assured him.

'They wouldn't say that if they thought she might not make it,' Tom had added.

Sue kissed him on his cheek, leaving her lips there for a fraction longer than a friendly peck. Her hand had gripped his arm as she said, 'Ring me on my mobile as soon as you hear anything. Give her my love when she comes round. I'll call in to see her.'

They were all being positive – they and Farmer Bacup. Sam needed that. It gave him the lift he needed as they left him to wait alone.

He had greeted Mr and Mrs Grover guardedly, wondering if they'd blame him for what had happened. They had every right.

'We weren't on a job or anything,' he explained, in mitigation. 'We were taking some time off. Going for a break in the country.'

'Our Sally's told us all about you,' said Mrs Grover, but she didn't elaborate.

There was a long awkward silence then Mr Grover said: 'I imagine things might have been worse for her had you not been with her. She's always held you in high regard.'

Sam felt unworthy of his praise. Mrs Grover added her own opinion: 'Which is not to say we fully approved.'

'I understand, Mrs Grover.'

They all waited in worried silence as the life of

the hospital went on around them. The two constables were relieved by a uniformed constable and a detective sergeant, who took Sam to one side for a statement.

'I'll say one thing for you, Mr Mad Carew,' he commented as he read through Sam's account of events. 'You're well named. I don't know what I'd have done in such circumstances but I'm pretty sure I wouldn't have gone for an armed man with just a lump of rock in my hand.'

'Sometimes, people thinking you're deranged is a weapon in itself,' said Sam. 'It makes them stop and think – gives you that extra few seconds.'

'Is that what you are, deranged?'

'Not really. It's usually an act.'

'And was it an act today?'

'No, today I was deranged.'

'Remind me not to get on the wrong side of you. By the way, we picked Roscoe up about a couple of hours ago.'

'Did he give you any trouble?'

'Well, we had had two helicopters, a dozen of our troops and an armed response unit crawling all over the Dales. I think everyone enjoyed themselves – it's good to have a day out in the country now and again. He fired a couple of shots at us then he threw his gun down before we had a chance to fire back – spoilsport.'

'Pity,' said Sam. 'He's the one who shot Sally. He also killed Paul Smith.'

'Well, Morrell's dead as you probably know,' said the sergeant, looking at the dried blood on Sam's shirt. 'We'll need you down at the station to make a proper statement.'

360

'I'm not going anywhere until I know Sally's all right.'

It was just turned nine o'clock that night when a surgeon came through to see them, still clad in his green theatre clothes. He looked at Sam.

'Are you Sally's husband?'

'Er, no. I'm her – partner.'

'We're her parents,' said Mr Grover, anxiously. 'How is she?'

'Well, the good news is that she's out of danger.' There were sighs of relief. The surgeon went on: 'She lost a lot of blood and we've taken a bullet from her pelvis, which was shattered – but we don't know yet what other damage has been done.'

'What does that mean?' Sam enquired.

'I can't be precise, but they may be some loss of movement in her lower limbs.'

'You mean she could be crippled?' said Mrs Grover, shocked. 'In a wheelchair?'

'I mean I don't know yet. She's incredibly lucky to be here at all. Had she not been brought here in a helicopter we'd most certainly have lost her. That was a bit of quick thinking on someone's part.'

'Can we see her?' Sam asked.

'If you don't crowd her, she's very fragile at the moment.'

Sam looked at Sally's parents. 'You should go in first.'

Mr Grover put an arm around his wife. 'She'll be all right, will our girl.'

'I know she will,' said Mrs Grover, with her eyes once again fixed on Sam. 'And even if she isn't, she's always got Sam Carew to look after her.'

'She'll always have me, Mrs Grover. I just hope I'm good enough.'

'Time will tell,' she said, but she didn't seem very convinced.

A nurse came and said Sally was ready to see her parents now. Sam asked if he could see her afterwards and the nurse said, 'If she's not too tired.'

'We won't tire her out,' promised Mr Grover, but within five minutes Sally was asleep, her parents were asked to leave and Sam told to come back tomorrow.

'It's been a sod of a day,' Sam said.

He and Owen had made last orders in the Clog and Shovel. Owen signalled the order to Dave and returned his attention to Sam. 'You should shake today's events from your mind, if only for the time being.'

'Oh yeah,' said Sam, 'and talk about what?'

'About the annual pub trip to Bridlington. Two days of fun, fishing and fornication – if you're lucky.'

'No one ever gets three out of three,' remarked Sam. 'Not in Bridlington.'

'The most I've ever had is two,' admitted Owen. 'Mind you, I never was much good at fishing. Eight hours bobbing about in a small boat off Flamborough Head plays havoc with my bowels. I might request shore-leave this year.'

Sam was lost in thought. 'I think Eileen can say goodbye to her insurance money,' he said. 'And we can wave goodbye to our commission.'

'Why's that, boyo?'

'Because Morrell was the central figure in Ron Crusher's murder and with him gone I can't see any way forward. There may be other people who know what happened but unless someone volunteers information I think we're goosed.'

'What about Roscoe?'

'Roscoe's going down for life. He won't want to do his time as a known grass.'

'Even for grassing up a dead man?'

'My guess is that there'll be a few live ones out there who'll want him to keep his mouth shut.'

'I'll break the bad news to Eileen then,' said Owen. 'What about the trip? It's week today. There's a couple of places going spare on the coach.'

'I can't, Owen. I want to keep myself available for Sally when she comes out.'

'Fair point, boyo.'

'Pity,' Sam said. 'I've always enjoyed the annual piss-up. Caught quite a few plaice last time I went. No – can't commit myself to two days away.'

'You could go in your own car,' Owen suggested. 'If you get a phone call you can always go back under your own steam.'

Sam had a sudden flash of what might have been inspiration but it vanished when Dave laid two pints on their table. It had come and gone and he'd no idea what it had been about. It was annoying because it had been such a great thought – whatever it was.

'Cheers, Dave. No, it's not the same. The coach trip back's one of the best parts. Stopping off at the Kings Head in York. You getting up on stage blind drunk, singing "When You Come Home Again to Wales".'

'Strongest beer in Yorkshire,' remembered Owen. 'The next day I'd have an arse like a Labour Party rosette.'

Sam's shoulders suddenly dropped. Tears began to flow and he held his head in his hands. 'I really need to see Sal,' he said.

Owen put an arm around his friend's shoulder. 'And so you shall, boyo. First get a good night's sleep.'

She was the only patient in a two bed ward. Sam had been sitting by her bed since ten o'clock, waiting for her to open her eyes.

'I know you're there,' she said, after a while.

'I thought you were asleep.'

'I was, but when I woke up I knew you were there.'

'How?'

'I don't know. I just knew.'

'How are you feeling?'

'Numb. Have they said anything to you?'

'Not much. They wouldn't let me see you last night. Only relatives.'

'Who then?'

'Your mum and dad.'

'What, Mum and Dad came up from Bourne-mouth? Was I dying?'

'You've been better. They came in to see you. Don't you remember?'

'Maybe – I've been struggling to sort out dreams from reality. Was I in your car with Morrell chasing us and shooting at us?'

He nodded. 'That wasn't a dream.'

'I remember being really scared. Then there was this farm tractor, then some sheep, then nothing. What happened?'

Sam related the whole story. She listened with mounting incredulity. 'You went for him with what?'

'A lump of rock.'

'He had a gun and you went for him with a lump of rock?'

'He wasn't expecting it, which is why it worked,' Sam explained, patiently. His methods always seemed to make more sense to him than they did to other people. It was a source of annoyance at times. But not now.

'I suppose it's fair to say,' she summed up, 'that if I'd been with anyone else, I'd have been dead.'

'If you'd been with anyone else it wouldn't have happened,' Sam pointed out.

She managed a smile. 'Sam – am I going to be all right?'

'You're not going to die, if that's what you're saying.'

'It's not exactly what I'm saying. I can't feel anything from the waist down.'

'That'll be the anaesthetic. The bullet shattered your pelvis. It'll heal but they don't know what other damage may have been done.'

'Are we talking wheelchairs or walking sticks?'

'Sal, they honestly don't know. We could be talking marathon running for all I know.'

She lay quiet for a while, digesting this information. Then she started to cry copious tears. He put his arm around her and held her as close as

365

he dare. 'It's okay, Sal. There's no point worrying about something that might not happen. Whatever the outcome, I'll always be around.'

'That's what's bothering me,' she sniffed.

Chapter Thirty-Two

Alec hovered by Sam's shoulder as he was studying the plans of the Dalby Parade site. It was three days later and they were standing on the top lift of scaffold.

'I don't suppose there's any chance you're back permanently?' he asked.

'I've closed the office down for the time being,' Sam told him. 'Without Sal there's no point in keeping it open.' He tapped his pocket. 'I'm having all calls transferred to my mobile – which is switched off for the time being.'

'Sam,' said Alec. 'I know you've got my share of the business tied down with this golden hand-cuffs contract – and I don't want you to take this the wrong way – but what happens to my share if anything happens to you?'

'It's a fair point,' conceded Sam. 'If I die the cuffs are off. You get forty-nine per cent, my boys get the rest. I'd like to think you'll keep it going for their benefit.' He picked up a brick and spread it with mortar. 'By the way, I've no plans for dying just yet.'

'You could have fooled me. You're daft getting mixed up with criminals, you know. You just haven't got the powers the police have.'

'I don't get mixed up with them on purpose. It's they who get mixed up with me – could you tighten this line, it's sagging.'

Alec walked along the scaffold to the corner of the wall and was tightening the line to which Sam was working when a thought struck him. 'There's a new building inspector started the other week – used to work in Huddersfield. He was asking me if I knew Ron Crusher, with him coming from round here.'

Sam stopped what he was doing. 'What's his name?'

'Rastrick.'

'Thin feller with a moustache?'

'That's him.'

'Did he ask for a bung?'

Alec looked uncomfortable and asked, 'Where do you know him from?'

'Morrell's site in Huddersfield. The man's bent. What the hell's he doing on our site? Can't be a coincidence, surely?'

'They do happen,' said Alec.

'Ron Crusher used to bung him. He wanted me to, but I fettled him. What the hell's he doing here?' Sam studied Alec's face. 'He tried it on with you, didn't he?'

Alec gave an embarrassed nod.

'Alec we don't give bungs. My dad would've rather lost money on a job than bung anyone. He'd have been straight round to the council shouting the odds, whether they believed him or not.'

'I'm not your dad – I wasn't sure what to do. He could have slowed the job down to a halt if I hadn't gone along with him. I've arranged to give him a hundred a week to keep the job running smoothly.'

368

'You should have told me.'

'Sam, you'd left me to run the sites. You had enough on your plate recently, what with people shooting at you and stuff.'

'When does he collect?'

Alec looked down over the scaffold rail at a council van driving on to the site. 'Round about now. He'll be giving the job a once-over, then no doubt wanting his wages.'

'Go and see him,' said Sam. 'Don't mention me. When it comes to money take him into the cabin and start arguing the amount with him.'

As Alec climbed down from the scaffold, Sam took out his mobile and rang Owen.

An hour later, Rastrick had completed a full inspection of the site in the company of Alec, and was in the site hut, having a very heated discussion. The door was partially open; Sam and Owen stood outside, listening to Rastrick:

'Fifty quid? – we agreed a hundred. Fifty quid a week's no good to man nor beast. If you want this job to run smoothly it'll cost you a hundred as agreed. You scratch my back, I'll scratch yours – that's how it works in this business. I'm not used to contractors arguing over pennies.'

'But we do a good job, why should we pay you at all?' Alec was arguing.

'You do as good a job as I say you do. If I made you work strictly to regulations I can have you jumping through bloody hoops and you know it.'

Eventually Alec came to the door and called Sam in. Rastrick's eyes narrowed when he recognised the builder from Huddersfield; and his jaw dropped when Owen followed Sam into the cabin. Owen showed the building inspector his warrant card.

'I believe you know Detective Constable Price,' said Sam. 'Well, it seems you're up to your old tricks, Mr Rastrick.'

'He wants me to pay him a hundred a week to keep the job running smoothly,' snapped Alec.

'I know,' said Sam. 'We heard him. Would you two gentlemen mind if I had a quick word with Mr Rastrick in private?'

Owen and Alec left, grudgingly, both unsure what Sam was going to do. Sam introduced himself.

'I'm Sam Carew of Carew and Son. Why are you trying to steal my money again?'

'I – I'm not–'

'I heard you – you were asking for a hundred pounds a week, so did DC Price. What's up, doesn't the council pay you enough?'

Rastrick was stuck for an answer. Sam took him by his collar. 'If you want to keep your job tell me about Ron Crusher.'

'Ron Crusher? I – I don't know much about him. What do you want to know about him for?'

'You took bungs from him. He fell off a high building. You demanded money from Paul Smith – he was murdered by Milo Morrell. Why did you move here? I want to know about you and Ron Crusher and Milo Morrell. I want to know who killed Ron Crusher? If you don't tell me all you know I'll just throw you to the wolves. You'll end up inside for sure.'

Rastrick was quivering with fright. Sam had switched into his deranged mode. The building inspector was shaking his head, violently.

'I don't know anything. If I could help you I would. I left Huddersfield because I was worried what might happen if Morrell ever found out I was taking money from his builder. This job just came up. That's all there is to it. There's no more money – just a better car allowance.'

'Car allowance?' said Sam, a bit stumped at this odd non-sequitur. 'What the hell have cars got to do with anything?'

'I don't know,' muttered Rastrick, miserably. 'Please call the copper off. I don't want any trouble.'

Sam stared at him and frowned as his eyes became focused on the cabin wall behind the building inspector – on which was pinned an A4 poster advertising the Clog and Shovel trip to Bridlington. Sam had offered to run the sites in his partner's absence so that Alec could go. His eyes flickered from Rastrick to the poster and back and he knew there was a connection. It was that same vanishing flash of inspiration from the other day in the Clog – and he was struggling to hold on to it. It was another piece of the jigsaw. But it was like having an elusive word on the tip of your tongue. Only it wasn't just a word. It was the key to finding Ron Crusher's killer.

He stared out of the window at the busy site and tried to get his mind to relax sufficiently for the thought to come back. Curly was driving a dumper across to a pile of gravel and he parked it in a spot convenient to him but inconvenient to everyone else. Someone cursed and told him to move it. Curly replied with two fingers. Sam closed his eyes, but the thought had buried itself in that place where they hide.

'Look, it's okay. I won't give any trouble,' Rastrick was saying.

'What?'

'I said forget having to pay me. Forget I mentioned it. I'll make sure the job runs smoothly.'

'Look, just clear off!' said Sam irritably. Rastrick was clouding his mind.

'So long as we know where we stan–'

'I said piss off!' snapped Sam, pacing up and down. 'Just go!'

Rastrick stepped out of the cabin past a bemused Alec and Owen.

'Are we letting the twisting bugger go?' asked Owen as Rastrick's van drove away.

'Do what you want. I've got some bricks to lay!' said Sam, walking away from them.

'What was all that about?' Owen asked Alec.

'Your guess is as good as mine.'

'He called me over here special and now he's being bloody rude.'

Sam was in his own world now. High above the site. Spread the compo on the top and sides, lay the brick to the line, tap it into position, scrape off the surplus compo, repeat the exercise, time and again. Constructive monotony. Constructive and therapeutic monotony. As the wall grows the mind is free to wander. Lunchtime approached and the compo had gone off sufficiently for him to do some pointing. He took a pointing tool from his bag, fashioned from a bucket handle, and ran it, expertly, along the vertical and horizontal joints.

Last night he'd taken another look at the CCTV tape from Ridings House and had spotted something else. It was something Sally wouldn't have noticed and anyway, he might be wrong. But he had played the tape through time after time and he knew he wasn't. For the life of him he couldn't understand it. Could it be yet another piece of his ever expanding jigsaw? There was one person who might be able to confirm what was on the tape, but that might prove tricky.

Below him he heard one of the joiners laughing that someone had stuck a joke parking ticket on Curly's dumper. And there it was again, the forgotten thought from this morning. Only it wasn't just another piece of the jigsaw, it was the last piece. This time there were no distractions. This time he pressed the last piece into place and viewed the whole picture. There were some indistinct areas around the edges but the picture was there, complete with its main protagonist – Ron Crusher's killer. There was a pile of compo lying on a ligger board. He flattened it with a shovel and wrote the name of the killer in it with the point of his trowel, lest it escape his mind again. But he knew it wouldn't.

With a deliberate lack of haste he cleaned off his tools and put them in his bag as he planned his next move. Then he climbed down the ladder and walked over to the cabin where Alec was studying a pile of delivery notes. Sam shouted through the door, 'I'm off.'

'Off – where to? Sam you can't just come and go like that.'

But Sam had gone.

Owen was in the CID office when his mobile rang.

'Owen, it's Sam – can I see you?'

'You saw me this bloody morning and wasted my time. I've got better things to do than run around after you.'

'I know who killed Ron Crusher – are you interested?'

Owen responded with a long silence.

'Did you hear me?'

'I heard you all right, boyo. The thing is, do I believe you?'

'You know you believe me,' said Sam. 'You got the credit for discovering Morrell's office and all the fake passports, didn't you?'

'I told them I got the information from a reliable source whose name I promised not to reveal. I felt a right pillock – everyone in this nick knows it's you.'

'They're only jealous. Tell you what, Owen, this is the big one. They'll make you chief constable after this.'

Owen relented. 'Okay – where and when?'

'First of all I wonder if you could do me a small favour and use your influence at the Leeds Register Office.'

'What influence would that be?' enquired Owen.

'All right, your personal charm.'

'That's more like it.'

Sam outlined what he needed, then added: 'I'm seeing Bernard Crusher at his house at five o'clock. He thinks it's to do with his drugs case.

In a way it is. Could you bring Eileen?'

'Eileen? Why does she have to be there?'

'Could you bring her?'

'I suppose so.'

'Owen, don't tell her why.'

'That won't be difficult – I don't know myself.'

'You'll find out soon enough.'

Eileen, Bernard and Owen sat in separate chairs like the suspects in an Agatha Christie dénouement. Sam sat on the arm of Bernard's chair and clasped his hands around crossed knees. Owen grinned.

'What?' said Sam.

'I'm waiting for you to fall over on your backside like Inspector Clouseau and tell us that everything you do is carefully planned.'

Sam saw the similarity and got to his feet. He spoke to Bernard. 'I really wanted Mariella to hear what I've got to say. Pity she can't be here.'

'I'd like to know where she's buggered off to, meself,' grumbled Bernard. 'I haven't seen her since first thing this mornin' – she had a face on her like a bad ham. Mind you, that's nowt new.'

Sam turned his attention to Eileen. 'I'd always suspected that you were the key to all this, and I was right.'

She frowned.

'I thought you said Morrell was the key to it all,' remarked Owen, sticking a toffee in his mouth.

'I was wrong,' said Sam.

'What?' said Bernard. 'Are you saying Morrell had nothing to do with the drugs?'

'On the contrary. I think that Morrell had everything to do with the drugs – I just couldn't prove it that's all. I don't think Morrell had anything to do with Ron's death, though.'

'What's all this about, then?' asked Bernard. 'I thought this was all about helping me.'

'In a roundabout way, it is,' said Sam. He took a video cassette from his pocket and gave it to Bernard. 'Could you play this for me please?'

'What is it?'

'It's a CCTV tape from the lobby of Ridings House at the time Marjorie Mutch jumped off the roof.' He looked at them. 'I assume we all know who Mrs Mutch is – or was?'

'She's the woman who cost me a fortune,' said Eileen.

'I never believed a word she said.' grunted Bernard. 'I reckon she'd been put up to it.'

'By Morrell?' suggested Sam.

'Who else?' said Bernard.

'Well, he's on this tape all right, but so is someone else. Could you play it for us, Bernard?'

Bernard inserted the tape and sat back down, not having a clue what to expect. Sam had set it to begin just as the panicking woman rushed into the building. He gave a running commentary: 'This is the lobby of Ridings House just after Mrs Mutch hit the pavement outside. In about a minute you'll see Milo Morrell come through the door. Now I must admit, when I first saw it this threw me, and I missed the important bit.'

Morrell entered and walked through the picture, to the accompaniment of caustic comments from Bernard. There was more commotion in the entrance door. People began to run out, including a woman with a very distinctive gait. She ran from beneath the camera towards the door, elbowing people aside. Sam looked at Bernard.

'I can't see her face, but the last time I saw a woman run like that was in Barbados.'

'By the heck that's Mariella!' exclaimed Bernard. 'Can't be anyone else. She runs like she's gorra broken bottle jammed up her arse. Anyway I recognise that coat. What the hell's she doing there?'

Sam took the remote from him and switched the tape off. 'I'm not sure how you're going to take this, Bernard, so I'll go through it bit by bit.'

Bernard sat on the edge of his chair as Sam began: 'I understand Mariella had an operation just before Ron died.'

Bernard shrugged. 'It was her adenoids. What the hell's that got to do with anything?'

'And on the day he died she went on a trip to Blackpool. It seems an odd way to convalesce.'

'It were my idea – got her out of me hair for a couple of days,' remembered Bernard.

Sam sat down on the arm of Owen's chair. He lit a cigarette and looked at Eileen. 'Did you know that Derek Fleming had a sister?'

She shrugged. 'No, I didn't. Should it surprise me? I imagine he's as much entitled to relatives as anyone.'

'Her name's Jean,' said Sam. He glanced at Bernard. 'Do you know who I'm talking about, Bernard?'

Bernard shook his head. 'Haven't a clue.'

'Did Mariella go on the coach to Blackpool?'

377

'You know she did,' said Bernard, bemused. 'What's all this about? I thought we'd just been talking about it.'

'No, I know she *went* to Blackpool, but I wondered if she went by car in case she felt she wasn't up to it, and might want to come home early – what with her just having had an operation?'

'Yes, she did go by car,' remembered Eileen.

'I think you're probably right,' said Bernard. 'In fact you are right, she went in my car. Have you any idea what he's on about, Owen?'

'Normally Carew's thought process is one of the great mysteries of the universe,' said Owen, 'but I think I'm following him on this one.'

'And where were all the women on the day Ron died?' Sam asked Eileen.

'Out and about – Pleasure Beach, mainly,' said Eileen. 'We all went on the Pepsi Max. I threw up.'

'Were you out all day?'

Eileen cast her mind back. 'Pretty much, I think. We went out after breakfast and came back in time for the evening meal. That's when the police came to tell me about Ron.'

'What about Mariella – did she go with you?'

'I imagine so. To be honest I tried to keep my distance from Mariella.' She shot Bernard a guilty look. 'She's not the best of company.'

'I know, lass,' agreed Bernard.

'Actually,' remembered Eileen, 'she didn't come with us. I remember everyone being relieved when she said she wasn't feeling so good and did we mind if she stayed in the hotel for the day and come out with us at night? Some of them

378

pretended to be concerned. Apart from anything else her breath stank like a sewer. I know it was something to do with her operation but she shouldn't have come. She couldn't talk properly either – it came out as more of a growl.'

'Why do you think I persuaded her to go?' said Bernard.

'I don't think you did persuade her,' said Sam. 'I think she persuaded you to persuade her – women are good at that.' He took Bernard's court summons from his pocket. 'Did you ever look at the date on this?'

Bernard shook his head. 'No, what difference does it make?'

'It would have told you that your car was parked in George Street in Unsworth an hour before Ron fell off Ridings House.'

Bernard examined it, then looked up at Sam. 'I don't understand.'

'I reckon Mariella drove it to Unsworth,' Sam said, 'and somehow killed Ron. Then she drove it back to Blackpool to give herself an alibi.'

'Don't talk so damn stupid!' exploded Bernard. 'Why on earth would she want to do a trick like that? This sounds like a load o' bollocks to me.'

'Then how do you account for the car being there,' Sam asked him, 'when it should have been in Blackpool?'

Bernard shook his head, then asked, 'What's all this to do with her bein' on this tape?'

'I think she killed Mrs Mutch as well,' said Sam.

'Why would she do that?'

'To stop her telling the police she'd been paid

379

to lie about seeing Ron commit suicide.' Sam looked at Eileen. 'The odds are that Mariella was the woman who killed O'Brien and ran Forbuoys down.'

'Why would she do that?' asked an amazed Eileen.

'Because she's Derek Fleming's sister.' Sam waited for this to sink in before he continued: 'I believe she wanted revenge for what they did to him. Forbuoys had received death threats and he thought he saw a woman driving the car that knocked him down.' Eileen was shaking her head as she listened. Sam continued: 'And a woman was seen leaving O'Brien's flat around the time he was killed.'

'His sister?' exclaimed Eileen. 'No, I don't believe this. I mean – how do you know?'

Owen cleared his throat and took out a sheet of paper. 'I contacted the Leeds Register Office this afternoon armed with the date of Derek Fleming's death and requested further information about his family.' He read from the sheet: 'He has a sister called Jean Fleming who, in 1984 changed her name to Mariella Storm. She was married in 1989 to Geoffrey Pilger and widowed in 1999. In 2001 she married Bernard Crusher.'

'Well, I'm beggared if I knew owt about all this,' said a baffled Bernard, who didn't seem overly concerned about his wife being exposed as his brother's killer. It was gradually occurring to him that all this might somehow get him off the drugs charge. 'I knew she'd called herself Mariella Storm when she were singing, but I never knew she'd ever been called Jean Fleming.'

380

'Next time you get married I suggest you should read the small print before you sign up,' advised Owen.

'I were probably pissed,' admitted Bernard. 'Yer'd have ter be pissed ter marry her. Anyway, who the hell's this Derek Fleming?' The phone rang, he went into the hall to answer it.

Eileen was still shaking her head at the revelation that Mariella was Derek Fleming's sister. 'I'm sorry, I can't get my head round this,' she was saying. 'I mean – why would she kill Ron? He hadn't done her any harm.'

Sam spoke as gently as he could under the circumstances. 'My guess is that she was trying to destroy you and watch you squirm – leaving you with nothing because of what you did to her brother. She'll probably see you as one of his abusers.'

'But she didn't know who I was.'

'People find things out,' said Sam. 'I did.'

Eileen was in tears. 'I didn't abuse him – I was only a kid myself. Oh shit, maybe I did abuse him! I was just thinking about the money – about my own survival.'

Owen had his arm around her. 'It's water under the bridge, look you. We've all done things just to survive. You didn't mean the boy any harm, that's all that counts, isn't it. Now, if you harmed him on purpose, then you'd have cause for self-recrimination.'

'When she's caught and found guilty it means you should get your insurance money,' said Sam. Eileen didn't seem impressed. She had been the indirect cause of Ron's death. Not only Ron, but

381

others as well.

There was a long silence, broken only by Eileen's crying. 'She probably only married Bernard to keep tabs on me,' she sobbed.

The same thought had crossed Sam's mind.

'Where does Morrell and the drugs come into the picture?' enquired Owen.

'I don't know. We won't know the whole story until we pick Mariella up, and there's no guarantee even then. Still, I think there's enough here to hold her.'

Own took out his mobile. 'I suppose I'd better pass all this on to Bowman.'

'Hey, this is *your* collar,' Sam reminded him. 'Bowman's had no part in this. Don't ring anyone yet. Let's wait until Bernard gets back – tell him what's happening before we do anything. I know she's a monster, but she is his wife. Anyway he'll probably know where she is.'

It was a further fifteen minutes before Bernard came into the room, ashen-faced. He sat down heavily in a chair, his head in his hands.

'Problems?' guessed Sam.

'I'll say,' muttered Bernard. 'She's only gone and cleaned out all the accounts – every last bloody penny. That was a creditor on the phone wondering why his cheque bounced. I said I'd ring him back. I'd sooner wring her bloody neck.'

'What – you mean you've checked the accounts?' Sam asked.

Bernard's head moved slowly up and down. 'We do this e-banking. I checked on the computer. She's been letting the bills pile up. Yesterday she transferred everything to this account I've never heard of.'

'But, isn't all the money hers?'

'Most of it belongs to the creditors – I'm entitled to some of it. Truth is, as things stand I can't even afford to pay meself any wages.'

'Might she be moving it for business reasons?' enquired Owen.

Bernard sighed, heavily. 'I very much doubt it. There's more, you see. I've just been looking through her papers to see if I could find some explanation.'

'And...?' said Sam.

'And she's just remortgaged the bloody house right up to the hilt. How the hell did she do all that without me knowing?'

'Because the house is in her name?' Sam suggested.

'Everything's in her name. The business will go bust. I'll have no money coming in, which means I can't afford to pay this new mortgage. Christ! She's putting me out of house and home – the evil cow!'

'I know the feeling,' said Eileen, without much sympathy.

'And you've no idea where she is?' Sam asked.

'None at all, but I know one thing. Wherever she is, I reckon she's got close on half a million quid with her!'

Sam went to the window and watched the evening clouds in the sky. The room behind was silent, all eyes were on him. He turned round.

'Would you mind if I took a look at Mariella's personal stuff.'

'Be my guest,' said Bernard, getting to his feet.

The whole party trooped to a small room at the back of the house. It contained a smart looking computer set-up, a desk and a chest of drawers.

'The top two drawers are hers,' said Bernard. 'They're not tidy. She's an untidy cow. What are you looking for?'

'No idea,' said Sam. 'Something incriminating. Something to give us a hint as to where she's gone.'

'Well,' said Owen, 'she's still in the country. This is her passport.'

'I suppose that's something,' said Bernard. 'At least she's not planning on going far.'

'I wouldn't bank on it,' said Sam. He was holding a sheet of what had been six passport-size photographs, taken by a photographer in Unsworth. Two had been cut out. The remainder bore only a passing resemblance to Mariella. The face was bland and expressionless, with neither smile nor scowl. Bernard took them from him.

'It's her, but it doesn't look like her,' he commented.

'Why would she have had passport photos taken?' asked Sam. He took Mariella's passport from Owen. 'This passport's got six years left to run.'

'No idea. They're not forced to be for a passport.'

'Bernard, how well did she know Morrell?'

'She used to sing in his club. I reckon she knew him pretty welt. What are you thinking?'

'I'm thinking that anyone who does a runner takes their passport. So, why hasn't Mariella taken hers?'

'You tell me,' said Bernard, knowing he wasn't going to like the answer.

'Morrell used to deal in forged passports,' Sam said. 'He kept them in his office in Ridings House, which is where Mariella killed Ron and Mrs Mutch.'

'What – you reckon Mariella's done a bunk on a dodgy passport? False name and stuff?'

Sam nodded.

'Bloody hell!' cursed Bernard. 'Half a million quid and a new name. How are we supposed to find her?'

'It's going to be tricky,' conceded Sam. He looked at Owen. 'Could be very expensive. I doubt if Bowman will bend over backwards to help.'

Bernard picked up a picture postcard. 'If I were to hazard a guess,' he said, 'I'd guess she'd head for this place. She hasn't travelled much and she'd want to go somewhere she knew, knowing her.'

'Where's here?' asked Sam looking at a photograph of a white beach, palm trees and blue sea. He turned it over and read on the back that it was Paradise Beach, Barbados.

'She once said it was her favourite place on earth,' said Bernard, 'not that she'd been to many places. I think she'd make for there, even if it's only for a couple of days, then she'd be off around the islands. She used to talk about that as well. We'd never find her.'

'Do you have any recent photographs of her?' Sam asked.

Bernard shook his head. 'None since I met her. She didn't like her picture taken. We didn't even have any wedding photos.' He picked up an old publicity photograph. 'This is her twenty years ago. She was quite a looker in them days. I don't think she wanted to be reminded of how much she's gone downhill.'

'Sam,' said Owen. 'What would you do if you did find her? You're not a copper, you couldn't arrest her. It's a police matter. If she's to be picked up quickly we'd need to send her description to the Barbados police.'

Sam nodded, gloomily. 'Trouble is, even if they wanted to, our police couldn't give Barbados a name or a photo that looked like her,' he said. 'That's if she's in Barbados. She could be in Timbuctu for all we know.'

'If you can't find her,' said Eileen, 'does it mean I won't get my insurance money?'

'That'd be up to the court,' said Sam. 'They might try the case in her absence, but I think that'd take a long time – years maybe. Even then the outcome's not certain. The only stuff we've got on her is circumstantial.'

'So, she's won then? We can't touch her. She'll be lying on a beach, gloating.'

Chapter Thirty-Three

Mariella stretched out on her sun lounger, gloating. It had all worked out so well. She had $840,000 in a Cayman Island bank and a wallet full of gold and platinum cards, all in her proper name, Jean Fleming – the name on her forged passport and the original birth certificate that she'd treasured since she was a girl. Milo had set this up for her several months ago. Once Ron was dead there was nothing to hang around for. Derek had been fully avenged and a girl with this much money could live a long time in the Caribbean, especially once her broker put her money to work for her.

Sam Carew had been getting too close. The minute she heard about Milo's death she put all her plans into action. Although he didn't know it, she was his ultimate target, and she didn't like being the target of someone so unpredictable.

She leaned up on one elbow and looked out from beneath her brightly coloured beach umbrella as she sucked, noisily, at a long straw protruding from a glass of rum punch. She allowed her thoughts to drift back to the events of last summer. The sparkling, turquoise sea lapped on to the half-deserted beach, inhabited only by leaning palms and three black boys playing cricket. Anchored about seventy yards offshore was a white catamaran. A topless woman was stretched out on the deck and a bronzed man was practising his diving. A pelican swooped around in a wide circle before gliding to an untidy halt on the water. It folded its wings and seemed to go to sleep.

But Mariella didn't see any of this. What she saw was Ron Crusher's car parked at a meter near Ridings House in Unsworth. A man walked quickly up to it. The boot sprang open. The man dropped a holdall inside. He slammed the boot shut and walked away. That was half the deal done. Milo never handled gear himself. All he handled was money. Never got his hands dirty. Ron was now in possession of the coke. Milo would now require to be placed in funds.

In her bag was a revolver that Milo had given her some years ago for her own protection. It wasn't loaded. She'd never fired a gun in her life, and anyway, to shoot him would have looked like murder. That wasn't her plan.

Ron got out of the car. He had a bag as well. But his bag contained the £150,000 he was to pay Milo for the cocaine now in the boot. He was a reluctant drug dealer but it was, in fact, a bargain, with a street value of more than a million pounds. Although crack was the fashionable drug – with its short-lived but high powered hit – coke never went out of fashion. She didn't have to follow him, she knew exactly where he was going; after all it was she who had set Ron up. She'd bumped into Milo in Leeds. He'd told her how he was going legit and did she want to buy twenty kilos of blow? He'd been joking of course but Mariella could see possibilities. Why didn't he just sell it on to the street dealers? she asked.

Because the filth are sniffing too close to my arse, he told her, and they're picking the dealers off like flies. His eyes had grown serious when she mentioned that Ron had a lot of equity in his house and a second mortgage would buy a lot of coke. Milo needed no further information. He made Ron an offer he couldn't refuse. Without realising it the gangster had become a part of Mariella's plan. All she had to do was wait outside Milo's office and approach Ron from behind.

She smiled as she remembered how well it had all gone. Every act of revenge she'd carried out on Derek's behalf had been charmed, as if someone was guiding her – Derek maybe. The adenoid operation had been a godsend. It had given her a voice that even she found scary. Normally she wouldn't have dreamt of going to Blackpool with all those cackling women with their Kiss-Me-Quick hats and candy floss. But they'd turned up trumps for her. She had always figured it would be an alibi the police would never see through. But this Sam Carew character was a different kettle of fish. It was a pity Milo hadn't succeeded in bumping him off.

Just for a second, when she'd held the gun alongside Ron's face, she thought he'd turn round. If he had she'd have been ready with a joke. There had been a time when she'd wanted Ron Crusher desperately. She had been a resolutely unfaithful wife and when her first husband died of a heart attack she had asked Ron to shack up with her and her money. He'd been the best lover she'd ever had. Attentive and sensuous. Not a bit like Milo, who was as selfish in bed as he was in general.

But Ron had reminded her that he was married, and with his wife being an ex-prostitute she was brilliant between the sheets. 'A brass?' Mariella had said. 'How can you live with a fuckin' brass?' Then, when Ron had told her Eileen's prostitute name – Zola Gee – she flipped. The man she loved had turned her down for the woman who had abused her brother. Her revenge days were in the past, so she had thought. But as time went on, her hatred festered and she knew she couldn't allow Zola, or Eileen as she now called herself, to go unpunished. Of course she didn't tell Ron this. No one knew about her past. That would have been too dangerous.

But Ron didn't turn round. She guessed her voice did the trick. It sounded evil to start with and she added to it. He thought she was a man. On top of which she knew her breath stank – also a handy side-effect of the operation. Bernard had reminded her often enough. Bernard, what a prat. After her first husband died she'd only married him to stay close to Ron and wait for the main chance.

Ron had climbed on to that parapet like a lamb to the slaughter. She'd let him think he was a decoy for a robbery that was going on elsewhere; lulled him into a false sense of security. That was a brainwave; she'd only thought of that at the last second to stop him turning round. Taking the car keys from his pocket had been clever as well. Had the police found all that coke in his boot they'd have suspected something other than suicide. It had to look like suicide or it would have been a waste of time. She knew Ron had plenty of insurance, he was that type. No way was Zola Gee going to cop for a small fortune after Ron's death. Zola Gee had to suffer bereavement and poverty and misery. With a bit of luck she wouldn't be able to handle it and she'd commit suicide.

All Mariella had to do was pull on one of Ron's legs and send him off balance. Easy as that. Far easier than killing O'Brien or running Forbuoys down. It had all gone so well.

There had been a downside. It wasn't until after she'd killed Ron that she realised how much she had loved him, despite him being married to the brass who'd abused her brother. Apart from Derek he had been the only other person she'd ever had any feelings for – and Zola had taken both of them away from her. So it had to be done. Zola had to suffer the same loss as she had.

Marjorie Mutch had practically flung herself over the edge to avoid being shot through the back of her head as Mariella had threatened. Silly cow. Point a gun at some people and they lose all common sense. All it had taken was a slight nudge and over she went.

At some point in the near future Sam Carew might figure out who she really was and would want to question her about certain mysterious deaths. It might even occur to that husband of hers where she was right now. But he'd have to find the money to come after her – and all she'd left in Unsworth was a mountain of debts. Her mouth twisted into a grin at the thought of his face when he realised what she'd done. Poor sod. Anyway he'd never find her, no one would. Tomorrow she was off to Tortola – after that, who knows? She lay back, closed her eyes and nodded off.

'Mrs Mariella Crusher, as I live and breathe? We meet again. He said you might be here an' I'm the only person on this island who knows what you look like. Now ain't that a stroke of luck? I hope you're not goin' to give me trouble this time, Mrs Crusher.'

For a few seconds the voice became a part of Mariella's dream. She opened her eyes and saw a familiar figure standing over her.

'Do I know you?' she said.

It was a black woman. There were two policemen with her.

'Your very good friend, Mr Sam Carew, asked me to look you up. He's very naughty feller that Sam Carew – not the marryin' kind. When you see him you can tell him that from Miss Francine le Bon, who *is* the marryin' kind.'

'What, what d'yer want?' Mariella was beginning to panic. Why was this woman talking about Sam Carew? This wasn't how it was supposed to be.

'Me afraid we have to arrest you once again.'

'Arrest me – what d'yer want to arrest me for?'

'For enterin' our country on a false passport. I know it's a false passport because the last time I saw you, you was Mrs Mariella Crusher. It's a name I wouldn't forget in a hurry. But now you're plain ole Miss Jean Fleming – Sam said that might be the name you was usin'. We's goin' to have to put you on a plane back home. Where, I believe, some policeman or two is jus' dyin' to have a word with you.'

Mariella recognised her now. She began to bluster. 'I can give yer money. I've loads o' money. How does ten thousand dollars sound?'

'It soun' like you tryin' to bribe us, Mrs Crusher.'

'I mean each. Ten thousand each. I can get it for yer today.'

As she spoke one of the policemen stepped forward with a pair of handcuffs. Marietta's temper got the better of her.

'Come one step closer with them you fuckin' nigger and I'll stick 'em up yer arse!'

She swung a vicious fist at his head and sent him sprawling. Then she pulled the beach umbrella out of the sand and held them at bay with it, swinging it round in a circle like some wild novelty dancer. The couple on the catamaran got to their feet to watch, the woman displaying her naked breasts. The three black boys paused in their game and didn't know which was the best show on the beach, but they favoured Mariella. The noise woke the pelican up. It gave an ill-tempered squawk, flapped its heavy wings and made off to quieter waters. Francine stood back. It wasn't her job to tackle this mad woman again; she was here for identification purposes only. The downed policeman got back to his feet, wiped the blood from his nose and, together with his colleague, he circled the angry Marietta, who was backing towards the sea. Suddenly she threw the umbrella at them, dived into the water and began to swim in a wild half crawl, half dog-paddle. The boys began to cheer her on. Both policemen were fully clothed and wearing heavy shoes. They looked at each other, uncertainly.

'Don't just stand there, get after her!' screamed Francine.

For reasons best known to her, Mariella was heading for the catamaran. Its two passengers were beginning to look nervous. The man began to wind up the anchor as his topless companion stood guard with a long boat-hook. In a wild, cursing, flurry of foam, Marietta splashed towards them like an angry wasp trying escape a summer puddle. As she neared the boat her energy began to drain, she stowed down, sank, bobbed up, sank again, bobbed up again.

'Get her!' yelled Francine at the man on the boat. 'She's drownin'!'

The man looked at his topless companion, who seemed to be saying, 'I wouldn't go anywhere near her, if I were you.'

Mariella went under again. The watchers on shore held their breath. The man on the catamaran looked at them, then at the water, then he gave a sigh, then he dived in. After a worrying thirty seconds two heads bobbed up on the surface. The boys cheered, the policemen breathed sighs of relief – they'd have had some explaining to do had she drowned. Fortunately for her rescuer Mariella had no strength left for a fight. The man brought her back to shore where the two police, neither of whom could swim much, accepted her safe return with gratitude. They laid her on the sand, just clear of the washing waves. Francine placed her in the recovery position until she had coughed up all the sea water in her lungs. Then she stood over her and chatted as if Mariella were an old friend.

'That Sam Carew has a real way with him if you axe me, Mrs Crusher. He don' look like nothin' much, but he has a way with him.'

'Sam Carew – how d'yer know Sam Carew?'

Francine gave broad smile. 'I know he was the one who stole you cruise card that time – caused us all a tot o' trouble.'

Marietta was still gasping with exhaustion, but she managed to splutter, 'What – that bastard stole me card – it was him, was it?'

'It was indeed, Mrs Crusher. He was just sayin' to me over the telephone how different both your lives would have been if he'd stolen someone else's card.' She gave a hearty laugh. 'Ain't that the truth, Mrs Crusher? Ain't that jus' the pure an' simple truth?'

As the two policemen marched Mariella off the beach Francine smiled to herself at the memory of Sam's face when she'd played her marriage game with him in the Plantation Restaurant. The best way to punish a man who has given you trouble is to mention the word marriage to him. Her smile broadened when she decided that Sam hadn't been punished enough. She'd leave it for a while and take him by surprise. He deserved a nice surprise now and again did Sam Carew.

Epilogue

'I wiggled a toe today, what sort of a day did you have?' It was late afternoon, two months later. Sam had just come into the office where Sally had been doing the accounts. 'Wiggled a toe?' he said. 'That's great. What did it feel like?

Sally thought for a while to work out the best way to describe her first toe-wiggle since the shooting. 'Better than sex,' she said.

'What – are we talking about sex with me or just ordinary sex?'

'Less of the smut, Carew. I've still got the use of my arms. I can still give you a crack around the ear.'

'By the way, Alex is going round to your house this morning to finish everything off himself. Your place'll be fully wheelchair friendly by the time you get home.'

'I'm not wheelchair friendly myself yet. Anyway I hope to have graduated to a zimmer soon.'

Sam grinned. 'I'll get you some roller boots for Christmas.' Then he went quiet and said: 'I was in court this morning for Mariella's sentencing. Four life sentences with a twenty-five year recommendation.'

'So, pleading guilty didn't do her much good.'

He shook his head. 'Not really. Her counsel put in a pretty good plea in mitigation, otherwise it would have been life with no parole.'

'Ron and Mrs Mutch never did her any harm,' said Sally. 'The other two probably had it coming.'

Sam nodded his agreement. 'She had a hard time as a girl – enough to twist anyone's mind. Trouble is, they don't let you out unless you show genuine remorse, and Mariella doesn't do remorse. She's locked up for good.'

'Was Bernard there?'

'He was, and he's not so suited.'

'Well, she is his wife after all.'

'It's not that. She's still got all that money locked away in some offshore bank account and she won't let him have a penny. He's got himself a window-cleaning round.'

Sam sat down at his own desk and looked at the post. Sally had opened it all except for one large, blue envelope that didn't look official. Sam opened it. 'We're invited to Sue's wedding – September 4th.'

'Hmm. She obviously looks on us as a couple.'

'Fancy it?'

'So long as she doesn't ask me to be a bridesmaid. How do you feel about it?'

'Okay, I suppose,' Sam said. 'She deserves a settled life. He's not a bad bloke, isn't Jonathan. The boys like him well enough.' He flicked through the rest of the post. 'Anything of interest in these?'

She gave a nonchalant shrug. 'Phone bill, cheque for a hundred and three thousand pounds, letter from our local councillor.'

'Eileen got it then? – good girl.' He found the cheque and read it with a big grin on his face.

'She rang this afternoon,' Sally told him. 'The insurance company transferred the money to her account as soon as Mariella pleaded guilty. She's as pleased as Punch. Her mortgage is paid off and she's quids in, to quote her.'

'So are we,' said Sam. 'Fifty-one thousand five hundred quids each, less expenses. You can afford a new pump for your wheelchair.'

'I don't intend being in it forever. I'm going to wiggle my bum out of this thing if it kills me.'

Sam grinned at her tenacity. 'Today the toes, tomorrow the bum, eh? Which reminds me, do you think Eileen'll kick Owen out, now she's a woman of independent means?'

'Sam, she's really happy with Owen. You don't have a clue about what goes on in a woman's mind.'

'I know when a woman's serious and when she's playing games – and I think Eileen's playing games with Owen. It's not just women who have intuition you know.'

'Fancy that,' commented Sally. 'By the way, your friend Francine Le Bon rang this morning from Barbados. We had a lovely chat about you. She seems to be under the impression that you and her are engaged. I congratulated her of course. Apparently she's coming over in a few days to finalise plans for the wedding.'

Sam blanched. 'WHAT? – what did you tell her? I hope you told her that that there's been some terrible mistake.'

'No mistake Sam, she was adamant. She's apparently bought the dress.'